ALSO BY DAVID DANIEL

ARK
THE TUESDAY MAN
THE HEAVEN STONE
THE SKELLY MAN
MURDER AT THE BASEBALL HALL OF FAME (WITH CHRIS CARPENTER)

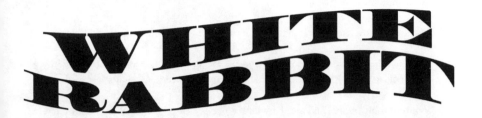

WHITE RABBIT

DAVID DANIEL

THOMAS DUNNE BOOKS ≋ ST. MARTIN'S MINOTAUR

THOMAS DUNNE BOOKS.

An imprint of St. Martin's Press.

www.minotaurbooks.com

Book design by Jonathan Bennett

Library of Congress Cataloging-in-Publication Data
Daniel, David.
    White rabbit / David Daniel.—1st ed.
        p.   cm.
    ISBN 0-312-30429-3
        1. Police—California—San Francisco—Fiction.   2. Haight-Ashbury
(San Francisco, Calif.)—Fiction.   3. San Francisco (Calif.)—Fiction.   4.
Women journalists—Fiction.   5. Serial murders—Fiction.   6. Hippies—
Fiction.   I. Title.

PS3554.A5383 W48   2003
813'.54—dc21

                                                                    2002032501

First Edition: March 2003

10   9   8   7   6   5   4   3   2   1

*For my nieces Susanna, Abbie, Andrea, Alyse, and Jacquelyn—
and for my own dear Alexandra. Flower children all.*

ACKNOWLEDGMENTS

On the long, solitary journey of this novel, I found helpers along the way. I would like to acknowledge them with sincere thanks. They include:

Ruth Cavin for her editorial alchemy. Dewayne Tully and Sherman Ackerson of the San Francisco Police Department, who were generous with their time and with their memories (any factual errors are my own, guys). My ground guides in the city by the bay: Tim Coats and Linda Hennessey.

Ed Ford, Judy Loose, Kathy Mackel, Beverly McCoy, Kristi Perkos, Robert Sanchez, David Tuells, Patricia Updyke-Thorpe, and Gary Watkins, who read portions of the book and offered suggestions, and Daniel Kotler at St. Martin's. For her friendship and editorial contributions, Pamela Getz. My old friends David Cappella and John and Susan Ford for encouragement at the right times.

Finally, I thank my wife, Stephanie, for her enduring patience and love as I took the journey. And the music! Who can forget the music?

Ye Golden hours of Life's young spring,
Of innocence, of love and truth!
Bright, beyond all imagining,
Thou fairy-dream of youth!

—LEWIS CARROLL

When the mood of the music changes, the walls of the city shake.

—PLATO

PROLOGUE

HEADS

April 28, 1967, the desert

ENDING, THE SONG FADED. THERE WAS A SOFT CLICK AS THE TAPE PLAYER CHANGED tracks, a pause, and then music filled the cluttered van once more. It was an old delivery truck, and if you looked very closely you could still see KATSOUBAS'S BAKERY, ASTORIA, N.Y. lettered underneath the road grime and the Peter Max colors. Not that the driver or his old lady were looking closely; they'd been on the road near to a month, they were a *long* way from Queens, and at the moment they were pleasantly stoned.

It had been an afternoon of flaming light burning the buttes and red rock formations, igniting saguaro cactuses, sparking the tall spikes of Adam's Needle, setting fire to sagebrush. In the past hour, however, the light had changed, gone a fishy green as big clouds stacked higher and higher in the western sky. At the far-off horizon, lightning scribbled earthward through the heat. Even at this distance it gave the two travelers pause. With a quiver of vague uncertainty, the driver shut off the tape deck. The girl, lounging next to him on the tattered paisley print bedspread laid over the seat, drew in her bare foot from the open window and sat up. The thunder came in a loud clap.

"Wow! Jump back, baby!" squealed the girl.

"It's heading our way," the driver said.

A few minutes later they spotted the hitchhiker. He was squatting by the road alongside a dusty motorcycle that stood propped on its kickstand. A set of saddle-bags was slung across the rear fender, and lashed atop that were a canvas army backpack and a bedroll. The hitcher, in denim jacket, jeans, and boots, got to his feet now and veed his fingers at the van's approach.

"Far out place to be bumming a ride," the girl said to the driver.

The driver slowed, drew alongside, and stopped. The hitcher, whose dark hair just reached the tops of his ears, wore a bandanna faded nearly pink around his neck and a friendly grin on his face.

"Trouble?" the driver called.

"My cycle busted down." He pronounced it "sickle." He stepped up to the window. He was sun-browned except for the pale mask that sunglasses or goggles had left around his eyes.

"Where you aimed for, brother?" asked the driver.

The hitcher turned to peer down the long empty strip of two-lane blacktop, which had an odd blue-gray hue in the changing light. "To the first town where I can get her fixed in, I reckon."

The driver looked, too, imagining some little filling station with a glittering hubcap fence and a dusty window that faced the alkali wasteland. He thought of a joky sign he and his old lady had goofed on: DON'T PASS GAS! LAST FILL-UP FOR MILES! And it had been, as he thought of it now. Civilization hadn't presented itself for some time, which meant that sooner or later it would have to. At that moment fat drops began to splat slowly on the windshield. He looked back at the hitcher, deciding. "If we shift some of this gear around," he said, "we can fit the both of you."

The hitcher bent nearer. "For real?"

"Come on, before the hard rain falls."

Some minutes later, with the motorcycle in back propped up by a camp stove and sleeping bags, they set off, riding three abreast on the paisley seat cover, the rain falling hard and fast now, drumming the van. "It's probably the magneto," the hitcher declared.

"What?"

"Electrical system. Foolish things are finicky as hell."

"What kind is it?"

"Y'all know bikes?"

"Harley-Davidson."

"This here's a Vincent Black Shadow. British. They quit making 'em in '55.

Most powerful bike ever built, but it don't mean Bo Diddly when she's dead on the road on account of a three-dollar gizmo."

"We came along in the nick of time."

"I'll say you did. How 'bout you all? Where you headed?"

The girl smiled. "Like the song says—'Be sure to wear . . . ' " and she began to sing it.

"San Francisco."

"I'm Christine, by the way. This is my old man, Ned." They all shook hands, the new way people did—upraised fingers curled, palms cupping—which settled things, and the girl slid open the dashboard ashtray and plucked out a half-smoked joint. "Had to be sure you weren't some motorcycle pig."

"Not me," the hitcher confirmed.

"Too late now, anyway." The girl lit the joint and passed it over. In unison, she and the driver said, "First time's free," and giggled. She turned on the tape player.

The miles went by, and beyond the streaming glass, where the wipers labored to swamp off the torrents, jags of lightning sizzled across the sky, leaving afterimages of desertscape. Tumbleweeds scuttled before them, urged by the wind, which in its bigger gusts rocked the van. But despite the storm, they were cozy inside, and soon all three were singing with the Youngbloods, " 'Come on people, now, smile on your brother, ev'rybody get together, try to love one another right now . . . ' "

Forty minutes later the rain seemed to be behind them, and though the sky gave forth with the occasional rumble of thunder, the storm was receding. But the elusive repair station still lay somewhere ahead. Now, however, dusk was falling. The driver didn't like the idea of traveling out here after dark. The van was old, after all; things could go wrong. He announced his intention to look for a place to camp for the night. The hitcher said it was fine with him; he was obliged to them for picking him up, and in no hurry to be anywhere special. At last, with sunset a red knife on the horizon, they spotted a cluster of boulders off the road, which all agreed had promise.

They found a turnout and parked. In the turquoise light they made camp. They built a fire, then stood by it and smoked another joint for appetite. The girl rooted in the van and emerged with a bottle of Boone's Farm, twisting off the top. The hitcher grinned. "First time's free."

With the van's doors open so that music drifted into the encircling dusk, they fixed a simple fare of beans, bread, cheese, and apple wine, and with the firelight and shadows playing on their faces they tucked into the meal.

"What's your name, friend?" the driver asked at length.

"Did I forget to tell you? Call me Bug Tooth."

The driver was puzzled by the name, but he accepted it. Why not? Hell, he was thinking when he got to 'Frisco he might become New York Ned, something he'd dreamed up. He tried it on the others now, and they said they dug it. Everyone out here had street names, his old lady said. She was going to find one, too.

"Y'all really from New York?" the hitcher asked.

"The Big Apple, born and bred. Christine's from upstate."

"We've been on the road a month now," she said. "A friend of Ned's wrote him saying he had to make the scene, that Haight-Ashbury is a beautiful happening. It's going to be the Summer of Love."

"Yeah?"

"I'm thinking I might hook up with the Mime Troupe. They do this like really wild Zen street theater? Or write a cookbook." She smiled. "I'll call it *Pot Luck*."

Occasionally a stick of burning wood snapped, sending sparks into the deepening indigo sky. They sipped wine. The man called Bug Tooth pointed. "There yonder's Orion the Hunter. Them stars in rows? That one line's his sword, but I always see a box with its bottom open. I keep thinking something freaky's gonna crawl out, sure."

The driver had never seen so many stars as here. Each night as they had moved west, through Pennsylvania and Ohio, into the flatlands, and now through the honest-to-God Southwest, the sky seemed to grow more crowded with them, glittering like diamonds, as if promising that what lay ahead, farther west still, was bright with possibility, a fresh beginning, a grand adventure, a place for new identities.

Christine burped.

"Bring it up again and we'll vote on it," he said, and they laughed stoned laughter.

Later, when the campfire had embered to salmon coals, the two men rolled the black motorcycle out of the van. The driver and his old lady didn't bother with the tent; there were no bugs, and the sky was clear. They spread a tarp and unrolled sleeping bags. The hitcher laid his bedroll on the flat ground with the silver-studded leather saddlebags for a pillow. As he drew off his boots, he said, "You two balling?"

They looked at him, startled, then at each other, and the driver laughed. Bug Tooth did, too.

Sometime in the night the driver opened his eyes, not immediately aware of what had wakened him. The sky was washed with stars, though the configuration

Bug Tooth had called the Hunter was gone, set below the desert rim, taking his sword with him. The fire was dead. Ned pushed himself up on an elbow. In the cold air the silence was a deep, solid presence. Christine lay asleep. He looked at the van. Wind stirred the paisley curtains. A voice startled him.

It was the hitcher. But he wasn't up; he was just lying over there in his bedroll, a shape. Beyond, the fuel tank of the bike mirrored starlight. Uncertain, Ned listened. The hitcher mumbled, "I care no more" or "I can no mall," something like that, the words scared-sounding. Ned realized that he was talking in his sleep, deep in some nightmare, perhaps. Ned experienced a wobble of uncertainty. Should he wake him? Just let him be? Then the man called Bug Tooth spoke again, and the hairs on the back of Ned's neck prickled, for this time there was no mistaking the words. *"I killed them all."*

ONE

GOD'S EYE

I don't want the news blues. . . .
—*The New Riders of the Apocalypse*

A month later

THE TELEPHONE WOKE JOHN SPARROW. FROM THE ANGLE OF SUNLIGHT IN HIS SMALL apartment he knew he had overslept. It was nearly ten A.M. He was due in court in an hour.

"Inspector? Change of plans." It was one of the assistants from the San Francisco DA's office. "The judge wants to take this under advisement."

Sparrow rubbed sleep from his eyes. He'd been out cold.

"Maybe we'll hear about it in a week or a month." Or never, Sparrow thought. "Nobody wants to go to trial on a vice case. Too much legal quicksand. You're off the hook for today." The prosecutor chuckled. "Hey, you could have it worse— like those poor bastards on your old detail."

Despite himself, Sparrow felt a flutter of interest. "Know something I don't?"

"It came on the radio just a few minutes ago. They found another body in the Haight. That's the second flower child in a few weeks."

Hanging up, Sparrow experienced a nag of frustration. As a cop you gathered evidence, systematically built a case, and you expected the courts to see it through. Too many of the cases he worked these days ended up lost in the system, consigned to some judicial limbo. With the homicide detail, at least there had been definite bad guys. And a regular shift—none of this staking out peep shows in the Tenderloin till all hours. Was that where he had been last night? God, he could hardly remember.

Resisting an urge to lie back, he swung his feet to the floor. On the nightstand stood a framed photograph taken on his wedding day, he and Helen smiling brightly. Sometimes, as now, it took him by surprise, and for an unguarded instant he could not believe that she was no longer in the world.

As he shaved, scraping morning shadow from his jaw, he assessed the stubborn face with its dark blue eyes, at the outer corners of which lines had begun to gather, the swatch of coarse brown hair that even a night of dreamless sleep never seemed to rumple much. He thought again of the man in the photo on the nightstand. He tried on a smile now, but he wasn't fooled for a minute. It felt like someone else's face.

On Fisherman's Wharf the striped awnings over the restaurant tables flapped in the cold wind, but June, still a few days away, was in the air. Amy Cole tucked strands of her blond hair behind her ears. She could smell the chocolate from Ghirardelli's. She sat with her parents, Dad, at Amy's suggestion, with a schooner of Anchor Steam. He sipped the ale without comment, though he probably wished it were a can of Pabst. Mom, who never drank except when she was dressed up and out to dinner, all of twice a year, had somehow gotten the idea that a frozen strawberry daiquiri was the thing for every occasion, and certainly for her first visit to her daughter's adopted city. She was hinting at Amy's failings, which, in her mind, began with Amy's having left Boston, fled west, and fallen among "agitators and bohemians." The words had a *Look* magazine sound when her mother said them, somewhere between disdainful and campy.

"Have you found a church?" It was Mom's attempt to confirm what she already suspected: that her youngest daughter had sunk to godlessness, too.

"There's one I've been to," Amy said, neglecting to add that it was an unconsecrated old sanctuary where members of the Haight-Ashbury met to discuss community matters.

"And this business with birth control pills . . ." Mom's expression said at least she hadn't gone *that* far.

"Well. Some things are changing."

"People don't believe in bathing, and women aren't shaving their legs? That's no change for the better."

"Some people just aren't hung up on everything being antiseptic." Bad choice of words, Amy realized at once.

"Hung up. Is that what I am?" Mom asked, widening pale blue eyes, which Amy had inherited. "Because I've kept a clean home for you and your father and your sisters?"

"I didn't mean it that way, now come on."

Dad was surveying the bay now, where the fog was creeping in under the majestic span of the Golden Gate Bridge. "Chilly here for almost June."

"The door isn't closed with the newspaper back home," her mother said. "They adored you."

Amy sighed. This was not working. "Let's just agree to respect each other's choices," she said quietly.

"What *are* your choices? That's what I'm trying to understand, have been since we got out here. Can you explain them?"

And hadn't Amy been trying? Saying yes, they had given her opportunities that they'd never had; but having graduated with a degree in English and finished a newspaper internship, Amy was not eager to be a beat reporter in her own backyard. She wasn't sure *where* her future lay, but she knew she wanted to write and that her writing must come from her life. She believed that living here would help. This set her mother off on the dangers of Amy living in the Haight-Ashbury. Hadn't the news carried the story of a murder there just days ago? Amy looked at her Timex, a graduation gift that she had disinterred from its box just for this meeting. "You've got to go. You don't want to be late meeting Everett and Jen." Her uncle and aunt were driving up from Ventura for a reunion.

"Why don't you come with us? You could change clothes at the hotel."

"I can't. I told Seth I'd meet him." She didn't volunteer anything about Seth's speaking that night at a rally to oppose the city's new riot control squad, nor say that she liked her antique dress just fine, thanks, had in fact chosen it over her customary work shirt and patched jeans ("dungarees," in Mom's parlance) in honor of the occasion. "I'll phone you at the hotel later."

She insisted on paying the tab, wanting to make it clear that she was supporting herself (just barely). Dad stayed in his frozen silence, responding only to pat her shoulder as Amy leaned across the table to kiss him. Mom, however, could not let the afternoon end without a parting shot. "We sacrificed for you and your sisters," she said with a wounded smile. "I hope you appreciate that." And Amy knew that it was time to walk away before she said something she'd regret. "Because it's almost like we don't know you anymore."

Her chest tightened. Just go, she told herself, smooth this out later; her parents would be in town for several more days. But she could not move. "The truth is," she said, speaking through the quiver in her voice, "you don't want me to be your daughter. Not really."

"Oh, my goodness." Eleanor Cole's eyes rolled.

"What's that mean?" asked her father, genuinely puzzled.

"Let's go, dear," said her mother.

"I'm curious," Dad insisted.

Amy could feel a vein throbbing in her neck. "You ran off, Dad, and joined up for the war—you were seventeen. You were a kid! You both were. I've done the math. When you got married, Katy was already on the way!" The words came in a rush, and then her mother was on her feet, upsetting the daiquiri and slapping Amy's face.

The blow lit a dazzle of stars. Amy took a stunned moment letting her head clear. Neither of her parents had ever struck her before. Refusing to put her hand to the burning spot on her cheek, she backed away, bumping chairs. Her last image, before she fled, was of her dad sitting awkwardly before the opaque red pond of spilled drink, and her mother standing there with her arm still out.

2

THE OFFICE OF THE CHIEF OF HOMICIDE INVESTIGATION ON THE FOURTH FLOOR HAD changed in incidentals mostly, one cop having substituted his trophy heads for those of another. Furniture, bookcases: John Sparrow recognized these as unchanged, like the hum of noise from the bullpen at his back. The civic awards and the commendations from a grateful citizenry were there. Missing was the photograph Moon had had of himself and Sparrow as eager patrolmen, though that had been gone even before Sparrow was. Occupying a spot on the wall instead was a photograph of Frank Austin standing with Mayor Alioto and Governor Reagan, the three of them in taxidermist's poses before the massive stone facade of the Hall of Justice. In another, Austin stood with his Nob Hill wife, proudly holding aloft his infant like it was a prize trout that would win him the fishing derby. Austin himself sat at the desk, but now rose, hand extended.

"Hello, John. Good to see you."

He was a lean, energetic man, clever with the politics of law enforcement. Sparrow's age, he had married well, risen to lieutenant's rank, and was said to have ambitions for more. If a clean desk were a predictor of success, Austin was on his way. Except for a single manila folder and a seven-day clock in a spotless bell jar, the desk was bare. "Sit." He didn't mention the message he had sent; it was understood from Sparrow's presence. "Coffee?"

When he had poured two cups—a gray brew that looked none too promising—Austin resumed his seat and laid his hands on the desk, flanking the folder. His eyes had a green sparkle that went with the neat navy blue of his suit. "So, how goes?"

"Vice never sleeps."

"You left some big footprints around here when you got reassigned."

"You didn't hear that from George Moon."

"No, I didn't. I've been going over some past cases, trying to prepare things for this computer we're supposed to get if the keypunch operators ever finish." He gestured vaguely toward the outer office where the paper files were kept. "Like the Reyes case, for one. That was a sweet piece of work."

"It was a group effort," Sparrow said.

"Ha. That's what Gale Sayers said when he ran six touchdowns against the 'Niners a couple years back. I didn't believe him either."

They weren't here to bask in old glory—or old failures, for that matter—and

12

Sparrow hoped his silence made the point. Austin asked, "Are you interested in this Haight-Ashbury business?"

For a moment Sparrow thought he was talking about the Summer of Love, the term the phrasemakers had coined for the silliness going on in the city; then he knew otherwise. Still, he hadn't seen any of the investigative work for the two recent murders. His sources were the same as every citizen who read the newspapers, with the added and not strictly reliable element of department gossip. "Is this informal?"

"Just us," Austin confirmed. "What's your instinct?"

It came to Sparrow that he had pushed a similar question from his mind more than once in recent days. With a sense of permission, he let it rise now, and in that instant he identified how working homicide was different than vice: it allowed you to believe that with time and persistence you could discover the truth. "Have we got a repeater?"

Austin's face stayed smooth as a stone. "Let's say we have."

Sparrow blew into the cup and sipped. The coffee hadn't improved. He set the cup next to the seven-day clock, close enough that it steamed a small patch of the glass dome. He began with what he knew.

Both victims had been young street kids, one male, one female. Both stabbed, no weapon recovered yet. No motive. Nothing, so far, to say that they had known each other. The killings had occurred within a six-block area in the Haight-Ashbury. So . . . instinct? "A male obviously. Maybe slightly older than the kids he's killed. A loner. Unmarried. Bright."

The killer had something that allowed him to bond with his victims, but he was different from them, too. And damned cautious. The crime scenes had been maddeningly clean, even beyond the news accounts, Sparrow had to believe, or Austin wouldn't be wasting his own precious time now, though there'd be details that Homicide was keeping to itself. Austin offered neither agreement nor particulars. Traffic sounds drifted up from the freeway.

"Victims," Sparrow continued, unconstrained by what he did not know, "multiple wounds. How multiple?"

"Six in the first, four in the other."

"That doesn't sound too angry. The papers haven't mentioned sex."

"There was no sexual assault."

Unless you wanted to go Freudian and make something of the use of a knife. In this work you got eclectic in your ideas, but Sparrow let it alone for now. "Mutilation?"

Austin chewed his lip, and Sparrow had his answer. The man was fussy about rules, and would be about sharing investigative data, too, even with another cop. "He's bent in some way," Sparrow said. "Psychologically."

Austin kept his counsel. "Of course," Sparrow went on, "there's grounds for seeing no link at all between the killings."

"But if there is a link?"

Sparrow tensed, aware that being here had drawn an unwanted memory out of his past. He forced it back. "Then, I'd say . . . he's just getting started."

Austin sat motionless.

"But, I don't know enough," Sparrow said, his interest bumping to a halt against the fact that he was no longer privy to the investigative goods, nor, today excepting, especially welcome on this floor.

Austin grunted. "The intelligence and the habit of operating alone work. Like the person profiled here." He turned the manila folder so the tab was visible. Unexpectedly, Sparrow saw the name typed on it was his own.

"I thought internal files are confidential."

"With this new computer coming, there's been a little drift. But you're safe. Actually there's a part left out of that. The shrinker part."

Sparrow stiffened. "Psychologist."

"What?"

"He wasn't a psychiatrist."

"Right. Anyway, this gives me enough."

"Am I a suspect?"

"God, I hope not. How would you like to come work here again?" The man was full of surprises today. "For this investigation, to start with. I'm cleared to add an inspector."

And that was another surprise. "I thought everything was going to Moon for his TAC Squad."

"George has been good at selling the threat of revolt in the streets," Austin granted. "After last year's riots, now this hippie thing . . . maybe he's right. We've become Mecca for longhairs. We're news. The Summer of Love slouches toward us."

"And the city doesn't want the focus to shift to another string of unsolved murders."

Austin frowned. "That's past. I can swing the temporary reassignment. I need somebody good. Of course, I'd have to have your written request saying you want back."

"So George Moon wouldn't see it as a political override?"

"Because regs require it." Austin was losing patience. Part of his success was his understanding that the toes you stepped on today could be attached to the ass you kissed tomorrow. "Look, John . . . I understand there may have been bad blood between you two. I refrain from judgment. As far as I'm concerned, that's history. Moon has new troops to keep him occupied. But there's no point pissing him off." He drew a tortoiseshell fountain pen from his pocket and set it on the desk. "You make a formal request, I'll get it okayed. If we've got a repeat killer on our hands, I can use you."

Sparrow's gaze went to the pen, then to the domed clock with its brass spheres turning inside, the cycles growing fractionally smaller under the forces of friction, gravity, and inertia. He allowed silence to build, such silence as ever existed in this world of ringing telephones and the constant coming and going of people tied by the common bonds of trouble.

Austin said, "Have you seen that poster with the little girl gazing at the ocean? 'Today is the first day of the rest of your life.' It's June first. What do you say?"

Sparrow had no beef with Frank Austin. The man was ensnared by policy, and a bit too nakedly ambitious for Sparrow's taste; still, he was reasonably adept for all that. But there were complexities at issue here that went deeper than Sparrow cared to go into. He was a good detective, he knew that; but there were other people on the force who could do the job, too. "Thanks for thinking of me," he said, then felt compelled to add, "I like what I'm doing well enough."

"Vice? Ha. That's not what I hear."

Despite their sparkle, Austin's eyes had an irksome force. He had put effort into this. The personnel file lying there said so; apparently he had talked to someone in special services, too, all done within PD regs. The possibilities galled Sparrow, though what bothered him more, he realized now, was that his own discontent was so bare. It gave hint of a man hanging on for weak reasons, drifting resignedly toward a pension. Seizing a temporary return to his old job could only underscore that discontent, and rekindle the fires that had brought it on.

"Look," said Austin, "if it's pride, I understand that. I've got mine, too. After all, I asked, right?"

And Sparrow was given to understand that the offer would not be made again; an ambitious administrator had to limit his defeats. He even entertained briefly the idea of mounting an explanation for his refusal, but it was complicated.

"I've got to get back to work," he said.

"Busting another burly show?" Austin sighed and pushed the manila folder across the gleaming desktop. "You can have that."

Sparrow waited until he was at his own small, paper-littered desk two floors below before he opened his personnel folder, and the extent of Frank Austin's deception was laid bare. Had it been a bluff? Or meant to imply a fresh start? Either way, the only reasonable reaction was to laugh. Inside the manila jacket was a single sheet of blank paper.

"You heard it yet, Ames? It's blowing my mind!"

The Jester's grin was sizeable and infectious, like the Jester himself, and it made Amy smile, too. He was sunk in a big beanbag chair in the front room of the apartment she shared with him and Seth and Tess. Others of their friends were there too, ringed around the Moroccan hookah which stood in their midst. The Beatles sang about turning everyone on.

"It's great," Amy cried over the volume.

Jester had cut out the little paperboard badge from the sheet inside the album jacket and had it pinned to his scarlet belled cap, identifying him as a member of Sgt. Pepper's Lonely Hearts Club. He said they'd been sitting there all afternoon, playing the record over and over.

They weren't the only ones. The album had been released that day, and radio stations had been spinning it nonstop. Amy had listened while driving back from the airport after dropping off her parents. She lowered the volume on the record player. Jester made a mystical sign in the air. "Join us, child, in paying liege to the lords of Liverpool and the great goddess Cannabis Sativa."

"Thanks, but I'm feeling unfaithful at the moment."

Jester beamed hopefully. "Does that mean you've finally realized you can't resist me?"

"No one can, but I've got an article to write."

"Ah, labor before leisure. You're getting bad as Seth."

"Is he around?"

"Went down the corner for wine," Tess said. She was a beautiful black street artist they had met when they first moved to the Haight. Now she did drawings for the *Rag*.

"It was an excuse to leave," Jester said. "He's on his 'music is the opiate of the masses' trip."

"But secretly he's digging it," one of the others confided. "He said 'Lovely Rita' shows a Marxist dialectic."

"I would've said Liverpudlian." Jester shrugged and rubbed his large belly. "As long as he brings munchies."

Amy restored the volume and went into the kitchen. When Seth came back a while later, she took the grocery bag from him, set it on the table, and kissed him. "Your folks make their flight?" he asked.

"They did," Amy said simply, not wanting to break the mood with elaboration.

The three of them had sat in the airport waiting area where Dad, figuring to avoid confrontation by keeping his head in a newspaper, had picked one whose front page revealed that the Haight had two unsolved murders and that the U.S. military in Vietnam had 313 combat deaths, the highest one-week total yet. The news was hard to ignore, but they did their best until finally, Mom interrupted her own small talk. "I'm worried sick at your being out here, and Aunt Jen is just as worried about Glenn being over there."

Glenn was Amy's cousin, a year younger than she, and a marine. "Of course Jen is," Amy agreed. "We all are."

"I hope you're not saying anything negative to them."

"Me?"

Perhaps convinced that, given the shortness of time, subtlety was doomed, her mother was using the crowbar approach to probe her daughter's meanings. "Your little newspaper and all."

"Did they say something?"

"What are they going to say? They're too polite to say anything. What do you think your actions say?"

"I don't know what you mean?"

"About Glenn. About his serving his country in Vietnam."

"I write him. He writes me."

"And you send him issues of that paper?"

"I send him the *Rag*, yes. He's asked me to."

Her mother frowned. "That can't be a good thing for the soldiers to read."

No, they can kill and be killed but not read a newspaper, Amy thought but didn't say. In truth, she and Glenn corresponded often. Every few weeks she would receive a letter, full of details of his long days in a place named Khe Sanh. After reading his words, Amy would tip the envelope upside down and a silty red-orange dirt would sift out, as fine as talcum powder. As some kind of organic link to Glenn, she poured it into her potted plants, especially the Mary Jane flourishing there by a sunny window in her apartment. Amy didn't offer this information to her parents, either.

"Those guys can't be left out of what's happening here," she insisted. "It affects them, too."

"But they need positive messages. To uplift them."

Like "U.S. Casualties Hit New High"? Some lift. "I agree."

"Ev and Jen are terrified about this whole thing."

"It's needless," Amy said.

"To worry about their son?"

"The fighting! It's needless our being there. It's a civil war."

Dad set the newspaper down. In spite of her intention to stay calm, Amy hadn't kept a fervent note out of her voice. She glanced toward where several people sat in blue molded plastic TV chairs, then back. "I'm not against Glenn," she said more quietly. "Or any of the soldiers. They're just trying to stay alive."

"You disagree with the war."

"But I'm with *them*."

"It doesn't sound like it from what you write. You criticize Congress, for goodness sake. Our own president."

"What I object to is his making them go! No risk to him, but telling those guys to put their lives on the line. Either that or go to jail or flee to Sweden. I hate the hypocrisy! As for Glenn—" Amy faced her mother straight on. "I love him. And the day he comes home safe, I'll be there to give him a parade."

Some people sitting in the busy waiting area nearby looked over. Nobody, including her parents, spoke. Mercifully the silence was soon broken by a public address voice announcing departures and arrivals. Then, the role of peacemaker having fallen to him, her father said, "Well, we'll just hope this thing is over soon."

On that, at least, they had staked a small piece of common ground, and spent the last minutes being studiedly pleasant until the flight to Boston was called.

Seth twisted open a jug of Ripple red. On the kitchen wall was a mural that Tess had begun to paint, a kind of Henri Rousseau primitive: animals and flower children in a peaceful jungle Eden, though in one corner, she had sketched in the small outline of what might be a B-52. Tess wasn't saying, but for the moment Amy chose to see it as a dove. Soon, Seth's hugs and the music from the other room had soothed her. The hassle with her parents faded. Her article could wait. Bringing the wine and Cracker Jacks, she and Seth joined the party.

At twilight, carrying a toolbox, John Sparrow made his way out the marina dock and down a gangway to the branching finger piers. In the distance, he could see the dusky outline of the Marin Headlands and the sweep of the beacon on Alcatraz.

Along the piers, lights were beginning to shine in the cabins of some of the big cruisers, and from several came music which sounded like the Beatles but at the same time didn't. He could smell meat being grilled on hibachis, and the brine of a turning tide. Near the end of the outermost pier he paused, taken as he often was by the sight of his own boat.

A weathered sloop, at thirty-two feet not the smallest, though far from the largest, craft in the basin, she was certainly one of the most proud, even now in her dotage. With her sleek, deep green hull and mahogany decks, she had a long history of voyaging, though an aging history now, Sparrow reflected. She hadn't been to sea in two years.

He stepped onto the transom mat, unlocked the cabin, and ducked inside, not wanting to be reminded of the unattended-to chores. There were bearded lines, canvas to patch, a rail in need of fastening . . . the list went on. He set the toolbox by the hatch.

In the galley, he opened a can of Chef Boyardee, and while it heated he poured bourbon over a pair of ice cubes. He switched on the Admiral black-and-white TV and watched the scant local report on the police investigation of the Haight-Ashbury killings. Afterwards, on *Huntley-Brinkley*, came the day's clashes with North Vietnamese Army troops near Da Nang. There was footage of a helicopter loading American casualties and lifting off in a whirl of palm fronds and dust. When Chet and David had said their good-nights, he watched a few minutes of *Gilligan's Island*, but found no laughs in it and shut the set off.

The marina was quieter now, settling in for the evening. The tide had ebbed and he could feel its pull. On the pier, a man and a woman strolled past, their voices soft and intimate. In the stillness that followed, a familiar loneliness tweaked his heart. It was a feeling for which TV or work sometimes served as antidote, but not tonight. He left the toolbox where it sat and poured more bourbon.

The *Blind Faith* had been bought at auction, intended as a boon for him and Helen, an outlet for the sense of adventure both shared and yet perhaps felt they had endangered in getting married. Not that either had been sorry; on the contrary, they had been fulfilled in each other and Sparrow had found special joy in being a husband, and yet, through their work, their lives had taken on a certain gravity. In his spare time, over a span of several years, he had restored the boat, and they sailed it weekends on the bay. Gradually, the notion of something grander, a voyage along the lines of those recorded in the craft's original log, came to them.

The plan was for an unhurried sail south to Santa Catalina, maybe even Mexico.

Helen loved to swim, and moved with a dolphin's grace. They would gunk-hole in coastal towns, homing with warm winds toward new harbors, taking summer at its leisure. Helen had the break from her first-grade teaching, and God knew Sparrow had accrued abundant vacation leave in his years on the job. For a time, the anticipation alone was sufficient to excite them. There were the inevitable preparations that a long voyage demanded. Helen took seamanship and piloting courses. In the joint planning for the sail there had been giddily happy evenings with cocktails and charts, plotting runs, selecting anchorages, stockpiling, then winnowing, supplies to fit limited spaces.

But as embarkation neared, Sparrow found himself consumed with the killings in North Beach. Then June was gone, and July, and when August, too, began to wane, it was clear that the voyage would not happen, and as if its failure had been his own, he faced a somber speculation that something was wrong, Helen had changed, though it would be some weeks before he found out how.

The boat's telephone ringing startled him.

It was an assistant DA named Yamamoto informing him that a judge had thrown out a case they had developed against a maker of blue films. "Technicalities," Yamamoto said simply. "Nothing you did or did not do." Sparrow didn't press for more.

As he hung up, he realized for the first time that he was sitting in nearly full darkness, so gradually had twilight seeped away. He made no move to turn on a lamp. He listened to the creak of lines, the scrape of fenders, the soft cyclings of bilge pumps and fans. He heard the liquid trickle of a woman's laughter. He was aware of ships in the bay, their passing relayed to the *Blind Faith* in her gentle rise and fall.

His eyes grown used to the dark, he made another drink, listened to a side of Coltrane, savoring the pure, radiant energy of the man's horn, as if it might infuse him with some of its drive. As he filled the glass a fourth time, he caught himself. How perfectly quaint: a man settling in for an evening of lonely-hearted drinking. He switched on the lamp, tipped the undrunk bourbon back into the bottle, and lockered it for another occasion. Securing the hatch, he discovered a stripped screw. He added it to the list of things to do. On the bay, night was bringing a shimmering mantle of fog . . . and with it, perhaps, a killer?

In his apartment, he got ready for bed. He looked again at the wedding photograph. Helen wore ribbons in her black hair and was every bit as luminous as Coltrane's horn: sweet and lustful and alive in his imagination. He put out the light and lay motionless, pretending that she was there with him. Being aboard the boat had brought it on. He could almost hear the whisper of her breath. For some reason he thought of the prosecutor's phone call. "Nothing you did or did not do," the man had said, and it occurred to Sparrow that that was the cold truth at the heart of his malaise: that sometimes actions could make no difference. It must have been what the doctors had known about Helen's illness.

For a time, after she died, he had maintained an exhausting regimen of upkeep on the boat, as if through sheer effort he could bring Helen back for a last sail, or as if the *Blind Faith* were one of those craft that Egyptian kings prepared for the voyage of afterlife. But he never sailed her again, and when he was transferred out of homicide his energy faded.

He thought about the chores unattended to, aware that their very number had brought on a paralysis and in that moment he came to a decision. It was time to sell the boat. She was too proud a craft to be left to decay by a dock. He would speak with a broker in the morning.

While this decision brought some peace, it didn't bring sleep. He lay there feeling the drum of his heart. For something to do, he began to imagine. What if he and Helen had taken the sail? Suppose she had told him at once and they'd seen still other specialists, demanded other diagnoses? What if they'd had kids? He thought of Frank Austin and his Nob Hill bride, holding their baby aloft. What if he had abandoned the North Beach case sooner, before it took on the weight of obsession? Or solved it?

And therein lay something he had overlooked earlier in the homicide chief's office. Frank Austin wanted him back because Sparrow had been good, yes; but what if, in the fog-stained afternoons of all those days since, he had lost the knack? Suppose he tried but this time, too, he could not find the killer?

Waiting for sleep, he watched headlight patterns splash the ceiling and slide away like ghosts. As his eyes closed, he heard the whine of guitars and singing from a passing car's radio, sounding vaguely like the Beatles again, but different, warped and enigmatic, not the bright clear ringing of "Good Day Sunshine": kids out driving in the night and maybe parents somewhere wondering, Are they all right? Are they smoking pot? Will they come home safe? *Stay out of the Haight,* Sparrow thought, drifting away.

On Monday, June 5 at 4:40 p.m., Sparrow parked along the panhandle in the block between Central and Masonic. In front of him was a truck fashioned like a log cabin, complete with chimney, and a bumper sticker that said JEFFERSON AIRPLANE LOVES YOU. He didn't know who or what Jefferson Airplane was. In fact, he wasn't sure about much of anything in this neighborhood anymore.

Once home to European immigrants and USF professors, with its handsome gingerbread houses, the Haight-Ashbury had taken on an air of dilapidation in the past decade, become a place where drifters and beatnik burnouts came to ground, and students found cheap digs. Now, as if fluidity were its birthright, the district had shifted shape once more and become a latter-day Sutter's Mill for the disaffected young, whose ethos, as near as Sparrow could make out, included smoking pot and sitting around probing the lyrics of rock 'n' roll songs, looking for hidden answers. But to what questions? What was the gold they sought?

Several of the unmarked black Fairlanes the homicide detail used were in view. He had driven his own four-year-old Impala. As he locked the car and started across the grass, he felt a shiver, though it wasn't due only to the cold fog drifting along the street. There had been a giddy undercurrent of fear in the dispatcher's voice. Sparrow had just returned to the Hall of Justice when he caught the report on the scanner. He instructed the patrolman he worked with to go up to vice and file the day's paperwork. Alone, Sparrow hesitated for a moment, then he took out his notebook and wrote something.

At this hour, the Haight's frenetic energy had ebbed. People in clothing they had fished from St. Vincent de Paul huddled in small groups along the sidewalks, talking quietly. Later, resuscitated with night and neon (and drugs, Sparrow had little doubt) the district would spark to life again. At the moment he didn't have to remind himself there was death to deal with.

The Victorian had seen better days. Its brown shingles were faded and loose, threatening to drop away like October leaves. The front-facing windows were grimed, like eyes no longer wanting to see what lay before them. The front door was boarded. Next to the house was an alley with an odor of refuse coming from it. Sparrow read graffiti scribbled on the side wall.

Frodo Lives!
Venus meet Jess at I/Thou 3/22
Off the pigs!
Jefferson Airplane Loves You

Broken bottles lying among the weeds crunched underfoot as he entered the alley. Chained to a fence, with a lock that looked like it hadn't been opened in years, leaned a flat-tired old bicycle. He paused at the foot of a fire escape that ran down the side of the house like a zigzag of rusty lightning. At the top was an open door. A murmur of voices spilled from it, and every few seconds the flare of a flashbulb.

The killing had come much sooner than he had feared. Since speaking with Frank Austin the other day, he had found it possible to imagine that he was wrong, that the two previous murders were unconnected. But this made three. At the top of the fire escape, he wiped his feet and stepped through the door.

The activity was familiar: homicide inspectors in their dark fedoras, gold stars flapped over their suit coat pockets; several uniforms; Stan Hoagland, from the coroner's office. He was glad to see that one of the inspectors was Rocco Bianchi, though it surprised him, too. Hadn't he retired? Other cops Sparrow knew glanced his way and nodded. A young man he didn't know came over.

"You're John Sparrow."

He was short, good-looking, with an olive complexion and hair as dark as Sparrow's own. He wore a gray suit and a black tie. "Pedro Sandoval," he said. "Pete. I've heard about you, sir."

They shook hands. "Inspector?" Sparrow asked. The man seemed too young for the elite homicide detail.

"Just a few months now."

Rocco Bianchi limped over. "Hey, John, you back?" Rocco's days with the detail went back long before Sparrow's own. He was an old man now, with a smoker's cough and bad legs.

"I thought you'd retired."

"Ha." Rocco poked Pete Sandoval's arm affectionately. "You like our college boy?"

The two veterans chatted a moment, then Rocco said, "You're going to wish you'd stuck to ogling tits and ass, John. This is bad."

Rocco caught him up. The building had been apartment units until the landlord was forced to shut down for code violations. It appeared the victim had come in to crash; not a novel idea, Sparrow mused, given the litter of trash and old paper coffee cups strewn about the otherwise bare floor. "A handyman the owner hired to patch the ceiling found the body. Male, stabbed, no ID yet, no weapon. Hoagland guesses early yesterday as time of death."

"What kind of violations?" Sparrow asked.

"Huh?"

"Of code."

"Not enough toilets, Mickey Mouse. What's creepy, though"—and saying this, Rocco Bianchi actually shuddered—"same as with the others . . ." He broke off and pinched at his tired face.

Sandoval spoke up. "Shall I show him, sir?"

Rocco looked relieved. "Sure, College Boy, do that."

A sour odor of dirt and decay made Sparrow's nostrils pinch as he followed Pete Sandoval into the room. Battery-powered flood lamps steamed in the cold air and gave a hard light to the angular walls and scant furnishings: a wooden chair, four stained mattresses, a shaky pyramid of wine bottles, a tatami mat covering a portion of floor. The woven straw creaked as investigators moved about.

Simon Chang, the dry and ageless evidence tech, hovered over the scene with a sober presence. He would be sure to sift the room for the slightest evidence, but Sparrow doubted it would yield much. It had the look of a place where people came and went and left little of themselves.

Beyond the glare, seemingly forgotten in the swirl of activity, the deceased sat stiffly upright in a corner, arms at his sides, head tilted away from the light. He had on an unbleached muslin peasant shirt, with birds embroidered on the front. The birds had been blue once, a shade deepened to purple now by the blood that greased the fabric and shone dully in the lights like dried jam. The mat beneath the man was stained in an irregular starburst pattern, as though someone had set out to paint it but had grown weary of the task and abandoned it. A burnt-down candle had puddled on the floor nearby, the wax hard. Edging closer, Sparrow squatted and looked at the face.

A cobweb of horror brushed him. His flesh went to goose bumps.

For a tipsy instant, he had the impression he was looking at a mask. But it was no mask. The man's eyes had the smoked look of burnt-out flashbulbs, and the cheeks were swollen and gray; but what gave the face its chilling appearance, and set his heart to pounding hard, was that the nose had been cut away, exposing the gaping air holes of the skull. Sparrow drew a fast breath and glanced away. After another look, he rose. As if it were a tether to reality, he produced a notebook, clicked a ballpoint to life.

Details: time, location, names of personnel on the scene. He sketched a floor plan and added the body, little more than a stick figure. Finally, he began to draw the face. He was thus intent when Sandoval stepped near and whispered, "*El hombre esta aqui.*"

Frank Austin stood in the doorway. Hands in his trench coat pockets, cordovan shoes buffed to a shine, he conferred soberly with several of the cops before coming in. He squinted against the flood lamps and saw Sparrow.

"Hello, John," he said, leaving the words to hang somewhere between greeting and question.

Sparrow flipped back a few pages in his notebook. Hesitated, then tore out the note he had written less than an hour ago. Taking it, Austin raised his eyebrows.

"First day of the rest of my life," Sparrow said.

Slipping the page carefully into his inside jacket pocket, Austin glanced finally at the dead man.

As was his weekday habit of late, Captain George Moon arrived at the Presidio at six P.M. He undid his tie, yanked his damp collar away from his neck. Driving from downtown, he had leaned on the horn several times for slow-moving pedestrians. Earlier, at the Hall of Justice, he had wanted to shove people. His meeting with the chief had not gone well.

Soon, more comfortable in a loose-fitting SFPD sweatsuit, Moon made his way onto the central parade ground carrying a canvas bag that looked like it might hold baseball bats. Indeed, portions of the field were chalked for games, though none was in the offing now. A lean U.S. Army sergeant in fatigues was leading twenty TAC police trainees through a warm-up drill. At Moon's approach, the man blew a whistle and the cops in his charge quit bouncing.

"Thank you, Sergeant," Moon said, dropping the canvas bag. "How are they doing?"

The soldier was assigned to the state National Guard, now temporarily attached to the SFPD as a fitness and martial arts trainer. "Coming along. There'll be some bellyaching about having to jog."

"Good."

The sergeant grinned. "You want to stretch, sir?"

"I'm loose."

"Well then, they're all yours."

For the next twenty minutes Moon ran the volunteers around the hilly compound, glad for the chance to burn the fuse of his earlier fury. That morning he had made a request to mobilize the TAC Squad at a demonstration planned for next weekend in Golden Gate Park. It would give his men a chance to experience a real crowd control situation, he argued. The chief had given the request a summary denial, writing in his terse memo that such a mobilization could be interpreted as a hostile gesture, adding the small, needling detail that, in any event, the gathering was to be a celebration, not a demonstration.

Considering this now in the flush of exercise, Moon found that his anger had thinned. Overall, such an event promised to be pretty tame. Mostly the hippies seemed content to be in the 3-H Club—hairy, horny, and high. Still, there were underground factions whose aim was the disruption of civil order. So far it was just street antics—blocking traffic with a game of catch, picketing the federal building—but that could change. The long days of summer were coming, and one of these times the kids flooding into his city from all over the country would reach critical mass. There would simply be no place for them, no toilets, not enough free food to dole out, no jobs. Their mood would turn foul.

Already there were leaders looking for followers. In the Haight there was the Summer Mobilization Group—Mob Grope, they called themselves—and Black Panthers across the bay in Oakland, armed to the teeth. How long before weapons began to stockpile in the Haight-Ashbury, too? How long before anarchy sprang forth? And when that happened, when the mob was howling at the gate, no one could blame George Moon for not having warned them, or not having been given ample chance to blood his young troops beforehand. And they definitely needed blooding. They were volunteers, and except for a few who'd been in the military, most had no experience with this kind of duty. That's what he had to change.

Back on the parade ground where they had started, he allowed the men a smoke break, then put them in squad formation and took his place before them.

"Gentlemen," he began, pointing toward the bay, "eleven thousand miles that way is Vietnam. I don't have to tell you that American boys are dying there for your freedom." Turning, he pointed inland. "A short way in this direction we've got another war getting ready to break out. Only this one's not about freedom. It's about lawlessness and revolt."

He took his time, choosing words. "Tactically, it makes sense for us to strike first. But the city council doesn't agree. There's chaos in the wind. Already there have been two killings in the Haight and—" He broke off. A hand had gone up in the formation.

"Cap, I just heard on the way here now there's been another."

Moon's jaw clenched. He was riled by the interruption, but angered more that he hadn't heard the report. "Pay attention." He rolled his shoulders, pumped-feeling under the fabric of his sweatshirt. "All winter, City Hall has known an invasion was coming, but have they made preparations?" A few "no's" came from the assembled men. "No," Moon echoed. "All they've done is arrange more handouts. Give these freaks the key to Love City. Let them 'do their own thing.'" He could see the restless stir of some of the trainees. "That's the price of freedom, they say. Wrong. That's the price for having candy-asses in power, eager to please and appease."

"And get reelected," someone called.

"The time's coming when they'll see their mistake. I only hope it isn't too late."

He squatted, unzipped the canvas bag, and drew out the truncheon. The look of it alone brought a stir. Not the standard white ash, it was a black, almost three-foot length of hard rubber. Each member of the TAC Squad would be issued one when he'd completed training. George Moon whacked it into his palm. It gave off a crack like a gunshot. For a moment he savored the sudden stillness. Then, his gaze roving across the flushed and waiting faces of his troops, he said, "Okay, listen up!"

"Creepy, huh, sir?" Pete Sandoval handed Sparrow coffee in a mug with Chinese symbols on it. Photographs from the first two murder scenes were spread across a desk in the homicide detail: the unclaimed desk that Sparrow assumed was his, though no one officially had said so. The other inspectors had welcomed him back with good wishes, and now it was late; only he and Pete Sandoval remained in the fourth-floor room.

In addition to the facial mutilation, the noses having been cut away in each case, creating bizarre effects, the photographs showed crime scenes much like today's: shabby, isolated locales in the Haight-Ashbury district. What Sparrow found surprising, given the nature of the crimes, was that beyond the blood and a few smudged prints there was no clear evidence. It was a maddening detail, and in his experience a near impossible one, but Chang, the evidence tech, had confirmed it.

"We've sent requests to Sacramento and the FBI," Sandoval said. "We're looking at recent prison and state hospital releases."

"Round up the unusual suspects."

Sandoval flushed. "Sorry, sir. I don't need to tell you how things are done."

"It's helpful to walk through it. Go on."

He did, recounting what Sparrow pretty much knew. If Frank Austin had a failing, it was his imagination, not his routines and procedures. The investigative bases would be covered. Austin had partnered Sparrow with Sandoval, and Sparrow was relieved to find he wasn't going to have to teach the young inspector the basics. The kid was sharp.

"Don't let them get to you with that 'College Boy.' They chose well."

"I don't mind the label. I don't think I'll hang my diploma on the wall, though."

"Berkeley, Rocco said."

"I got lucky and they gave me a small scholarship. Psych." Sandoval shrugged dismissively. "I always figured to raise hogs with my father, but I'm not half the worker he is. College seemed a smarter option. I probably would've done just as well at a JC—every other day it seems there was a demonstration about this or that." He stopped as if he'd said too much, then added diplomatically, "It certainly didn't hurt you, sir."

"We're going to be working together, let's make it first names. Or last. Whatever's comfortable."

"All right. John, then."

They went back to work. The files on the killings lay on one side of the desk, in thin folders, though Sparrow had yet to open them. He was still occupied with the photographs. Now something in one of them seized his interest. He held up a photo, pointing to something on it. "What's this?"

Sandoval brought a magnifier. Sparrow studied the photograph, staring at a small pale shape that lay on the chest of the first victim. It was a flower petal. Suddenly he was struck with awareness. It was a detail the police were holding for themselves.

"There was a flower at each of the three scenes," Sandoval confirmed. "A daisy and two roses. Mr. Chang bagged today's before you got there."

"Anyone planning to tell me?"

"I thought Lieutenant Austin must have. Sorry." Sandoval fidgeted. "Um . . . on the topic of flowers . . . at that first scene, I was too eager. I thought I'd discovered the big clue. I picked the flower up before Mr. Chang came."

Sparrow laughed. Sandoval's look went hangdog. "Welcome to the club. We've all compromised a crime scene."

"Even you?"

"Famous for it. You're not in until Chang's read you the riot act."

Sandoval appeared relieved.

Half an hour later, Sparrow had finished examining the photographs and was just starting the folders. The usual shift in homicide was nine to five, with a rotating on-call schedule, but the three killings had changed that. Sandoval said, "Are you going to work much longer?" His eyes were glassy with fatigue.

"You go on home. I want to get through these files. I'll see you in the morning."

At the door, the young cop turned. "I think we've got a bad one here. When does it stop?"

"I'm not sure yet."

After refilling his coffee cup, Sparrow went back to the photographs. Spending time at the places where death occurred helped you learn things you needed to know if you were going to find a killer, taught you what you could anticipate, *what to be afraid of* . . . He wedged this thought away and went over to a large wall map of the city. There were red pushpins in the Haight-Ashbury district, numbered one to three. In North Beach, the number had risen to four over a span of five months and ended there, unsolved. Here the first murder had occurred on or about May 3; the second had been on the 27th. Now this. Three in barely a month.

Multiple stab wounds and facial disfigurement. A flower in each case. Otherwise, an almost total lack of physical evidence. He thought about the sinister care this suggested, the resistance to discovery. He tried to pursue the threads of several ideas, but they had no substance and were quickly lost.

Deal with facts.

Okay. Two men and a woman, ages seventeen to twenty-two. But while they were almost definitely linked in death, there was no suggestion as yet of any connection between them in life. He read the crime scene data again, his notebook at hand. In the silence of the bullpen, his pen made small scratching noises, like an insect trapped in a matchbox. Fighting fatigue, he rolled his shoulders. Coffee was useless. He went back to the wall map, trying to achieve some angle he had not yet considered, to coax a new perception from his brain. What came was unwanted: a memory of other nights spent thus, in the months when he and Helen ought to have been sailing south.

Helen accepted his absence. Ever his support in his dedication to the job, however late he returned, she would waken and listen if he wanted to talk. Usually he didn't. One night, however, perhaps sensing something more in him, she asked, "Is it the woman in black?"

He looked at her, surprised. She was referring to a woman who had presented herself a few days prior, with some psychic claim to having foreseen danger in North Beach. Sparrow had mentioned it in passing. "Now how did you know that?"

Helen's smile was coy. "I'm a bit of a witch myself. Is that what she is, Johnny? A witch?" He didn't know what she was, he admitted, but he had to consider everything. The woman had come to the main desk asking for a cop: not him in particular, just someone familiar with the North Beach killings. He had been there.

The woman in black, he thought now, trying but failing to come up with her name. He went into the closet where cabinets full of past case reports were kept. He tried to locate the summary folder for North Beach, but the files seemed to be in disarray. The telephone rang.

"I knew I was right getting you back," Frank Austin said. "Anything?"

In the background, Sparrow could hear a faint clinking and imagined crystal glasses being raised in toast, though at this hour the notion was absurd, and the idea that his return would be the occasion for high spirits even more so. "No. Frank, those old case files in the closet . . . what's the story?"

"Rocco's been taking stuff for the keypunch operators to put onto cards. When it's done it'll make things easy. Are you looking for something particular?"

"Just spinning gears."

"It's late. Get some sleep. I want you bright-eyed at a press briefing in the morning."

Sparrow groaned. "Necessary?"

"I want a show of force to reassure City Hall."

And the public? Sparrow wondered. Can we reassure them they're safe? When he hung up, he realized Sandoval was right about Austin feeling pressure. An ambitious man always did, mostly from himself. He thought again of the woman in black, but he wasn't going to wade through drawers full of paper in search of what might not even be there. When he got on the street he found he had recovered a measure of energy. He wasn't tired after all.

Amy Cole sat hunched over the old door that served as a desk and layout table in the editorial office of the *Rag*. Donovan sang his soft mysticism in the background. Ignoring the IBM Selectric in favor of a pencil, she wrote:

June 5th / late

Lance Corporal Glenn Torrey
Bravo Company / 1st Battalion
3rd Marine Division

Dear Glenn,

   Sorry for not writing sooner. I've meant to. Not a day has gone by that I haven't thought of you and of the question you asked yourself in your letter: "Why am I here?" I didn't want to answer too quickly.

When I saw you here in San Francisco before you left, I hinted that you could still go to Canada. That was dumb of me. You had your reasons for joining and they're not mine to judge. Still, your question . . . it's one I ask myself, too. So in responding, I'm trying to answer both of us.

To pick someplace to begin, I choose a gray Friday afternoon in late November almost four years ago. I was back in Massachusetts, sitting in class as the professor droned on. I was anticipating a sorority party I was going to that evening, how I'd grab supper in the dining hall, go up and iron my white ruffled blouse (no gaudy gypsy here), put on knit skirt and makeup and . . .

Then word came. The president had been shot.

Everything changed. It was as if we'd all been pushed underwater and were being held there. Time slowed to a hazy crawl. We watched the TV in the student lounge . . . images of Parkland Hospital, of Oswald gunned down, Air Force One, a stricken Jackie, LBJ being sworn in, and eventually the funeral and that black horse, jumpy and scared, with no rider in the saddle . . . Instinctively, we knew that nothing would ever be the same again.

A few days after that—surely no more than a week—I heard the Beatles for the first time, and that next February I sat with Mom and Dad and my sisters and watched them on Ed Sullivan's rilly big shoo.

Somehow, that confluence of forces—the fear, the gray depression, the wretchedness after Dallas, and now the bright simple joy of this music—made me begin to think and see things differently. I didn't tell you this—I even debated not telling it now, but you asked. A year and a half ago, when I was working as a newspaper intern, still with some notion of writing for a city paper, I was assigned to do obituaries. One day I came across a boy I'd known in high school, who was killed over there. Briefly, all over again, the fear was back.

But it can't win. We've all got each other and the music and love.

Writing this I realize how trivial it must sound, but I tell you, Glenn, I changed, am changing. A lot of us are. This scene happening here is really something: buzzing with good vibes and as colorful as a Moroccan marketplace! You'll know when you come home. I pray it's soon.

The little macramé-and-feathers thing I'm enclosing is a God's-Eye. Our housemate Tess makes them; she says it'll bring good luck. Seth says hi, too. He works constantly to help end the war.

As to your question, there may not be an answer right now. What I do *know——and you listen to me, Cousin!——is that you've got to pay attention to your officers and NCOs and do what you have to do and be the best soldier you can be.*

STAY SAFE!! And know I love you.

Amy signed the letter, hesitated, then added:

PS: Mom thinks I'm infecting you, so I won't send the latest issue of the Rag.
PPS: No! I want to know what you think! Rag enclosed.

Honey B's was sedate in contrast to some Tenderloin clubs, with their flashing marquees: TOPLESS! BOTTOMLESS! GIRLS GIRLS GIRLS, in case you were slow to get the idea. It had only its name block-lettered in blue neon; and if it offered smaller temptations, it was, as a consequence, a place of smaller troubles, too. Sparrow had become friendly, sort of, with the owner, one of the few he'd never had official occasion to bother over city obscenity statutes.

The shill in front, a pale moth in a trench coat, fluttered near, recognized Sparrow, and raised his eyebrows. Sparrow shook his head to indicate he wasn't working, and the man opened the door without a word.

Rock 'n' roll and smoke met him. Honey B's had a cowboy decor: fiberboard cactuses, wagon-wheel lamps, and studio stills of Gary Cooper and Randolph Scott on the walls. On a runway behind the bar, a woman was dancing, moving her arms as though she were swimming; indeed, her upper body appeared buoyant there in the smoky blue-green light, as if she were submerged in water. The few patrons were scattered at tables. As Sparrow took a stool at the bar, the owner, serving as bartender, came over.

"If this visit's official, Inspector, relax and have a drink. The only law we're defying is gravity." He was a lean man of middle years whose Western vest and sideburns fit the motif, if his Bronx accent did not. He gestured at the dancer on the runway. "Science has done it again. We've got knockers full of silicone."

"It's a good line," Sparrow said, "but I'm not in vice."

"You quit the force?"

The only other patron nearby was a man in a fedora at the end of the bar, hunched over his glass and looking as lonely as one of Edward Hopper's nighthawks. In a lowered voice, Sparrow said, "Reassigned to Homicide."

"Well, I'll be." The owner set a napkin on the bar. "What'll you have?"

When he'd poured bourbon and refused money, he said, "You working the hip-pie murders?"

"You know anything I should?"

"Only what's on the tube. Some kind of slasher, huh? Another good reason to stay out of freakville."

Today had been Sparrow's first venture to the Haight-Ashbury in some time, and he recognized that he didn't have a clue about the district. *Venus meet Jess at I/Thou. Off the Pigs!* The Beatles, it turned out, did have a new record, but it wasn't anything he knew. "I was trying to recall a dancer you had here a couple years ago," he said. "My age maybe, thirty-five. Nice looking. She always wore black?"

It rang no bells. The owner attended to customers. He returned carrying a loose-leaf binder, which he set on the bar. "This is the talent I've used."

Sparrow went through the pages, clear plastic sheets containing publicity stills, standard cheesecake mostly. The woman Sparrow sought was toward the back, in a come-hither smile and a black diaphanous nothing. Star Fleming was the name scrawled in gold script across the bottom of the photo. The owner nodded his remembrance. "She's one of the few who can actually dance."

"Is she still doing it?"

"I haven't seen her for a year or more. Why the interest?"

"Did she have a sideline?"

The owner drew the binder away.

"I know," said Sparrow, "you don't pry into your talent's private lives. The fact is, she was helpful when we were working the slashings in North Beach."

"No kidding? She was involved with that?"

"She came to us with some ideas. Now I'm just curious."

"Yeah, well, if I hear anything . . . I hope this turns out better than North Beach did. I get the creeps every once in a while thinking that guy might still be out there."

"I say draft 'em all." The drinker at the end of the bar had roused himself and glowered under the brim of his hat. "Longhairs. Scalp 'em and ship 'em off to Vietnam."

He said it "Veet-nam," the way the president did.

THE SIXTH-FLOOR CONFERENCE ROOM AT THE HALL OF JUSTICE WAS CROWDED WITH families of the victims, and probably other families, too, whose children had run away to join the ragtag army of hippies. Their anxious phone calls flooded the switchboard daily, pleading for information. Sparrow stood near one of the doors at the back. On a dais in front, behind a podium hung with the city and county seal, gleaming brightly under spotlights, a deputy chief was concluding a welcome. Along the sides of the room were reporters. No ghouls yet, Sparrow saw. Good. There'd been ghouls with North Beach, showing up at every chance, like spectators at an execution. Ignoring a flurry of questions from the floor, the deputy chief surrendered the podium to Frank Austin with ill-concealed relief.

In contrast with his elaborately uniformed superior, Austin wore a banker's suit, his red silk tie cinched into a neat knot. He blinked at the pop of a flashbulb and began without fanfare. The audience listened raptly.

"Each victim died of multiple stab wounds, inflicted by the same or similar weapon—a heavy, double-sided knife with a blade approximately ten inches long." Austin spoke for five minutes.

"Is there a suspect?"

"Not at this time."

"Do you believe it's the same killer in each instance?"

"It's looking that way."

"Were the victims sexually assaulted?"

Sparrow knew the questions. With slight variation they tended to be the same for every investigation where a suspect wasn't immediately caught. Moreover, he knew the answers from having probed the case files last night.

That morning Sparrow had stopped by the marina office and filled out a work request to get the *Blind Faith* ready for market. It would be a few weeks before the tasks were completed, but by late June she would be done. Part of him was glad for having taken action: the boat deserved better than he'd been giving her; but another part of him was sick over the decision.

Frank Austin was revealing that toxicity tests on the victims showed they had used drugs. "Marijuana?" the reporters wanted to know. "LSD?" The briefing went on. Austin stayed cool under the lights and questions. Sparrow, by contrast, felt overheated and removed his jacket. He admired Austin's deft handling of inquiries, his unapologetic admission to having no witnesses, suspects, weapons, or motive: precious little evidence of any kind, in fact. What he did convey was sorrow for the dead, concern for the living, and assurance that the killer would be caught. It was no wonder he was a favorite with City Hall. There was one uncertain moment when a young blond woman sitting near the front said, "You revealed that there were no signs of sexual assault, Lieutenant. Beyond the stab wounds, were the victims . . . marked in any way?" With a discreet hand Austin touched his tie, and it bought him enough time so that when he said "No" the lie was undetectable. He hadn't mentioned the mutilations. Nor the flowers.

The rest was easy, and just before Austin concluded, he paused, with the effect of bringing a hushed expectancy to the audience. "We're well aware," he said evenly, "that the social chaos in the Haight-Ashbury may be a breeding ground for social deviance and violence. Rest assured that we are going to protect the public and pursue our investigation with vigor." It was at that moment, as Austin turned the limelight back on the deputy chief, that Sparrow spotted George Moon.

He was standing by the opposite door. Like Sparrow, he wasn't fully committed to the room or its events—an observer, his arms-crossed stance said, though an interested observer, for all that. He had formerly been the man to give these briefings. How much was he privy to now, Sparrow wondered. Was he aware of Austin's evasion? The thought occurred to Sparrow that Moon had learned of his reassignment and had come to protest. It had been George Moon, after all, who had banished him from Homicide.

Perhaps sensing Sparrow's scrutiny, he turned. Their eyes met, Moon's narrowing with what might have been malice. Sparrow glanced away at hearing his own name in the tally of personnel assigned to the murders. When he looked again, Moon was gone.

As the briefing ended, Amy resisted the forward surge of reporters. Representing dailies and TV and radio news, they felt a deadline urgency she was spared. The *Rag*, after struggling through six months of sporadic publication, had finally achieved a tenuous weekly regularity. Seth, as editor, drew salary, as did Amy and Tess, though compared with even the least well paid of the journalists clamoring for a story now, the money was a joke. The main reason she didn't rush forward, however, was that she hadn't been officially invited today—though that hadn't stopped her from asking her question.

She made her way to the door and waited. Zephyr from the *Oracle*, equally uninvited (or too stoned to carry on), flashed her a peace sign and went on out, his blue espadrilles padding softly on the municipal tile. Zephyr was happier penning zonked ragas about astral planes and the zodiac, ideal copy for a paper which appeared at random intervals on jasmine-scented paper—not that the *Rag* was very much different, though it had not gone to rainbow color.

As she debated her course, she saw a man with a tan suit coat hooked over his shoulder exit through a side door. She checked her notebook for the names she had jotted; then, on an impulse, she followed him. She caught up as he paused to drink from a water cooler in the hall.

"Detective?"

His face was hard-jawed, she saw as he straightened, alert with a faint quality of menace.

"I'm Amy Cole. I'm with the press." She showed him the badge, glad for her insistence on this bit of professionalism at least. He gave the pass a wordless glance. "We're a weekly," she said, trying not to sound defensive. "Alternative news. May I ask you a few questions?"

"You're the one who asked if the victims had been marked."

"Guilty," she said. "Now, about the rest of it—"

"I thought Lieutenant Austin covered it okay," he said.

True, if no's were all one was looking for. No clues, no suspects, no arrests, no comment, apparently. "Can I confirm your name, at least?"

He glanced toward the corridor where people were crowding into an elevator. "John Sparrow."

She found it in her notes and corrected the spelling. Like the bird. But there was nothing birdlike in his appearance. He was six feet tall, lean, with wide shoulders that pushed against the seams of his shirt. He had dark blue eyes and a resistant swatch of brown hair. Despite his rough look, however, she detected something vulnerable in him, and restless right now.

"Do you think the killer will be caught soon?" she asked.

To his evident disappointment, the elevator closed without him aboard. "Hopefully."

"Lieutenant Austin said you're new to the investigation, Detective. What were you doing before this?"

"Inspector."

"I'm sorry?"

"For some reason, out here we're called inspectors. Detective is back east. Boston?"

The question caught her off guard. "Near there, yes," she admitted.

"Ever since Kennedy, I'm charmed by the accent."

"Thank you." Her cheeks warmed. "About your being new to the case——"

"Is this what's meant by alternative news?"

"The *Chronicle* and the *Examiner* keep carrying the city's promises for vigorous action to stop the killings. If I do a story, I'd like to give readers something to interest them while we all await results."

His half smile acknowledged her point. "What you can tell your readers is to be careful. They're in danger. I'm serious. And if any of them have seen or heard anything suspicious, contact us." He drew a card from his pocket and handed it to her. "Excuse me," he said, and turned for the elevators.

Thanks for nothing. As Amy wandered back toward the conference room, a burly locomotive of a man in a tweed sport coat stepped into her path, stopping her. He nodded after the departing cop. "Did he tell you how he's going to do it?"

"I'm sorry?"

"Sparrow. Did he say how he's going to bag the killer?"

Her curiosity was aroused. "Do you know him?"

The man's eyes followed the homicide inspector a moment more, then he turned. "You from one of the underground papers?"

There was no need for a press badge today. "The *Rag*," she acknowledged.

"What's your name?"

She told him.

"Well, I've got a news flash for you, Miss Cole. A big banner headline." He framed it with his hands. " 'Go Away.' The Summer of Love is over. Give your readers fair warning."

Only after her composure was restored and she was on her way downstairs did she realize she had seen the big man before and knew who he was. Captain George Moon. He headed the riot cops.

The crush of people got off at the fifth floor, leaving the elevator to Sparrow and Rocco Bianchi. The old cop's shirt collar pinched his neck. "Headed back to the detail, John?"

"I'm picking up Sandoval. We're going to the Haight."

Rocco sighed wearily. "All that BS upstairs just now . . . the 'team'—what a crock."

"A lot of it," Sparrow agreed.

Rocco glanced around as if he suspected hidden microphones in the elevator, and then said, "Between us, I'm not sure the city wants this one shut." Sparrow's attention sharpened. "Like maybe the killings will keep all these long-haired kids from coming." Perhaps hearing how cynical he sounded, Rocco frowned. "The truth is, I don't think we're ready for this one."

"What do you mean?"

Rocco scraped a hand through his hair. "The lack of evidence, for one thing. How can that be? It doesn't square with the way murders happen. And where are the witnesses? Somebody must know *something*. Problem is, we don't have the resources. Moon's getting all the juice for Tactical. We're lucky we got you back. Don't get me wrong, some of the guys are good. Lanin's a pain, but he's okay. College Boy is green and he makes mistakes, but no one works harder."

"There's you," Sparrow said.

Rocco's lungs rattled with coughing. "Nice try. I could've taken the handshake in May. I only stuck because Frank asked. But why? I should be going over there with you guys right now, but I just can't swing it anymore. My blood pressure's through the roof, my piles hurt like a bastard."

For years, Bianchi had been the model of a good cop: hard-bitten, thorough, and concerned. He'd been with Sparrow as they'd worked the North Beach case. John hadn't realized how spent he was. "Don't get me wrong," Rocco insisted again. "I'll still bust my hump . . . but hearing Frank up there just now, the 'team.' Hell. You'd think we were the 'Niners getting jazzed up for the Super Bowl." He gave in to a fit of coughing.

As the elevator opened, Sparrow said, "Can you still find your way around the files in that closet?"

"Pretty much. Why?"

"In the North Beach case, we built a profile."

"Of the killer?"

"Do you remember that?"

"Not the details." Rocco frowned. "These hippie killings are pretty different. Anyway, the files have been jockeyed around to put them into this fancy new computer."

"You're probably right. I was just curious."

Rocco's dull, groping eyes brightened a little. "I could have a look."

"Yeah?"

"Why not? I'll let you know." Rocco trudged out, then reached back to hold open the door. "It's a new world, John. Few more months and there won't be a scrap of paper in the whole building. It's all going to be little cards with holes in them." He shook his head in wonder. "Every file in this entire damn place is going to be in one contraption no bigger than my living room."

"Imagine," Sparrow said.

"I'm trying to give it a mariachi beat." Pete Sandoval's hand swept the air to include the crowded sidewalks, the cars inching along around Sparrow's Impala stymied in the midday clog of Haight Street. "It's noise," he said, "but it doesn't play."

The district was a carnival midway of flower children, cowboys, jugglers, freeloaders, magicians, speed freaks, chalk artists, swamis, beat poets, and panhandlers, all intent on purposes known only to them. A Gray Line bus motored along, belching fumes and giving out-of-towners the hippie tour. Soap bubbles, marijuana smoke, and music floated in the cool June sunshine.

"What happened to zits and sock hops?" Sandoval wanted to know. "Drive-ins and mini golf? Two, three years ago kids were racing GTOs and doing the Surf Stomp."

"And life was sleepy sweet all over," said Sparrow. "I don't think we're in Kansas anymore."

Sandoval grinned. He was a slender, handsome man, with his dark hair and low rider's slouch. "These kids are *from* Kansas."

And Dayton, Detroit, and Des Moines. The newspapers and TV were full of tidings of the coming summer. The influx of people to the Bay Area had risen to sixty thousand by some estimates, with more coming—driving in, hitching, turning up at the bus station downtown—and the season not even officially begun. Maybe there *was* something in the air, or in the water.

"You missed all this, no?" Sandoval said.

He meant the work, the probing of a criminal case; certainly not this place. In truth, Sparrow had not been here in a long time. Neither, by his own admission, had Sandoval; though he at least had been at Berkeley not many years ago, and so was familiar with the countercultural tilt of things.

Comic book–colored shop fronts with names like the Quasar's, the Free Store, the Blushing Peony, Mnasidika, Blue Unicorn, I/Thou, and the Freeque Bouteak lined Haight Street. Placards proclaimed free food at area churches, free clothes at secondhand shops on Divisadero, free love wherever you found it. Street hawkers offered just about anything else.

Telephone poles and tree trunks were tacked thick with flyers, walls papered with handwritten notices: Love Burgers for 40 cents; a Be-In on Hippie Hill;

broadsheets of poetry; an offer for free kittens; bongs (whatever they were) "$3 Cheap"; a demand for U.S. withdrawal from Vietnam; a job hotline number; "Drop Acid, Not Bombs"; a parental plea for a daughter to please call home; and the weird art nouveau proclamations of bands playing at the Fillmore, Winterland, the Matrix, Avalon, Masonic Hall, even the old Cow Palace. Music was in the air, apparently. And protest. There were petitions to sign: ban this, resist that. Was it all about opposition? Sparrow wondered. On the stop sign at the next intersection, someone had added the word "war." A million bits of information vying for the attention of passersby.

Feeling as if his own senses had reached an unmanageable density, Sparrow drew into a vacant space at the curb and parked. Sandoval got them take-out coffee.

"The Love blend," he explained, handing Sparrow a cup.

As Sparrow pried the plastic lid off, he sniffed the brew. Expecting what? For it to be laced with LSD? Or Spanish fly? This place made him prickle with prejudices.

Pete Sandoval seemed more attuned to it. Their initial formality having worn off, Sparrow found them comfortable together. Pete sipped his coffee without complaint, watching the scene through Wayfarers. "Maybe it is some eerie cruiser from out in the Valley," he offered. "He sits around until he gets the bad itch, then comes here to scratch it. He puts on a costume to fit in. Wouldn't be hard, John. Check this scene!"

Far from narrowing possibilities, Sparrow saw the prospects spiraling outward to the accompaniment of the music which enveloped them, changing block to block, issuing from storefronts, open windows in apartments above the shops, even from street musicians giving it away on corners. His mind wanted to shrink in inverse proportion.

"So, which one is he?" Sandoval went on as they edged back into traffic. "Moses on the corner there, waiting to part the Red Sea? Or catch the guy in feathers and face paint?" He was drawn in, sitting up now, scanning the teeming sidewalks.

Sparrow had begun to entertain the idea that the species was finally taking its cue from other animals, with the male preening himself to attract the female. It seemed to be working. Many of the young women were truly pretty, resplendent in costumes of their own. The idea of manhood appeared to be changing, causing him to wonder if some torch were being passed. John Wayne, who'd been a favorite at the drive-in theaters of Sparrow's youth, evidently was gone. Even the astronauts seemed destined to be left behind. The new man had hair below his ears, wore beads, strummed guitar, smoked another kind of cigarette.

A rap on the Impala's fender brought him back.

He braked. A woman who looked to be his age flitted past, showing them veed fingers. She wore a purple velveteen vest and an orange satin jumpsuit, looking misplaced only in her cocktail-party jewelry. He tried to picture Helen in like outfit, but the concept was absurd.

"Revolution hasn't changed a thing," Sandoval observed at the next intersection, nodding at a pretty teenager in a crocheted halter top and hip-huggers who was hawking newspapers. "They're still using cha cha cha to sell product."

"Get one," Sparrow said. He drew to the curb and watched his partner stroll over and say something to the girl that made them both smile. Sandoval brought back the newspaper, an odd-sized affair, some of it typeset, other parts typed, and some even handwritten in a florid, stylized script. The *Oracle*. "Twenty-five cents. A deal, huh?" Opening it, he began to read. Sparrow edged back into the flow of people and cars. After a time, Sandoval said, " 'The Zephyr Report.' Are you ready?"

"Give it to me."

"Uranus and Pluto are conjunct in Virgo. We've got some heavy psychic weather to get through, amigo. Zephyr, whoever that is, lists today as a dog."

"Ruff ruff."

They worked a slow route through the grid of streets, and Sparrow was aware that, as they observed, so they were observed, glances more curious than hostile, but alert to two men in suits lingering here where they were so obviously out of place. His high mood had been brief, and only as they left the district and headed back to the Hall of Justice did he realize that he had been holding himself tight. He felt the tension ease now, leaving in its passing a sullen thirst for a drink.

TURNING THE HANDLE, AMY SLIPPED BACKWARD THROUGH TIME (AT LEAST THAT WAS how she had come to regard the use of microfilm). Doing her internship at the Lowell *Sun* back home, she had often used a microreader to spool through old volumes in the newspaper's morgue, conducting research. Slowly winding the crank, she had come to consider the device a time machine. She still did now, in the library reference room at Berkeley.

Coming back had been Seth's idea, a blast-from-the-past visit to Terry Gordon, who had been Seth's favorite professor. Terry had been the catalyst for Seth's evolution from crew-cut, tennis-playing prep to president of Berkeley's chapter of

SDS. Terry had combined an incisive mind, firebrand politics, and personal style to become one of the most popular profs on campus. Now Seth wanted his advice on expanding the Mobilization Group and on dealing with the city's new tactical police squad, which seemed equally bent on expansion. Amy was interested in seeing Terry again, too, but she decided to let him and Seth get caught up first. Meanwhile, there was some research she wanted to do.

"Into what?" Seth had wondered.

And she could say only that she'd know when she found it.

She had not given up on the idea of writing a story on the killings, though clearly there was no purpose in replicating what the city dailies could do. She needed an angle, something beyond a "Just the facts, ma'am" approach. That's what she was looking for now as she scrolled through microfilm.

It was quiet in the reference room except for a few solitary students plugging away. Were they the last of a breed? God knew she'd spent her share of hours in classrooms, but slowly, steadily, she had found herself drawn away, pulled by the siren song of the streets, where truth was measured in the intensity of one's commitment to ideals. As for her writing, she had had to choose: either to go on grinding away at research papers, whose goals were void of any connection to some larger whole, or to write the stories *she* wanted to tell, finding the words and images that, if she worked hard enough and was good and lucky enough, would connect things into bigger meanings. The choice had been simple.

Yet here she was, back in a library carrel, searching for something, though she had no idea what.

After twenty minutes she was ready to give up, and it was then that something caught her eye. She bent closer to the viewer. On the front page of an edition from two years ago was the headline: POLICE SEEK TO ALLAY NORTH BEACH FEARS. What interested her more, however, was the accompanying photograph, which showed two men standing by a dark Ford sedan. Impelled by a new curiosity, she dug through her bag a moment.

There was a pay telephone in the library foyer.

"Special services," a tired-sounding man answered. "Vice."

Off balance, she glanced again at the card that John Sparrow had given her after the press briefing the other day. "Is Detec—Inspector Sparrow in?"

There was a pause. "He's back in the dead squad."

"I'm sorry?"

"Homicide detail. Fourth floor."

The man hung up before she could ask another question, and she was left to consider again Sparrow's reticence to talk the other day and George Moon's advice to her afterwards. And now there was the photograph in the two-year-old newspaper. Back at her time machine, she looked at the photo once more. The cut line only confirmed what she already knew: the men standing by the car were John Sparrow and George Moon.

From the marble steps of Sproul Hall, Amy saw Seth striding across the sunny plaza, but the rigid set of his shoulders told her at once that he wasn't feeling sunny at all. She hurried down the stairs toward him.

"He's gone," Seth called.

"What do you mean?"

"Gone. He resigned."

The idea struck her with force, and she stopped, still half a dozen steps above Seth, who stopped, too. As he angled his face upward, she saw anger in it, and pain. Terry Gordon was a campus mainstay, one of the poles around which student energy sparked. More important, he had been Seth's hero.

"When?"

"Right after commencement."

"Maybe he took a sabbatical."

"He quit. He went up north somewhere."

"To another school?"

"To the land, for Christ's sake. A farm. Figure *that* out."

"It's probably a political commune." She was looking for explanations, too.

"The Windflower Love Farm? We'll see him in *Zap Comix*."

Seth's sense of betrayal gave his words a caustic edge. Terry Gordon had been like the older brother who takes the risks, blazes the path, and sends back dispatches of such thrilling discoveries that you can't wait to follow. "I ran into one of his students, okay? She talked to him before he left. Terry decided all this politics was just bullshit! Time to grow up. Oh, yeah, and I quote—'The revolution is over.' We lost, baby."

THERE WERE SIX OF THEM BESIDES FRANK AUSTIN CROWDING THE OFFICE OF THE Inspector-in-Charge, their chairs arranged in a tight arc around the desk. They were Sparrow, Sandoval, Inspectors Bianchi and Lanin, the crime tech Simon Chang, and Stan Hoagland, a deputy coroner. It was Austin's delivery on his promise of a vigorous investigation: the Haight-Ashbury Task Force. They would meet daily, though earlier, tonight being an exception. The seven-day clock showed 9:35 P.M. This would be the core unit, though the full contingent, with various other personnel and the staffs at the crime lab and coroner's office, would be twenty, a good solid number for the newspapers.

Dr. Hoagland clicked a lighter, adding cigarette smoke to a room already dense with it. Austin and Sandoval were the non-smoking minority. "Talk to me," Austin said.

There was a report on paroled killers going back two years, ditto for state hospital releases, an update on FBI fingerprint checks, and additional data on the victims' backgrounds. Austin listened with ill-concealed impatience. "The net result," he summarized before Rocco Bianchi had fairly concluded his own report on information requests sent to police departments throughout the Southwest, "is still no suspect."

As if this were a judgment on him personally, Bianchi pulled a gloomy face and fell silent. Austin looked at Sandoval and Sparrow. "What about you two?"

Glancing to see if Sparrow wanted to speak—he didn't—Pete said, "It's frustrating talking to people in the Haight. We've been going door to door, but to them every cop is a narc."

"What do you expect with hopheads?" Bianchi observed.

" 'Hopheads?' " Paul Lanin jumped on it. "Jesus, Roc, that term went out with Tony Bennett. Dopers, we're talking now."

"Who says Tony Bennett's out?" grumbled Bianchi.

"It isn't all just paranoia," Sandoval said. "There have been a lot of drug busts, and I'm not sure every officer is following proper search and seizure, Lieutenant." Austin grimaced but kept quiet. "You've got runaways, transients, no one eager to cop any real tips. The merchants want to help, but they've got their hands full just managing their shops. And folks use street names—Marigold Girl, Zenith, Ruby Tuesday, Candle Jane. Try finding them twice."

Lanin sparked an L&M. "How come all you talk to, College Boy, are women?" He had bloodshot eyes and a small mouth, like some vestigial orifice, which had scaled down for smoking and drinking and just enough food intake to keep him alive.

"This one *guy* I talked to, Paul, quit being Jeff Wilson and decided he's 'January' now."

"January."

"That's his name."

Lanin snorted. "With hair down to his ass, I bet."

"If they're not living in crash pads or over at All Saints, they're moving around constantly."

"More often than they change their clothes," Lanin said. "If we're going to be working down there, Lou, how about issuing gas masks?"

"Give it a rest," said Hoagland. He wore a mustache, but not the fashionable kind: it made him look more like Andy Gump than any of the Beatles, though that suited his bland facade. Lanin showed him his middle finger. Sparrow quelled a yawn. He felt removed from the caffeinated flow around him. Outside, the sky was darkening by slow degrees.

Austin said, "How about lab evidence?"

Simon Chang might have been asleep, so silent had he grown; but he wasn't. In his humorless manner he said, "Only fingerprints we find so far are victims'." He sent an unreadable glance toward Sandoval, perhaps silent reproof for the young cop's having touched the flower on the first crime scene. "We have possible footprint—some kind of treaded boot. Also a roach to check for prints."

"A what?"

"A stub of marijuana cigarette."

"And that's your evidence?"

"I thought the shiftless bastards ate them?" said Bianchi.

"Or turkeyed them," Pete Sandoval said. "Pot is like gold over there."

"Seriously, don't they eat them?" Bianchi asked.

"Check a book, or make a phone call, Rocco," Lanin said. "Call up Tony Bennett."

Chang gave Austin a look of long-suffering appeal. "Finish up," Austin said.

Chang did, though he probably should have quit while he was ahead, for admittedly what he had was meager. Lanin was all over it. "You sit around playing with your test tubes. When're you going to come up with something we can use?"

"When you going to find a suspect?" Chang said evenly.

"A suspect?"

"I cannot catch guy in a laboratory. You've got to find him on streets."

"What street?" Bianchi shrugged. "You heard College Boy. The longhairs won't talk to us."

"If you inspire paranoia," Chang said, folding his arms, "there is nothing I can do."

Lanin butted his cigarette disgustedly. "You guys couldn't find your dicks with tweezers."

"But I hear you can," said Hoagland.

Lanin got halfway out of his chair before Sparrow's hand on his shoulder stopped him. He sank back with a sigh.

"All right." Austin's patience was fraying. "We won't get anywhere fighting ourselves. We've got a killer to catch."

"And a killer roach to catch him with," Rocco Bianchi stage-whispered.

When it was the deputy coroner's turn, Hoagland said, "I'll keep it brief, Lou, I know we're all busy," and talked for twenty minutes. At last he got to the faces. Something in the room changed, as subtle as the shifting smoke, but palpable. Everyone there had seen the mutilations. None of the severed noses had been found. Hoagland said, "I've detailed it all in the reports, but as to what it means"— he looked around the table—"I leave that to you."

Lanin said, "Could be symbolic some way. The killer reacting to all these people coming, maybe saying they don't belong, they should keep their noses out."

"Maybe he's a freak, you know, deformed," Rocco offered with a shrug. "Wants the victims to look like he does."

Or was it about sex, impulse, rage, retribution, madness? Sparrow began to drift. There was still too much data they lacked, evidence and witnesses they didn't have. The clock showed an hour gone. Outside, the sky had blackened. He said, "Along the Ho Chi Minh Trail, I've heard they have these fruit tree bombs they drop into the jungle."

Everyone's attention was on him.

"Not exploding bombs," he went on. "These little items sink nose-down into the ground. In the tail is a microphone that picks up sounds of trucks and troop movements on the trail."

"Gook bastards." Rocco Bianchi shook his head in disgust. "They have those?"

"*We* do. To tell us where to drop real bombs."

Austin was staring at him. "Interesting, John. We know you were in Korea and all. Your point being?"

"We need something in the Haight-Ashbury to tell us just what the hell is going on."

Pete Sandoval waited until they were in the parking garage before he said, "*En boca cerrada, no entran moscas,*" and grinned. "Old saying—'Flies don't go into a closed mouth.' You were quiet up there, John."

"I never learn much by talking."

"Your last point was on the money."

"It's another world in the Haight. How do we penetrate it? It's—" He broke off. He felt a sudden swim of wooziness. His vision went pale. He braced on the roof of his car.

"Hey, you all right?" Sandoval asked, hurrying around.

Thankfully, he didn't pass out. A wave of nausea swept him, dizzying him as it rolled through. It left his brow damp. Breathing deep, he blinked the parking garage lights into focus. "Yeah."

"You sure?"

"It must be that coffee on an empty stomach."

"Don't you love it? A twelve-hour shift and no time to eat. You hungry? There's this taco stand . . ."

"Rain check," Sparrow said. "I'm going home to fade."

At the rear of the stage, away from where liquid patterns of light moved on the wall like jellyfish in a dark sea, Circe stood among the shadows and let the band jam. With each gig they grew tighter, and she took pleasure in stepping out for a time just to listen, the music swirling about her like a sorceress's cloak.

It wasn't a big crowd—or a big club—but there were starting to be regulars, trailing the New Riders of the Apocalypse from gig to gig. Like the guy in denims and the leather kepi, some old North Beach beat poet type; the albino spade who dealt on the corner of Haight and Stanyan; the tall woman with the flamenco shawl and heavy eye paint; the girls in pigtails; the boys with suburban haircuts and fuzzy new mustaches. The bikers along the bar were familiar, too, watching her with hot Dexedrine eyes when she sang. But mostly the people coming to see the Riders play were flower children.

Potentially there were thousands of them, *tens* of thousands. She knew them by their look of hunger and pent-up longing. Once channeled and allowed to flow toward some common end, there would be no stopping them. But first they needed to find the channel. Circe turned her regard to the band.

Eric Lindgard, blond hair fringing his chiseled face as he bent over the Stratocaster, was wringing sounds from the wood and gleaming steel, sending feedback and distortion rising like furies. He found the notes that drew listeners into the heart of the music, holding them mesmerized so her singing could seize them. The beautiful, silent Eric, infecting listeners with his guitar . . . she had given him the name Pestilence.

Vince Russo stood to Eric's left, unmoving but for his hand plucking the bass in a rhythm that pounded the chest, awakening something primitive within. In tight black pants, dark T-shirt and sunglasses, he watched the crowd with a gaze that missed nothing, divining any curious glance, show of vulnerability, momentary fascination, as all the while he fingered the strings with the same detached artistry he would use later on the girls he picked up. Circe had come upon him in the Crypt one time with a pair of teenagers, their naked sweaty bodies intertwined. Insatiable as a satyr, gaunt with hunger, Vince was Famine.

Offstage, Joe Williams had an easy street charm, but here he might have been an African tribal warrior, resplendent in his dashikis and hand-carved beads, lights sparking in his fine-wire Afro. He wielded the ebony-black Rickenbacker like a weapon, firing dense salvos of chords. He liked to keep a burning cigarette clamped among the tuning pegs—"Old street trick," he said, "from when you didn't take no breaks, waitin' for folks to throw you nickels an' shit"—the orange tip gleaming like a tracer round. Ready and reliable as a soldier, Joe was War.

And back there on the drum riser, half concealed behind his kit, was Toad Madden, consumed with his sticks, and with mixing his mind poisons in the basement of the big house on Ashbury that they all shared. The newest member of the Riders, he was eager to prove himself. Circe watched him, his arms a blur as he pummeled the skins and cymbals, banging out the beat like a black hole into which everything else was drawn. Loyal, homely, warted little Toad, who longed for her with a desire bordering on despair, and who would do anything for her. Toad was Death.

She made five as singer. And Desmond Raimes—out there in the fog of smoke working the mixer, absentee angel and electronics wiz, who wrote the lyrics and the checks—Dez was six.

But the New Riders of the Apocalypse was much more than the sum of its parts. She shut her eyes, feeling the music take her, carrying her along as dizzily as a bit of stardust on a solar wind, building in a force that intensified around her, and with each passing day threatened—promised!—to explode them out of this little club and sweep away all that lay before them.

With the guitars screaming, the bass thudding like pursuing hoof beats, Toad's drums pounding, Circe opened her eyes and stepped through the watery slide of light. She gripped the microphone and brought it to her mouth, about to sing, when a tiny shape flew through the shimmering light, bounced softly against her dress, and fell to the stage.

Puzzled, she glanced down. It took her a dizzy moment to realize what it was, then she reared back with a prong of panic, for lying at her feet was a human nose.

Even now the memory has power sometimes to wake you in the night. You lie damp with sweat, heart *a-whumping* as the dream fades. The dirt, the soft, moist fingerfeel and rooty, rich nosesmell of it always the same, land that has been lived on and fertilized and farmed for a thousand years and more, and you know its coolness as you slide over the lip of the hole, slither inside, and you're gone, for hours sometimes, crouching, duck-walking, at times crawling through the secret dark behind the shine of the flashlight, emerging at last to be greeted by the others, who're full of questions, smiles and friendly insults, and you're big in their eyes in a way you never are when you stand among them.

But the dream concerns itself with one time, and here, awake, your heart quickens with recall.

Let it alone.

But you can't.

It's past.

It's now.

No. God, no.

Moving through blackness on all fours, rounding a turn. Ahead, a frail flicker of light. You freeze.

A moment passes, ticked off with the drumbeats of your heart. A spider scuttles across the back of your outstretched hand. Slowly, fearful of making any sound, you creep into the gauzy light of a single candle. You turn to stone. Squatting there, just visible in the frailest reach of flame, is a man.

His eyes are closed. He's small and brown, dressed in black, and he's alone. He begins to murmur something. *"Nam mo a nhi da phat . . ."*

Prayers? God Jesus. There in the one place where there is some peace for him, is he praying?

"Nam mo a nhi da phat . . ."

Now he's sensed you. His eyes pop open. For an instant there's surprise in his face, as there must be in your own! But it goes, leaving only . . . what? Bemusement? Knowledge?

Neither of you moves. The candlelight wavers. Shadows shift. Suddenly, the man turns, reaching for something there beyond the light.

The sensation—still so vivid after all this time that your arm will sometimes rise in the dark of your room, riding the drumroll in your chest—the sensation of raising the knife . . .

You give the scene three, four replays; sometimes a dozen, though far fewer than the hundred it used to require.

And then, perhaps, sweat-soaked and exhausted, you sleep.

A PAIR OF PLAINCLOTHES COPS LOOKED UP WHEN AMY WALKED INTO THE HOMICIDE detail. After a momentary appraisal, one asked, "Can I help you?" She gave Inspector Sparrow's name, and the cop pointed to the rear of the room, where she saw Sparrow on the telephone. "Go on over when he's done," the cop said.

"Thank you."

The room was unexpectedly small: a bullpen with half a dozen desks and file cabinets, a wall map of the city, WANTED flyers, a single window, and stale air. The "Dead Squad," the person on the phone had called it. On a table in a corner was a seven-day clock, which struck her as quaint somehow, a touch of elegance in an otherwise drab world. The main effect, however, was of confinement, and she was uncomfortable in it. She hadn't given up her idea of doing a story on the killings, however, and she hoped that she might find an angle that hadn't been covered yet. When Inspector Sparrow cradled the phone, she went over and gave her name.

He rose, straightening his tie, but from his expression, she realized that he didn't remember her, or if he did, he couldn't remember from where. "We met upstairs the other day," she prompted. "At the press briefing."

"Right. The underground journalist." He scooped a stack of manila folders off a chair. "Have a seat." He took his own. "I saw your newspaper. The *Oracle,* right?"

"The *Rag.*"

"Oh. How many are there?"

"Three or four."

"Really?"

"Surprised?"

"Well, those papers don't seem quite . . . real somehow."

"Compared to the *Chronicle* and the *Examiner.*"

He shrugged. "Maybe it's just me. I'm behind the times."

"Your cup's pretty hip." She nodded at a coffee mug with Chinese characters printed on it.

"That came with the desk. Any idea what it says?"

"Someone told me the word for 'crisis' is the signs for 'danger' and 'opportunity' together. I think that's it."

"Perfect." He gave a faint smile. "So, what brings you, Miss Cole?"

"I'm curious about what kinds of leads you have."

"We don't have many," he admitted. "We're convinced it's the same killer. Same weapon—some kind of heavy knife. There's some physical evidence that's being examined. Beyond that . . . not much. Lieutenant Austin is the one who releases information."

She held his gaze. "Not to everybody, or in equal measure, apparently. So I guess I should read the *Chronicle*."

"His office is right there if you want to speak with him."

"Or maybe the underground press isn't legitimate enough."

"You said it, not me."

"No, you did. 'Not quite real,' remember?"

"I wasn't speaking officially. Anyway, the one I read was on rainbow-colored paper and smelled like a beauty parlor. If the medium is the message, as this McLuhan is telling us, I don't think most people are going to stake much confidence in what they read there."

"Why does the news have to be one size fits all? Who decides that? The Hearsts? NBC? We serve a community. The truth is, our readers don't believe half of what's in the straight press—or what *isn't*." She was aware that her voice had risen, carrying in the enclosed bullpen. She lowered it. "I heard that a severed nose turned up at a music club last night."

The sleeves of his white shirt were turned back, revealing lean, strong-looking forearms. He crossed them and sat back. "Okay. I'll take your word for it that the people in the Haight-Ashbury do more than just navel-gaze."

"So it's true."

"The truth is nobody down there has been much help to us. No one wants to talk."

"Have you considered the way the police present themselves?"

"We've tried to avoid that in this unit. We're just investigators. Still, if people are breaking the law . . ." He let the thought hang, but it was plain that he didn't approve of what was going on in the Haight.

It was also plain that her idea that this could be a simple give and take wasn't going to happen. She played the card she had told herself she wouldn't. "Is that where Captain Moon comes in?" she asked.

For an instant, something in the cop's dark blue eyes changed, grew wary. He recovered, but not quickly enough. "You worked with him, didn't you?" she said.

Sparrow glanced around as if conscious for the first time of how small the office was. He bent nearer. "Danger and opportunity, huh? Let me buy you coffee. The stuff here isn't fit to drink."

Since Amy Cole had hitchhiked downtown, Sparrow offered to drive her back. She suggested a place for coffee. The I/Thou was on Haight, in a stretch of brightly colored shops. Seeing it, Sparrow recalled something: *Venus meet Jess at I/Thou.* Graffiti on a wall at one of the crime scenes. *Jefferson Airplane Loves You. Off the Pigs!* He followed the young woman inside.

The aromas of coffee and tobacco smoke rose above a clatter of cups and the murmur of conversation, creating a congenial atmosphere Sparrow didn't expect. A man with a year's-long beard worked a hissing espresso machine. En route from the Hall of Justice, Sparrow had quizzed the journalist about the murders, though beyond her sense of their tragedy, she knew little. They settled at a table in a sunny window, with coffee that was ink-black and rich tasting, as different from the cop house brew as Dom Perignon was from Thunderbird. He brought up George Moon this time. "Is he the subject of your story?"

"I don't know. I don't really have a story yet. I came across a photograph of the two of you working in North Beach."

He nodded. "Moon was head of the homicide detail—my boss before I went to Vice." It wasn't classified information, but neither man had done much advertising about his past. Even if she had spoken with Moon personally, he doubted Moon would have mentioned him in any detail: certainly not that they'd once almost become brothers-in-law. "Now the bureau's got need of another inspector in Homicide, so I agreed to help—for this one case."

"And we all know where Captain Moon has gone."

"So, you see? No dark secrets. My turn now." But he didn't go on because something had caught his eye. Beyond Amy's shoulder, a young man was surreptitiously stuffing muffins into the recesses of his threadbare serape. An empty cup and a pack of cigarettes followed these. Excusing himself, Sparrow rose.

The young man was slow in looking up, alerted finally by Sparrow's presence at his side. In a whisper, Sparrow said, "You're doing that to free your hands to get your wallet, right?"

Something unreadable flickered in the man's bloodshot eyes; then, awkwardly, he turned to run. Sparrow gripped the serape, which started to rip away in his hand. He took hold of the man's arm, startled at how thin it was under the fabric of his shirt. It was like clutching a stick. The young man quit struggling at once. But the commotion had drawn the counterman, who asked, "What's going down?" Sparrow looked at the young man, inviting him to make a clean breast of things, which after a moment he did, hauling out the items he had stashed. He launched into a manic account of how he had arrived a few days ago from St. Paul but he hadn't been able to find some friends he was supposed to hook up with and, like, start a business with, and he'd crashed in the park last night and been hassled by cops and he hadn't eaten in, like, two days, and by the way, his name was Kenny. The counterman listened thoughtfully, threshing fingers through his beard. Finally, he said, "You want to work, man?"

"Here?"

"We can use help."

Kenny nodded slowly, giving it thought. He was a candle maker, he said— that's the business he was planning to start, because folks always needed candles, right? Let there be light. Sand candles were his specialty—*scented* sand candles— but yeah, it sounded cool. He paused. "Do I punch a time card?"

The counterman laughed and told him he could eat and could start working today if he wanted. When the kid had gone off to the kitchen, the counterman clapped Sparrow's shoulder. "All's well that ends well."

Left with neither victim nor crime, apparently, Sparrow went back to Amy Cole, who looked amused, having watched the whole drama. He returned to their purpose and pressed her about the killings, but she knew nothing more. "What about rumors, gossip?"

"Only what I've told you. If anyone knows more, they may be afraid to come forward, afraid of the cops."

"Okay, people won't talk to us, but what about you? Don't you people talk to each other?" He was growing restless. "What the hell do you do all day?"

"Besides not working, you mean?"

"Enlighten me."

"We sit around stoned and groove to the Beatles. We get it on randomly with strangers, because life's a trip. But you know that already, don't you."

He let out a long breath. He was an easy target for irony. He knocked a Winston out of his pack and offered her one. She declined. He quelled a comment about the kind she might prefer. When he got the cigarette going, she said, "With the first death, I thought, okay, bad vibes, bad drugs, a money trip. But it's not those things, is it?"

"I don't think so."

"It's something . . . darker."

She was plain looking, but there was a sparkle to her features, an intelligence that shone through. She wore patched Levis and a fringed suede coat over a denim shirt whose faded blue accentuated her eyes and made them all the more piercing. "Go on," he said.

"I've begun to wonder if for a lot of people here the killings aren't happening."

"Aren't happening? Like that fellow wasn't stealing."

"I know, it's weird. I was at a gathering the other night, on community issues. The murders had to be on everyone's mind—I know they were on mine—but they didn't come up once. Okay, some people are scared, I understand that. But we're also scared of narcs and what we've been hearing about the TACs. I think there's something else. You mentioned people having street names. What does that suggest?"

"That they're hiding out."

"In some cases, yes. And there are runaways, and maybe some draft resisters."

"And a killer."

"I don't know that for sure."

"Which part?" he said sharply. "The killer?"

"Okay, there are people here who want invisibility. But not everyone. There's a whole other situation, too, that's not about hiding. In fact, it's just the opposite. It's facing up. It's . . ." Trailing off, she glanced past the glass.

He followed her gaze to where longhaired people strolled by in the dappled sunshine on Haight Street, in no more hurry, apparently, than she seemed to be. In fact, he had begun to suspect her notion of herself as a journalist was a delusion, a vestigial clinging to an old world where people still worked, a cover for druggy thoughts.

"A lot of these people," she said, "are . . . molting."

He drew his eyes back to her, and discovered that hers were on him now with a degree of focus he found unsettling.

"They're shedding old identities, casting off chains, looking for something beyond the empty longings that were making them unhappy." Perhaps reading skepticism in his expression, she said, "Dismiss it if you want, but they're evolving."

"They."

"*We*. It's why we've come here, why *I'm* here. It's what I'm trying to do, too."

But he didn't dismiss it. She was so earnest in fact, that he found himself interested. Molting. If you got beyond the oddness of it, the notion had a certain appeal. As did the idea of giving someone a chance to work instead of having him steal from you. But the more pressing reality reasserted itself. Four people had been hacked to death. He butted his cigarette. "I have to go."

"Wait." She gripped his arm as he started to rise. "Hang on a second. Okay, you're right, I know. There's a real killer out there." As if suddenly conscious of her hand on his arm, she drew it away, momentarily flustered. Recovering her composure, she said, "What do *you* experience here?"

He didn't have to think. "Craziness."

"Is that really what you see?"

"Only when I look."

She sighed.

Did she want a list? All around, the quirks of the district announced themselves with the subtlety of semaphore flags. Like the fact that no one seemed to cut their hair or bathe. That a lot of folks were obviously stoned. And what were they? Bead artists and candlestick makers. He couldn't walk without having to skirt around someone making chalk drawings on the sidewalk, or juggling colored balls. No one wore a watch; he'd noticed it the other day: there were no clocks. But if time wasn't a concern for anyone else, it was for him. He felt it spooling past, and while he stood here entertaining goofy notions, a monster was out looking for its next prey.

"Do you know the word 'chiaroscuro'?" he asked.

An art term; she did know it. Shadows and light. "If all this is light," he said, "I'm definitely in the shadows."

"That's honest, at least. My mother thinks she understands the scene from having read *Look*."

He felt a jab of remorse for having spoken so bluntly before. "You came to me on your own," he said. "I appreciate that. I am over my head. I admit it. What can you tell me?"

She hesitated, then shook her head. "Nothing really."

"Why? Because I'm not part of it? What if I put a flower in my hair?"

She gave a quiet laugh. "That might be premature."

"So what, then? Really." It occurred to him that it wasn't only remorse he felt; this was as near as he'd come to making a link with this place. Her eyes were on him again, penetrating and direct, and he saw that he had been mistaken in thinking her vague and distracted. She was probing him every bit as much as he was she, had been from the moment they met.

"You've got too much resistance," she said.

"Resistance."

"To ambiguity and . . . chaos."

More hippie lunacy. This was not a good idea. He turned toward the street now himself: looking for what? An accident, a scuffle, some act of physical conflict to pull him safely back to the world he knew? A string of soap bubbles wobbled in the air like tiny crystal apples. Let her go, he told himself. But she sat there, watching him. How old was she? Twenty-two? She seemed older in some way, wise, and briefly he had the idea that she was manipulating him, playing with his head, had been from the first. But when she spoke, there was a note of suppressed urgency in her voice.

"You're right. The killings are real. Of course they are, and they're terrible. But people here aren't reading the city papers or watching TV. They've tuned that out. If they see cops, they avoid them. Information passes through different channels."

The tarot deck and the *I Ching?* The "Zephyr Report"? More than ever this whole situation struck Sparrow as absurd. In his mind he could see the blood-red pushpins on the wall map in the homicide detail. From here he could walk to the actual crime scenes in minutes—down Ashbury to the Panhandle, or along Haight to the park—even considered doing just that, taking this woman on a macabre tour to give her a jolt of reality, and remind himself he was dabbling in foolishness just talking to her. As if she read his thoughts, she said, "Dismiss it if you like, but it's how people think. For someone who's taken a long look into the void—"

"Tripped out, you mean?"

"—to that person, the idea of physical death isn't so menacing."

He thought of Helen in the days of her radiation and chemotherapy, and it occurred to him that she might've agreed. Her focus had been on him, his happiness. He swept the thought aside. "Just another turn of the cosmic wheel," he mocked.

But she was pledged to her idea. He couldn't rattle her. "Walk with me," she said.

"What?"

But before he could ask where, she put down money for the coffees and went outside. Pausing just a moment, he went after her. She started down Haight. "I do know this," she continued in a lowered voice, as though not wanting to be overheard by passersby, "there's more to the killings than meets the eye. I think you know it, too."

His pulse quickened. "What do you mean?"

"Do you agree?"

Did she possess some knowledge after all? Had she learned about the mutilations? Having set in place the intricate rhythms and steps of this dance, was she about to enlighten him? Or was she just playing a hunch, trying to gauge what he knew? She turned left onto Masonic and they headed toward the Panhandle. "Go on," he urged.

"For one thing, the person you're after isn't one of us. He doesn't share our values. Violence is the language of people who can no longer express themselves in other ways, with words and colors and sounds."

"But he comes here."

"People here are trusting. But I think there's something else drawing him. And while you're looking for clues and evidence, asking cop questions, he's looking to find it. The killings are a response."

A flame of adrenaline had ignited Sparrow's nerves. He was walking in daylight, but even so he felt a shadow chill him. "To what?"

She stopped walking. "Are you willing to tell me what you know? I've read the newspaper accounts, they're empty. I mean your investigation, any leads you've developed. Profiles. Whatever you're keeping back, whatever you've really found. Like that severed nose, for instance."

So she did know some things. "In exchange for what?"

"My help."

For a moment, he weighed the offer; but only for a moment. What she was asking for he couldn't provide. Policy precluded it, of course, but he wasn't ruled by policy the way Frank Austin was; no, his position in the homicide detail was tenuous enough as it was without adding risks, most of all the risk to her. She was part of this community, and therefore she was vulnerable. He simply couldn't involve her in a hunt for a killer—especially if she might herself fall prey. "I can't."

"No, I suppose not. Anyway, you and Captain Moon have your own time-proven methods."

He sensed that he had failed a test, fallen short of something she had hoped to find. Unaccountably, this pained him. He wanted to point out that he had no link with George Moon—no present link, certainly—but it seemed a quibble just now. In her view, cops were cops: narcs and TACs and homicide inspectors alike. Pigs. No friends to her or anyone else here, and he had no words to counter that. When they had covered the last slow block to his car in silence, he said, "Let me pay for the coffees," but she wouldn't let him. "Can I offer you a ride home, at least?"

She looked at him, tucking a strand of hair behind her ear. "In⟩   "
she said, using his name for the first time since at the Hall ⟨
unfondly, "you really don't get it, do you? This *is* home."

In the coming afternoon fog, the waterfront had a gray s⟨
removed from the gaudy tumult of the Haight. Masts an⟨

tral forest, and the gangway chirped as Sparrow went down to the pier. Since his decision to put the *Blind Faith* on the market, he had avoided the marina. His hours consumed by the labors—thus far fruitless—of investigation, there was no time; nor did he want the memories that he knew seeing the boat would bring. But perhaps, after his failure in the Haight-Ashbury, he needed something to reassure him that his life had roots.

He wasn't prepared for how quickly the yard crew was bringing the craft back to shipshape. With her upper hull clean and the deck clutter gone, she had regained her contour, like a once sleek beauty on a new regimen of exercise and diet. And he realized that this, too, was why he had stayed away, for now it was apparent that some irreversible course had been charted. He didn't go aboard. In the marina office, the foreman reported that the boat was scheduled to be hauled in a few days to have her bottom scraped. After that there would be some mechanical repairs, but with those done, the *Blind Faith* should sell quickly. Did Sparrow want to order a new set of sails?

That evening, doing paperwork at the Hall of Justice, he found himself thinking of Amy Cole's visit, and from there it was only a short trip along memory's path to another day when another woman had come to the homicide detail. She showed up and asked to speak with anyone assigned to the North Beach case. Sparrow introduced himself. She was Miss Fleming, she said, and she had come to offer something she'd experienced in a trance state, which might relate to the killings in North Beach. "I see a house, even the street. I don't have the name of the street, but I'd know the house if I saw it."

"In the city?" She thought so, yes. He was mystified already. Out of courtesy he offered a chair. With a swirl of her black shawl—she was clothed entirely in black—she sat. "Go on," he encouraged, "tell me about the dream."

Not a dream, she said.

A trance, then.

Self-conscious, possibly aware of how it must sound, she told about the house being shabby and large, with a lot of people living in it. And outside in the yard, she said, there was always a man. Very tall and wearing a bathing suit.

"Doing what?"

"Sunbathing, I think. And . . . watching."

Though that was another curious thing, the woman said. Each time she had an age of the man, he was paler, as if he were sick. But the important part, the rea- was there, was the girl. The girl. Sparrow seized on that. She might have although that was a guess. What the woman was sure of, what had prompted her visit, was that the girl was in danger, and the threat was getting more serious. Although Sparrow had his pencil ready, he had not yet taken a single note. Now he wrote the word "danger" on his pad.

What sort of danger? The woman in black didn't know; only that there was a girl and she was in jeopardy somehow. From the tall man in the swimsuit? She wasn't sure. He drummed his pencil and sighed. Did Miss Fleming want to fill out a report?

"A report?"

"Well, we'd like some more details."

She didn't *have* more details, and she resisted offering anything further about herself. She felt that what she had given was information the police ought to know. "You'll look into it?" she asked. She gave him a city number. "You can call me."

But no one ever did, even after a follow-up note from the woman addressed to Sparrow a week later; and whether or not she had any more trance images of the house or the girl or the tall man, Sparrow never knew. Two weeks after the woman's visit, the fourth and final victim of the North Beach Slasher was found by kids looking for returnable soda bottles. She was wrapped in a blanket and hidden in some bushes in an alley, her throat cut. When an address check took Sparrow to a housing project in Hunter's Point, he happened to glance out the tenement window and find himself face-to-face with a man in blue swim trunks. Rocco Bianchi and George Moon were there, too, going through the victim's few possessions. "John," Rocco said. "Our guy's been here."

But Sparrow was staring at the man in swim trunks, who was reclined on a chaise. He was fifty feet long in a billboard ad for tanning lotion. Exposed to months of sun and freeway grit, his image had paled to a jaundiced green.

It would be another day before background checks on the victim revealed her to be a seventeen-year-old runaway from Boise, who had been hooking in the city for a month. Two days later, as an afterthought, Sparrow would call the telephone number the woman in black had given him and discover that it was for Honey B's Lounge, where a Star Fleming—not her real name—was an exotic dancer. But that evening of finding the young victim, Sparrow felt for the first time in the case an acute need to talk about his day when he got home. However, Helen was not there. She had been taken earlier to the hospital for what would prove to be her last visit before doctors declared her cancer untreatable.

IN LETTERS FORMED OF FLOWERS, THE POSTER ABOVE THE IBM ELECTRIC TYPEWRITER, keeping company with a wild-bearded Karl Marx and an idealized Che, urged:

```
TURN ON * TUNE IN * DROP OUT.
```

Amy no longer recalled the circumstances of the choices—the Marx and the Che were definitely Seth's—but this poster had come to have special meaning to her. There was other adornment on the walls of the converted theater that served as editorial office for the *Rag*: a "Keep on Truckin' " figure that Robert Crumb had presented to them on the publication of their fifth issue; pubescent-looking Beatles in a Liverpool doorway—but the floral Timothy Leary mantra always seemed to Amy especially apt. She envisioned the glossy three-by-four-foot broadsheet as an escape hatch there in the wall, should what she did as a writer become overwhelming.

The task of getting the newspaper to press on deadline, given its small budget and smaller staff (never mind the distractions of the Haight itself), was a big one. Seth and she had been at it nine hours today already, and there was always more to do. Now, in the face of the tensions threatening to split the community, and the dark menace of the killer, she saw her job as going far beyond writing.

Not Jester though, apparently. He seemed ready to take Dr. Leary's advice. He was hunched over the old door that served as the *Rag's* layout desk, using the *December's Children* album jacket as a chute to clean a lid of grass he had scored from the albino Negro on Stanyan. He had actually paid ten dollars for it, twice what he'd paid only a month ago, but it was what you had to expect this time of year as the supply began to dry up. Seeds spilled across the bony English faces of Jagger and Co. and bounced onto the door like BBs.

Seth sat on one end of the door-desk, blue-penciling copy. He was editing Amy's Open Letter feature, this week addressed to "The Tribes," an appeal to unity versus factionalism. The Open Letter was among the paper's more successful features, and the one that generated the most reader response. Her letter to Mayor Shelley a few months back had even elicited a note from Hizzoner, albeit a patronizing one. Seth made a couple of notations on the pages and handed them back. "Okay?"

The changes were small cuts that tightened and improved the piece, mostly. She'd have stuck with "togetherness," but she let his substitution of "solidarity" stand. "Okay."

Done cleaning the dope, Jester put a few pinches into a leaf of paper, which he rolled crisply between his fingers, spilling crumbs from both ends. He licked the seam and presented his handiwork to Seth. Seth lit it. "Like the dormouse said . . ." He took a small hit. Amy laughed. "What's funny?" Seth asked.

"I just had a flash of the two of you at thirty, holding up the shaker and asking your wives, 'Cocktail, my dear?' "

"Bullshit." Seth frowned. "I don't plan on seeing thirty."

Jester took the joint and toked deeply. A seed that had escaped his detection flared briefly like a miniature blowtorch. When they had smoked the joint down and Jester had swallowed the roach, he produced a king-sized Hershey's bar, unwrapped it, and began snapping off squares of chocolate.

"How can you eat that right now?" Amy cried.

"An ounce of prevention . . . I wanna ward off the munchies."

Afterwards, as he sat sucking his fingertips, Jester asked when they were going to leave to catch some music. Seth declined, insisting he had work to do. "Come on. What are tomorrows for? You've got to hear this band I've been telling you about."

"Can't. I've got another clock to punch."

Amy looked at him. It was Seth's way of saying he had something to do for the Movement. He kept certain of his activities private, even from her. He claimed he didn't want to put the *Rag* at risk of a bust by aligning it too closely with Mob Grope, but Amy suspected he got off on having a secret, like a lover. He kept a mimeograph machine and other equipment in a locked janitor's closet at the rear of the building. The few times she'd mentioned it had led to disagreements, so she let it be. While her interest was in recording events, Seth seemed to harbor some grander, if vague, scheme for inciting them.

Clearly bummed at Seth's defection from the plans for the evening, Jester was nevertheless up for fun. "Ames?" he said hopefully. "You still in?"

She had just about talked herself into staying to work on her feature, but all at once the pulse and promise of the night beckoned. If Seth wanted to stay in, that was his thing; she'd had enough for one day. Turn on, tune in, drop out. "Yeah," she said. "I'm in."

They took the Volvo, an old gray affair that Amy had owned at Berkeley, but it was communal property now, share and share alike. Thor's Hammer was across the city on Grant. Although it continued to carry itself like a coffeehouse for folkies, with espresso still the drug of choice, it was apparent that the club was metamorphosing. Greeting them as they walked in was a light show, big amoeba shapes squirming and dissolving on the wall behind a low stage where a band was producing barely serviceable folk rock. When the set ended and the band Jester had come to see was ready to appear, the room had grown more crowded. Without fanfare or even an introduction, four musicians took the stage and began to play. They were called Raven, Jester said, and though he had never seen them perform, he had heard about them from a friend.

More than rough at the edges, the music was neither skillful nor very good. There were missed cues, a broken guitar string, and ragged vocals by the rhythm guitar player, a black man with a red feather boa and a hovering cloud of hair. Amy found herself with second thoughts about having come. As if sharing them, Jester caught her eye and bent near. "The lyrics ain't much, but the malady lingers on." He pointed to the bar and made an interrogative tipping motion to his mouth. She shook her head. He waved and drifted off into the smoky dimness. She kept her spot by the back wall.

When the next song began, announced by several sinewy chords that the lead guitarist wrung from his instrument, a woman emerged from the shadows at the rear of the stage. She had dark hair and a long black dress, which seemed to flow in the breeze of an unknown wind as she stepped forward. In the changing light it was hard to see her face; still, she had an immediate impact on the crowd. Some bikers along the bar whistled. The woman paused a moment; then, gripping the microphone in ring-spangled fingers she began to sing.

Her voice was a husky whisper that lagged a moment behind the music, then got ahead, and finally found the tempo beautifully. The crowd quieted.

The band took a step up, too, their musicianship suddenly surer than it had been, as if they'd only been tuning up before, or hustling the audience in some way—*Don't expect much, we're just a bar band*. The guitar work started to sparkle, and the drumming had gone from simple-minded thudding to something more compelling. The crowd seemed aware of the change, too; the dancers quit but stayed on the floor, giving the band their attention. Amy looked around for Jester but didn't see him.

The music had a distinctive something she couldn't name, like a dark undercurrent flowing through it. And indeed, Amy felt an odd vibration. The more she listened, the more she was drawn in, until her focus on the stage was total.

Leaving the *Rag* office, she had been mildly buzzed, but now she felt herself soaring, carried along by something headier than weed. On the floor, crowded and humid with people, the current seemed almost electrical. And yet for all of her excitement, she realized she had also begun to feel faintly uneasy, given over to a sense of being hemmed in by strangers, backed into a dark corner. Her breath came a little faster.

Not for the first time she had the impression that the lead guitarist was familiar, yet maybe it was just a familiar *look*—the shoulder-length blond hair and hungry features. His guitar glimmered with light as he worked it, and it was as if his entire body, not simply his fingers, was drawing out the sounds, which seemed to take physical shape there in the swirling smoke-filled room, seemed almost to writhe like snakes.

The rhythm guitarist had his eyes shut, his dark face knit as though he were in pain, while the bassist looked like he had turned to stone: all but his fingers, plucking the strings. Breaking her attention away from the stage, Amy looked around for Jester, who had yet to reappear, and that's when she noticed the man perched behind a console at the left of the stage, just visible in a spill of cool blue light. He was tall and thin, with a fringe of pale, longish hair ringing his bald crown. Although he was clearly mixing sound for the band, he seemed oddly detached from everything else going on, intent on the rows of knobs and dials on the console, like a scientist experimenting with a laboratory effect. After a moment, the blue light faded and he was returned to the shadows. Amy edged closer to the foot of the stage to watch the band.

Their playing was frenzied, the music seeming to unwind out of the air as the singer's voice wove in and out. The blond guitarist was totally into playing, his lead changing with deft speed: light and shimmering one moment, taking on a flamenco crispness the next, now uncoiling dangerously like a quicksilver serpent. The other musicians, too, were performing with a new intensity, and this close to the stage the volume seemed sufficient to shred the speakers, but Amy stood her ground, spellbound.

Then, slowly, as if through some weird alchemy, the show began to move beyond just spectacle. Amy glanced around to see if others felt it, too. The amoeba shapes of the light show were moving across the faces of the crowd. There was still no sign of Jester. One man in a beret appeared to be the figure of Che in Seth's poster come to life, here to bring chaos. And chaos it seemed. Under the distortions of the light show and the pall of smoke, people seemed otherworldly somehow: some adorned with body paint that glowed in the dark, giving the impression that they were aflame, others with winding garlands of flowers in their hair, whirling dizzyingly around the floor until they began careening into other dancers. Amy found herself in the grip of a vague paranoia. She continued to scan the faces, but she recognized no one.

The musicians were oblivious. On the tiny stage, the drummer hammered away; the guitarists tortured their instruments; and the singer wailed: "I went down to the cavern—oh, yeah—the cavern of the . . ." *trees*, it sounded like.

With mounting alarm, Amy's reaction to the spectacle grew physical, a revulsion that twisted her stomach. She felt herself starting to free-fall, like Alice tumbling down the rabbit hole, and the panicky thought scratched at her mind that she'd been dosed. Somebody had slipped her DMT or acid, and now it was coming on and she wasn't prepared and she would lose it and freak out and start to scream. She began to hyperventilate. She had to get to the door, get outside.

Her heart was pounding. Her brow felt fevered. She pushed past people, side-stepping roughly, though no one seemed to notice or to care. She was near panic, her hands clenched so tightly she could feel the nails carve into her sweaty palms. A man stepped to block her. He had on a black vest with German military regalia dangling from it. His bare arms were stained with tattoos: leering skull and crossbones. Grinning, he yanked her close and kissed her. Without even thinking, she punched him in the stomach. He gasped boozy cigarette breath in her face and staggered back. She fled past. As she neared the door, someone grabbed her arm. She whirled, her fists balled.

"Running out on me?"

Jester. His round face was flushed and smiling. Some of her fright subsided.

"Dig it!" he shouted. "What do you think of the band?"

"I hate them."

"Whoa. You serious?" He seemed honestly dumbfounded.

At that instant the song ended in a clash of cymbals and drums. "Let's get out of here!" Amy cried.

Another song had begun. The tempo was slow, the chords minor and peaceful, in stark contrast to the one just finished. The dark mood of only moments ago was suddenly gone, wisped away like smoke. Amy found herself trying to conceive what had spooked her. Beyond the few tokes of grass, she'd had nothing to eat or drink all evening. So what then? Had she only imagined it? Tired from her long day at the *Rag*, had she driven herself to the brink of panic by mere thoughts?

The music had slipped into a soulful groove. People were slow dancing. Where there had been grimaces only moments ago, now there were smiles. "You still want to go?" asked Jester. But Amy didn't move. Raven was a more interesting band than she'd at first thought. She said so. Jester shook his head. "I was wrong. They were that first group. This is the band I wanted you to hear. The New Riders of the Apocalypse."

She and Jester began to dance to the smooth flowing music, and she was further convinced that her panic had simply been the result of the long day and no supper. She'd been ready for a bummer, primed from the hours of writing, the conduits of her imagination open. And the explanation seemed to satisfy her. Off to the left of the stage, as she danced, she saw again the tall bald man with the fringe of hair, working intently at his console. When the song ended, Amy noticed several small, crescent-shaped stains on the shoulder of Jester's shirt. It puzzled her a moment, until she looked at her palm, then at her other hand. In them she could see the little cuts her nails had made beginning to bleed.

Ears still ringing, hair and clothes fouled with cigarette smoke, Toad Madden sat where he had collapsed in a nest of velvet floor pillows, surrounded by the other members of the band. They were in the dark-paneled room on the ground floor of the house on Ashbury, the room they called the Crypt. Candlelit, decorated with big vases like Egyptian burial urns, and thick oriental carpets underfoot, the Crypt was the place where the band gathered. With only an hour or so till dawn, they all ought to have crashed by now, but except for the little chick with zebra-striped bellbottoms (Crystal, she called herself), whom Vince Russo had scooped earlier and who now leaned groggily against him as he fondled her, none of them seemed ready to sleep. Nor, owing to the heavy drapes over the windows, were any of them particularly aware of the paling of the night outside. Toad knew the hour because he *felt* it, like the heavy-gravity burn after a Dexamyl rush. He was experiencing the sensation he always got after playing for hours: phantom motions, his arms invisibly bashing out rhythms he still heard in his brain—*boom bah boom bam!* In reality, he occupied his hands shaving flakes from a Nepalese temple ball into a little brass pipe.

"What I'm saying, it's an opportunity. Bill Graham needs to hear us." Joe Williams was advancing the cause of playing bigger gigs, appealing to Circe, who sat in her chair. The shifting candlelight on his face as he paced the Crypt was like licks of cream on dark coffee. "We need to be jamming with the Quick and the Dead." He was talking about Quicksilver Messenger Service and the Grateful Dead, though he might well have named any number of local bands. On almost any night now there were concerts somewhere in the city, Bay Area bands and groups from elsewhere playing Winterland, Masonic Hall, and the elegant old Avalon, over on Sutter and Van Ness. "Hendrix is doing the Fillmore next week."

"We'll get heard," Circe said, in that quiet voice that was always a surprise to anyone who'd heard her sing first. Seductively feminine, it had a raw edge now after four sets in the smoky club. "By everyone." In her luminous black dress, she occupied her antique mahogany chair. Given his present stoned state and the uncertain light, Toad could almost imagine that she and the surrounding darkness were one.

"When?" Joe Williams wanted to know. His shimmering 'fro gave him the truculent look of an African warrior.

"The music isn't quite there yet. When it is, we will be."

"We cooked tonight," Williams insisted.

"At a hole in the wall. That ain't the Fillmore," Toad felt compelled to interject, out of loyalty to Circe, though he bent to pass Williams the pipe to keep it fraternal.

Williams dragged deeply, and went on talking through a held breath. "You want to go on jammin' for nickels and beers to a bunch of stew bums, Toad, fine. Go back to L.A. We're losing time."

"No, I don't want that. I want what you want, just as bad."

Williams exhaled. "Bands around here are signing for serious bread! You think Moby Grape's better than us? Sopwith Camel? Give me a break."

"Have you been disappointed so far?" Circe asked, still speaking quietly, not being drawn into any drama. "Any of you?"

None of them would have said so; though Toad realized the measure of success was different for each of them. For Williams, who had grown up playing street-corner blues on a hawk shop guitar, it was increasingly the prospect of money coming their way, the way it was starting to come for a lot of bands up and down the peninsula. He was a good musician, and maybe he felt he was missing his chance. There was a sound growing here in the city, a wild, hairy explosion of music, and he longed to be part of it. They all did.

For Eric it was the chance to play, that simple. Flamenco-trained, honed razor sharp with his disciplined hours of daily practice, he was by far the purest musician. His movements right now weren't phantoms: he stood by the marble fireplace, still fingering the unplugged Strat. It was the introvert's perfect soul mate.

Vince Russo's motive for being in the band was chicks, the groupies who were starting to come around. Hell, balling was part of it for all of them.

Except Circe. Toad couldn't figure her. For all her witchy black gowns and her dark musings with the tarot deck, she might well have been a nun. She lived a life apart, never partaking of the weed as it went around; sleeping in that room upstairs which was off-limits to everyone, and as far as Toad could tell, a chastity chamber. Toad had been hot for her since the day he'd auditioned for the group. But that wasn't happening for him, which was okay for now. Didn't he still get to live in this great house, and have the little chem shop he'd set up in the basement, not to mention the sheer chance of being here, just being part of the whole crazy, tripped-out scene?

"Our time is coming," Eric said, so softly he might have been speaking to the Strat.

Joe Williams had stalked to a window and parted the drapes. "I'm waiting," he said to the paling day beyond.

"You trust me?" Circe asked.

Williams let the drapes fall and turned from the window, giving up the fight. He said yeah, he trusted her. "Forget Hendrix and Moby Grape and the rest of them. They're just a bunch of cheeseball bands. The New Riders of the Apocalypse are where it's gonna be at!"

"Right on," the little chick on Russo's lap chimed in sleepily.

Dawn was seeping through the stained glass panel above the door, making faint colored patterns on the wall. Circe ran fingers through her long hair and stretched. "Time to rest." She rose. She gave each of them a quick kiss, her lips only the barest touch on Toad's own, then withdrawn—but it was enough. He felt himself grow hard. Sucking the pipe, he watched her float off in a swirl of gowns.

The others sat for a time longer, the physical toll of four sets having finally overtaken them. Joe Williams said he was going to crash. Toad pushed out of his pillow nest and got to his feet, too. Eric headed for the stairs, clutching his guitar. Vince Russo tickled the midriff of the little chick in zebra-striped bellbottoms, who yawned and asked was there any dope.

"Yeah, like you need any more," Williams said from the foot of the stairs. "What's your name again?"

"Crystal."

"Right."

"Used to be Christine. I'm thinking of adding 'Blue' on account of I had this vision? When I was tripping on Blue Cheer? I saw that everything is like . . . Oriental? Does that make sense?"

"That's heavy."

"No, it's like, you know . . . *Japanese* or something."

"Yeah," Williams said. "Later, all."

Vince Russo rubbed his eyes. "Toad, you got any of that last batch left?"

Toad gestured to the ornately carved mantelpiece. "In the medicine jar."

The former Christine, now Crystal—soon, perhaps, to be Crystal Blue—giggled. "First ride's free, right?" Helping themselves to whatever was in the Blue Willow china bowl on the mantel, she and Vince Russo climbed the dim stairway behind the others.

The girl walked along the beach in the dark, listening to the ghostly whisper of surf. Her name was Carmen and she had come from down on the border in El Centro, where her parents told her she needed to break the cycle of migrant work, had to finish high school, get a good job. She had avoided getting knocked up and married, but in the end she guessed she hadn't gotten away from that migrant blood. She had run away with a girlfriend. They'd spent a month in L.A., hanging out with some pachucos, but when things started to get rough and the girlfriend got strung out, Carmen said forget that and hit the road again, thumbing north with some vague idea of going up to Washington to the apple country she'd always heard tell of. She'd get rides with friendly strangers. "You're from El Centro?" they'd say, and she'd grin, "Yeah, the *farther* from the better."

The journey was stitched together by songs—not the Latino songs playing on tinny little transistor radios in picker shacks—but wonderful news songs, "With a Little Help from My Friends," "Lucy in the Sky with Diamonds," "Light My Fire." In late spring she found herself in Lompoc, where the fields seemed to froth with sweet peas and marigolds. She needed money and hired on at one of the big farms, and for two weeks she rose before dawn to go out into the starlit gardens to tend the blooms, and it came to her at last that she was what she'd been coming to all along—a flower child. From that moment, her destination had been set.

She'd thumbed a final ride just that evening, and now the sky was a clear dark pool flecked with stars. Up the beach she could see people scattered along the seawall in small groups, could hear their muted laughter, but she didn't approach them. Something in the flickering half shapes made her think of the migrant workers gathered around lanterns singing their sad *campesino* songs. She was through with that. This was going to be home.

But she was tired from a day of traveling, and it was late. She'd crash here tonight, then tomorrow make her way to the Haight-Ashbury. She drew her coat tighter. The night was becoming *frio.*

Off to her right, the surf broke in low, foaming lines. Farther down the beach were the dull orange glows of other fires, welcoming and at the same time spooky there in the dark. She made her way in that direction.

One small campfire was untended, though someone had left a pack by it. She stood warming herself, and soon a man appeared, walking down from the dunes. He smiled.

"Is this your fire?" Carmen asked.

He was good-looking, with a nice grin. "Mine, yours, ours." He chunked an armload of firewood onto the sand. "Sit." She did. "You hungry?"

She was, she said. Kind of.

"I've got some grub in my pack I'm going to do up. Where you from?"

From El Centro, the farther away from the better. "Lompoc," she said.

"Cool."

"You know Lompoc?"

"Not really."

"It's full of flowers."

"I love flowers."

He knelt and started feeding sticks of driftwood into the flames. Colors she didn't usually associate with fire began to rise. Carmen remarked on this and he said it was the sea salts in the wood.

"That makes me think of a lady I met down the coast who's a driftwood artist," she said. "I never heard of one before her."

"A driftwood artist, huh? Me neither. I'm just into keeping warm tonight."

"You sleeping here?"

"Oh, yeah."

She wondered if she should ask if she could stay, too. He was nice-looking, older than her; in his late twenties, maybe thirty. She'd ball him if he'd let her stay.

"I like to keep it big," he said. "The fire. To scare the predators away."

"You mean like animals? On the beach?"

He looked at her. "You haven't heard about the Ripper?"

Gooseflesh prickled the back of her neck. "What?"

"He's killed three kids. It's been in the papers."

She hadn't heard. She'd been avoiding news. He told her about it, going into some detail. Later he went to get more firewood and brought back several pickets of broken fence. "And this, for you." He handed her a flower. "I don't know what it is."

Carmen didn't know what it was either, some kind of beach rose. It was pretty. "What about this?"

She looked up and saw he was holding something else, turning it this way and that. In the firelight, it glowed like a long piece of amber. He smiled. Suddenly she felt a wallop of panic. She tried to stand.

He shoved the blade into her chest.

A flower burst into brightness there . . . or so it seemed; it was really behind her eyes, as if the night had been wired with strobe lights, so swift and bright she was sure people all over would see it, too, and come running and save her.

The ground tilted underfoot, as if the tide had come in unexpectedly and swallowed the land. She managed a few steps, then collapsed. She lay there twitching and cold . . . *mucho frio.*

TESS WAS IN THE KITCHEN WORKING ON HER MURAL WHEN AMY GOT HOME. THE flower children figures in the jungle Eden were taking form. "Have you decided yet whether that's a dove or a bomber up there in the corner?" Amy asked.

"Uh-huh." Tess grinned. "I'm just not declaring yet. By the way, girl, you got a letter there on the table."

Amy found the piece of mail and felt a surge of excitement. Barely containing it, she went to her room, put on a Ravi Shankar record, and looked again at the envelope with her name on it. Glenn's APO address was in the upper left corner and the word "free" scribbled where a stamp would customarily be, in one of the government's concessions to young men living in a war zone. She slit open the envelope and drew out the letter. It was dated six days ago.

> *Dear Amy, thanks for your letter and the issue of the paper. They're good reading when I'm not out humpin' the wild & woolies, maybe going somewhere or maybe not (no one seems to know). Got to say, "The Rag" makes me think of the song by Country Joe and the Fish. "Yippee! We're all gonna die!"*
>
> *Tell your friend Tess thanks for the God's-Eye. I've got it pinned to my pack—to ward off unwelcome bullets, punji stakes, or other unholy surprises.*
>
> *Seems like SF is a happening. That's likely where I'll land when I get back. I can't wait to see you and check it out. Maybe you've got some girlfriends who won't mind a guy with short hair (but at least no strange jungle diseases).*
>
> *Sound a little weird, do I? Maybe because I am. I'm changing. I'm not smoking dope or even drinking much more than a few cans of brew once in a*

while (c-rats and Carlings Black Label! That's high living!) No, I'm chang-
ing 'cause I'm LOOKING & THINKING. Risky, huh?

Like coming up here from Da Nang on Route 1, "riding the snake" they
call it, and I see burnt-out vehicles off to the sides, painted with names of
guys from places all over the States, and I'm back to wondering WHY AM I
HERE? What's this got to do with me? But when I hear the news from home I
feel like, do I dare go back THERE??

A guy in my platoon from Ann Arbor told me he went home for leave after
boot camp and was hiking from the bus station, and college kids saw him with
his duffle bag and called him "Baby Killer!" He wanted to shout, "Six months
ago I was where you are, assholes! I'm no different than you!" I like what you
said about how maybe we can get all the wounds healed, that what's going on
there in H/A might spill over to other places, like Saigon and Hanoi . . .
hey, maybe even Washington isn't a lost cause.

I think my dad is starting to wonder about the war, though I don't guess he's
singing along with Country Joe yet. If I'd just lit out for Canada, he never
would've talked to me again, but little by little I tell him I'm not sure we belong
over here, or at least we ought to think about why we are, and he listens.

It's not all bad here. The friendships are #1.

Friendships, yes, Amy reflected. She didn't really know Glenn well, growing
up on opposite coasts as they had, yet there had been that one summer when they
became close. Glenn and his parents had visited New England. She must've been
nine or ten. He was like a son her dad never had. By the time his parents came to
pick him up, Glenn had become very attached to her dad, so when his mom said,
"What are you going to be when you grow up, Glenn?" showing off a little—she
thought she had him primed for something highfalutin, like nuclear physicist—he
said, "A farmer like Uncle Pete." Looking back, Amy saw it was a moment of
uneasy truth for all of them. But everyone was cool and they had fun. She saw
Glenn once after she got out here, just before he left to go over, and it was like she
was seeing this man, with the crew cut and the broad shoulders, in a marine uniform; but he was still the boy she taught how to swim, and she knew they were
joined—not only in blood but in friendship, too. She went back to his letter.

Intense and loyal friendships with guys I'd probably never meet otherwise:
brothers from Watts and Motown, with picks in their hair, who hang loose lis-
tening to Isaac Hayes; ol' boys from down South who dig Merle Haggard and

Jack Daniel's, not necessarily in that order. And guys from up your way near Boston—they're the ones reading Hesse in their spare time (ha). There's even a few guys like me. And we all get along.

Intense, loyal, yep. And did I say sometimes doomed?

Like this one sergeant I first saw at the induction center when I took my physical. I couldn't believe it! He'd already done a tour here and got stateside duty, so what's he do? He re-ups and he turns up in the next unit as a platoon sergeant. Not that we were really friends, but we talked some. He could've stayed where he was, processing poor dumb recruits like yours truly, or just got out when his hitch was up, get a job, get married, have kids. But nope. He's back, and last week he got killed. It makes zero sense.

Timothy Leary may be right telling people to turn on, tune in . . . but dropping out, over here that's a tall order. We talk about the Million $ Wound—one that won't kill you or screw you up too bad but'll get you sent back to the world WIA. But it's mostly just talk. Best way to get there is to listen up, be a good sojer, do your time, and get home in one PEACE.

And I will. 65 days and a wake-up!

Love & prayers, Glenn

Sixty-five days—minus the six since the letter had been written, Amy calculated. Glenn would be home in fifty-nine days! "Love and prayers to you too, cousin," she whispered.

With a slab of pizza, Dr. Stan Hoagland waved Sparrow and Sandoval into the coroner's office. "What do you two want?"

"Wisdom," Sparrow said. "Enlightenment."

The ME twitched his Andy Gump mustache in Pete Sandoval's direction. "I thought *he* was the college boy."

"You were removing the victim as we got there this morning."

"I don't like a body lying around on a beach. It spoils fast. Like pizza. Have some."

They declined. "Did you get an ID on the victim, sir?" Sandoval asked. "Or any new evidence?"

"So it's not really my mind you're after, it's my bodies." The ME pushed his food aside, burped discreetly into his palm, and rose. "It's our guy," he said as he led the way out of his office and they started down a corridor. "The stab wounds are consistent. The nose is gone. Same knife, probably. If no weapon's turned up," he said, glancing back at them. Close-handed with his own information, he suspected others of holding out, too.

"No weapon yet," Sandoval confirmed.

"My best guesses are some kind of chef's knife or a dagger."

At the end of the corridor, Hoagland unlocked a door and took them into a room that glowed with white ceramic tile and stainless steel. He shut the door behind them. Only slightly larger than his office, it nonetheless comprised the centerpiece of his world. On a table, concealed by a sheet, lay a human form. As Hoagland pulled on rubber gloves, Sparrow caught Pete Sandoval's uncertain glance and recalled their conversation about getting used to the work. For his own part, he drew a steadying breath. But the ME wasn't in any hurry, apparently. He picked up a clipboard lying nearby.

"Carmen Gonzalez, seventeen. Left El Centro in February and drifted north." He gave physical dimensions, then went on to enumerate the contents of the stomach and cite analyses of urine and blood, including the detail that, like the previous victims, the girl had used pot. He gave the weights in milligrams of various organs, measures of this and that: stats, Sparrow realized, which couldn't be called vital in these circumstances. So here she lay, a wasted weed of the Summer of Love. With a twinge, he was given to reflect that there'd probably been other summers, not so long ago, when she had ridden piggyback on a father's shoulders, sold lemonade at the roadside, laughed with friends, tasted her first kiss.

"No sexual assault," Hoagland said. "Five wounds, the depth consistent with the others. I want you to see something." He turned off the overhead lights. In a moment, a tube of purple light, about six inches long, glowed in his hand. He folded the bottom of the sheet partway up to expose legs and lower torso. In the dark room, the two cops edged closer to the table. Holding the light tube a few inches from the girl, Hoagland ran it over her body. Small objects fluoresced on the bottom sides of her legs and hips, like tiny glowworms.

"Fibers of beach grass," he said, "wood splinters."

"Meaning what, sir?" asked Sandoval.

"That she was lying on the sand before she was killed, that she was comfortable and relaxed there on the beach when she was murdered," the ME said, drawing the sheet back into place. He put on the overhead lights and switched off the ultraviolet tube. "And then there's this."

With the practiced motion of a chambermaid turning down a hotel bed for a valued guest, Hoagland folded the top of the sheet down to reveal the young woman's head.

As with the previous victims, the flesh and cartilage of her nose had been carved away. But there was more. The cheeks had been slit an inch or so to either side, so that the lower lip hung in a flap, baring the bottom teeth. In his peripheral vision, Sparrow saw Pete Sandoval turn away. His own impulse was to do the same, but the astringent smell of antiseptic braced him, and he stared at the pale, mottled face, willing himself to understand. He gave the task another moment's attention, then gestured for Hoagland to replace the sheet.

"What do you make of it?" Sparrow asked when they had returned to the ME's office.

"All I can tell you is that, like cutting the noses, it was done after death."

They spent another twenty minutes with Hoagland while he reviewed his notes for them. As they were leaving, he said, "By the way, has Austin cleared anyone outside the task force for access?"

Neither of the cops knew, but said they didn't think so.

"That's what I thought. So I said, show me written permission from on high, or get the hell out of my morgue. I said I didn't want him here him unless he was dead." Hoagland scratched his mustache. "Of course, maybe it was just from old habit. George Moon did used to be the bull goose, after all."

The sea was a sheet of rusting steel as the sun angled westward. Turning out of the intermittent flow of cars on the Great Highway, Sparrow pulled into the lot on the Golden Gate Park side. There were a handful of privately owned cars there but none of the earlier official activity, when the homicide unit had been out in force. Even Rocco Bianchi had abandoned his desk to make the trip, as if drawn by the sea after the string of killings within the shabby perimeters of the Haight-Ashbury. Sparrow, too, had spent the better part of the day here before being called away. Now, after his session with the coroner, he was back. He left his suit coat in the car and donned a windbreaker. When there was a lull in the traffic, he jogged across the highway to the beach.

Off to the right at a distance, a cluster of hippies sat cross-legged on the sand, facing the Pacific. Were they waiting for the sunset? Meditating? He doubted they were holding a vigil for Carmen Gonzalez. Something in their stillness unnerved him. They might have been carved wooden totems.

He swept all that from his mind as he turned and started down the beach in the other direction, plodding through the sand with some sense of looking for something, though he could not have said what.

The onshore wind of earlier in the day had died, but with the sun westering there was a chill now. A beachcomber had come upon the body at dawn, lying beside a fire ring of stones. With a phalanx of twitching blue lights, the SFPD had descended on the scene and grid-searched the area, taking away whatever evidence there might be; though once again the killer had left little beyond the violated corpse and his signature flower—a beach rose, Chang had declared.

Sparrow came at length to the ring of stones.

The site was abandoned. Certainly he wasn't likely to find anything Chang's hawk eyes hadn't, and he stood there smoking, shoulders drawn up against the chill. Was it possible, in the quiet now, to draw some message from the site itself, as though it might retain an impression of what had happened here hours before? Squatting by the circle of stones with the scorched bones of driftwood within, he imagined flames, and then a flickering light ringed by darkness. Who sat here in its glow with Carmen Gonzalez last night? A friend? Is that what accounted for the fibers on her body and no sign of struggle? Likewise with each of the victims. Was the killer a friend to them all? A background check had so far revealed no link between the victims. The hippies were trusting, Amy had said. But what else was drawing their killer?

"Got some bread, hey?"

The voice startled him. He turned to find himself confronted by a shabby, wild-eyed man. Gray hair sprang in stringy snarls from under a filthy watchcap, and his face was crimson with boils.

"You fuckin' deaf?" the man railed. "What the fuck you doin' on my beach?"

Sparrow showed his star. The derelict glared at it balefully a moment, then hissed. "Screw that. I wanna get a bottle."

Sparrow offered a cigarette.

"The hell am I gonna do with a smoke?" the man snapped, taking it anyway. "You with the cops here earlier?"

"I didn't see you," Sparrow said.

"Then you ain't no hotshot dick."

"You can say that again." Sparrow lit both their cigarettes.

"I hate cops. Always have. This whole stretch"—he waved a grimy hand—"is mine."

"The state's going to be surprised to hear that."

"Fuck the state. My ancestors was Tamal Indians. They had all this, one time. They're dead, now it's mine."

"So you keep an eye on things. Did you know the young woman who was killed last night?"

"Never seen her before. Not one of the regulars."

"Who are they?"

"Useless longhairs, people call 'em, but I like 'em. They share."

"Did you see anyone with the girl?"

"Did you hear me? They *share*."

Sparrow took out his wallet and came up with a five-dollar bill, which he removed but held onto. People he had spoken with that morning had seen almost nothing. The derelict drew a hand across his cracked lips. "Yeah, she was with a dude. Never seen him before, either. The pair of 'em was sitting around this fire."

"You're sure it was the same woman."

"Dark hair. Mex. I seen 'em, right here."

"What time was that?"

"Late."

"Were they friends?"

"How the hell do I know?"

"Were they talking?"

"Yeah, but I don't know about what. I was gonna come over, but the fire was this little piss-ass thing, and I seen they didn't have no wine. I went down the other end. The hippies always got wine."

"What did the man look like?" Sparrow asked, still holding the five-dollar bill.

"Shit, I don't know. More hair than you, but he wasn't a longhair. And he didn't build much of a fire. He was burning big chunks of wet driftwood. I split."

"You remember anything else?"

"Yeah." The derelict snatched at the money, and Sparrow let him take it. "The wine was good." Turning, he shambled off in the direction of the park.

Sparrow thought about calling him back to get his name, but the man wouldn't be hard to find. He squatted by the fire ring again and began to sift the cold sand with his fingers. He found a small piece of wood, charred except for the unburnt stub end, which was red.

On a direct line inland from the site was a low fringe of dunes, which cut off the beach from the highway. He had wandered the area earlier, but had stopped at the dunes, having found no evidence of footprints. Now he field-stripped his cigarette and started in that direction.

The light had grown golden, and he followed a kind of trail, though it was really little more than formless indentations in soft sand. He walked into the low dunes, which were bearded with the coarse, bushy vegetation that survives in such places. When he reached the top, maybe ten feet above the beach elevation, he looked toward the highway and saw what he had imagined he would. A twisted wind fence snaked along the highway edge. Its pickets snarled with vines, half buried in sand at some points, it might have been the fossil spine of a sea serpent. He waded down through the grass and beach roses to it. Holding the bit of charred wood up for comparison, he saw that it was the same material. So even if the results were piss-ass, last night's fire-builder had at least tried something other than wet driftwood.

As he returned to the crest of the dune, Sparrow noticed a slight rectangular depression in the sand, as though something had been set there. The sand had been compacted, and not that long ago, considering how little of the loose granular sand the wind had sifted into the bottom. The rounded corners suggested a briefcase, perhaps, or a knapsack.

A soft whistling distracted him. He looked up. Approaching in a southbound direction on the highway was a camper trailer. It was coming fast. With its aerodynamic contours and silvery skin, it might have been a space capsule gone way off course. His eye caught a blip of light skimming over the dune tops, igniting brush and sparking mica in the sand, heading his way. It was reflected sunlight thrown by the vehicle's windshield, and as it streaked by him, just feet from where he stood, something in the sand winked; then it was gone, and so was the camper trailer, which whistled on past, oblivious. Squatting, he reached for whatever it was that had winked.

It was a small diamond of chromed steel. He turned it over and inspected it, and his heart quickened as he recognized what it was. He considered the sheer chance of his having been here now. By tomorrow the wind would have sifted in enough loose sand to bury the piece of metal. Even a few *seconds* earlier or later, and neither he nor the camper trailer nor the sun would have been at that precise conjunction which had made discovery possible. His spirit rose with the idea that perhaps luck had broken well for the first time in the case, for the one discovery now led to a second. He stepped over to the depression in the sand, and bending close he was able to see there were actually a series of even smaller indentations within the large imprint. The diamond-shaped nugget of steel fitted easily into one of them. And now the bigger depression presented itself not as something caused by a briefcase or backpack; no, it had been left by a pair of saddlebags, the studded kind favored by bikers. This realization actually prompted Sparrow to survey the highway in half-expectation of seeing a cadre of motorcycles cruising this way, but for once the road was empty, the blacktop and the greenery beyond it lacquered with amber light.

After another moment's reflection—a moment which had him wondering how the chrome stud might have come loose, and to whom the saddlebags belonged, and what that person was doing there last night—he pocketed the stud. But standing there now, in what might justly be a moment of triumph, he experienced instead the stirring of a tiny bloom of foreboding. He shivered. Was the person who had been here the killer? Or was there perhaps a second person, who might have witnessed what went on at the beach? As he made his way back to his car, it occurred to him that if his small uncovering shed ever so faint a ray of understanding, what still remained was a vast and faceless dark.

Two

THE TRIBES

Ev'rybody get together. . . .
—The Youngbloods

You want the head shop?"

Sparrow wasn't sure what was being asked until Pete Sandoval pointed at the storefront. Hand-painted on the window in thick rainbow squiggles was the name Freeque Bouteak. "You take it. There's another place I want to try. I'll meet you at the car." They set off in different directions.

As usual, the district teemed with bright hordes, and there was music in the air: rock 'n' roll songs overlaying each other in a noisy collage, as multiform in its way (and as resistant to his understanding) as everything else here. Amy Cole had been more than right: not only didn't he grasp this place's ambiguities, he hadn't even known what a head shop was.

He and Pete Sandoval had spent the morning canvassing businesses in the district, some for the second or third time in a week, speaking to anyone willing to talk about the murders. He was also on the lookout for a motorcycle with chrome-studded saddlebags. So far, useful information remained scarce.

The address he sought proved to be a two-story building that had once been a theater. Seated on the wooden steps in front were a cluster of people. One boy was thumping a pair of bongo drums, though it was apparent everyone was listening to a chubby kid in a bright red fool's cap who slouched against the railing, evidently telling a story. He broke off as Sparrow stopped at the bottom of the steps. They all looked at him.

"Is this the editorial office for the *Rag?*"

"This is it," said the kid in the cap, "but I don't think they're hiring."

The quip got smiles. The kid shrugged and pointed the way. Sparrow climbed past them and entered a foyer. On the door that the kid had indicated was a poster which depicted a red clenched fist, and across it the words:

RIOT CONTROL—HELL NO!

SUMMER OFFENSIVE COMMITTEE. STAY TUNED FOR DETAILS.

In the office a young black woman was sitting cross-legged on a table, working on a sketch pad, a dab of pink tongue visible in the corner of her mouth. On the walls, Karl Marx and Che Guevara grimaced from their beards, giving him to wonder what their appeal was. He had had Marilyn Monroe to grace his dorm room, sweet and surprised-looking as a sidewalk vent whooshed up her dress.

"Hi," the young woman greeted him.

"Hi. What are you working on?"

She showed him the sketch pad. On it was an intricate geometric shape done in colored pencil. "Getting the symmetry right is a drag," she said.

"It looks good from here."

She held the pad at arm's length, reexamining her work. "I'm not into using a protractor or a compass. If a mandala's going to have good vibes, it's got to just flow from the heart."

"It's good," he said again. "Is Miss Cole around?"

The young woman twisted and called over her shoulder, "Seth!" She told Sparrow, "It's full of spiritual meaning, the mandala. You meditate on it and things become clear." He took another look at the drawing, but it was just an elaborate doodle to his eye. "I'm Tess, by the way. Seth, there's a straight here looking for Amy."

After a moment, a lean man with dark curly hair and the suggestion of a beard appeared in the doorway of a back office. He was in his early twenties, good-looking, with intense dark eyes. He came over. "What can I do for you, officer?"

Sparrow shook his head. "Maybe I should grow a beard."

"Won't help. What's up?"

Good; cut right to it. "Is Amy here?"

"Who's asking?"

Sparrow told him.

"You have a badge or something?"

Sparrow showed his ID. It appeared to satisfy him. "I'm the editor. Seth Green." His beard grew in crisp whorls on his cheeks and chin and looked like he hadn't quite committed to it yet. "Amy's out," he said. "Covering the news."

The reception committee from the steps had drifted in. The kid with the red cap nodded, making bells jingle. "It's happening all around. Within you and without you. How's that feel?"

"Not good if it means people are getting killed to make it."

"Like the undeclared war in Southeast Asia," Seth said.

"Closer to home. Do any of you have information about the murders? Anything that might be helpful?"

There was brief discussion among the group about whether anyone had seen or heard anything. There'd been rumors of a nose being found at a concert, but no one knew for sure. If he sensed a faint undercurrent of fear among them, there was also a chill of resistance to him. He printed his name on a sheet of his notepad, tore it out, and put it on a desk. "Tell Miss Cole I was by. Maybe she can call me when there's a lull."

As Sparrow started for the door, he stopped and turned, overtaken by a thought. "This summer offensive committee—is that you?"

"Offensive committee?" Seth gave the others a look of consternation. "Is someone being offensive?" Dumbfounded expressions all around.

Sparrow shook his head. "You might pass it along to be careful," he said. "The TAC Squad leader isn't nearly as friendly as I am."

Seth followed him to the door. "Are you suggesting the people haven't got a right to assemble?"

Sparrow was out of patience. "I don't give a San Francisco damn what you do, it's a free land. But four kids are dead. I'd have thought that would concern you. Foolish me."

Pete Sandoval was waiting by the Chevy, staring at the hood. In their absence someone had plastered a bumper sticker there: DRAFT BEER, NOT MEN! Sparrow felt another jab of anger.

"I just arrived," Pete said. "I didn't see who did it."

Anyone might have applied it; the streets flowed with people who looked like they would share its trite sentiment. Any one of that crowd Sparrow had just left certainly would. He tried to peel a corner of the sticker, but it was firmly in place. Screw it.

"How'd it go?" Sandoval asked as they climbed in.

"I feel like *I'm* wearing a sign."

"I know what you mean. 'Pig.' "

As Sparrow started the car, a man crossing the street came over and peered in. He was short with gnarled ginger hair and an air force uniform shirt bearing the three-star rank insignia of a lieutenant general. He might have been twenty. "Couple button-down guys, you're dicks, right? Working those murders?"

Sitting nearest, Sparrow said, "We're not looking for Uranus. What've you got there, General?"

The kid cackled. "That's me, yeah. General Alarm. I've got a theory about all this."

"If I beg you, will you tell us about it?"

"Let me give you a list of suspects. Try . . ." He squinched his eyes and gripped his temples in an exaggerated show of remembering. "Okay, it's coming to me.

Try Lone Star Lyndon, for one. Then McNamara, Westmoreland. That don't pan out, check Melvin Laird, Dean Rusk—they got their mug shots hanging on the draft board wall, and they ain't draftin' beer."

"Okay, asshole," Sparrow said, "we'll get right on it."

Their shift having ended, Sparrow proposed a drink. They found a place on Powell whose sign was a lavender neon martini glass. He got bourbon, Sandoval beer. "Do you suppose Frank Austin imagines we're winning hearts and minds in the Haight-Ashbury?" Sparrow asked.

"I hope he doesn't think that."

"We're not very groovy, are we?"

"Though measured against Inspectors Lanin and Bianchi . . ."

They laughed. Sparrow told about his encounter with the group at the *Rag*. He considered telling about having had coffee with Amy Cole, but he decided not to. Loosen his resistance to chaos and ambiguity? Sure, that would help. In fact, most of his interviews so far were reducible to notebook scribbles, as intricate as Tess's mandala, and ultimately as meaningless.

"General Screwup back there in the uniform," Sandoval said. "Do you think he had anything? Someone targeting victims because of politics?"

"Tell me again what you studied in college?"

Pete smiled. "Psych. Answer my own question. I'll be back." He went to find the men's room.

Murder and mutilation for ideological reasons was a reach, and Sparrow wasn't prepared to make it. What constituted the counterculture's belief system anyway? Drop acid, not bombs? Gandalf for president? Jefferson Airplane loves you? He swirled the ice cubes in his drink, watching them as if to divine answers. The hippies were probably a finger in the eye of some people—he wasn't overly fond of them himself—yet they didn't appear to represent any consistent view. "Hang loose and do your own thing" seemed about as close as they got to a philosophy. Which made them ideal quarry for a predator.

As though the cold glass had chilled him, he set it down. The killer had waited more than two weeks between his first and second victims, whereas the gap between victims two and four had narrowed. Why? Having established an MO that worked, was he growing confident? Or was he in the grip of some mania, working against an inner or outer deadline? Sparrow didn't know, but grimly he saw that the killer's increased activity might be their best hope for finding him, because maybe in his haste he would make a mistake, and they would find it. Maybe, in fact, he'd already made his mistake and Sparrow had it in his pocket. He drew out the chrome stud and examined it.

But what if this wasn't enough, or wasn't even linked, and the killer didn't make a mistake? The streets of the Haight-Ashbury swarmed with potential victims, thousands of them, with more arriving each day as the start of summer loomed. Sparrow signaled for the check.

Amy watched Seth standing at the podium of the old church hall that the community used for meetings. "Come on," he declared over the volleying voices of those gathered, "we're not going to get anyplace hassling each other!"

Coming through the PA system, his words provoked an uprising of veed fingers above the motley congregation sardined into the worn pews. Amy saw an almost equal number of fists clenched in a symbol of complex meanings that the Panthers had begun to make popular. Light from the chandeliers suspended in the arched space overhead sent shadows spoking off in all directions.

"Solidarity!" someone cried.

Amy hadn't mentioned Terry Gordon again since the other day at Berkeley. Nor had Seth. He'd apparently shaken off what he considered Terry's defection and redoubled his efforts in the cause of what he liked to call the Movement. He had helped organize tonight's meeting, and although Amy was never quite sure what exactly the Movement was, she nevertheless was proud of Seth for his ability to take charge when needed. "Let's do this in an orderly way," he said and pointed. "Red, you were first."

Near the front, a needle-thin man with untamed clock springs of copper hair bounced to his feet. "It's why some of us left North Beach—on account of things got to be such a downer. Now it's happenin' here, man. All this heat sniffin' around."

"Busting our stash, man!" someone called, and touched off a small amen chorus.

A black man in a bright dashiki rose from a pew. "Is drug busts all you're sweating?" Amy recognized Nat Evans. She and Seth had known him at Berkeley, where he'd been in a doctoral program. " 'Cause if so, you've got yourselves eye problems! I'm talking *color*-blind. Brothers in Oakland are getting rousted. For exercising their rights, same as you all doing, it's 'Up against the wall, nigger!' "

"Come on, Nat," Seth protested. "You know that isn't the view of anyone here."

"I *don't* know. Like Eldridge's been saying, if you ain't the solution, you the problem."

"The brother's right!" yelled someone else. "And if we aren't cool, it's going to be heads breaking next time. The cops are itching for a trash-in."

More voices rose, and Nat Evans, looking grim, sat down. There were predictions of kangaroo courts and midnight shootings. Others insisted that all was well, that flower power was the way, a view that was painted by still others as naive. Amy kept waiting for the topic of the murders to come up, but so far people were staying away from it. Then, during a moment's lull, a voice called, "Eat me, drink me."

The voice came from the back, causing heads to turn. It was Emmett Grogan, Amy saw; one of the Diggers' leaders. He was leaning against the wall at the rear of the sanctuary. With an easy movement, not taking his hands from the pockets of his army surplus duffle coat, he tipped away from the wall and sauntered forward along the aisle. "A nice *Alice in Wonderland* fantasy you're spinning here. Off with their heads!"

Ah, no, Amy thought. This was going to lapse into street theater. She looked anxiously toward Seth. But oddly the room had quieted, the hubbub falling away. Even Seth's friends seated in the front pews—veterans of the Free Speech Movement, some of them, who loved contention and verbal strife—kept their places, waiting for Seth now, too. In Grogan's chiseled face a streetwise skepticism cohabited with a cosmic grin, an awareness of the dramatic possibilities in every moment. He was intelligent, charismatic, and unpredictable; and Amy didn't trust him. Still, Seth remained calm. "What fantasy you got in mind, Emmett?"

"All of them."

"That's pretty vague."

"Take the one about the storm troopers coming-zee here."

"The threat is real," Seth said.

"Oh? Says who? Because unless you're getting it from man in the sky"—Grogan glanced upward—"I don't hear nothing but a bunch of bullshit hallucinations keeping folks uptight."

"You'll have to take my word for it," Seth said.

"Yeah, well, you see, I can't do that. And I don't think you can expect others here to accept a lot of downer talk unless you can back it up."

There was a rush of energy in the crowd, like a spark arcing from one pole to another, from Seth Green to Emmett Grogan and back again. *Whoosh!*

"Yeah," someone called. "Put up or shut up, Green!"

Seth let the challenge hang a moment, before he said, "We've got a bad moon rising, folks."

Grogan smiled and shook his head. "With all due respect to Zephyr and other astroglodytes, I think that stuff's looney."

"The moon I'm talking about is blue," Seth said. And all at once Amy understood what he was doing, where he was taking this. "Captain George Moon. He's got a squad he's training."

The name hadn't achieved household status yet, but it was known among some of the group and it brought a stir. Emmett Grogan spread his duffle coat in a kind of shrug. "Riot cops, so big deal. A little tear gas adds to the fun."

"This is a special unit. Headbangers." Seth held his hands several feet apart. "With sticks like this. They've been training at the Presidio. It'll be in this week's issue of the *Rag*, complete with a copy of an internal PD memo detailing what their mission's going to be."

Grogan was struck silent. Seth caught Amy's eye, perhaps regretting that he'd revealed what was intended as a journalistic coup, but she wasn't thinking about that. She was remembering the first time she had seen Seth speak, full of passion as he addressed an antiwar rally from the steps in Sproul Plaza. She had been aware at once of two things: that he was the same guy who was in her poly sci class, and that he was very sexy standing up there with his blue work shirt and red bandanna, thick dark curls and tanned face. She felt the same electric tingle of warmth now as Seth asked, "Any guesses?"

A hush settled on the crowded hall. People had believed that here in the Haight, at least, they were on home ground, in a haven where the agents of the municipal structure ventured out only for the occasional pot bust, and the neighborhood was tolerated because, if nothing else, it lent color to the city. But apparently that was no longer true, and the perception of safety was only that, as Seth had just made plain: an illusion, like oil rainbows on dark water. Tension eddied in the sluggish silence of the sanctuary. But people didn't need long to mull the implications.

Voices leapt, and Seth attempted to recognize speakers one at a time, but they were impatient and not to be contained. Questions, speculations, and accusations volleyed across the room, and in them Amy heard an edge of barely contained volatility. Over the past few months she had listened and observed, sensing an erosion of the deep foundation of purpose that had held the community together. When she had first come here early last year, there had been a feeling that she could only describe as love. When people greeted one another as "brother" or "sister," or the all-inclusive "man," flashed the peace sign, shared a joint, there was a small physical sensation, a rising warmth, a feeling of being bonded in some new and exciting way.

But that had begun to change.

Now, almost as if the spring rains, the heaviest in years, had started dissolving the glue, paranoia ran through the community in livid threads, giving people over to irritability and mistrust, fracturing them into small, jagged alliances. Instead of just being one, people attached labels: Diggers, Krishnas, politicos, druggies (which family had its own factions: potheads, acidheads, the tense, hassled speed freaks). There were Leary devotees, Merry Pranksters, Marxists, Maoists, plain old—and new—lefties; the HIP merchants, bikers, Panthers, and on and on, each brandishing an "us" versus "them" conviction. As Nat Evans had said, "You're part of the solution or part of the problem . . . on the bus or off the bus." It occurred to Amy that it was fitting that tonight's meeting was taking place here in a church, because what was at stake went to the very heart of belief. Back in January, at the Human Be-In in the park, she'd truly felt a spirit moving. Though her mother would've been aghast at the idea, the experience had felt *holy*. The question now was, could they remain a congregation, joined by some common faith?

"Let the storm troopers come!" someone shouted. "We need a good trash-in!"

"That ain't the purpose of the Summer of Love," cried a kid in a purple robe that gave him the look of a runaway choirboy. "That's buying into their sick jack-boot trip!"

"So we give it to them!" rang a voice. "Get solid, man!"

"Screw Moon and the tank he rides in on!"

"Kicks! Not riot sticks!"

"Off the pigs!"

The old church hall filled with yells, "Right on!" where "Amen!" might once have risen, and indeed the mood took on something of a prayer-meeting fervor. Amy felt pulled in many directions: she wanted to speak, to warn against buying trite slogans, wanted to laugh (so crazy-sounding had some of this gotten), wanted to tremble. She needed to be a voice for unity, because if this whole brave notion that people could be free and responsible and self-determining was to work, they had to reason together. Yet it came to her with an eerie awareness amid the din that she could never fully be part of the events around her. No matter how much she identified with the Summer of Love, she also stood outside it, a spectator, a recorder. Her earlier thought was back. *No one has mentioned the killings.* Some of their own were dead, cut down right here on their turf. As a community, they ought to have been breathless with outrage, yet it was as if the murders hadn't occurred at all! No, that wasn't it. She sensed that the knowledge *was* here, but it lay below the skin, scraping nerves raw, metastasizing in silence, offered up in no shared plea to deliver them from evil.

She stuck up her hand, ready to raise the topic now, but a cry rose from nearer the front. "Wait!"

A buxom woman about Amy's age, in a tie-dyed halter top and jeans, had climbed onto a pew and was being hoisted higher by eager people around her. "Hold on!" she called over the noise.

"Cool it!" someone shouted. "Hear the chick!"

"What we should do—"

"Tell it, sister!"

"Wait! What we should do, when we gather in the park for the solstice, get this, we should all strip bare-ass and just frolic! Make love, not war!"

And as if to have it begin here, she yanked up her halter top and her breasts sprang free. This brought cheers, whistles, and then happy laughter. The strident voices fell away. Somebody put *Surrealistic Pillow* on the PA system. Soon joss sticks were lit, and as though to apply some ecclesiastical seal to the bargain, joints and a few pipes made appearances. The mood lightened, and people began to boogie in the aisles. Amy got into it, too, clapping her hands to the music, and for several minutes she had a return of her former sense of joy. They were a community after all, a new tribe.

But later, as she picked her way around the edges of the sanctuary to where Seth stood talking with some people, she heard more argument than agreement, more confusion than confidence. Walking home with a group of people afterwards, with Gracie Slick's voice still floating through the back of her mind, she found the foreground beset by conflicting images of flowers and rifles, incense and tear gas. And haunting it all, detached and drifting like a shadow in fog, loomed the ghost image of a killer.

You've had the dream again.

The dark breath of earth as you creep through the labyrinth, so many passages, bewildering in their profusion. But aside from the physical discomforts, spooked at times when something unseen brushes your face, you don't mind. You're powerful here, a dark knight entering an enemy's realm, bringing death. Now, coming upon the candle flicker, the small man there . . . *Nam mo a nhi da phat . . .*

The sensation of your hand lifting the weapon . . .

You bang awake with the cries in your ears. Yells, curses, and prayers. You cover your ears, wanting to stop them, but it never worked before and it doesn't now because the voices are coming from inside, in the tunnels of memory. You gape into blackness, breathing hard. Only gradually do the sounds subside.

Too tense to sleep any longer, you rise.

Moonlight seeps around the edges of the window shade. You raise the shade a few inches, giving the tiny room enough light for you to see in. You pull on your trousers and shirt and boots. Taking care to be quiet, you use the adjoining toilet. The cracked mirror on the medicine chest gives back a split image. What time is it? Two A.M.? Three?

You slip into the garage, where the air smells of gasoline and grass clippings and mustiness. You step carefully amid the garden tools, old tires, and boxes, to the Shadow, poised on its kickstand. The gleam of its tank touches you and you run a hand over it, reassured by curved surfaces of steel, as smooth as a girl's cheeks. You drape the saddlebags over your shoulder, hear the soft tinkle as objects shift inside. You slip outside. With footfalls as silent as fog, you cross the backyard. In the house, the landlord's dog doesn't bark. Moments later you're on the street, pulled toward the beating night-heart of the Haight.

IN THE HAIGHT-ASHBURY IT WAS COMMON TO TALK OF FATE. BUT IN CONTRAST WITH its meaning elsewhere, Amy knew, here it was seen as an outward manifestation of karma, the deep underlying principle that steered the universe and held that every action has consequence. *Go with the flow,* people were fond of saying; *What goes around comes around; We have all been here before.* People spoke earnestly about *samsara,* the Hindu idea of the eternal round of birth, death, rebirth. It was with something of all this in mind, therefore, that Amy approached the pink Victorian house on Ashbury shortly before nine o'clock that evening, for it was here on these front steps, seven months ago, she had first encountered the New Riders of the Apocalypse, though she hadn't known it then—nor, in fact, had the band had that name.

That meeting had occurred on the day the *Rag* opened its office. Keyed up from moving furniture and typewriters, and not inclined to join the others in an office-warming smoking of the big Moroccan hookah, Amy had set forth to explore their new neighborhood. Climbing Ashbury, she heard live music issuing from the open windows of a pink house, obviously a band rehearsing.

Hearing musicians wasn't unusual, especially in the Haight; but some distinctive note in this music seized her attention, and she paused to listen. After a time the music quit, but so entranced had she become, she didn't move on. Just then a guy wearing an Edwardian coat of turquoise velvet, with blond hair to his collar, came out the front door carrying a red guitar. He had an unlit cigarette in his mouth, and he patted his pockets in a fruitless quest for a match. Seeing Amy, he looked at her hopefully, in one of those momentary, wordless (fated?) exchanges between strangers that happened all the time in the Haight. She smiled and shook her head and he shrugged humorously. As she moved on, he plucked the cigarette from his lips and called, "Not a drummer, are you?"

And all at once she was aware of what it was about the music that had struck her: there were no drums. "Sorry," she said.

The man looked bashful, almost surprised at having spoken. "Ours split. Overdosed, you could say."

"Really? That's sad."

"He's not dead. He just OD'd on trust, I guess. Ripped off our good will and split." The man didn't seem bitter, merely factual; as though this was the kind of hassle you had to expect when dealing with people.

"Well, you sounded good anyway," she said. "I'm sure you'll find a new one."

She started by again, and abruptly he blurted, "I'm Eric, by the way."

"Hi. I'm Amy."

"You want to watch us jam sometime, Amy? We don't have any gigs yet, but we practice every day. You'd be welcome to listen."

"Sure," Amy said.

"We live here. Come by anytime."

She waved. She was several strides away when she thought of something and turned. "What's your band called?"

"We haven't got a name yet, but we will have. And you'll hear it."

And he'd been right. She had heard of the New Riders of the Apocalypse exactly once since then. She had seen them play, new drummer and all, at Thor's Hammer where the Jester had taken her, though she hadn't recognized Eric, the guitar player, until after the show. The music had affected her, and she had written about it in the *Rag*, not because of any technical understanding of its merit, but purely because it had had such an impact. It was only a brief notice, hardly a review (she hadn't even mentioned anyone in the band by name because she hadn't known their names), but someone in the group must have seen it. That morning, an elfin teenager in a green mini-dress and yellow suede boots calling herself Crystal Blue turned up at the office with a message from the lead singer, a woman named Circe, saying she'd like to meet Amy.

So, in a sense, Amy had cause to reflect as she climbed the steps, this visit marked another turning of the cosmic wheel. Though it was possible, of course, as Seth had suggested, that the band simply wanted free publicity.

Crystal Blue opened the door and greeted Amy with a loopy grin. She led the way into the old house. At the far end of the huge front room, lounging on big floor pillows, was a group of people, several of whom Amy recognized as band members, though at this distance her impression was mostly of hair and smoke and the babble of voices.

"C'mon up," her escort said. Amy trailed her up a flight of broad stairs. "The Riders've got a gig later. We like to mellow out before playing."

Amy considered asking about the "we," but let it go. On the third floor, Crystal Blue opened a door and they went through. Amy found herself in a dim room, lit only by several tapers burning on a low table at one end. There was a bay window, hung with gauzy curtains, which let the ebbing daylight in: enough to reveal that the room, though large with a high ceiling, was cluttered with ornate furniture. There was an arched doorway to the left, hung with a bead curtain. Dominating the dimmest corner of the room was a canopy bed.

"She'll be right with you," Crystal said, and exited.

Left alone, Amy peered out the bay window, which looked onto Ashbury. This upper end of it was quieter than where it met Haight, though it still pulsed with street life. Looking around, Amy saw that, in addition to the furniture, the room was cluttered with an assortment of objects: antique lamps with fringed silk shades, an oval mirror in a gilt frame, an ornate crossbow, small inlaid ivory boxes, old silver. There were oddly formed gourds, archaic stringed instruments blackened with age, rams' horns. In one glass-topped box was a display of tarantulas. Amy shuddered. It was as if the band had simply taken over a museum.

At the sudden *click-clacking* of the bead curtain Amy turned, expecting Crystal Blue, but it was another woman who came in. Amy recognized her as the singer in the band. She wore a dark, flowing gown, as she had on stage. She was about thirty, slender, with glossy dark hair and an exotic beauty. In her arms she held a gray tabby. "What sign are you?" she asked.

"Taurus," Amy told her.

The woman smiled. "You like old objects. I do, too. Sit." She gestured to an ornate couch whose brocade fabric was threaded with exotic hues. She sat on the bed facing Amy and put the cat down. They introduced themselves.

"This is fascinating." Amy made a sweeping gesture to indicate the furnishings and displays. "You must be a collector."

"Most of these belong to a friend. He likes to collect, but has no patience once he owns something. I like having them around."

Crystal Blue reappeared carrying a bamboo tray with a china teapot, two cups, and a plate of cookies. She set the tray on the edge of the bed. Circe thanked her and the teenager bobbed her head and went out. Circe poured tea and handed Amy a cup. "I read what you wrote about us."

"Well, you gave me an experience," Amy said. "I wanted to respond."

"I'm glad you did. There're lots of bands springing up around the city; it's nice to get noticed. I thought we should meet. I had a sense we would." She was looking at Amy through the steam rising from her tea. Beside her, with jade-eyed interest, the tabby cat watched, too. "Was I wrong?"

Amy smiled. "Tell me about the band."

And Circe did, talking about the musicians, who had come together for the first time less than a year ago, through a series of odd links. "Though odd only if you didn't know better," she qualified, "if you didn't believe things happen for a reason. Like getting our drummer."

Amy recalled his hypnotic pounding at Thor's Hammer. Speaking in her soft, unhurried voice, Circe told about Toad Madden joining the band, completing the mix that had begun with Eric Lindgard, Joe Williams, and Vince Russo. She came at length to herself. "I like to sing. Where else would I get the chance at thirty-five?"

Amy was surprised. "You certainly don't look it."

Circe smiled. "Thank you."

"Who writes the songs?"

"We all chip in. Desmond, our manager, is involved, too. We have ideas about music."

Amy edged forward on the couch, partly to better hear Circe's soft voice, though she was thinking again about the strange experience she'd had the night the New Riders had played. "What kinds of ideas?"

"Well, like there are certain things you can do to . . . *intensify* the experience."

"You mean with the spotlights and the liquid slides?"

"That, too. And our sound mix. At root bottom, rock music is about expression, about sex . . . and freedom. Of the mind and the senses, the body, yes . . . but what if music could rearrange everything we know, and recreate it as something brand new?" Circe leaned forward so abruptly that the cat jumped to the floor. Her eyes were alight with hope. "When you sit with your friends, listening to the Doors and the Dead . . . partly it's the sense of shared experience, but aren't you also looking for another path? Isn't there a longing that the music will show you the way to something better? I mean, could it change the world?"

Amy smiled to cover her sudden uncertainty. Music for her had always been about feelings. Circe sighed and sank back. "It's probably better just to experience the music and leave the talk alone. More tea?"

They went on talking for a while, and the subject changed, but it had become clear to Amy that there were topics other than the New Riders of the Apocalypse that Circe wished to discuss, though she was in no rush to get to whatever they might be.

"You're courageous," she said. "I like the open letters that you write."

"You read them?" It surprised and pleased Amy.

"Every time. You feel a real connection to the community, don't you."

Amy was embarrassed, as though she were being called upon to voice some platitude from an Intro to Journalism course: " 'A newspaper's responsibility to the community it serves is blah blah . . . ' " While she didn't doubt that was true, it was an abstraction. Her foremost aim in writing was to move people. "I like that there *is* a community," she said. "I'm worried that it's starting to fragment."

"It's the killer doing it, isn't it?" Circe said.

"You think that, too?"

"It's hard not to."

"Yet no one's talking about it. It's like it hasn't really hit us."

"Who's in charge of the investigation?"

"For the police, you mean?"

"Have you spoken with them?"

"I've talked with a detective named Sparrow."

It was difficult to be sure—one of the tapers had begun to flicker, making shadows dance—but Amy thought she saw a reaction of surprise. But Circe rose then and moved out of the candlelight, and her voice was calm when she said, "Well, I hope they're clever enough to find the answers."

She returned and handed Amy a small picture in a gilt frame. Amy angled it toward the light. It was a figure painting, decidedly Indian. Done in coloring-book hues, it showed a dark, many-armed figure of a woman. She was nude and drinking red liquid from a cup. She didn't look happy. "Kali," Circe said. "The Hindu goddess representing the untamed energies." Amy remembered it from a comparative religions course in college. "We're in a state of contraction," Circe went on. "A pulling inward." Her strong, lean hands illustrated, drawing together, fingers interlocking like teeth. "When things contract, fierce energies occur. *Dark* energies. The Vedas say there'll be great tribulation. Kali is the dark goddess who lives in the cremation ground surrounded by corpses, and drinks blood. Hers is a time of destruction."

Amy felt an odd disquiet. Was she referring to the killings? The candles wavered, giving a strobe effect to the objects in the room: gourds, rams' horns, and antique instruments appeared alternately to vanish and rematerialize.

"Of course," Circe said, and smiled, her hands relaxing. "Kali is also Mother of liberation. It'll be beautiful. The Age of Aquarius. But first there's the darkness to be gotten through."

Amy felt a churn of excitement. There were discoveries to be made here, beyond the music and the mysticism. "What do you think will happen?" she asked.

There was rap on the door. "We're ready to roll," a man called.

"Do you really want to know what I think?" Circe asked.

"Yes."

With her head tipped slightly in an attitude of listening, Circe lifted her hand and held it in the air, fingers curled. "He's here, among us. He wasn't, but he is now. He's come for the summer."

A shiver worked up Amy's spine, as if the surrounding darkness had drawn closer. The candle flames flickered. She gave the room a furtive survey, more aware than ever of its dim nooks and corners, the paraffin scent of the candles. Circe's long-fingered hand shadowed the ceiling, like one of the mummified tarantulas in the glass case. "They've all been programmed to come—everyone, whether they proclaim revolution, give out free food or drugs or parking tickets. Or play in a band or write letters. Everyone is here for a reason."

"But you said, '*He's* here.' "

"Everyone. It's all part of a plan." With a puff, Circe extinguished the candle. She stood silent for a time, staring into some vague place, then faced Amy and whispered, "And he wants to kill us."

12

ON THE TWENTY-FIRST OF JUNE THE MOON WAS IN SAGITTARIUS, GOING INTO CAPRI-corn, and that night it would reach the full and beam down on San Francisco. Zephyr had predicted the day would be a Lion. Pluto and Uranus were conjunct in Virgo, which was symbolic of transition, he said, a time of upheaval and change. Make of that what she would, Amy couldn't shake what Circe had told her; nor could she forget that four people were dead. Still, as counterweight to that, or per-haps out of respect to it, the cosmic powers had seen fit to deliver up a glorious day for the summer solstice.

The celebration had begun before sunrise, a mile to the east of the Haight, atop Twin Peaks, where people had gathered to greet the dawn. From there the crowd, already several thousand strong, had hiked here to Golden Gate Park, where their numbers had been growing all morning. And what a morning it was.

Today was the longest day and shortest night of the year, and with so little time to sleep, Amy imagined, it seemed possible to confuse dreams with waking reality. Magic was in the air. It was as if overnight the sidewalks, streets, trees, and houses of the Haight had been pulled up, crinkled and dipped into big vats of bright paint. Mist off the ocean, a mile to the west, drifted in translucent fingers up the long wooded stretches of the park, carrying the mingled tangs of cold ocean, eucalyp-tus, and manzanita, scented oils, flowering plants, barbecue pits being fired up, and the languid, pervasive musk of burning hemp.

Amy and Seth held hands and made their way slowly along, exchanging peace signs and smiles with people. Their destination was a meadow where there would be bands playing later.

She had put on a long ivory-white dress of soft Madras cotton and drawn her hair back in an antique tortoiseshell clasp. She had tied a blue silk scarf around her neck and tiny bells on her ankles. Barefoot, she made music as she walked. Seth wore a forest-green velour vest over his denim shirt, his jeans tucked into Spanish leather boots tooled with red birds. Jester, in Farmer Johns and his belled cap, bopped along at their side talking an antic rap about everything in general and nothing in particular.

Stretched across the park lawns was a carnival of people. Amy watched a girl of about seven dancing with swirling purple ribbons, like a Maxfield Parrish sylph. A man in Merlin garb, complete with tall conical hat emblazoned with stars and moons, juggled gilded eggs. Dogs bounded after thrown balls. Bikers lounged by their gleaming Harley-Davidsons. Chalk artists graced the paved walks with fanciful creations.

And there was music in the air.

It moved in crosscurrents, as mingled and layered and evocative as the aromas. People thumped conga drums, spanked tambourines, strummed guitars, played renaissance flutes, accompanied on jaw harps, finger cymbals, mandolins, harmonicas, and clapping. A group of black men were harmonizing a cappella, moving sweetly from gospel choruses to soul songs. Under a tree, ringed by entranced listeners, a bare-chested man was plucking shimmering arpeggios from an ungainly sitar. There were Celtic and Indian chants, folk ballads, mantras, rebel yells, hymns, even wild barbaric yawps, and whether or not they went soaring over the rooftops of the world, Amy couldn't say, but one thing she knew with a growing joy was that the tribes had come in peace to greet the official start of the summer of love.

Tantalized by the day's prospects, Jester said, "There's got to be *one* chick out here for this latent heterosexual to love. Or at least a double cheeseburger with my name on it." Pointing to the rising smoke of a cook fire, he named a spot where he would meet them later and sauntered off.

As they resumed walking, a man with a goatee tapped Seth's shoulder. "Hey, brother, gotta rap." He drew Seth a few feet away and began to talk. He seemed edgy, Amy thought, pulling at his spiky tuft of beard as the two conferred in low voices. After a moment, he whisked off into the crowd like smoke.

Seth rejoined her and she took his hand. "Was he a dealer?"

"Just a guy. They want me to say a few words later."

"Here? Talk to the crowd?"

He shrugged. "There's a stage set up in the meadow."

Her reaction was puzzlement. Not that she doubted Seth could do it, he was a wonderful speaker; it was just that she had thought today would be free of speeches.

"The guy who was supposed to do it dropped some bad acid," Seth said. "They reserved a little slot of time between bands. Somebody's got to say something. For the Movement."

It was a phrase that fell from people's lips, though never without a certain hushed tone of secrecy and reverence. Amy could almost see the words in the air, hovering ephemerally to the strains of a Phil Ochs song. *The Movement.* Despite its vaguely furtive sound, however, it was nothing anyone seemed able or willing to define with any precision. Notions like the Left, antiwar, liberation, the underground and revolution seemed to cluster around it in a loose constellation, but it was all of these things and none of them.

"Do you want to?" Amy asked, sensing some ambivalence.

"As opposed to what?"

"Just let it be, let the bands play. It's a day for music."

"As opposed to what?" he said again.

As opposed to the bombast that tended to invade too many speeches, she thought. She said, "Politics."

"Shit, don't you get it? *Everything's* politics. There's a war on!"

Amy stepped back, stung by his attack. "Lecture me about it, Seth! I know there's a war. My cousin's there, remember?"

"I don't only mean in Vietnam."

"Okay, there are hassles," she agreed, "but look around. We're all together. We're happy. For one day, can't we just hang out? Why do there have to be factions and speeches? First speeches, and pretty soon demands, and then—"

"Confrontations," he broke in.

She fell silent. It was as if the man with the goatee had infected him, and now his edginess touched her, too. "Why does it have to be you?" she said, a rising note in her voice, one she didn't want there. The hectic pace of their days had been pulling them apart. She felt disconnected from Seth. They hadn't made love in a week. She wanted just to be with him today, to be close. "You ran the meeting the other night," she said, adopting a quieter tone. "Why don't *they* speak?"

"They're scared."

"Oh, great. Of what?"

Seth glanced toward a hillside at the eastern edge of the field. She looked, too. Beyond a line of bushes on the slope, she could make out dark forms she hadn't noticed before. It took her a moment to realize they were Tactical Police Squad vans. Despite the growing warmth of the sun, a sliver of ice slipped down her back. Perhaps Seth felt it, or maybe he wanted to be sure he had made his point, for he looked at her with new meaning in his eyes. "Want to tell *them* to just hang loose?"

After a moment, he put his arm around her, a gesture at once conciliating and protective. "Come on, Jester will be waiting."

The blanket of exhaust fumes on the 30th Street edge of the park gave way to other smells as Sparrow walked the fringes of the crowd. The cool air carried incense, cooking food, stale bodies, and the smell he had come most to associate with the Haight-Ashbury, marijuana. Though his impulse was to identify who was smoking it, he resisted. He hadn't come here today on cop business; at least, not officially.

For that reason he had donned faded chinos, a plaid flannel shirt, and deck shoes, such clothes as he might wear working on the *Blind Faith*. And indeed, the thought had come to him that morning that he might well spend the day aboard, boxing his belongings before she went on the market; but after breakfast and checking with Austin for an update on the investigation, he found he had no heart for seeing the boat. So he was here, wandering among the hippies in all of their belled and tie-dyed pulchritude, though he wasn't sure why. Curiosity, perhaps. Or maybe this was a way to get an appreciation for ambiguity. Once inside the park he simply joined the unhurried tide, assuming that in time it would take him somewhere.

"Hash, acid, weed, speed?"

This time he succumbed to impulse and, turning, saw a man in a buckskin jacket with long fringes on the sleeves. "Hash, acid, weed, speed?" was his chant. Gauging Sparrow's interest (or the notion that someone who looked the way Sparrow did was interested at all) the man grinned and added, "Pepsi-Cola?"

Sparrow roamed, taking in the scene without making much sense of it. Small children ran nude, and some of the adults, too, were doffing clothes as the day warmed. One voluptuous woman strolled past naked, causing him briefly to stare and bringing to mind the old nudist camp joke line, "Bet she'd look great in a bathing suit." Everywhere, people danced to music of their own making. To say he was relaxed would have overstated it, but no one bothered him, few even gave him a second glance, and he was content. WAGE PEACE read a banner he saw, and it didn't seem like an unreasonable idea.

They were a mob. They called themselves a gathering of the tribes, and the newspapers said a crowd. Somebody on TV that morning had cooed about a "celebration." Bullshit. George Moon was not to be coddled with semantics. What you had here, he realized, was trouble looking for a place to happen. Fifty thousand? Seventy-five? On a Wednesday, yet; nobody at work. It was a goddamn mob.

From atop a rise on the eastern side of the park, he slowly scanned binoculars across the grotesque tapestry of people befouling the meadow below and saw:

A circle of longhairs passing a feathered pipe.

A banner that read WAGE PEACE, AMERIKKKA!

Some kids who looked about fifteen drinking wine.

A Negro with an American flag draped around his grungy body like Superman's cape.

A couple lying bare-assed under a bush, and although they were too far away to see clearly—or even tell what gender they were—Moon didn't have to guess what they were up to.

He lowered the binoculars. A gathering of the People. The hell with that, it was an expanding geometry of violations, and before the day was out there would be civil disorder, he would bet on it. It didn't matter that most of them were just lost, aimless kids looking for a chance to belong to something; that was pathetic enough. But it took only a small number of agitators with their minds set on mischief and worse, like the SDS and the Mob Grope crowd, who met in their secret cells, jacking themselves up with the ravings of communists and Malcolm X— those were the dangerous ones who ran like combustible rivers through the dark heart of the district, threatening to burst forth in conflagration.

Moon reached through the open window of a police van and gripped the radio microphone, intending to check in with the units he had arrayed around the park. And that's when he saw it.

Leaving the mike to dangle, he stepped back from the van.

Not two hundred feet down the slope from where he stood, someone was waving a flag. Red and yellow, it struck him with a shock of recognition. It was Ho Chi Minh's National Liberation Front flag. Right under his goddamn nose.

He experienced a flare of such rage that he was ready to charge down and rip into the flag-wavers with his fists. And he might have done just that if at that moment the two-way radio had not crackled to life.

"Cap, this is Bravo. Come in."

It was one of his men, positioned a half mile away near the outdoor amphitheater where a stage was set up for music. Moon jerked the hand mike from its hook. "Go ahead, Bravo."

"Got a situation here I want your opinion on." The cop tried for a seasoned nonchalance, but Moon heard apprehension in his voice. He was a new recruit to the squad. "There's a group of people moving this way."

"Coming at you?" Moon's eye stayed on the NLF flag wavering in the distance, like a guidon for an insurrectionary force.

"Well, kind of . . . meandering. They got off a truck just now, maybe a half dozen of them. They're carrying things."

Tension began to congeal at the back of Moon's neck. "What things?"

"Something . . . long. Damn, is it rifles? Wait. Sonofa—" The cop gave a little huff of breath and said something Moon didn't catch.

"What?"

"*Guitars.* Get this, it's a band coming to play."

"That's it?"

"Shaggy-ass bastards with guitars. You want us to do anything?"

"Do what?"

"I don't know. Hose them with deodorant?" The cop chuckled.

"Do nothing. Stand your ground. But stay alert!" George Moon slammed down the microphone. For the first time since he had begun training his men at the Presidio a month ago, he felt his confidence slipping out from under him, being wisped away on a breeze of reefer madness. Guitars, for Christ's sake, and—

He turned, remembering something, then cursed again.

The NLF flag was gone.

Amy's disagreement with Seth was forgotten. He'd bought her a nosegay of violets wound with pink velvet ribbon. She held the little blooms to her face and savored their subtle fragrance. The chill had gone from the air and the day glowed with golden light. They were sitting with some friends, just grooving.

At the far end of the meadow, the Dead were performing on a plywood stage. At the moment they were into a flowing, easy-tempoed raga that gave no sign of ending anytime soon. Jerry Garcia was resplendent in a stars-and-stripes shirt, seeming almost to nod over his guitar. Even baby-faced Bob Weir was subdued, his normally manic energy evident only in his occasional bluesy runs. The crowd was riding the same easy wave, their bodies gently swaying, and Amy realized that today it was as if all of them—she and Seth, this circle of friends, the people up there making music, the crowd, straight, stoned, young, old, and in-between—were one big family.

Sparrow was surprised to discover that it was only two P.M. He felt like he'd been here a long while. It had been long enough for him to feel the burnish of sun on his face and to have eaten a hot dog grilled over charcoal—when he had dug out a dollar to pay, the woman had laughed and waved it away—but it was as if the day had slowed down, that a time warp had occurred in Golden Gate Park and he had slipped into it, his watch inadequate to the task of measuring the flow of events.

The crowd had expanded. He could no longer smell pot, though that was probably due to the fact that it had become so pervasive. There was something childlike in these people, some of whom flew kites, tossed balls, played tag. The music, too, though raw-edged at times with what at first he had taken merely for poor musicianship magnified by public address equipment, had begun to sound different. Its oddities were a deliberate facet of the performance, and it was capable, as now, of inducing a restful, almost hypnotic state. From a distance he watched a band play. On the left side of the stage, a man with tangled dark hair and a flag shirt was standing with his guitar, singing. Around him, stacked like the toy blocks of a baby giant, stood piles of speakers and amps, but his voice had a surprising softness.

Continuing to gaze around, Sparrow stopped, taken by a sudden throb of paranoia. No, it wasn't paranoia at all; it was real. Standing on the crest of a knoll, scoping the crowd through binoculars, was George Moon. And if he was here . . . yes, there were some of his troops, too.

This recognition was followed by another: that Moon would come up dry because the crowd, tamed now by sun, music, wine, and who knew what else, would wind down into passivity. There would be no eruption, no riot, no field day for the TAC Squad. Feeling heartened, Sparrow turned back to the music.

The sun was like a baked brick on the back of George Moon's neck. Periodically he made radio contact with his men at their locations around the park, including the stage area where a succession of so-called bands were performing, each louder and more mindless than the preceding one, apparently, but still nothing was happening. Restless, he unhooked the mike. "Bravo," he inquired, "who's playing now?"

So far it had been a tally of weird names like Quicksilver Messenger Service, Country Joe and the Fish (if you could believe *that* one), Big Brother and the Holding Company, the Grateful Dead.

"Guy Lombardo."

"What?"

"Only kidding, Cap. There's a break, some guy just got up to talk. A bunch of crap it sounds like. Love and peace."

Moon looked at his watch. Five past four and not a damned thing happening. "Start checking for runaways," he said determinedly. "Check draft cards. Anyone resists, bust them."

When he was announced, Seth let go of Amy's hand and she watched him cross the stage to the microphone. She puffed a breath to calm herself. This was by far the biggest crowd he had ever addressed. At Berkeley he'd spoken to hundreds of people gathered in Sproul Plaza and held them spellbound; but there were tens of thousands today. She was nervous. Jester stood by the foot of the stage, gnawing a pretzel.

"Greetings and hallucinations," Seth said. "What a day for a daydream."

His words drifted across the amphitheater and floated back, and with them came cheers.

"You, too." Seth pointed and waved. "We see you up there on the hill. Peek-a-boo." People standing near the stage turned to look. "It's the *Tact*less Squad. But, hey, we're cool."

More cheers. Amy glanced at Jester, whose grin was studded with crumbs. She looked out at the sea of faces and she smiled, too, and thought: well, okay, it was going to be just fine. Say a few things, keep it light, and Seth was going to have a whole bunch of new fans.

He said, "You probably heard the governor's hippie joke. 'Who dresses like Tarzan, has hair like Jane, and smells like Cheetah?' What a wit, huh? Hey, he ought to know, man. His hottest bedmate was Bonzo."

Amy caught Seth's glance from where she stood at the edge of the stage, and it occurred to her that that's what had eluded her in trying to define the Movement part of it, at least, was *flow*. Seth understood flow.

"What we're doing today is showing the gov', showing the country, showing the fuckin' world that—"

He went on talking—or at least, he *looked* as if he was talking. She couldn't be sure because suddenly no sound was coming out. He appeared to recognize at the same moment as Amy did that the PA system had quit. He tapped the microphone a few times, then stepped back from it and looked over to the side of the stage, an uncertain expression on his face.

Someone yelled, "They cut the juice!"

From where she stood, Amy could see the generator in the bed of a pickup truck, along with a mixing console. A man with a ponytail bent to pick up a power cord that had been pulled loose. As he did so, a biker in a denim jacket with the sleeves cut off to reveal big, tattooed arms, grabbed him and yanked him off the truck.

Angered, Amy started toward them, but there were a lot of people in the way. Still holding her violets, she edged among them. As she neared the truck there was an explosion of glass. She spun, half prepared to see the biker holding a jagged beer bottle, but she saw the truck's windshield had been shattered. The biker was gone. There was a scurry of people, and raised voices. Then, seemingly from nowhere, cops.

In their black helmets and Plexiglas visors and shields, they had a beetling look, like dark creatures from Tolkien. Amy was amazed at how fast they'd appeared. And frightened. She heard her name called and turned. Seth vaulted off the stage and grabbed her arm. His face was red, and for a horrid instant she thought he had been hurt, but he was flushed with excitement.

"This may be *it!*" he shouted over the rising din. "The start!"

She was trying to keep steady in the crush of people shouldering by. "We've got to stop it!"

"Stop it?" His incomprehension matched her own. "It's happening."

"People are going to get hurt! Where's Jester? Can you get to the microphone?"

He looked at her as though she'd suggested something alien.

There was another shattering of glass. Suddenly she and Seth were forced apart as bodies slammed past. She reached for him, but she was yanked away and swept backwards. People were running. At the back of the panicked crowd was a line of the helmeted cops, prodding forward with their truncheons. She twisted free of fleeing people and managed a few steps toward the advancing cops. She waved her arms, shouting to get their attention. In their visored helmets, and half hidden behind their shields, they were oblivious. She might as well have called to an onrushing wave.

It took Sparrow a moment to realize that the speaker had quit abruptly. He looked toward the distant stage, but nothing there appeared to have changed. Problems with the PA system, he thought, which was fine; he didn't need to hear the governor knocked. He started to turn away again when another sound came to him. It seemed to float from a great way off, a cry where moments ago there had been words and laughter, and before that songs. He grew alert.

At the far end of the meadow dust had begun to rise, yellowed by the late sun. Emerging from it, like Bedouins from a sandstorm, were the shadowy apparitions of people. From this distance, some hundred yards away, they seemed almost to be moving in slow motion. Then more voices reached him, high-pitched shouts, and suddenly he realized the people were fleeing in a dead run. Something was stampeding them.

Sparrow discovered that the afternoon had induced a languor in him. Sun and fresh air and music had given him over to a pleasant lethargy. He shed it now. People around him, lounging on the grass, began to stir, too. Breaking into a jog, he started toward the stage.

People bumped past her: a bright blur of clothing, tangled hair, open mouths, shouts. A bewildered dog raced by. Feet trampled her bare toes. Amy squirmed, twisting sideways in an effort to move forward against the charge, but it was impossible. She was barely able to hold her ground.

The line of cops was shoulder to shoulder, just yards away now. She raised her hands, desperate to wave them off. A woman trying to cradle an infant was screaming. Amy took her by the shoulders and steered her in the direction of the flow. But as Amy turned, she was knocked backwards. Dropping her violets, she went down.

As he neared, Sparrow could see a scuffle in front of the stage. People were pushing, shoving, but he couldn't tell what was causing the confusion.

"Somebody was murdered!" called a voice.

Panic clawed his gut. Had the killer struck?

He began to run hard, moving against the charge of people like a swimmer in a rip tide. As he got nearer to the stage, the current thickened. He was forced to slow. At some points he had to stop and brace against rushing people, standing to try to see over them. The air was choked with dust, shrill with sounds. Overhead, an elaborate Chinese dragon kite wobbled as someone hastily dragged it earthward. When a youth of about sixteen ran into him, Sparrow seized his arm. "What happened?" he demanded.

"The cops! They've lost it totally!"

He understood. He struggled forward until he was near enough for a view. Through billows of dust he could see the black helmets of the TACs. They were advancing in a line, shoulder to shoulder, shields and truncheons in hand. One wing of cops had boxed several hundred people between an old pickup truck, the stage, and a second line of cops. There was a flailing of arms and bodies as the hippies, left with no means of escape, tried to climb onto the stage, like bathers trying to get aboard a raft ahead of frenzied sharks. Some couldn't scale the five-foot side of the stage. Their cries filled the air as they slid or were pulled back, some literally stepped on as others clambered over them. But now a new perception came to Sparrow, and his stomach tightened at the sound of falling clubs.

Amy shielded herself with her arms as people fled by, howling as they ran. Legs and feet buffeted past. On the ground, a beautiful Chinese kite was trampled, its frame snapping like tiny bones. Dizzied, disoriented in the pandemonium and the blinding dust, she nevertheless knew that she couldn't lie there. Any minute she'd be injured in some way, knocked unconscious, perhaps stomped to death. This was no family anymore; people were in stark confusion.

With effort, using her hands to fend people away, she got to her knees. At last, the crowd thinned slightly, and there was Seth. She had to blink to be sure. He saw her.

"Come on!" he shouted, pulling her up.

"My flowers." The thought had risen dizzily to her mind. Stupid. There was no time. The TAC police were practically on top of them. "Stop!" she cried.

Seth spun to the halt. "What?"

She was looking at the nearest cop, treated to an image of her own panic in the Plexiglas visor of his helmet. Seth tugged at her to go.

But she still faced the cop. Shelled as he was in his armor, it wasn't at all clear that he saw her. She reached to touch his shield. He flung her off. This time she touched his shoulder, acutely aware of the engorged muscle beneath the damp fabric of his shirt, alert even to the rush of his adrenaline, which matched her own. She yelled again and he swung his head; through the plastic visor their eyes met. With shock she saw he was young, her age. It seemed to hit him, too. His eyes widened with something she couldn't read.

"It's a mistake!" she cried. "Please!"

For an instant she thought the tense expression softened to something that might've been understanding. His breath fogged the visor. Then, amid the melee all around them, came a grunt, followed by a series of quick, soggy sounds, like large stones falling on packed earth. The cop pushed by, and before Amy could run, Seth's hand was gone from hers.

Shouts. Curses. Screams.

Dust forced Sparrow to squint. His progress had slowed almost to a standstill. He lowered his shoulder, and a wedge of fleeing people broke around him and flung past. Somewhere ahead, he knew, were the TAC police. He had some blurred notion of finding George Moon, of stopping this.

To his right he saw a young woman, like himself, facing the flood tide of rushing people. Angling her way, he was astonished to see it was Amy Cole. Her hair was awry, her dress grass-stained, but she held steady against the buffeting of the crowd. She didn't see him. Her attention was riveted elsewhere, and he looked up to see a TAC cop advancing toward her. Amy was shouting at him. The man loomed so near Sparrow could see his knuckles, as large as lug nuts, gripping his black truncheon as he raised it.

Grabbing Amy from behind, Sparrow yanked her backwards just as the club fell. He had half spun around and it crashed onto his shoulder. His arm went numb. Amy broke free and rounded on him, ready to throw a punch—then her eyes widened with recognition. For an instant, neither moved. Frozen, as if time had stopped, they stood like statues against a diorama of battle.

"Sparrow!" she cried.

He wheeled and saw another cop, club raised. Snatching hold of each other, Sparrow and Amy lunged out of range.

But they were quickly hemmed in by the crowd. A woman cradling a puppy against her torn peasant blouse screamed hysterically. Coughing from the dust, a man in a dashiki, carrying a broken sign that read NO VIETNAMESE EVER CALLED ME NIGGER!, swung the sign at a cop and instantly was clubbed. "*Nat!*" Amy yelled in apparent recognition of the man, but he was swept away. They, too, found themselves being pulled along by the flow. Sparrow grabbed Amy's hand so they wouldn't become separated. He could feel hers trembling, but her grip was strong. They got past a pickup truck whose front and back windshields were shattered. Standing in its lee as people crushed past, he saw the stage and made for it.

He lifted Amy onto the platform. One of her feet was scuffed and bleeding, and the hem of her dress was torn. He hoisted himself up behind her. She sat there, breathing hard through parted lips. She looked at him. Her cheeks were flushed and there was a swipe of dirt on her forehead. Her hair, which evidently had been done up, had come undone and hung in loose disarray, but her eyes were bright, and Sparrow thought how wrong he'd been in once thinking her plain. She was beautiful, incandescent. It had not struck him before this moment, and now, all at once, he couldn't take his eyes off her. Nor had her eyes left his. They were searching him as if she sensed what he was thinking.

She turned away suddenly with a look of fright and got to her feet. "Seth," she cried. "He was with me."

Sparrow rose, too. The area below the stage was pandemonium now. Someone had tumbled the big amplifiers down onto the ground, where they lay like monoliths, around which people dodged in their panic. Hysteria shrilled above the din. The cops were clearly carrying the battle, the hippies offering little resistance beyond the simple fact of their being there. Some of the TAC cops, reacting to this, seemed to moderate their attack; others pressed their advantage. The black truncheons rose and fell. Sparrow was at a loss as to what to do.

He whirled at Amy's cry.

"Seth!" She pointed.

The dark-haired editor of the *Rag* was struggling past. Sparrow called to him, too, but the kid seemed not to notice. Sparrow climbed off the stage. When he reached him, he saw Seth's head was bleeding, his hair pasted to his forehead with rivulets of blood. His green vest was spotted with it. Sparrow grabbed his arm and pointed to Amy. With dazed comprehension, Seth made his way to the stage. When he'd climbed up, Amy threw her arms around him.

"How bad is it?" Sparrow asked. Some of his blood had stained Amy's cheek and hair.

"It's not what it looks like."

Sparrow produced a handkerchief. "Press it on the wound."

Seth took it and did so. Sparrow ushered the pair of them behind some amplifiers for added safety. He righted an overturned drummer's stool and got Seth seated, then he went to the edge of the stage again to look for a route of exit.

The battle was breaking as the TAC cops slowly regained order. One cop was talking on a military field telephone which gave the scene a disconcertingly martial attitude, Sparrow thought, and it wasn't difficult to superimpose on it one of the nightly TV images from the CBS news. In the pall of dust, he could not see far, but at the distant rim of visibility, he did make out the slowly approaching wink of patrol car lights. He went back to Amy and Seth.

She was tending him. The handkerchief, only a red wad now, lay on the floor. Amy had stripped the blue silk scarf from her own neck and was pressing that on the wound.

"How bad?" Sparrow asked.

"I think the bleeding has stopped." She didn't sound quite sure.

Seth looked at Sparrow as though seeing him for the first time, then remembering they'd met before. Amy said, "This is John Sparrow."

"Who cares?" he sneered.

"He's not with them, Seth."

"He's a pig, goddammit!"

"He saved me."

Just then a rock landed on the stage with a thump, startling them. An instant later a beer bottle crashed. "We better get out of here," Sparrow said. "There's a medical tent—"

"I'm okay, dammit!" Seth pulled roughly loose as Amy tried to reapply the silk scarf.

"Let's get it checked," she pleaded. "You may have a concussion."

But Seth wasn't interested. He stomped to the edge of the stage. Amy went after him. "It's starting to bleed again," she said with alarm.

Seth's curls were sticky, his forehead streaked. The wound was probably more bloody than dangerous, Sparrow guessed, but he couldn't be sure. "Come on," he said, reaching to take the kid's sleeve, "that might be worse than—"

Seth jerked away. "*Fuck off!*" he shouted, his face contorted. He rounded on Amy. "You want to make friends with people who do this?" He gestured at his wound, though he made no move to mop away the gore. "For Christ's sake, Amy, get your head straight. I told you. It's war!"

Oblivious to her stricken look, he leaped from the stage and stumbled off in the direction from which he'd come. Amy looked helplessly at Sparrow, torn; then she tossed aside the bloodied silk scarf, jumped to the ground, and went after Seth.

Sparrow picked up the scarf and stuffed it in his pocket; then he did the only thing he could think to do. He got to one of the Park Station prowl cars that had come across the field. Upon seeing Sparrow's star, the patrolman at the wheel said he didn't know who was in charge, he'd got a report of a disturbance and come to investigate. "Some kind of hippie riot, huh?"

Sparrow used the radio and got the dispatcher, who patched him through to the office of the chief. Speaking to a secretary, he started to explain the situation as he was witnessing it. Before he'd fairly begun, Chief Cahill himself came on, listened briefly, then told Sparrow to hold. From that point on the matter was handled quickly. Evidently contact was made with the TAC command vehicle and orders given for the squad to stand down. Left with no choice, someone (presumably George Moon) carried out the order, and soon the TAC police were withdrawing.

Sensing they had somehow endured—and having no interest in further trouble—what remained of the crowd kept its distance. Sparrow had a thought to try to find Amy Cole, but the likelihood seemed remote. He had the Park Station cop drive him back to the JFK Drive entrance. As he got out, a dark blue van came bucketing past. In the passenger window, a face turned and Sparrow saw George Moon. The expression on Moon's face went from surprise to recognition, and Sparrow guessed that his own role in things was now known. Moon's final look, before he turned away, was one of thwarted fury, the impact of which, even at this distance, was palpable.

Twilight. A rim of moon just starting to rise. Down below where you stand, the meadow fills with shadows, and an owl hoots to the coming night. For the moment, thank God, it isn't screams. But things are beginning to break down.

From here on the ridge top, you marveled at the gathering, listened to music, saw the afternoon skirmish unfold. You watched the advance of the police, the small pockets of resistance around the stage, but mostly the longhairs scattering in clouds of amber dust. You can still see the flicker of lights as the last patrol wagons and an ambulance leave. What had that astrologer, Zephyr, predicted? A Lion? Today was a sign. A foretelling. The flower children were here, and then the men with boots and clubs came. Nothing serious yet, some bloodied heads, a few arrests, but a lot of confusion and uncertainty now.

And fear.

With the turning of the earth, summer has come. But summer is a season of waning, the days shortening now—in the smallest gradations, it's true—but shortening nonetheless as the long darkness approaches.

And you know about darkness.

Unlike these children, you understand its dimension, have plumbed the black contours of it. But these folks will learn. Their season has come. And yours, too.

The owl *who-whoos*. You make your way down the path, saddlebags flapping on your shoulder, a soft jingling coming from inside. At the foot of the slope you start across the meadow, empty now in the enfolding night. Something lying on the ground catches your eye. You pick it up. A cluster of small, broken flowers tied with a velvet ribbon.

THREE

BLACK LIGHT

When logic and proportion have fallen sloppy dead
And the White Knight is talking backwards . . .
—Jefferson Airplane

13

THE DAY AFTER THE SOLSTICE, AMY AND SETH DROVE ACROSS THE GOLDEN GATE Bridge, heading north to look for Terry Gordon. Ocean and sky were shades of brilliant blue, and the sun gave vibrancy to the flowers and grasses that waved from the Marin headlands, made lush by the heavy spring rains. To Amy it was a perfect day by every measure, save one. She glanced at Seth at the wheel of the battered Volvo, his forehead swathed in a bandage. He had required twelve stitches to close the cut on his scalp.

Her temptation was to dwell on the rift that was growing between her and Seth, a rift that had been brought into sharp focus yesterday, but there were larger issues, too. Just a short time ago there had been a real sense of quiet revolution taking place in the land. Part social experiment, part cosmic adventure, it was there in strangers greeting each other on the street with a smile, a quickly flashed peace sign, a shared toke, an exchanged flower, a hopeful feeling that collectively they could change the world. But now something was different, and she could no longer pretend otherwise. She was aware of a faint seismic shifting, like the first pull of sand underfoot as a wave is drawn back to sea. And while the Haight had been a relatively calm eddy in the turbulence of greater waters, where war and oppression raged, that was changing, too.

If yesterday told the shape of things to come, the authorities, it seemed, were more intent on committing crimes than stopping them. Or solving them, she thought with a shudder. Four people were dead, and she was convinced that the police were no closer to finding the killer than they had been before.

With good reason, folks were afraid. Didn't she hear the edgy talk at Lynell's coffee shop mornings? Granted there were already threads of tension among the tribes, but so far they stopped well short of outright hostility. Now she had to wonder, for how long? Last night, after having his wound treated at the Free Clinic and declared superficial, Seth had gone off with some of his Movement friends, telling Amy only that they needed to rap. Her attempt to probe him on the nature of their talk—and her urging that he take some aspirin as the doctor prescribed— had led to a hassle at breakfast. Even Jester, usually immune to larger concerns, had been subdued; and when given a chance to come with them today—something he would ordinarily have jumped at—he'd drifted off to his room to smoke a joint instead.

So today was a perfect day if you were able to leave such things behind. Amy couldn't.

The idea of finding Terry Gordon had been hers, conceived in the sleepless hours before Seth had returned from his meeting. Her hope was that they could gain some perspective from their old teacher. And maybe the ride itself would mend things between Seth and her before they worsened.

In college, Seth had revered Terry Gordon, taken all his classes, studied Terry's book on the psychology of revolt the way a religious adept pored over sacred texts. Yet, when Amy proposed today's quest, Seth declared darkly that Terry had changed since those days, had copped out. In the end, Seth consented to the trip, she suspected, simply to prove his point. In his view, Terry had dropped the banner of revolution and sold out to the System. "He's become a landlord!" he railed as they got farther north, waving a hand at the trees, beyond which rose the spectacular upthrust cone of Tamalpais.

"He inherited the farm," Amy pointed out.

"He was *against* property. He could've refused it."

"That's a bit dramatic."

"Or given it away." Seth snorted. "A farmer. I can see it. Kids and animals underfoot, no electricity."

Amy was reminded of her own childhood on a small apple farm. "Doesn't sound so awful."

Seth's sour expression said he wasn't buying. For all his open-mindedness, there was an intolerance in him. He and his Cal friends talked fervently about people mapping their own way, but had little patience for any path that branched very far from their own.

"The back-to-the-garden trip is a fantasy. Where the hell was Terry yesterday? He should've been on the barricades."

"Breaking heads?"

Seth glanced over.

"Is that better than baking bread?"

Seth scowled. "Someone's being a wiseass."

"Or breaking beds?" She laughed. She couldn't help herself. She scootched over closer to him. It was a big bad beautiful day, and it felt good to have left the city behind. Even Seth didn't wear the mantle of angry politico very snugly today, despite the white gauze headband. He put his arm around her and they puttered north.

In her single graduate year at Cal, Amy had become friends with Terry Gordon, who was a decade older than she. He was Seth's senior advisor, and each in different ways had been responsible for Amy's friendship with the other. She and Seth had taken Terry's Modern Social Ideas course and gotten to know each other there, sitting in the back of an amphitheater, sharing lecture notes, which led one day to a cup of coffee. Soon they were holding hands in class, listening to Terry Gordon, all six-feet-four of him, as he paced storklike at the front, stroking his unruly Fu Manchu, brimming with an intense New York energy and spinning out words that held the entire audience—some three hundred students strong—rapt. Those were good days, Amy reflected now, and she found herself clinging to her own quiet hope that Terry had not changed *too* much.

They chugged up increasingly narrow roads, navigating by secondhand directions. After several miscues, they found the turnoff, marked by a wine bottle propped on a stump in the undergrowth. The dirt road was only just passable, and they jounced along it for some time, brush whacking the Volvo's doors. At last the lane snaked across a dry creek and opened into a meadow. It was clear how Windflower Farm had got its name. The meadow was studded with yellow and white blooms that danced in the breeze. Ahead, some kind of archaic farm implement, stripped to its rusty ribs and hub-deep in weeds, marked the end of the trail. They climbed out.

In the quiet, sounds emerged: birds singing in the dappled gloom of woods, the *crack-crackle* of locusts in the high grass. Across the June meadow stood a weathered ranch house, several outbuildings and a small corral. As they neared, a white retriever came loping out, the flop-eared advance unit, it was quickly apparent, of an amiable, mismatched trio of dogs, and then a woman stepped into the doorway, peering under the flat of her hand at the approaching strangers. "Hi," she called, at once welcoming and wary. The dogs quieted.

Seth explained that they were old friends of Terry's. The woman was Clover and said they'd come to the right place. She was pretty, in her mid-twenties, with long wavy brown hair, a long flower print dress, and bare feet. Terry's lady? Amy wondered. The woman ushered them inside.

The house was larger than it had appeared, opening into a big all-purpose space of splintery wood and sunlight streaming through skylights, with overhead areas suggesting lofts. Potted plants hung in macramé slings from the rough-hewn joists. At one end were a woodstove and an open kitchen where a second woman stood at a counter, shelling beans. She was older than Clover, weathered from country living, though her grin was broad. She was Sarah. She wore an apron over farmer's jeans, which didn't hide a very pregnant stomach. A toddler sat nearby on the plank floor, chewing a wooden spoon.

"Terry ought to be back before long," Clover explained. "He's out hauling stove wood on the tractor."

Amy caught Seth's "I told you so" look.

"Make yourselves comfy. You want tea or anything. Smoke?"

Seth and Amy said some tea would be good.

"Herbal okay? Most of us are into a caffeine fast—except Terry. He still likes his black coffee."

The women seemed more talky than curious about visitors. They revealed that there were seven adults and three children and "a bun in the oven" living at Windflower. "That's what we call it. Windflower Love Farm. I'm going to make a sign." The others were away for the day at a livestock fair clear up in Humboldt County. The child here was called simply Girl, no clear line of parentage offered, though the question came to Amy: Was Terry the father? When the women realized that Amy and Seth were from the Haight, they nodded with a kindliness of experience, like travelers farther along a road encountering new pilgrims. Sarah brushed back a cloud of hair with her wrist and looked up from her beans. "I was doing mushrooms one day and found myself on Lombard, and it came to me, the city is a crooked path. The land is where I'll find love. Just like that, I understood I had to split. So I linked up with some people at Morning Star and did that scene about six months, then someone said Terry was starting a thing."

"You knew Terry before?" Seth asked.

"I studied with him back in '62."

"Does he still get down to the city?"

"Hardly ever," said Clover. "I do from time to time, for the music. I'm going down next week to see the New Riders of the Apocalypse. You heard them yet?"

Amy said she had but didn't elaborate, for just then the door opened and a tall figure ducked in, backlit momentarily by a patch of bright sky. Girl looked up and cooed.

"Friends, Terry," Sarah announced.

Terry Gordon stopped, hands on hips. "Well, what do you know?"

He had changed. The John Lennon glasses, which had been a trademark, were the same, but his face was fuller, and the Fu Manchu had given way to a tangle of beard, threaded lightly with gray. He had added weight to his lean frame, and he wore overalls and a black T-shirt, a bandanna wrapped around his head pirate-style.

"Seth, cool to see you." Their handshake was the power clench. "I figured you'd make it up sooner or later. Jesus, what've you been using your skull for? An LZ for cop batons?"

Seth told briefly of the trash-in and looked a little disappointed when Terry merely clicked his tongue. "Pigs don't change." He turned to Amy. His gaze moved across her, and she momentarily doubted that he even remembered her. But then he grinned. "God, Ame, you haven't changed either. Except to become even more of a piece."

"And you're still full of it, Terry."

She hugged him and was aware of the firm angularity of his body, aware too of his warmth. Her hopefulness about the visit grew.

He pulled off the bandanna and shook out his hair, which was longer than she remembered and starting to thin on top. All in all, he was still a striking specimen, not at all the kind of latter-day Grant Wood figure Seth had seemed determined to paint. "You met part of the family," Terry declared, and to the women said, "Hey, don't you offer our guests some sacrament?"

This time Amy and Seth accepted, and soon a chillum packed with homegrown was circulating. Terry washed up and they made plans for an afternoon meal together later, then he took his visitors outside to show them Windflower Love Farm. He asked about the Haight, said he hadn't read a newspaper in weeks. Even so, his interest seemed perfunctory. As they were walking, a popping explosion rang out from the woods. Terry stopped.

"What's that?" Seth asked.

"There're some squatters down on the edge of the woods."

"Was that a gunshot?"

"Afraid so."

"What're they shooting at?" Amy asked worriedly.

"Targets. Squirrels. They're hillbillies. They give off pretty hostile vibes. One of the sisters got chased by their dog last week."

"Why don't you evict them?" Seth said. "It's your land."

"Yeah, well, that's doing a pretty possessive number. Live and let live. Come on, have a look at the garden, then we'll go eat."

The meal was a fragrant stew of turnips and potatoes served with a jug of Gallo mountain burgundy, small, misshapen loaves of bread, and a wedge of cheese, all of which seemed to be imbued with a flavor of garlic, patchouli, and woodsmoke. Girl burbled happily, using chubby hands to eat, and the dogs lounged nearby. Overhead, the skylights framed a moving scape of bright clouds.

"This is how it should be," Amy remarked appreciatively, relishing the congenial mood that had settled over her.

"It all gets down to bread," Seth declared.

"And wine," Terry laughed.

Amy didn't point out that she meant the vibe, the warm, homespun comfort. "There's enough food for everyone," Seth went on. "It's a matter of distribution, getting it to the people. The man's got distribution locked up."

"The Diggers have been trying that number and getting shit on," Terry said.

"Community action has to be political action! The Diggers are existentialist buffoons. They've got no agenda."

"Well, first things first, man. Feed your own. Cheers."

Seth stared at Terry. It wasn't Seth's first attempt to fire up a discussion, but this got no further than earlier efforts and he gave up. The burgundy dwindled and conversation rose, going to recipes, planting seasons, music. Politics wasn't mentioned again. At one point Terry looked around paternally and declared that they were all members of Sergeant Pepper's Lonely Hearts Club, and despite the images of yesterday's clash, still fresh in her mind, Amy felt a measure of the hope and promise of the unfolding summer return.

The telephone receiver looked like a lump of coal where Frank Austin pressed it against his reddening ear and listened. Sparrow couldn't hear what was being said, but it was clear from Austin's expression that he wasn't enjoying it. At last he made conciliatory sounds into the mouthpiece and hung up. "Tell me about yesterday," he said coldly.

Sparrow gave an account of the events at Golden Gate Park as he had seen them. Austin listened with impatience. "For your information," he said when Sparrow finished, "Moon went to the top to complain about interference in his operation. I just got an earful from the chief."

Sparrow apologized. He'd hoped to keep a few kids from getting their heads split, but in truth he hadn't had much success at preventing anything. He pictured Seth Green with his head streaming blood and Amy Cole mopping it with her silk scarf; but it wasn't just blood he was thinking of now. There was the look in Seth's eyes as he leapt off the stage, and the look in Amy's as she had gone after him. He worried that the whole dynamic would change and the TAC squad would find its cause. Yesterday had been only a test. A few of Moon's troops might decide this wasn't for them and would request transfer. For some of the hippies, too, this would be the end. Having tasted terror, they'd be homeward bound, eager to be back in their safe beds, and in a week they'd be in summer school or getting haircuts and looking for jobs. Others would shake yesterday off as yet another kick, a cosmic upper or downer, and the trip would go on. Some would forgive and forget, seeing the violence as further proof that they were right in dropping out of the System, with its coarse brutalities and undeclared Asian war, and they'd be stoned and placid once more. But a few—and it would only need a few, Sparrow reflected soberly—had been given their badge of courage, and yesterday was the call to arms they'd been listening for. Moon would know it, too, and press his case for more men, more power. A collision course had been set. Now, as if the inhabitants of the district weren't spooked enough already, the TAC squad had unraveled whatever small gains at community relations Homicide had made. Sparrow felt further away than ever from finding the killer. He thought of saying as much to Frank Austin, but the man wasn't looking for dialogue.

"Moon is trouble," Austin complained. "You should know that better than anyone. Wasn't I clear when I brought you back? 'First day of the rest of our lives,' I said. No old baggage. The chief doesn't want his tit in the wringer again," Austin concluded. "Nor do I. You stick to what you're supposed to."

"Bummer what happened to those people who got killed," the sister named Clover said as she cleared plates following the afternoon meal. "How many is it now? Four?"

"Yes, it's terrible," Amy said.

"What's going on with that?" Sarah asked. "We're out of touch up here. They know who's doing it?"

Talk turned to the murders, though from their questions it seemed that the women were looking for excitement more than enlightenment.

"You mentioned a band before," Amy said, shifting subjects. "The New Riders of the Apocalypse."

"Have you seen them?" Clover asked excitedly. "Aren't they great? I got these incredible visuals! And a feeling like I was coming. Wild! A sister who lives here, Naomi, knows one of them. We're going down to visit soon."

Dessert was served, which in texture and color resembled the stew, though it was sweet and delicious. They ate amid volleying conversations and afterwards drank hibiscus tea while a joint the size of a Churchill cigar made the rounds. Clover began a discussion with Seth about Che Guevara in Bolivia. Terry Gordon showed no interest, and after a while, out of restlessness, Amy sensed, he said why didn't he show her the goats. They took the dogs.

Shadows had lengthened with the coming of evening, and the wind had a cooling edge. As the dogs headed for the woods, Terry plucked a stem of grass and stuck it in his mouth. "The sisters are pretty new to politics," he said. "Clover won't get that Stalinist charge Seth was making. She likes Che because she thinks he's cute."

Amy smiled. "He is, although I imagine you're teaching them other dimensions."

"Nope. That's not why I'm here."

Amy kept her surprise to herself. "Well, Seth likes a challenge."

As they walked, Terry showed her a few skinny goats and some chickens, the firewood he'd been cutting, pointed out ground that had been tilled and was awaiting seed; but his manner was halfhearted, like a tour guide with little zeal for what he was showing off. Amy spied a dusty automobile parked by an outbuilding.

"Terry, is that——? It is!" she cried. "The Blue Lunch lives!"

It was the Citroen he had had at Berkeley, which he would leave parked near the social science building, key in the ignition. When Amy once pointed out the risk involved in this, Terry was philosophical: "Someone needs it more than I do, it's theirs." Although no one staked a claim that deep, people did take to borrowing the car on occasion, generally returning it to the same spot, sometimes with a bonus of gas in the tank. Once, as campus legend had it, someone had gotten sick on peyote buttons and flashed their Technicolor visions all over the upholstery, and the car had been given its name. Seeing the Blue Lunch again now, Amy had to laugh and Terry joined her. But the merriment was short-lived and, like the sky, his mood was darkening again as they wandered toward the meadow.

"Is Seth still in touch with any of the SDS crew?" he asked.

"A few. They're in a mobilization group against the draft and the riot police."

"The struggle goes on," Terry said in a tone so neutral she wondered if the words were facetious. "You and Seth still making it?" he asked.

"We're together. The focus has changed a little," she said, surprising herself with the response. She hadn't ever voiced it, and now she felt Seth ought to have been the one to hear it. But then Terry had always inspired honesty. "Putting out the paper is pretty consuming," she added by way of brief elaboration.

"Yeah, well, like I said, I haven't been reading much."

They walked in momentary silence, feeling the wind. Amy shivered. "It gets chilly up here when the sun fades."

"You want to go back?"

She sensed there was something on Terry's mind that he hadn't gotten to, wouldn't get to if they returned now to the house and the others. "No," she said. "I'm okay."

Terry went back to the Blue Lunch and returned with a worn peacoat, which he handed to her to put on. It swam on her. Like the car, the coat had a history for her, and she had a sudden image of Terry showing up at her place one wet winter night wearing it and a Greek fisherman's hat with a small red star pinned to it, his mustache streaming rain. He'd been out walking and had seen her light, he said, and wondered if she wanted to rap; which surprised her because she didn't know Terry knew where she lived. She was only one of his students, after all, and he had hundreds. They opened a bottle of *leibfraumilch* and talked for hours, and then they made love, the one and only time. Neither had tried to make it happen again, and it had become a secret between them, still there now, she realized, although buried deeper by time.

They had started down the dirt road flanking a meadow on one side, sloping to forest on the other, in the direction the dogs had gone. Abruptly, Terry stopped walking and turned to her. "Leave the city," he said. "Come up here."

His animation surprised her. Was it a joke? A cryptic declaration of love? But no, he was in earnest. "There's room," he pressed.

"We can't produce a community newspaper in the woods."

"The hell with that. Why bother?"

"What?"

"What's the point?"

She was startled that he of all people would ask that. At Berkeley he had helped found the *Barb*, had been a pillar of the Free Speech Movement when it was a serious matter, before it devolved to sloganeering and a sophomoric preoccupation with talking dirty. "What's going on, Terry?"

He ignored her and resumed walking. She had to catch up. "Seth's been trying all day to draw you out, and you haven't risen to the bait. Why? I don't believe you came up here to be reborn as a farmer, like your family back there want to believe."

"No? What about you? You were never hot for the Movement."

"We're not talking about me. Politics was your blood. You used to live for a good fight. What's changed you?"

His eyes met, and then evaded, hers. "I've smartened up is all."

"On campus some people are saying you just quit."

"Quit. Doesn't have much ring." Terry's smile was mirthless. "I was hoping for a more dramatic epitaph. How about, 'Firebrand prof driven into exile!' "

"Is that what happened?"

"Or how about, 'Uncle Sam wants you, boy!' "

Amy quit walking. "How about the fucking truth, Terry?"

It stopped him, too. She almost never swore. The word had sprung from raw emotion. He turned. Alight with the fading sun, his glasses were copper disks. She couldn't read his eyes behind the lenses. Finally he nodded. "The truth. Yeah. But tell me first, do they say I'm hiding out in the hills? A Marin County Lenin awaiting the right moment to return and lead a popular revolt and smash the system?"

Amy held him with a stare. "I don't know what the party line is. Seth believes something like that."

Terry sighed, as if he, also, had grown tired of the performance. "Yeah, well, sorry for that. And that he had to take a riot stick on the head. It's not the same as your doubles partner's racquet out at the country club—but between me and thee, he is a tad naive."

She knew it well, but having it said openly and without Seth present made her want to come to his defense. Seth was her lover after all, not Terry Gordon. "He's disappointed, I know that much."

"Because he figures I sold out. Christ, Amy, are you reading Ayn Rand novels again?"

"Did you?"

He didn't answer, but she kept silent, too, waiting him out.

"Did I quit? Is that what you're asking?"

She hadn't gotten anything of what she'd hoped to get by driving up here today; still, she believed Terry had wisdom to impart. She chose her words tentatively. "I understand people change. As long as there's growth in it, and you're happy with things, it's fine. This is a beautiful place." She gestured with her hand. "But you seem real iffy about being here."

"What's Seth think?"

"He's confused."

"When I first knew him, the poster on his wall was Raquel Welch, just like every other horny freshman. Okay, so it's Che now—and I know he's sincere, I'm not saying that—but he'll change, he'll find his way. Getting clubbed is a dividing line. It thins the ranks. This year's radicals wind up fighting next year's, and yet we all start out with the same shiny ideals. My advice, tell him to bail."

"You tell him."

"I will."

"I want to watch." If naiveté was a failing in Seth, he certainly didn't lack fervor or courage. He was the toughest-minded person she knew.

Terry turned away. When he faced her again, she still couldn't quite see his eyes, but his expression was pained. "Would it be better to hear that his idol has feet of clay?"

"I don't believe that." She was aware of Terry's past; everyone was. He'd been teargassed and clubbed, bitten by police dogs. In Mississippi, he had spent time in a jail cell and been threatened by night riders for his commitment to his ideals.

"I mean maybe it is all bogus . . . politics, revolution, the 'Movement.' " He gave the word an uncharacteristic mocking twist. "The whole schmeer."

Quietly she said, "Do you think so?"

"Do I think so?"

"Repeating questions." Amy shook her head. "A bad sign. It means you know you're on shaky ground." He didn't reply. "Because I never got the feeling, Terry, that you were anything but sincere."

He frowned. "Let's drop it."

"No," she persisted, though part of her was willing to—even wanted to. She had come here because she needed something, some word; and perhaps, she thought, this was it. Was the Summer of Love an utter dream? A will-o'-the-wisp? She desperately wanted to believe otherwise, but she was prepared for the truth. "No, let's not."

He stalked swiftly away. She moved to keep up with him. "What's wrong, Terry?"

As though worn out from resisting, winded from his own pace (or simply convinced he couldn't outrun whatever was pursuing him), he heaved a sigh and slowed. The dogs loped back with drooping pink rubber tongues, then were off again. Terry said, "For a time there was this feeling . . . that ideas and ideals mattered. You remember that? Before Dallas? But it's changing. The White House has dug in its heels on Vietnam; nobody wants to talk to anyone who's different from themselves—black, white, young, old. The dialogue's become dogma. But there's a piece only a teacher sees."

Amy waited for him to elaborate, but he paced away again, as if he'd said more than he'd wanted to, or was being pushed to reflect on things he'd rather not. Amy went with him, his shadow, and after several strides he rounded on her. "If you won't stay, go home. Back to New England. Maybe you can still be safe."

"What do you mean? From what?"

The fading sun was no longer in his face; she could see his eyes finally, and in them was something she hadn't seen before, though she could not name what it was. "I can't tell you the students I've had come to my office to plead for a passing grade, saying if they flunk out they'll be drafted. I've had guys break down and bawl like babies."

"Seth never did that," Amy said, more sharply than she intended.

"No. No, he never asked for anything."

"Except for honesty."

"These be times which doth make liars and cowards of us all."

"Cut it, Terry. I never bought the cant. Forget the words. The *feeling* behind them, that's what was real. You said it yourself. Caring and concern and closeness. Hope. I felt them again at the table today."

"You were stoned."

"No," she said insistently. "We learned them from you. It's the part of you we carry still. Don't cast it away."

He looked toward the woods where earlier the sounds of gunfire had come, silent now, thickening with dusk as the sky faded faster. Wind stirred the treetops. Terry drew up his shoulders. Speaking softly, with a tone of revelation, he said, "I gather from what Seth said earlier that you're familiar with the TAC police . . . with Captain Moon?"

It startled her. No one had mentioned Moon, and if Terry didn't follow the news . . .

"He's made himself known on campus, too," Terry went on. "Not in person, but he's behind it. He's got a network of connections—at Berkeley, State, USF."

A chill clenched her.

"It's pretty simple, really. Bust a few kids for grass, lean on them a bit . . . They don't want to be expelled and lose their deferments, sometimes they become compliant."

Her reaction to the idea was physical: a pressure clutching her heart, like a small convulsive fist. "Students are informing?"

"It beats wearing stripes—or jungle green."

"That's repulsive."

"The way of the world."

"No, it isn't." She felt compelled to protest. "It stinks that the cops would trade on people's fears, but they don't all do that." She was thinking of John Sparrow; he wouldn't blackmail kids, would he? "And most students don't rat. You can't condemn the whole for the part."

"It only takes a few . . . and for a few more folks to do nothing about it. A few lily-livered frauds like me."

"You're wrong. That doesn't describe you. You'd fight it. You'd confront the—"

She broke off. Something was closing in, she felt it: a perception she wasn't sure she wanted to have.

"Go ahead," Terry said. "Ask your question."

"I want to go back."

"Ask it, dammit!"

"Terry. I'm cold."

"Or I will."

"All right. Why are you here?"

He kept a fierce posture for another moment, then his shoulders sagged, and all at once he looked like someone contemplating forsaken honor and haunted by the act. Above them the sky had grayed considerably, alive with fast-moving dark clouds that presaged night. Just visible through the pine boughs, a pale yellow moon had appeared. Finally Terry said, "I didn't make a mistake by coming up here. But you did. You came looking for a tourniquet. It's too late."

"No."

"The Hashbury trip, the Summer of Love . . . it's done."

"The Haight is still a good scene."

"*Finito.*"

"How do you know? If you never go there, how do you know?"

"*Time* magazine and ABC are there! Harry Reasonable. Sociologists are writing books about it, for God's sake. That dead enough for you? You brought vibes with you today. You roused the sisters, all that talk about murder and rock bands." He spat the words. "But that's not the point. The point is you should get out. You still believe in trust and sharing and peace and rebirth and—" He broke off, as if he had lost track of a litany. He said, "You're worried about the murders."

She didn't move, *couldn't* move, as if she were being held by Terry Gordon's gravity. "They have to stop," she managed. "They're going to rip everything apart. The good that's happening in the Haight may be our best hope."

"Amy, you really are a sweet New England girl at heart."

"Don't, Terry. Don't patronize me."

"Dreams die hard. People are still flooding in, but they're running *from* something, not *to* anything. The 'love' generation doesn't have any experience of love; it's a word to them, something from TV. You see real love going down? The systems are at the limit. The mob's taking over dealing. The bikers are a bunch of sociopaths, the Panthers want to burn everything. Anarchy's coming. Moon sees it, *wants* it. And there're a lot of kids who are going to get hurt when it all goes bad—which it will do, and soon."

"Unless what?"

He narrowed his eyes. "What makes you think there's an 'unless'?"

"You do. I'm hearing passion again."

"I quit. There is no 'but.'"

"There has to be," she said almost pleadingly, unwilling to surrender. "It isn't too late."

Terry started walking. She pushed after him with effort, as if she were being called upon to overcome forces beyond inertia and gravity, to contend with the very dark itself. The wind had risen, threshing the meadow like a large and unseen being were moving there. After a few strides, Terry whirled and gripped her arm. "Come on up here!" he said again, urgency in his voice. "Both of you, if you want. Get away from there."

"Seth won't leave." Which was true, but evasive; *she* wouldn't leave either.

"Come alone, then."

"And be another sister on the love farm?"

"Write poems," he hissed, "or a book. String beads, for God's sake, spin wool. Have a kid! Get out while you can. It's turning."

Angrily, she pulled free of his grasp and stepped back. And too late it came to her with a jolt of recognition that what she had seen in his eyes was despair. It was an emotion she just didn't associate with Terry Gordon, and that quickly her anger was gone, like a swarm of sparks up the flue of a chimney.

She realized how his experiences must have shaken him. For as much as his students had been like younger brothers and sisters, and he the older brother, they had betrayed him. His was a personal reaction, not some generalized perception. With a Judas kiss, a handful of students had traded his safety for their own. And though he could accept that, he wasn't prepared to face the idea that his own actions would put them at risk. If Terry had stayed and fought, Captain Moon would have made certain that students were expelled, subject then to the draft and the war, or jail; some, perhaps, consigned to death. Terry had offered up himself instead.

Amy put her arms around him and held him tight. After a moment he put his arms around her, too. Perhaps it was just the cold wind, a promise of coming night, and Terry without a jacket, but she felt him shiver.

It was ten P.M. by the time Sparrow left the Hall of Justice. As he was unlocking his car in the semi-dark parking garage, he heard footsteps on the concrete, then a voice. "Hey, shitbird." Familiar. He turned and something bashed his face.

Fireworks burst in his head. Half blind, he stumbled back against the car, bracing to stay up, but a blunt force speared his gut. He gasped. As he buckled, a third blow crashed onto the back of his neck. With his vision streaming tracers, he collapsed.

Hunched in a curl, he fought to stay conscious. He lay on the concrete, his stomach sucked tight, blinking to clear a red mist behind his eyes. He could lash out with his feet, try to kick whoever must still be standing there. Or reach for his gun, belt-holstered under his jacket.

"Roll on your back and fucking *freeze!*"

It wasn't the same voice as before; there were at least two of them. Aware that he was vulnerable no matter what he did, he obeyed. Pain settled deeper into his gut. A flashlight lit, pinning him there, wiping out everything but its own harsh eye. His heart thudded madly.

"I don't like what you did," a voice said, the same voice as the first time (*"Hey, shitbird."*) and now he knew the speaker. A boot prodded his ribs. "You hear what I said?"

Sparrow coughed. He put away the thought of drawing his gun. They were cops. One of them, in fact, was George Moon.

"Well, hear this," said Moon. "Don't get in my way again."

The light dredged his eyes a moment longer, then it clicked off. In his blindness, he heard the diminishing beat of the men's boots as they walked away.

After he'd wobbled to his feet, blinking back the afterimages the attack had left in his mind, he considered going up and reporting it. Frank Austin, with his devotion to regulations, would deal with it. But Sparrow remembered Austin's warning not to make trouble. More than that, however, he knew the action would be futile. There'd been two of them to his one; and he'd never actually seen a face. No, whatever he did, it could not be through official channels. For the moment, though, he was too shaken to think of an alternate means. Moon held the cards. Sparrow drove to his apartment, where he took four Anacin tablets with a glass of bourbon and stood a long while in a hot shower.

Afterwards, he was calm enough to see that the attack was instructive. On the heels of his discussion with Austin, it had come to him that a second front had opened in his war with the killer stalking the Haight-Ashbury. The irony was that in giving Sparrow the blank personnel folder that day, Austin had seemed to declare that the past was of no consequence, and while that may have been the case as far as Austin was concerned, Sparrow could no longer pretend it was true. On the contrary, it was now clear to him that his current problem with George Moon had to do with that past, and perhaps with the unsolved killings that had terrified North Beach two years ago. The question was, how?

He didn't have long to mull this before the telephone rang. "John?" It was Pete Sandoval, and as though it were an evening for brief communiques, the young homicide cop trumped even George Moon. "*Cinco,*" he said.

14

"WHY THE CHANGE OF HEART?" AMY DEMANDED. "BECAUSE THE COUNT IS UP TO FIVE?" Her anger felt serrated. "Why not wait till it hits ten? Or a dozen?"

On the other end of the line, John Sparrow's silence was eloquent. "I'm sorry I didn't get back to you sooner," he said. "I do think an article might help reassure some folks over there."

"About what? You haven't found the killer."

"That we're not looking to bust them, anyway."

"Can you speak for the TAC Squad? Or the narcs?"

"No."

"How about Captain Moon's campus crusade? Is he hoping to get an ROTC building named after him?"

"What?"

His bewilderment seemed genuine. Anyway, she found no joy in her sarcasm. And he had taken the initiative to phone, when she'd hardly expected it; she could at least listen. "All right," she said more equably. "What's your plan?"

Ten minutes later she rolled what she had written out of the typewriter and handed it to Seth, who read it. "I don't like it."

"What's not to like? It's an appeal for information, with a hot line number. He promised all calls would be anonymous."

"The whole idea, I mean. I don't see the *Rag* as a pulpit for the pigs."

For a moment she didn't respond, convinced he was joking. But his expression was humorless, "*I* wrote it," she objected.

"And I'm the editor. I just don't see it, Amy. Sorry." He handed it back and returned to his office.

She sat motionless. The tall windows of the old converted theater were open and a breeze moved through, inflating the curtains, bringing sounds from the afternoon street: hawkers' cries, fragments of talk, car horns, a siren, noises more jarring now than harmonious. The news of the fifth death had shaken her badly. A 23-year-old woman had discovered a pair of jeans missing from her laundry and had told her roommates she was going back to the laundromat. She'd never made it. The laundromat was on Amy's block. Maybe Terry had professed the truth, after all; perhaps the dream was doomed. Even Seth, with his growing partisan rigidity, was probably right. How could any partnership with the cops be possible? She crumpled the typewritten appeal and picked up the phone. When Sparrow answered she identified herself and said, "Inspector, I'm sorry. We've changed our minds."

Seth was in his glass-walled cubicle, sitting at his desk, using an orange grease pencil to mark photographs for cropping when she went in. "Did you call him, or vice versa?" he asked without looking up. "Just so I can keep it straight."

"I've been trying to get a story for over a week, you know that. This was the first cooperation the police have shown."

"I don't want cooperation. Not theirs."

"This is the guy who saved me from getting stomped, in case you've forgotten. And just so you can keep it *all* straight, he doesn't have anything to do with the TACs."

"He's a cop."

"It's that simple, huh?"

Seth tossed down the pencil. "Trying to grok pig logic is a waste of time! A cop's got one function—stomp anything that threatens the system."

"That's a bit doctrinaire."

"The fuzz are the system's attack dog."

"Not its 'running' dog? Dammit," she flared, irked at his pulling rank like this rather than hold open discussion, "if you're going to toe the old party line, why not just print the *Rag* on red paper and be done with it? At least it'd grab attention—even if there wasn't anything inside to hold it!"

She braced for an angry response, but Seth surprised her. "Will these do?" he said calmly, offering her the photographs he'd been marking. Frowning, she took the stack of prints. There were about a dozen of them, eight-by-ten black and whites. The shots obviously had been taken on the solstice, with a telephoto lens. The one on top showed a TAC van partly concealed behind trees on the crest of the meadow, where she had seen it that day. The next few photos were of cops making their way down the slope, donning their black helmets. The next grouping of shots, taken at closer range, were slightly blurred, as if the photographer had been running. They showed cops with clubs and shields advancing toward a cluster of people near the stage. Her heartbeat quickening, she sank into a chair.

"Lest you forget," Seth said.

"Where'd you get them?"

"A woman was supposed to shoot the bands for Bill Graham. She got those instead." He didn't volunteer how they had come to him and not to the rock promoter or to another newspaper, and Amy didn't ask. It was like the equipment that outfitted this office, like the internal police memo the *Rag* had run in the last issue; Seth had sources, and he liked his secrets. "Check the rest," he urged.

She went through the remaining prints. They were grainy and out of focus, having been shot at rushed angles and into the dust raised by the scuffle; but the best of the lot, which Seth had already marked for cropping, had captured the melee and conveyed the paroxysms of anger, confusion, fear, and ultimately chaos that had wracked the day. It was the last shot, however, that hit her hardest, and she realized Seth had intended it that way.

"Dear God," she whispered.

"You okay?"

She nodded mutely, but she couldn't take her eyes from the photograph. In sharp focus, it showed a TAC cop, his arm reaching out of frame but clearly holding his club. Mirrored in the Plexiglas visor of his helmet, her own arm upraised defensively, was Amy herself. Staring, she had a reawakening of the panic she'd felt when the cop had turned on her, a panic that was etched on her face in the photograph. But her reaction now was more than just personal. She felt a visceral churning of her story sense. The prints showed clearly that the aggressors had not been the kids, as the official sources had more or less maintained. "These are explosive."

"Yeah. We're going to run them."

She agreed. They represented a journalistic coup. This issue of the *Rag* could well attract national attention. But the paper wasn't going to curry any favor with the police, or with the city, and maybe they couldn't afford to alienate them just now. Perhaps it *was* time for an alliance, she said.

Seth leaned back in his chair. "Lock arms with the mayor and the chief of police. Shit, why didn't I think of that?"

She ignored his tone. "Give space to other issues, too. Show a bridge across our differences, a way for the community and the city to come together."

"Kind of a hip edition of Up With People."

"Quit it. Don't demean the deaths of those people."

"No. But I'm also not going to let that sidetrack us from the main issue here."

She fought her rising irritation. "The main issue?"

"Revolution."

"*What?* That isn't why we started the *Rag*. We wanted a voice. For solidarity, yes. Resistance, okay. But it wasn't about revolution. We never said that."

He backed off. "Look, our job is to keep people focused. We can't do that if we spread ourselves too thin. Let the city dailies cover the killings. They can do it better anyway."

"But maybe not. It's our community, Seth. We have a responsibility."

"We're meeting it. These photos prove it." He began gathering them up; it was clear he considered the matter closed.

Amy stared at him. Since the trash-in, his sense of balance had tipped sharply. His passion for the fight, that spirit which had drawn her in the first place, had hardened into something else, and it occurred to her now what it was. He was on a vendetta. He wasn't in pursuit of the truth anymore, or even news—though maybe he never had been. *She* was the journalist; Seth's field was poly sci. And yet he was in charge. For all his talk of community and sharing, the *Rag* was his paper. He had put up the money for it, paid the overhead, shelled out for secret memos and graphic photos, claimed editorial rights. It was a cooperative venture, but Seth was first among equals, and they both knew it.

"Congratulations," she said, rising. "The issue will sell like mad."

"What say you, Toad?" Joe Williams asked. "With us?"

Toad Madden considered the little entourage of his band mates Williams and Vince Russo and the groupie chick named Crystal Blue. "I don't know," he said.

Chewing coyly on a pigtail, Crystal Blue gave him her mock lascivious look. "First time's free, Toad."

First time for what? Russo was the one who'd end up rocking her boots tonight. Russo treated her like dirt, but she didn't seem to care—none of them did. Never mind that Vince was a crotch jockey, looking for just one thing. He was "cute." "Nah, I don't think so," Toad said. "Too cold."

"It's summer," Williams said.

"Too damp. Anyway, I want to mellow out."

They split, leaving Toad alone in the Crypt.

He had never fully adjusted to the climate up here, having spent his whole life in L.A.—the first nineteen years of it anyway—which was where he'd started playing music. Guitar had been his first ax—a pawn shop *f*-hole Les Paul—and his first band had been a surf group, Beach Boys rip-offs, with the Pendleton shirts, bleached hair, and high harmonies, all of it except one thing. They couldn't play for shit. Nobody seemed to notice, though, and they got gigs pretty much every weekend: sock hops, beach parties, stock car races in the valley. Then the scene changed. Bang, fast as you could tap the toes of your Beatle boots, songs about cruising burger stands and summer girls weren't where it was at. They tried the mop-top thing awhile, but so did every other band. When the group split, Toad came north, moving into a pad in the Mission with some guys he'd met. There was a new scene happening here, dance halls, light shows, crazy costumes—a little cranked up, yeah, but exciting. Acid was legal when he arrived, and he got into it. He met Owsley at one of the Acid Tests and decided, hey, if he could do it . . . So he'd set up a little lab and started cooking his own. But there was no money in it since people were doling out hits like Girl Scout cookies, and he realized that if he was going to work, it would be as a musician. Except he'd already sold his Les Paul for rent money, and anyway there was a shitload of guitar players around who were tons better than he was.

Then, peaking one afternoon on windowpane, he saw God (or *was* God . . . that part wasn't clear). What *was* clear was The Answer.

In junior high he'd played baseball. Because he was short and stocky, he'd become a catcher. It wasn't a sexy position, not like shortstop or pitcher. In fact, nobody wanted the job, squatting back there, getting your fingers split and your nuts thumped, putting on the gear, taking it off . . . no, you became a catcher because *someone* had to. But you got to play that way.

Like being a drummer.

No glamour there, set back behind the front guys, working twice as hard, out of the spotlight, poison with the chicks, unless you were Dennis Wilson or someone. But where was a band without a drummer? He had his folks send him some bread, enough to buy a used five-piece Ludwig kit, and he began his earnest pounding. He had a good sense of time from his guitar days, and he found he liked the work. In the little basement pad in the Mission he'd eat some mushrooms, sit down, start banging away, and hours would float by.

Just as his physique had been a plus in baseball, so it served him well on drums, too. He had arm strength and leverage, and he didn't mind crouching behind the action, releasing his compressed energy, like a clock spring coming slowly uncoiled. Nine innings or four sets, what did it matter? You got to play; and in an odd way, you controlled everything.

Or would if you found a band.

Then, last winter he heard talk of this group that might need a drummer. So he came over to the Haight, here to this house, where he was greeted by Joe

Williams, who led him into the kitchen where the others were. Williams said he played rhythm guitar and told Toad, "Welcome, man. What bands you been in?"

Toad had expected to kick tires, rap a little, maybe audition, though he hadn't brought his traps. What he had done, just to be mellow, was drop five hundred mikes of Sunshine. When he found out he was going to be interviewed by the whole band—and he had no paid experience as a drummer!—he almost split right there.

But then he laid eyes on the lady in black.

She was older than the others by six or eight years, the leader, though she hadn't spoken yet. Williams, the lone spade in the band, did the introducing that day. She was Circe, the singer. The silent blond dude was Eric, played lead guitar. The bassist, Vince Russo, sat there with a young chick on his lap (a dozen or so young chicks before Crystal Blue, this would've been) his hand fondling her under her T-shirt the whole time, a pastime that Toad would soon discover was more or less constant when Russo wasn't sleeping or performing.

"What hand you lead with, man?" Russo wanted to know, and Toad wondered if he was being set up, like the guy was going to tell him to go ahead, cop a feel.

"Left," Toad admitted.

The others looked at each other, and the blond guy—who hadn't said boo the whole time, just fingered his unplugged starburst Strat—nodded and said, "Cool."

Then they all came into this room, the Crypt, where there was a kit set up, a battered unit with a pair of toms, a snare, a bass, some hats. "Do your thing," said Williams.

Experiencing a little rush of nervousness, Toad sat. Reasonably, he figured they were going to lay some sound behind him—the blond guy hadn't plugged the Strat in, but he hadn't put it down either—but no, they wanted just Toad to play, and that was the second time he nearly split. For one thing, the drums were set up for a rightie. But he saw the dark-haired lady watching him, giving him a look that made his cock stir. So he settled in, checking the height and reach, adjusted the high hats.

He tapped around a few times to get a feel, come up with a riff, then he launched into something simple, starting slowly, the half hit of Sunshine just right, giving him a floaty dream feel, the notes soft-falling like snow, not too loud in the big drape-hung room, and as he warmed, time started to stretch and his hands moved faster, smoother, running around from toms to snare to cymbals, his foot hammering the bass pedal, building volume, speed, into it now, sweat beginning to roll from his face, and he was alone inside this little place, letting it all come through him until the sticks were a blur, like bobbins whirling a seamless yarn of sound that ran and ran, and finally when it got so long he thought it might snap, he went with a big splashy finish—*Bam ba-bam BAM!*—and cut it himself.

The brass shivered into stillness. Then . . .

Nada.

Silence. Could've heard cigarette ash drop.

The people sat there.

What? He'd played his ass off and that was it? Empty expressions, like zombies in a Jules Feiffer cartoon? Well, fuck you very much. He set the sticks down, mopped his brow, and stood up, definitely ready to split . . . when all of a sudden the others broke into cheers.

He'd blown their minds! The little chick climbed off Russo's lap and came over and tongued him. Joe Williams slapped him five. Even the blond guy grinned. But it was the lady in black whose reaction he was waiting for, sitting there in her carved ebony chair, where she hadn't so much as moved. The others observed this, too. Finally, when they settled down, she tipped her head to one side and asked, "What sign are you?"

And Toad had been stumped because he wasn't sure, saying finally that his birthday was late January, and the lady said, "Aquarius." She wanted him to toss a coin, and he thought, They're looking for a drummer and it's a coin toss? Who was the competition? Ringo Starr? Then she stepped over—*floated* was more like it; she was in this flowing black gown—to a table along one wall (a table no longer here in the Crypt), dark wood inlaid with ivory and copper moons and stars. She handed him three Chinese coins. So, what the hell: he tossed them.

After he'd done so several times, Circe noting the way they fell, she consulted a book, which she studied in silence a long moment, and he thought this was weird, even on Sunshine, till she looked at him and smiled this beautiful smile. "Hexagram ten," she said. And read: "The image is of the sky above, the lake below. 'When vapor rises from the lake it goes to the sky, and falls again as rain.' The oracle says, 'One who is humble seeking advancement among the powerful is permitted to rise when the principle of placement of the elements is observed.' The auguries are right," she declared, actually used that word—"auguries"— which he didn't even know the meaning of till later. And Joe Williams said, "We've been waiting for you, man."

And that was that. Auguries. Oracles. Hot diggity damn! He had a full stinger by that time, so turned on was he by the lady. They invited him to join, and three days later he moved in here with the band. When he asked what would they think of him having a little lab, you know, to cook some dope, Circe said, "No scag, no needles." And Toad said scag was not to his taste and he hated needles; no, just some nice clean lysergic acid diethylamide-25 is what he had in mind. It had to be cool, Circe said: for friends only, no partying with strangers, no dealing, no setting them all up for the Man; and Toad agreed. He was a drummer not a dealer.

So he had become one of the New Riders of the Apocalypse.

He later learned that the original drummer had died in that very room, sped himself to death shooting meth, and his replacement, after only a month, had ripped off a bunch of antiques from the house and hadn't been seen since. Toad learned, too, that as the New Riders, Circe had given the individual band members stage names. Not that anyone referred to themselves or each other by the names; they were intended more, he figured, as publicity fodder for when the band's time came. A gimmick. Joe was War, Vince was Famine, silent Eric was Pestilence, and Circe told Toad that he would be Death. Well, cool, he was a southpaw Catholic Aquari-ass day-tripper, yeah. That was far out with him, he said, and meant it.

Days, they practiced. Nights when the band wasn't performing (which at first was most nights, though that was changing), he'd hang with Joe Williams and go catch Hendrix or Moby Grape, the Charlatans, Big Brother, Country Joe and the Fish, the Great Society, Heavenly Blues, Loading Zone, the Young Rascals . . . so many groups, so much music going down it was a nonstop soundtrack. Admittedly, he sometimes got to wondering how come the Riders weren't happening the way some bands were, because, swear to God, a lot of the acts around were pretty piss poor at best. To his mind, there were L.A. bands, like the Doors, Buffalo Springfield, the Byrds, who could write and play rings around the groups up here; but maybe everyone was just too stoned to notice. Anyway, Circe kept telling them their time would come. The Riders needed to gel, to get the jams worked out in the layers she wanted, then they'd go far. The past few months they'd begun to perform often; and now Toad knew that Circe was right. He'd always *believed* her—she could make him believe most anything—but when she said they were on their way, he *knew* she was speaking the truth, that they were hooking into something potent. He felt it.

He felt something else, as well.

From the first moment he laid eyes on her, he'd had the hots for Circe. In his early weeks with the band, the feeling had become an obsession, though he got hipped by Eric—one of the few conversations of more than five words he'd ever had with the guy—who said that Circe was no one's old lady, said it kind of bitterly, in fact, leading Toad to wonder if the guitarist had made a play himself. It didn't lessen Toad's desire, any more than their age difference did, but it forced him to adopt a new perspective, made him realize he'd have to be cool because he didn't want to be out of the band and thereby away from her.

Since then Toad had seen a lot of men try her, at clubs and bars when she sang, moving with her witchy, quicksilver grace on the stage. Offstage he'd see guys try, too, including some of the local heavies who ran shops over on Haight, tomcatting around when Toad would accompany her to buy candles and herbs and bolts of madras cloth. At first their attention made him jealous; but in his ten months with the band, though Circe treated everyone with kindness—and Toad himself with a special affection—he had never known her to go with anyone. Why? He didn't think she was a lesbian. Had she been burned in a bad romance in her past? Did she hate men? Have a secret lover?

The questions returned, and all at once, with quick dazzle of curiosity, he wondered: *Can I find answers?*

The big house was hushed as he climbed the stairs. Circe's room was on the top, at the end of the hall. She wasn't in—nobody was—but nevertheless he knocked.

He waited, his heart thumping, his mind turning in directions he had not foreseen only moments ago. The house remained silent. Swallowing dryly, he palmed the antique brass knob and opened the door.

The first thing he was aware of was a flickering web of shadows on the ceiling and walls. Across the cluttered space, a stubby black candle burned inside thick glass. Did that mean she was going to be back soon? He drew a slow breath, aware as he did of the aromas he associated with Circe: an exotic, musky spice of incense and oils, and in an instant he was turned on. His pulse quickening, he went in.

The space was furnished with antiques: an ornate dresser, an armoire, a canopy bed. What drew him now, however, was a draped figure in a corner, head-shaped under a paisley shawl. *Leave*, said a silent voice, *this ain't your space*. And for a moment he listened to the voice, pledged to go back downstairs and forget he'd even thought of violating Circe's privacy . . . but he was *this* close to her. This close to *her*.

He tiptoed over to the draped figure. Carefully, he lifted the shawl, folding up the hem . . . and stumbled back, startled by the face that regarded him. He huffed a breath of relief. It was a big stuffed bird, an owl, gazing at him with glazed marble eyes. It perched on a stump of birch log that sat on a low table. Also on the table were a small animal's skull and a knife. He picked up the knife, some kind of heavy dagger. It had an ornate silver handle and a long tapered blade with double edges, which winked in the light from the black candle. *Enough,* the silent voice said, more insistent this time. *Anyone catches you, you're up the creek, out of the band . . .* But caution was hopeless in the face of curiosity, his tweaked now by the big brass bed that occupied the room. He set the knife down.

He went to the bed and touched the quilt, ran his fingers over the satin pillow slips, which had an almost electric effect, causing him to draw a shivery breath. And now he found himself fully, almost painfully aroused. He unbuttoned his jeans and let his cock spring out.

He sat down, feeling the mattress settle. Carefully, almost afraid he would convulse any moment into climax, he lay back into an ethereal softness of feather pillows and down quilt. The overhead canopy rippled with his movement. His body swimming with sensations, he shut his eyes and took hold of himself. He felt the throb of his heart.

In his mind, he was naked, spread-eagled; he began to form an image of Circe equally naked and here with him, bending over him . . . but what flickered into his brain wasn't Circe. No, he was seeing what he'd begun to see at some of the Riders gigs, off there in dim corners where snaky shadows coiled, couples dancing and . . . balling. It was like the band's long jams were switching people on, charging them with a force, *changing* them somehow, and it both excited and frightened him.

Then, one night, performing on a dose of home-cooked, he thought he saw someone get killed, stabbed to death right there in the crowd at the edge of the stage. Just a glimpse, a weird little peek under gelled light, but it was enough to convince him it had happened, that he'd seen it. His whole body began to shake. His timing went so to hell that Joe Williams came back and shouted for him to get it together. And he had, drawing not on professionalism nor will, but only the crazed idea that if he didn't, he would be killed, too. But when the set ended and the crowd had gone, summoning all his nerve he went down in front of the stage, actually got down on hands and knees. The floor was sticky with spilled soda and squashed cigarette butts and who knew what else, but there was no body, no blood. And the next day, there was the imagined "victim" walking around like normal. Obviously, Toad told himself, he'd hallucinated the whole thing. He'd sworn off dope for three days.

He sat up. His hand was still wrapped around his now limp cock. Jeez, where had he been? The candle flame still twitched and shadows leaped. How long had he been here? Only minutes? Hours? No, that couldn't be—the candle wasn't far gone. He hopped up, zipped his jeans.

He was on his way out when he saw something he hadn't noticed before. To the right of the door was an archway hung with beads. Parting the strands, he peered in. On a table he saw yesterday's edition of the *Chronicle*.

FIFTH SLAY VICTIM FOUND
Killing Linked to Others
Clues Continue to Elude Police

Just then he heard a door close downstairs. Someone else was in the house. He was at the door when he thought of something, and hurried back to draw the shawl over the dead owl, cutting off its stare.

Joe, Vince, and Crystal Blue were in the Crypt, settling into big pillows, as Toad entered.

"Hiya, Toad, how are ya?" Crystal Blue greeted.

"No action?" he said, hoping it sounded casual.

"We scored some Thai stick. Join us," she said. "First time's free."

He tried to read Russo's expression, gauge his welcome, but the bassist showed nothing. Toad shrugged. What the hell. A short while later, the four of them were ripped to the tits, the other three to the point of silly laughter, which Toad tried very hard to enter into. But he couldn't shake the very strange feeling that had settled on him.

As a sop for having pulled rank on her, Amy guessed, Seth had asked her to write cut lines for the photos of the trash-in in the park, which she had done, and he'd approved them before he left to post some Mob Grope flyers. She finished some other work, had a bowl of soup next door, and now, with daylight fading beyond the windows, she sat alone and gazed up at the floral exhortation to turn on, tune in, and drop out. She had read Timothy Leary's little book and knew that his actual sequence was drop out, turn on, tune in, which didn't scan nearly so well as the poster version.

Dropping out, according to the good doctor, was a starting point, not an end. She saw herself as having done that, left a system that was worn out. She'd felt it while serving a newspaper internship, seeing that one day's news was only a variation on the previous day's, the focus forever on the bad, shaping the tribal consciousness as relentlessly as a tooling machine bent steel, and causing people to give up hope.

Turning on meant shaping your own mind, based on your personal experience with the world. Music, meditation, drugs, and sex, too, were opening new conduits to consciousness. Maybe these could lead people to a resurgence of joy and hope and spirit, but words were still the way she knew best. Even when an editor was being a prick.

"Up yours!" she shouted and jabbed a middle finger in the direction of Seth's empty office. She laughed and immediately she felt better.

She switched on the Selectric and typed: "Open Letter." It was a feature she wrote each issue. Among the addressees so far had been Johnson, McNamara, the stockholders in McDonnell-Douglas and Dow Chemical, Ho Chi Minh, and the Tribes. Now she typed: "Dear Police Chief Cahill."

She stopped. She experienced a light sensation in her chest. Outside, a pale fog was coiling through the streets, bringing cold. She went over and closed a window. The pane was old and rippled like the glass in the big windows of her elementary school, but it gave back her reflection, like someone orphaned out there in the coming night. She saw a dwindled throng of people moving past. No one was sauntering as they might in daylight. They were hurrying, intent on Saturday night destinations, and it came to her that, with the approach of darkness, they were afraid.

The threat of narcs and the TAC Squad were obvious sources of concern, but the real, gut-gnawing fear was of a monster, and now Amy found that she was afraid, as well. She locked the window, hugging herself to ward off a sudden chill. She sent a final glance outside and went back to the Selectric.

She sat for a moment, then clacked a brisk "xxxxx" through Chief Cahill's name, taking a small satisfaction in it.

On a new line she typed: "To the Death Tripper . . ."

THE BELLS ON JESTER'S CAP KEPT A KIND OF CONTRAPUNTAL RHYTHM WITH DISTANT church bells as he strolled along the Panhandle, all but deserted this Sunday morning. It was early, and not for the first time he yawned loudly, his stomach responding with sounds of its own. Ahead, a slat-sided truck was parked on the grass and three lean, shirtless men were unloading loaves of bread in cardboard cartons, Diggers setting up for their food giveaway. The aroma of the bread made Jester aware that he hadn't even had coffee yet. But he headed for the park; he needed to get this done first.

The stack of flyers had been next to his mattress when he woke, along with a spool of tape, no note or instructions. Seth probably had said something to him when he left, but Jester had been dead to the world. The flyers were on heavy stock paper and bore a clenched red fist and the words: RIOT CONTROL: HELL NO! He would post some around the park, hand out a few to passersby, and then truck over to Blind Jerry's for breakfast.

"Hey, Jester," a voice hailed as he crossed Stanyan.

He turned and saw a street guy he knew, Andy something, who lived in a packing crate over in the Fillmore. Andy looked forlorn. "I'm feeling dragged, man."

"Yeah?" Jester said guardedly.

"My big chance, and I blew it. I'm bumming."

The guy was always looking for spare change, or dope to mooch. "What chance was that?"

"The tube." Andy shaped a twelve-inch square with his hands.

"TV?"

"Talk about a downer."

"What do you need a TV for?" He thought about using Seth's riff on the media of mind control, but he didn't really understand it. The main reason the guy didn't need a TV was he lived in a crate.

"No, man. Over on the street earlier . . . there was a crew there, Japanese or something. Lights, cameras, you dig? The guy with the microphone was the only one could speak English—'terribision,' he called it, would I be on terribision? Me! Sure, I said. The others stood around smiling and bowing. The guy asked me was I a hippie, and what did that mean."

"What'd you say?" Jester asked, interested.

Andy gripped his head dramatically. "Man, I dropped five hundred mikes of purple for breakfast."

"You *told* them that?"

"No, no, I like freaked. They had the camera rolling, and I must've given them fifteen minutes of boring-ass motor mouth. I couldn't stop myself. I couldn't find the right *words.*"

He seemed genuinely distraught; and Jester was convinced now he wasn't going to be stemmed, at least. "Relax," he said magnanimously; even clapped the guy's shoulder.

"But I wasn't like . . . succinct, you know?"

"Doesn't matter."

"But it was my *chance*, man. I could've *enlightened* them."

"*No problema*. They'll edit it down to the best five seconds."

Andy brightened. "You think so?"

"Absolutely. Five seconds. Viewers back in Japan will say, 'That guy is brilliant! A Zen master! I could listen to him for fifteen minutes.' "

"Yeah?"

"Sure."

"Wow."

"That's terribision."

"What a groove." Andy was beaming now. "Thanks, man." He started off, then turned. "Hey, Jester . . . got any smoke on you?"

In the park, a brother carrying a conga drum looped across his back approached, flashed Jester a peace sign, and went past, ignoring an offered flyer. Jester taped it onto a tree. He taped others onto benches and lampposts. A tall woman, the frayed hem of her bathrobe damp with morning dew, was holding a hank of rope while her dog watered the weeds. Jester gave her a flyer and she gave him a sleepy smile. Pass it on.

He headed down into the meadow, his cap flopping as he descended the slope. Later, there would be people out, having fun, though for the moment, except for a guy sacked out alongside a greasy rucksack that looked stuffed with every possession he owned, Jester had the meadow pretty much to himself. Winded from the walk, his stomach making hungry sounds, he paused to attach a flyer to a tree.

The words printed under the clenched fist were part code, telling members of the Summer Offensive Committee where and when the next meeting would be held. New people interested in joining had to ask around to learn the particulars. Seth didn't like to advertise openly because he wanted to avoid cop hassle. Jester taped a few more flyers to handy surfaces, and then fanned the twenty or so he still held. He sighed. Mobilizing people for stuff wasn't his thing.

He had started off at S. F. State with a clear notion of getting a draft deferment and some dim one of becoming a draughts*man*. But what he had really found in college was that while he was a fair card player, he was a lousy student. Then he got called up for his pre-induction physical and failed it for being overweight and having flat feet. He waited a few days to be sure it wasn't a mistake, that there wasn't a follow-up notice ordering him on Metrecal and Dr. Scholl's insoles and declaring him fit to serve; but when no notice came, he quit attending classes and took to sleeping late and food freaking. One day, looking to score a lid, he'd climbed aboard the No. 22 bus heading over to the Haight.

The bus was full and he sat next to a blond chick who was reading a book. At some point he grew aware that his bare arm and hers were lightly touching. He didn't know if she was aware of this or not. She seemed pretty into the book, something called *Trout Fishing in America*; in any case, she didn't move her arm, and he didn't move his. That feather-soft brush of her skin was a turn-on, and as the bus jostled along the stop-and-go blocks to the Haight, he settled into it.

The bright streets floated by, but with each passing block he began to worry: would she discover his secret and yank her arm away? He thought about speaking to her, asking how she liked the book or something, but he didn't have the sacks. Anyway, if he did speak, she'd definitely move her arm away, and if she asked if *he'd* read the book, he couldn't even fake it and say "yeah" because he didn't know diddly about fishing, and he'd be back to where he always seemed to be with women—nowhere. And this woman was beautiful, with her long hair swaying with the motion of the bus and tiny freckles on her nose (and he bet she'd look just as good *naked*), so he kept still, just sat there digging the electric prickle of their bare arms lightly touching, and when they got to his stop—hers, too, it turned out—he said, "Thanks for the ride!" Just blurted it out, nothing he'd have said normally to a pretty girl. And she surprised him. She laughed: with her mouth and blue eyes and whole face, with real pleasure. Didn't call him disgusting or slap him or look at him funny. This pretty girl laughed.

That was how he came to meet Amy Cole, and through her Seth and his SDS friends from Telegraph Avenue. He never did get to see Amy naked, but that was okay because he loved her in a pure way (cold showers helped, too) and he did discover that he could make people laugh without even trying. He wasn't going to be Mort Sahl or Newhart, there was no *message* to his humor, it was more just a being himself kind of thing. Doing voices—"Mah fellow Amurricans,"—telling stories— like the time he met Amy on the 22 bus, his "Catch-22" story, he called it—and okay, maybe it helped that people were zonked. Then it became, "Hey, man, do that guy hiding his stash!" or "Tell the one about your draft physical," or "Your father's backyard fallout shelter!"

Amy had dubbed him Jester, and bought him the scarlet cap and bells at the Freeque Bouteak on a whim. The politics was Seth's trip, and though Jester had sat through countless raps about social class, the exploitation of the masses, and the coming revolution, he never quite grasped what any of it had to do with them, especially since Seth's old man was a rich shrink in Beverly Hills with a tennis court in his yard instead of a bomb shelter. But so what? It was worth having friends for a change, so Jester didn't mind pitching in, distributing leaflets and such. And Seth and his "comrades"—as they liked to refer to themselves—could use a little humor. Not Amy; she knew how to laugh, but the rest could be a straight-faced bunch when they got going about the People, and the Movement—another word they liked, one that always made him think of someone taking a dump.

As he taped a flyer onto a wire mesh trash basket, he considered the thin pile still in his hand. Half a dozen. He canned them. Time to mobilize some breakfast. He was starting back up the long grassy slope when he heard the voice. He turned. It was the Man: a short, thickset unit with aviator shades and a crisp city uniform.

"Yeah, you. Hold it right there."

Okay, ossifer; whatever you say. He waited for the cop.

"What do you think you're doing?" the cop asked.

"Oh, just truckin' along. On my way to do up some coffee."

"Just like that, huh?"

"Well . . . yeah."

The cop pointed at the trash basket where the flyer, with its clenched red fist, was taped. "Defacing city property is what it looks like to me."

A hassler. It was too early. "Hey, how 'bout I buy you coffee," Jester offered congenially. "They've got this espresso at Blind Jerry's that'll put a twitch in your stick and a shine on your badge."

"I asked you about that flyer."

Jester sighed. The fuzz could be so dumb. "It's this right we've got? Called free speech?"

"Meaning you're free to stir up trouble, is that it? Or are you one of the ones who like to talk dirty? What're you, a Marxist?"

Jester grinned; he couldn't help himself. "He's the best. I love the one about shooting an elephant in my pajamas."

The cop turned and called, "Hey, we've got a comic," seemingly to no one.

Jester squinted, and that's when he saw the second guy. He was stepping out from behind some foliage. He was larger than the uniformed cop, dressed in a tweed jacket and brown slacks and what looked like army boots. He called, "I guess that explains the goofball hat."

That hurt. The cap was Jester's trademark.

Tweed Coat paused by the trash basket and looked into it. "You see him?" he asked the uniformed cop.

"I did. He spotted us and he ditched something."

Jester threw up his hands in mock surrender. "You got me. Guilty as charged. Don't tell Seth," he said, still not worried. They didn't even have him for littering. "Can I go eat now?"

"What's your name, son?" Tweed Coat asked.

"Jester."

"Chester what?"

"Not Chester, *Jester* . . . like in Shakespeare?"

"Your Christian name, asswipe."

Whoa. What was this guy's hang-up? Goofing on straights, even the occasional cop, was a game. Blowing people's minds, messing with their heads, freaking them out. But there was a time you didn't. Like now? "Francis O'Neill."

The cop repeated it, but neither man wrote it down. In fact, Tweed Coat scarcely seemed to be listening. His attention was drawn by something inside the trash basket. Frowning, he reached in. A quip about "law and odor" rose in Jester's mind, but something about the man doing this—deliberately reaching in among discarded soda cans, sandwich wrappers, and buzzing yellow jackets—made Jester nervous all at once. The guy straightened, and with sudden perplexity Jester saw that he wasn't holding the flyers as Jester had expected, though exactly what he did have Jester couldn't make out.

"Did you observe him drop this in there, Officer?"

"Certainly did, Captain."

Captain? What he was holding, Jester saw now, sealed in a small clear plastic bag, was a lid of grass.

"Aw, man," Jester said, "don't do this."

The captain drew open the baggie and sniffed the contents. He let the cop do likewise, and then offered it, as if for Jester to take it. Jester didn't.

"What's this look like to you, son?"

A cold, scaly hand clutched Jester's heart. He licked dry lips. "I don't know."

"It's vegetable matter, fool. Weed. Dope. Product. Goof grass, herb, smoke, tea. Are we talking? Cannabis, reefer, Mary Jane, hemp—"

Jester could see the guy took pride in his recitation, had the feeling he could go on rattling off names a long time, and in other circumstances Jester would gladly have entered into the fun—"*Don't forget gage, ganja, shit*"—but he felt a need to break it off now. He swallowed, trying to moisten his tongue, which felt thick in his mouth. "I wasn't holding. Honest."

The captain shook his head, as if truly pained by the situation, and Jester knew then that this couldn't end well. There were two of them to counter anything he might say. They'd bust him, and maybe Seth would be able to make his bail—any money Seth needed he could get from his old man—but even so he'd think Jester was a putz for getting busted in the first place, and his parents would find out, and it would be like failing his draft physical and flunking out of college all over again. No, he couldn't let this go down like this.

With his heart pounding his ribs like mallet blows, he judged the distance to the slope: up that, and over the top, there'd be people out. Maybe the Japanese news crew would be there. These guys wouldn't be so stupid as to make a bad bust with cameras around. But down here . . . With bleak recognition, he saw that, except for Sleeping Beauty with the greasy rucksack, there wasn't another soul besides him and the cops.

He bolted.

He got two steps before a blow banged his ankles together. He went down in a tangle of legs and feet, did a belly flop that sent his cap flying and knocked his wind out. Gasping, he tried to roll over, but a weight like that of a large rock pressed between his shoulder blades, pinning him. Then something prodded the back of his head. For a panicked instant he knew it was a gun, knew they were going to shoot him. Right here in broad daylight, execute him!

"So much as twitch your fat ass, I'll break you," the captain said. "You understand that, Shakespeare?"

Realizing then that what was at his head was some kind of billy club, Jester squeaked assent.

"Handcuff him."

As the cop bent to do so, he straightened suddenly and jumped back. "Sonofabitch! He pissed himself."

In his terror, Jester had lost control. Shamed, he puffed his humiliation into the dirt. With a snort of disgust, the captain said to forget the cuffs. He was allowed to sit up, which he did gingerly, his gut crimped with raw fear. "Honest," he said, "I didn't have that pot. I tossed away some flyers." He tried to steady his voice but was unable to, thinking: *The hell with it, just don't hurt me.*

"Riot control flyers?"

Jester choked out a weak yes.

"Mobilization Group?"

"Yes."

"Like this. That you were papering all over the park."

"That's what I'm trying to tell you. I wasn't holding any—"

"What's it say?"

"What?"

"Is this some kind of code?"

"It says there's . . . there's a meeting."

"When?"

"Tuesday night."

"Where?"

"I'm . . . I'm not sure."

"But you're a member of Mob Grope?"

"No, no, I just help out."

"Help who?"

"I don't know. It's a only a job."

The baton prodded his ribs. "Working for who?"

Too close to tears to go on, he made a choked sound, then sat there with his arms around his updrawn knees, head sunk. For a time no one spoke. In the Sunday morning stillness, birds chirped, and floating on the wind from far away came chords from an electric guitar. He wanted to cry.

"What are we going to do with this big fat baby?" the captain asked, more thinking aloud, it seemed, than wanting an answer. "Can't even control his bodily functions, but he's got no problem with distributing narcotics."

"I wonder if he's got a draft card?" the uniformed cop asked. "He looks the type to burn it."

"I've got one," Jester offered. "I'm 4-F."

"You flunked the physical?"

"Well—"

"My God," the captain said. "You are disgusting. Not only aren't you defending your country, but while other men are—some of them dying—you're spitting on the flag, ripping the fabric of democracy itself."

"But I'm just—"

"A dope-dealing anarchist turd-ass."

A few tears slid down his hot face, dripping onto his hands.

"What do we do with him, Captain?"

Jester's mouth was salty. He sniffled and wiped his cheeks. He looked up at the man standing there, and all at once he was afraid, more afraid than he had been yet. Captain *Moon*. The man Seth and Amy had talked about. His stomach cramped on its own emptiness. His bowels wanted to burst. He held himself tight.

"Of course, pushing dope is bad," said Moon in a measured tone, "but this other thing here, inciting revolution—that attacks the very idea of an ordered society. And with a war going on . . . it's treason." He paced, shaking his head, his boots puffing up little spurts of dust. Jester longed to be that dust, so he would just blow away.

"What a pain, you know it?" Moon went on. "I hate to get the FBI involved . . . all the other stuff they've got to worry about." He walked back over to Jester, who dropped his gaze. He was weeping again, but he didn't try to blot his tears. He was afraid even to move.

Speaking slowly, Moon said, "Maybe we can work this out."

Jester swallowed hard and looked up. He wanted a way out, a shower, food, a change of clothes. "Please," he whimpered, and wasn't ashamed when his voice broke.

To the other cop, Moon said, "Francis here mentioned a name a while back."

"Jester," the cop offered.

"No, another name. 'Don't tell so-and-so.' " Moon pinched up the fabric of one pant leg and got on one knee. "You told us before, Francis, you were just help-ing out. Who gave you the flyers? The same person?"

"Aw, no . . . that . . . that's someone else."

"Name?"

"I . . . can't even remember."

"You're looking at jail time. Federal, probably."

Stupid gosh damn politics! Why couldn't Seth just leave it alone, stay home, stack records on the stereo, make love to Amy, why, why, why? It was crazy to think you could ever change anything with these banana-heads in control. Seth was a fool!

"A name, Francis, and you can walk."

"I can't."

"No."

"My mind's all mush."

"In five minutes you can be sitting down to a stack of hotcakes."

"I can't."

"I ate already. I've got all day."

Jester felt miserable. He ached and he was starving. Finally, his whole body trembling, he said, "Seth Green, the editor of the *Rag*," then broke down and wept.

It was only a little past noon, but Amy felt encased in lethargy. Two cups of coffee hadn't dented it. She sat at the humming Selectric, her fingers hovering over the keys as they might above the planchette of a Ouija board, seeking inspiration. Zephyr, in his report on KPMX that morning, had said that one result of Mercury having gone retrograde would be fatigue. Her explanation was that she'd been out too many nights lately. The telephone rang. The *Rag* had just one line, with two phones, one here and a second in Seth's office. He was in there listening to a tape with headphones. He had the speakers turned off, but after several rings it was apparent he didn't hear the phone. Amy answered.

"Is this Miss Cole?" asked a soft, male voice. "Amy?"

"Speaking."

"You don't know me." Pause. "I mean, we've never met. In person."

"That's okay," she said encouragingly. He seemed awkward, like a shy boy calling for a date. "How can we help you?"

Outside, the morning fog was slower than usual in burning off. It nuzzled the windows, cool and milky as watered ouzo. "In the thing you wrote," the man went on, "you said we could call with information."

Information. She had the phone wedged between her shoulder and cheek. She straightened now and gripped the receiver. "Yes, that's right." Her lethargy was gone. He was referring to the Open Letter. "Have you got something?"

Another silence. She had to resist breaking it with more questions. She flipped open a note pad, seized a pencil. The caller said, "What is it you'd care to know?"

The hairs at the nape of her neck prickled. *Your name, for openers*, she thought. Where he was calling from. Why. What he knew. How he knew it. Everything. *Anything!* "Whatever you have that might be helpful," she said.

"Helpful to who? To you? Or the authorities?"

"To everyone."

"To me, too? Because you see, I know things that're . . . disturbing."

Her scalp tingled. In the hand clutching the receiver, her pulse throbbed. She forced herself to stay calm. "Well, if you could start with—"

"Not *everything*. I mean . . . some of it I just don't understand yet."

In the background—or was it in the connection itself?—she could make out sounds: traffic, it sounded like. She leaned to the length of the cord, wanting to catch Seth's eye. She could see him beyond the glass partition, headphones still on, tapping a hand on his desk.

"Are you there?" the caller asked.

"Yes," she said, too abruptly. "I am. If you're part of the community," she went on in more measured fashion, "would you consider coming here to talk? Just us?"

"I know where you are."

Good, so he was nearby. *Come on, Seth, look up!* She got an idea. On the note pad, in large block letters she wrote: I THINK I'M TALKING TO THE KIL—. The pencil point snapped. She tossed the pencil aside, tried to find another, couldn't. Seth almost never lost himself in music—too frivolous for him. Why *now?*

"Something you wrote in your letter, Amy . . . you wrote that the person could go to the Free Clinic, you said. The psych unit."

"What I meant is—"

"Would it do any good? Shrinks just mess with your head."

Seth looked up then and saw her frantic waving. He plucked off the earphones and poked at the front panel of the tuner. Noise exploded from the speakers— loud guitars, pounding drums—making both him and Amy jump.

"*What's that?*" the caller cried.

Amy sliced a finger repeatedly across her throat, signaling for Seth to cut the volume. Recovering from his own surprise, he did, and the office fell silent as abruptly as it had boomed with sound. "Are you there?" Amy asked, rattled.

"That song . . . Who's with . . . ? God, are *they* there?"

"What?"

His manner had changed; something had frightened him badly. "Oh, dear God Jesus," he moaned.

She was infected with fear now herself. "What is it? Are you—?"

But the connection was broken.

Seth was out of his cubicle, crossing the office. "I hit the wrong button. What's going on?"

Amy was still holding the receiver. A dial tone broke her trance. She cradled the phone.

"What was that? Who was on the phone?"

"Somebody about the letter," she said hollowly.

Seth frowned, not comprehending.

"The last Open Letter."

"The last . . . to the Death Tripper?" Seth slung a chair around and straddled it. "He? She? What did he say?"

What had he said? That he knew something about the killings. Had information. As Amy tried to recount the conversation, she realized he hadn't said much of anything. How long had the call even lasted? Twenty seconds? On the pad was the one note she had begun to write: I THINK I'M TALKING TO THE KIL—

Her weariness of minutes ago was gone. Her mind felt razor sharp. Seth was the rationalist. What did *he* think? He threshed a hand through his dark curls, a patch of which had been shaved away and was still covered by a bandage. "I never liked that letter," he said. "You're getting stoners."

Was that it? It hadn't even crossed her mind that the caller just now might be head-tripping her. He hadn't sounded like that. Still, that was the most likely explanation. Otherwise, why not share information? Or agree to meet? And why hang up? Cranks, paranoids, and fantasy mongers came with any big news story, a reality you dealt with every bit as much as rumors, unconfirmed reports, and reluctant sources. Someone with genuine information would have said so, would have said *something*.

Beyond the window, the sun was burning through the fog, making a yellow smear of the sky. "You're probably right," she agreed. She tore the page from her notebook and crumpled it.

Looking satisfied with this return to rationality, Seth squeezed her knee and headed for his office. And yet, Amy reflected, what had the caller said? *I know things that are disturbing.* His words came back to her. *Not everything. Some of it I don't understand yet.* But he had never gotten around to revealing what he knew.

"Seth!"

In his doorway, he turned.

"That music you were playing—"

"I said I was sorry."

"The band, who are they?"

"It's a bootleg Jester got somewhere. The group you two caught the other week. Talk about dumb names."

He went into the office and shut the door behind him, leaving Amy with a long-legged spider crawling up her spine.

Sparrow wandered quietly amid the aisles of the Freeque Bouteak, affecting an air of the veteran head-shopper. He gazed at clutters of beaded pouches, handmade jewelry, macramé belts, bandannas, peace medallions, scented oils, candles, and crystal amulets on rawhide thongs. A display case held more pipes than any tobacco shop, though Sparrow doubted they were designed for smoking Edgeworth. There were cigarette rolling papers, a dozen brands, in assorted widths, colors, and flavors, an array of alligator clips, and little plastic vials and boxes in a rainbow of colors. Despite its avowed anti-materialism, the counterculture seemed to embrace a goodly amount of commerce.

Along one wall stood racks of clothing in bright colors: granny dresses, T-shirts, vests, jeans, headbands, hats, and sandals. A perky girl in a cheerleader's jacket and wire-rim glasses was shopping for her boyfriend, a high school football type who appeared even more foreign to the hippie role than she was. She held a ruffled Edwardian shirt against him. Over his barrel chest the effect was ridiculous. She made several other tries before settling for a strand of Turkish beads. As he slipped them self-consciously around his neck, he caught Sparrow's gaze and something like fellow feeling passed between them.

In a bin on the opposite wall was an assortment of LPs. Sparrow fingered through them. The bands had strange names in strange lettering—the Mothers of Invention, Canned Heat, It's a Beautiful Day—and the covers were equally bizarre, so different from the rock 'n' roll albums of his own younger days, on which group members posed in high school sweaters and liner notes revealed that Chris, the singer, liked coconut sundaes, and Roy favored powder blue Ban-Lon shirts, while guitarist Jimmy dug old Mercs with curb feelers and baby moon hubcaps. He came upon the name Jefferson Airplane, and for the first time he realized they were a band. He picked up the album.

"Getting ideas for Christmas?"

It was Amy Cole. "I didn't know Jefferson Airplane was a band till just now. Or that they live here in the Haight. *Surrealistic Pillow?*"

She smiled. "They love you."

He slid the album back. His last image of her had been jumping off the stage in the park and disappearing into the chaos, an image that had a certain finality. But seeing her now, her hair woven in a thick gold braid, her blue eyes bright, stirred him in a way he hadn't anticipated when she'd telephoned.

Perhaps sensing his thoughts, she colored slightly. "You're out of uniform," she said.

He plucked at the sport shirt he'd donned with chinos and deck shoes. "John Sparrow lets it all hang out."

"You look fine." Unlike the high-schoolers, she seemed at home here, though her simple garb of jeans and a faded work shirt was more functional than fanciful. "Thanks for coming. Come on, we can talk back here."

They went through a doorway hung with a curtain. The inner room was dark except for the posters. They bore mandalas and pentagrams and announcements for the ever-present rock bands, all in vivid, glowing colors, which seemed to pulse from the walls and ceiling. Curious about the effect, Sparrow ran a hand in front of one of the tubes of purplish light. "Black light," Amy said happily. "Shows you things you didn't know were there."

Like her bra, he realized. Under her shirt collar he could see one strap gleaming whitely. He hadn't expected any woman under thirty wore one anymore. "It's ultraviolet," he said, putting the thought away. "This paint fluoresces at that wavelength."

She affected a frown. "Well, that sucks the alchemy right out of it."

He spared her the detail that the coroner used ultraviolet light to examine the dead, but the topic returned him to the reason for their meeting. Amy told him about the phone call she had received just an hour ago, which had prompted hers to him. When he showed little reaction, she looked doubtful herself. "Skimpy, huh?"

"I'm not sure."

"It was a feeling I had, something I grokked. Seth's convinced the caller was a crank."

"Do you get many?"

"Cranks?"

"Grokkings, if that's the word."

"Some. Don't we all?" She shrugged. "Cranks we get by the case lot. People want to lay their trips on somebody."

"Tell me again what he said about Free Clinic."

"They've got a psych unit to help people having bummers. In my letter, I suggested someone could turn himself in there. I thought it might be nonthreatening. He said shrinks only play with your head."

"Speaking from experience maybe."

Some people came into the poster room, bringing with them a thick aura of pot smoke. Sparrow led Amy outside. In the afternoon sun, Haight Street was a live version of the black light room, the street and sidewalks pulsing color. Each time he came here, there was more traffic, more people. He and Amy joined the flow, moving south, in the direction of the park. Ahead, a city employee holding a hose was watering a bed of marigolds and snapdragons, but he seemed preoccupied, and the stream of water occasionally strayed from the flowers, as though he were uncertain whether he wanted them to thrive or to wither. A white van painted with stars and moons eased away from the curb. Wanting to get focused again, Sparrow asked, "Did you have a sense of the caller's age?"

"Twenty-five, maybe? Hard to say."

He had more questions. When they reached the intersection of Haight and Masonic, he said, "This isn't a good idea."

She looked at him. "I'm sorry I wasted your valuable time."

"I mean the whole thing—printing your letter, taking calls from strangers. He sounds like a weirdo. He knows where you work, where you are. Doesn't that frighten you?"

"A little," she admitted. "But the newspaper is part of the community. I choose that. I won't hide."

"Suppose he had come?"

"Then maybe we'd have information and wouldn't need to be having this conversation."

"I just don't want you in danger."

"That's two of us. What should I have done? Seriously."

He felt exposed there on the busy sidewalk. "Let's walk," he said. As they did, he went on, "Why not just refer everyone to my office? Use that hot line number if you want. Let me handle the calls."

"Do you honestly think you'll get any? After the TAC Squad's performance the other day? I know that wasn't you—you get personal kudos for what you did—but people don't make distinctions."

He felt a prickle of frustration, a vague anger at cops working against cops, and Frank Austin using the rulebook to defend it. "No, we didn't win any friends," he said. Remembering something, he took out the blue silk scarf she'd worn around her throat that day and used on Seth's wound. She looked surprised—pleased, he thought.

"You washed it." She smiled. "You are a good shepherd."

"I wish I could say it opened doors around here."

"That word you used one time, for shadow and light . . . chiaroscuro. It's like that here, isn't it? You think you understand something, then you're not sure."

"Mostly not sure," he admitted.

She smiled. "I have my days, too. Anyway, the whole idea behind my letter was that people might come forward to the *Rag*. Yes, we are visible—*I'm* visible. It's a risk, but we're part of this place."

"And I'm not."

"I hate to say it, but . . ."

It was true. Painfully, it struck him that his casual attire today was as blatantly obvious as his suit. Moved along by the flow of people, they resumed walking in silence. Occasional passersby recognized Amy and said hello. A smiling youth handed her a red rose. Men eyed her with open sensual appreciation. And why not? She was a pretty woman. To give himself some purpose, he said, "Take me through the part about the music again."

She told it, told him, too, about her own experience with the New Riders of the Apocalypse, whom she'd heard play. Details went into his notebook, along with the growing list of notes that still added up to little. When they reached the next corner, she said, "Thanks for coming. I've got to get back to meet Seth."

"You live together?" It was out before he could stop it.

She looked at him. "Live, work . . . there're a few of us."

Unexpectedly, this bothered him. He had imagined her having her own apartment, or female roommates. Was it a commune? A *ménage* of some sort? "How's his head?" he asked, covering.

"On the mend. He's no booster of the 'authorities' these days."

"Not anymore, huh?"

Amy smiled and handed him the flower. "Thanks again."

With a wave she crossed Haight and started up Ashbury. Holding the flower, he started in the opposite direction, toward the Panhandle, where he had parked. He'd gone only a few steps when he pivoted, aware of something all at once. He scanned the street. There. Creeping along, out of phase with the traffic, was the white van he had noticed outside the Freeque Bouteak, painted with its psychedelic moons and stars. It lingered near where Amy was walking.

He called her name. She didn't hear him over the street noise. He started back toward her. Now, whoever was at the wheel of the van seemed to become aware of him. The van backed up sharply and swung a U-turn. Hesitating only an instant, Sparrow started across the street at a run. "Amy!" he called again. She heard him this time, and turned.

The van cut into the traffic, picking up speed. Afoot, he did likewise, weaving through the dense pedestrian swarms, after it. This was an unaccustomed pace here, and many people stepped aside; even so, he had to break stride often to avoid running into others.

The van swung onto Clayton when he was still half a block away. As he rounded the corner, there it was, a dozen car lengths off, stalled in traffic. He was breathing hard now, but he made for the van. With its curtained windows, it was hard to tell who or how many people were inside. There was some painted-over writing on the side, like the ghost of an ancient message. As he ran, traffic started to move again. A tour bus cut him off. Forced to a halt, he glared up at the passengers gawking from the windows, snapping photos. When the bus had wheezed past, leaving him in a hot blue haze of fumes, he saw just a flash of the van—paisley curtains in its rear windows—as it wheeled onto a cross street and was gone.

IN HIS WINDMILL-CREAKING-IN-A-MINNESOTA-WIND VOICE, DYLAN WAS TELLING A woman he wasn't the kind of person she needed, so Seth didn't hear the door to the *Rag*'s outer office open. He was intent on clamping a spirit master onto the roller drum of a mimeograph machine; but he looked up now as the door closed. Two men in suits were standing in the outer office, and although they wore no badges, he knew at once they were cops. One of them, in fact, was Captain Moon.

Seth drew a nervous breath. He had the mimeograph machine set up in this small back room, separate from the newspaper office. The sign on the door identified the space as a janitor's closet, which in fact it was, but it was also where he created flyers and other communiques for the Mobilization Group. He snapped off the overhead light, pulled the closet door gently shut behind him, and went into the outer office.

"Help you?" he asked over the record spinning on the little Columbia phonograph. He hoped he sounded calm. Given the gash healing on his scalp, being civil to cops didn't come easy. They were no doubt here because of the current issue of the *Rag*, which had hit the street yesterday, bearing its graphic photo essay of the TAC Squad's outing in the park.

"Evening," said Moon, flipping open a badge case to show his star. The other one, who was of the stocky, standard TAC issue, with lots of shoulder and neck, occupied himself gazing around, paying extra attention to the posters of Che and Karl Marx. *Have a seat,* Seth thought, *make yourselves uncomfortable.* "Want to talk to you about what you're up to," Moon said.

"Publishing a newspaper?"

"That's stretching it." Moon frowned toward the record player. "Can we put that whiny sonofabitch out of his misery?"

When Seth made no move, the stocky cop went over and lifted the tone arm, being none too careful, so that the stylus scratched across the vinyl, setting Seth's teeth on edge. "Better," Moon declared. "Now." He produced a sealed plastic bag and offered it for Seth's inspection. Inside was a fold of paper, and though Seth couldn't see the words, he recognized the red clenched fist. "Look familiar?"

"Should it?"

"It was printed here, wasn't it?"

Seth realized he could deny it; he didn't still have the original around, and he had given Jester the last of the batch to circulate; but why lie? There was no crime in having printed or distributed the flyer. He shrugged, again hoping he appeared calmer than he felt. "I guess."

"I *know*," said Moon.

"Well, then?"

"I can't figure you guys out. A rich kid, your old man puts you through college . . . probably has friends on the draft board."

A chill touched him. He crossed his arms, as if to ward it off. Did Moon really know things about him, or was he guessing?

"But has your father seen this?" Moon was still holding up the plastic bag with the folded flyer in it.

The stocky cop, who was standing by, watching, said, "Dad'd probably pass it off as another phase of growing up. Like pimples, or beating your meat."

"Probably he's scared because he never figured out how to tell you no, so he gives you this big leg up on life—"

"Wait a minute," Seth said.

"—but what do you do? You spit on it. Instead of taking a place in society, being grateful for all your advantages, you want to trash everything in sight."

"Hold it!" Seth was angry now. "I wasn't the one swinging a club in the park the other day."

"Neither was I," Moon said innocently. The other cop maintained his flat stare. "What do you hope to accomplish?" Moon went on. "Overthrow the government? *You* want to be the guy with the club?" He leaned forward with a look of exaggerated cunning and lowered his voice conspiratorially. "Or is this a way to get quim? Tell me. Hey, if it works, I might try it. Some of these hippie girls look pretty horny."

Pathetic. There was a killer loose and they had nothing better to do than lay a number on him. Seth shook his head. Surprisingly, Moon laughed. When he grew serious again, he pointed. "What's back there?"

"Janitor's closet."

"So it says. Were you getting ready to mop the floor? Or is that where you've got the negatives stashed?"

So there it was. This was roust. "Sorry, I've got no negatives. But if you want prints, something to frame for your bunker wall . . ."

The stocky cop walked to the closet door, nudged it open with his foot. Before Seth could find a way to distract them, the cop found the wall switch and put on the light. He let out a soft whistle. "Well, looky here."

Moon went over. Seth stayed with him. Taped on an inner wall was a poster of Mao. Mr. Potato Head, Jester called him. It hadn't made the cut for display out front. Moon gave it a passing glance and stepped over to the mimeograph. He peeled up the spirit master clamped to the roller drum.

"That's private property," said Seth.

" 'Bring The War Home,' " Moon read. " 'Create two, three, many Vietnams.' " He looked at Seth. "You come up with that all by yourself?"

"Che Guevara did."

Frowning, Moon put the master down. "Your old man buy you the machine?"

"Go ahead, take it." Shaken at first by the invasion, Seth was regaining control. He was already thinking of the next issue of the *Rag*, in which he would push even harder against the cops. "Take the typewriters, too." He gestured toward the outer office. "We've got phone extensions, a pencil sharpener. We're kind of short on pencils right now, all the writing we do, but do your thing. Grab the record player. You like Dylan? Take it all. You'll bring it back pretty quick when a judge gives you a crash course in democracy."

Moon grinned, but under the dark bristles of his crew cut his scalp reddened. "Nah. We just want to talk." His gaze was still roving the cramped closet, taking in the shelves stacked with reams of paper, a paper cutter, containers of copy fluid in blue, gallon cans, boxes of spirit masters. "This is an arsenal, when you think of it," he said. "Where you build your bombs."

"Sure, whatever you say."

"They don't have to be the kind with fuses and powder. Words can be just as explosive, and cause as much harm. Like the trash you've got on the street right now. You think people should read that?"

"I believe people should see what's going on."

"You do, huh? Power to the people?"

"Something like that."

"How about killing people? Are you the hippie killer?"

The question took Seth unawares. He grew wary, not sure where this was going. The stocky cop had picked up one of the blue cans and unscrewed the cap. Sniffing the copy fluid, he winced at the sharp smell. As he lowered the can, some of the fluid spurted from the opening onto Moon's suit coat.

"Goddammit, Fred!" Moon exploded.

The cop flushed. "Sorry."

Moon snatched the can, causing more fluid to splash out. The closet grew pungent with fumes, with the effect of clearing Seth's head. "This has gone far enough," he said sternly. "Leave."

"You kicking us out?"

"I'm calling my lawyer."

"Your old man's lawyer, you mean. Dad covers everything, from college tuition to co-signing the lease on this place."

How did Moon know such details? That day in People's Park in Berkeley when Seth and some others had burned their Selective Service cards, had someone had a camera? The alcohol fumes were stinging his eyes. "Get out!"

"Dad's a headshrinker," Moon went on, "but he can't figure you out, I bet. Has he seen this firetrap? Does he know where his money's going? Or is he too messed up with his own problems to bother? Paying alimony to two ex-wives and whatnot. Shrinks are known to be screwy."

"Fuck you!"

Moon threw up his hands, and for an instant Seth was sure the man was going to hit him. But he didn't. He turned his palms out, a gesture of concession. Seth's pulse was snapping painfully in his throat. "You're right," Moon said. "I don't know what I'm talking about. I've never been to a shrink. The thing is, this could be valuable, us rapping like this. Get to understand each other, you know? See each other's perspective. But I think we need some music, calm us all down. Fred, some music."

The stocky cop went into the outer room. "Same record?" he called.

Moon made no reply. In a moment Dylan began to sing again, a different track—"Chimes of Freedom"—but as loud as before. Moon gestured. "That's where I should begin. Listening to your music, so I can understand." He appeared to give the song his attention for a minute. "You know what he's singing about? Sounds kind of pissed off. Is that why you're angry? The music you listen to? Is that what's got the killer going?"

Like the first whisper of a rising wind, Seth's uncertainty grew. The man seemed on the narrow brink of explosion. His body radiated it, a heat coming through his clothes. And the thought came: Was *Moon* the Death Tripper?

Seth was scared now, frightened of the man's potential for violence. He wanted to get out of the room. The smell of the copy fluid was making him dizzy. But Moon was in no hurry. Absently, as though pondering his own questions, he drew a pack of Lucky Strikes from his shirt pocket. He tapped a cigarette out and held it between his lips. He put the pack away and produced a chrome lighter, but he didn't snap it open, just held it, as though far away in thought. "Now, your girlfr—oops, your 'old lady.' Isn't that the term? See, I'm trying. She's a good writer, huh? That letter she wrote . . . what was it, to the Hippie Ripper? Or no, the Hashbury Slasher. No, wait . . . the *Death Tripper*. That's it. The name's so good, even the city papers picked it up and are calling the sick bastard that now. You heard from him? Anyone come in to confess?"

Moon glanced at the other cop, who looked as uncertain of what was going on as Seth was. In fact, Seth felt an odd pressure mounting in the base of his skull, as if the fumes were collecting there. Moon snapped the lighter. He applied the flame to a corner of the small clear bag containing the flyer. The plastic began to melt. He was destroying it. Was it his way of making peace? The paper took the flame.

"How about a cop named Sparrow? You talked to him?"

Seth was watching the flame.

"Be careful of Sparrow. He's not what he seems."

When the fire brushed Moon's fingertips, he dropped the burning bag into a wastebasket. This broke Seth's reverie. He stepped toward the basket. As he tried to get past the stocky cop, the man hooked an arm around his neck and yanked back.

The force jerked Seth upright, cut off his breath. The cop started to drag him toward the door. Moon paid no attention, watching the flames in the wastebasket. The more Seth resisted, the more pressure the cop applied. He tried to still himself, but he was trembling. Smoke had begun to rise. Moon splashed the remaining contents of the blue can around the closet. When the can was empty, he tossed it aside and kicked over the basket.

The vaporized alcohol combusted with a *whoosh*.

Freaked, Seth struggled. The cop tightened the chokehold. Nearly invisible flames began to spread. Moon turned and, shoving the cop and Seth before him, they exited into the outer office.

Behind them there was a muted explosion, and almost at once the janitor's closet was engulfed in fire and smoke. Against the grip of pain and fear at his throat, Seth yelled hoarsely, "Douse it, for God's sake!"

The flames leaped from the closet and were dancing across a strip of ratty carpet, a relic of the building's days as a theater, moving toward the sawhorses that supported the old door that served as the composing desk, stacked now with papers.

The fire made a soft rustling, like bamboo leaves. Despite the mounting heat and smoke, Moon did nothing. Seth tried to break free but the cop tightened his hold. In horror, Seth watched the office begin to burn.

Finally, Moon said, "Let him go."

The cop holding Seth seemed hesitant. "You don't want to bust him?"

"For what? Turn him loose."

The cop pushed Seth away.

"Call the fire department," Moon shouted. The stocky cop reached for the telephone on Amy's desk, where sparks were igniting papers. "Not here, outside. From the car." The cop went.

The noise had risen to a low roar. Furniture and floor were ablaze. In the leaping red light, Seth watched the posters curling off the walls. Karl Marx's beard went yellow with flames. Che, too, took blaze, as though his own fiery rhetoric had hit the kindling point. Turn On, Tune In, Drop Out: Seth tried to snatch away Amy's flowered poster, but too late. The paper blackened to char and fell away in flakes, which spun up on the heat and fluttered off like moths. In the back room another can of fluid exploded, and there was a sound of shattering glass. Smoke was making Seth cough. Dizzily, he allowed himself to be pulled away and ushered out the door.

The street was already filling with people as Seth and Moon descended to the sidewalk, their faces aglow with the firelight visible through the windows of the old building. Voices called back and forth: "What's going down?" and "Are there people still in there?" and "Has anyone called the fire department?" But aside from the space Seth leased, the building was vacant. He could only watch, weak-kneed and sick.

The noise had risen to a raw crackling, and soon smoke and flames were billowing out the door. One young man darted up the steps waving a tattered serape at the leaping horns of fire, a crazed matador; but it was obvious that neither he nor anyone else had any idea what to do.

"Listen!" someone cried. "Is that who I think it is?"

"Dylan!"

Inside the blazing office, the troubadour went on venting his lonesome anguish. Seconds later he was cut off by a crash, as though the night itself were splintering. Curtains of sparks whirled into the air. After a time, the stocky cop drew an unmarked Ford to the curb. "Fire trucks are on the way!" he yelled over the rumble of the burning.

"No good," Moon called back. "He beat us. Or got lucky. Convenient how the evidence caught fire before we could get a warrant."

The words jolted Seth from his torpor. He rounded on Moon, his hands fisted at his sides. "You lying goddamn Nazi!"

Moon only looked regretful, playing for the bystanders. "Easy, son. You won. I've got no case, unless you're telling me you didn't start that fire by accident."

"He's lying," Seth cried to the people on the sidewalk. "*He* set it!" Faces turned, dazed-looking in the firelight, curious. "*They* trashed the office! They trashed the First Amendment."

But there was too much spectacle and noise to compete with. One by one, people turned back to the fire. Soon Moon, in a tone of authority, began urging them to move along.

But Seth wasn't ready to surrender. He could organize these people, get some buckets, a hose . . . there had to be a hydrant . . .

He scanned the faces, big-eyed in the wavering red light. A few were vaguely familiar; most, however, were those of complete strangers. But worse, he realized with heartsick force, despite their headbands and peace medallions, granny dresses and stash pouches, he had almost nothing in common with these people. Right now they were just gawkers on the carnival midway of the Haight.

Seth spun away, thinking to run to the corner, where he knew people, but abruptly he stopped, his attention caught by something at the rear of the crowd. In the reflected light, he thought he recognized a face, but it was lit only fleetingly before the person slipped behind some other watchers. Seth shouldered through the thickening swarm for a closer view, but after a few steps a fierce *crack* made him jerk around.

In the inferno, a beam collapsed. An outer wall let go, cascading inward, bringing an awed murmur from the crowd and sending flames hissing up into the night like enraged serpents.

When Seth managed to reach the street, the person he had seen was gone. He wasn't sure, and yet, for a moment there he could've sworn that the person watching from the distance had been Jester.

The heat rose to a baking intensity that drove everyone farther back. After what seemed an eternity, there was a distant whine and the goose honk of fire engines. Too late, Seth reflected bitterly. The building was a blazing ruin, the facilities for the *Rag* and the Mob Grope a total loss, and any notion of rights and freedoms gone. As George Moon watched the fire, he wore only the faintest hint of an expression, but Seth recognized it as a smile. Despite the heat, Seth felt a cold chasm open inside him; then it, too, filled with fire. Rising from it came a phoenix of bright rage.

18

"THEY BURIED IT!" SETH CRIED, TOSSING THE *CHRONICLE* ONTO THE KITCHEN TABLE, upsetting an ashtray and spilling roaches. "Buried on page ten, and what does it say? Faulty wiring suspected as the cause. One mention of the *Rag*! Nothing about my statement to the fire department." He hammered the table with a fist.

"At least Moon didn't give them that ridiculous lie that you started the fire," Amy said.

Seth had told her the full story, but it was as if seeing it in print, in a version other than his own, had fanned the flames all over again. He seemed ready to riot. He paced the kitchen, making the linoleum floor creak. From the wall, the lions and lambs in Tess's unfinished jungle Eden mural watched. "Should we call the fire marshal?" Amy asked. "Demand an investigation?" But she already knew the answer. A request for a formal inquiry would go nowhere. A ramshackle building in a rundown district, nobody hurt? Worse, a place where an underground newspaper was produced? It would be dismissed as a waste of taxpayers' money.

Seth shook his head. "I have to find new office space."

"I can do that. Why don't you forget about it for now," she said.

"We're not going to miss a single issue! I won't give the bastards the satisfaction."

With stuck-record insistence, Amy said that she would take care of locating a new home for the *Rag* and arrange for replacing equipment burned up in the fire, and gradually Seth's agitation calmed. But at another level, she understood with a dawning awareness, that something in him had shifted, some more reasonable part of him had been burned up, too. She was about to urge that he drive up and visit Terry Gordon at his farm for a few days when a scream made them jump. They exchanged a wide-eyed look. Jester.

A spill of daylight seeped around the edges of the drawn shade to reveal him huddled in a corner of his tiny room, atwist in the bedclothes, staring wildly at the mattress as though it were crawling with bugs.

"It's all right," Amy said calmingly, settling on the edge of the mattress, putting an arm around him. He had the ill-kempt appearance of someone strung out on heroin. "You were dreaming." He'd been asleep for more than twelve hours.

Seth watched from the doorway a moment, then said he'd go make some tea. "It's okay," Amy reassured Jester again. "Nothing can hurt you."

When she rejoined Seth in the kitchen, he glanced up questioningly from pouring boiling water. "He's asleep again," she said. "He's been crashed all day. I want to take him to the Free Clinic, but he won't move."

"You think he just tripped out?"

"*Something* freaked him, but I don't believe it was drugs."

Seth brought over teacups and sat. "What then?"

"You said he acted strangely when you saw him last night watching the fire."

"*If* I saw him. I can't swear to it." Seth frowned. "But why wouldn't he have come right over? He'd have known what was going down the minute he saw Moon."

"Unless something happened to him or—" She stopped.

"Or he'd already talked to the cops," Seth said, finishing her thought. "And that's why they showed up."

Amy clutched herself, as if a chill had touched her. "I don't even like thinking it. He worships you."

"Moon linked that flyer to me, Jester was handing them out. If the cops got to him, threatened him . . ."

She found the idea repellent, even for the TAC police. And yet she knew what Terry Gordon had told her about cops leaning on students to snitch.

"If Moon is responsible, in any way," Seth vowed, "it's one more thing I owe the bastard."

She didn't want that kind of talk now. Images of the solstice rout were still clear in her mind; but clearer still, superimposed on them, was the image of their friend pressed into the corner of his bed, gaping at unseen things. "We need to wait for Jester to tell us," she said. "And I think he will when he's ready. For now, let's just be here for him."

They drank their tea in silence; and after a few minutes Seth picked up the newspaper again and opened to the commercial real estate rentals. When the phone rang some time later, she was a moment identifying the voice. Then she did, and a cold fist squeezed her heart.

Sitting on the narrow bed, under the feeble light from the overhead bulb, you wait for the screams to fade. When they're gone you unbuckle the saddlebag and remove the knotted red bandanna. You open it carefully, peeling back the folds. One by one you take them out, setting them on the worn bedspread in order, always in order. Adair, Fischetti, Ford . . . Names. Lately you've been seeing faces, too, in fog and smoke; in the display of a jukebox's lights. Practically every-place. Like portents. Heite, Kornstein, Molloy . . .

In the backyard, the landlord's dog barks briefly and you hear the old man opening the screen door to let her in, hear the door close, the sounds muted in the blue gloom of dusk. Pena, Worden . . . Yours goes in there, too. You sort through the tags again, counting them off; then you return them to the bandanna and put the bandanna back in the saddlebag. Later, when you wake again, the crickets are singing. Quietly you slip out, cross the yard, and wander over to the district.

Red neon makes zigzag shapes in the deep sheen of the teardrop tanks of the choppers parked along Haight Street. None of the bikes are as good-looking as the Shadow . . . or as noticeable, which is why you keep it stashed. For now, at least, until you've finally done what you need to do.

"Step back from the machine, asshole."

It's one of the Angels, a fat growler in denims. You'd like to go head-to-head on the Shadow, leave him and his hog in the dust, but you move on, the neon reflections whispering to you with hieroglyphic meaning as you pass. This is nothing new, this knack for seeing signs everywhere, in the markings on the walls of gas station bathrooms, or sitting in the Pancake Palace and discovering a face in the floor tile pattern, and next to it, bleeding into it like smoke, another face. Maybe it began when you met the couple who stopped in the desert to pick you up when the Shadow broke down, and sometime later, up there in God's own corner of Arizona someplace, you understood that things were starting, though you didn't know how or why yet. That took awhile, traveling a few days with them, camping out, smoking weed.

The girl always seemed to have some handy, little twig-thin numbers in pink strawberry paper sometimes—New York needles, she called them, like calling her old man New York Ned—but you didn't care, passing the J but no judgment because something had begun to speak to you, telling you that you would see a sign, so you rode along, listening to the music, "Light My Fire," "Somebody to Love," "Get Together," and the bootleg tape of the band you'd never heard of before, wouldn't hear of again till you got out here and started to realize that in bolting from Fort Sam, you'd set in motion a way to take away the faces, erase the names, and maybe, at last, stop the screams.

Pete Sandoval made eating with his fingers seem fastidious. He sat at the squad room table, breaking an enchilada into small pieces and putting them into his mouth. Sparrow, by contrast, was making a mess. He had juice running across his hands in greasy streams, dripping onto the absorbent pages of the *Rag*, spread before him. A notice there, in the gaudy rococo style of the head-shop posters, had caught his interest, and he was puzzling over its message. He would have paid no attention except that it was for the band Amy Cole had mentioned to him when she'd received the phone call about her open letter. "New Riders of the Apocalypse," the notice read, "appearing . . ." and gave a date and location, someplace over in Sausalito, two nights from now.

"Jeez, you guys," Rocco Bianchi said, "something wrong with American food, you gotta eat that stuff?" He set a yellow Telex on the table, away from the greasy mess.

"What's this?" Sandoval asked.

"Something else to look for. A cop called from upstate New York, asking about a couple kids that set out from there back in March and haven't been heard from."

Sparrow looked at the unfamiliar names. Neither had turned up as a murder victim, at least.

"They're teenage sweethearts," Rocco went on. "*Ozzie and Harriet* kids, not the type to forget to call home, the cop told me. Anyway, there's the info, and a VIN on their wheels. 'We'll add it to the list,' I said. 'Oh, you'll know this one,' he told me, 'one of those hippie vans, with stars and planets painted all over it.' 'Sure,' I said, 'can't be more than a few hundred of those around.' " Rocco went to answer a telephone.

Sandoval was reading the Telex from New York when Rocco said, "For you, John."

He took the receiver, listened to a moment's silence, and then a young woman said in a whisper, "John? It's Amy Cole."

Which was all she got out before her voice broke apart and she began to sob.

19

THERE WERE LILIES AND FREESIA AND SWEETHEART ROSES SURROUNDED BY A SPRAY OF baby's breath. Amy doubted John Sparrow would know the names, but that didn't matter; he presented them along with his condolences, seeming awkward in both acts, but sincere. "They're beautiful," she said. "Thank you."

"I don't know if they'll keep till Ventura."

They were standing in the parking lot of the marina, the spars and masts of sailboats forming a spare calligraphy in the morning fog. "You can change your mind," she said, and meant it. She was feeling guilty, as if her tears on the phone yesterday had made him uncomfortable and he had said yes, he would go with her to her cousin's funeral, because he didn't know what else to say. "You were kind to accept, and I thank you. I'm stronger today. I can make the trip okay alone."

Sparrow had put on a dark suit, and his shirt collar looked tight. "That's got to be up to you," he said.

"Seth won't come, because I won't let him be angry," she offered. She didn't want rage. Not yet, not now.

John Sparrow's faint smile was doleful and ironic. "So he said go with your mild-mannered friend the cop?"

"I didn't tell him I called you. But I'm just thinking this was dumb of me. You've got your work to do, your investigation."

His rough-hewn face was not handsome, certainly, but stolid and dependable. In his dark eyes she sensed the faint melancholy she had seen before. "There're other people on the case," he said. "And I can check in by phone. So the question is, Amy, do you still want me to go?"

She'd asked herself the same question. Seth had let her cry and spill her grief, comforting her in his fashion. He said he would go with her to the funeral; but his outrage at Glenn's death and at the burning of the *Rag* office had pushed him into a mania to get the paper going again. She had insisted he stay. And poor Jester hadn't emerged from his bedroom. She had other friends . . . so why this man, a dozen years older than she, whom she knew only slightly, and as he said, was a cop at that? The fact of the matter was she had called simply because she thought he would understand, and perhaps the proof of that was right in her hands. She drew the flowers to her face, breathing in their scent. "Yes," she said.

They took his car and made their way out of the city and got on the highway heading south, Amy holding the flowers, Sparrow smoking quietly. Their brief conversation had angled into silence, and she was alone with her thoughts. Yesterday's call from her uncle Everett, with his terrible news, had felt like something falling on her from a great height. She had telephoned her parents, who'd heard the news and were devastated. There was talk of their flying out, but they'd spent their money on their visit last month and simply could not afford the trip again. Amy would represent the family at the funeral. Finally, she had taken out Glenn's letters from Vietnam and reread them all, probing the words for some comfort, some inkling as to what had happened. But it wasn't there. No voice came from beyond the tear-dampened pages, and now death had silenced the speaker. She slept in a deep, dreamless dark.

She wore a pale blue Indian cotton dress, sandals, and a simple strand of ceramic beads, and had put her hair in a chignon. As they got farther south, Sparrow opened the glove box, reaching for cigarettes, she imagined, but he got out sunglasses and offered them.

"I look that bad, huh?"

He smiled. "You look fine. It's getting sunny."

The fog was vanishing, the last wisps of it marching off like a ghost army in retreat, and soon the sun was raying down in bright shafts.

They were too late for the cortege. The service was being held outdoors, graveside, for which Amy was grateful. The emotions she was feeling would not have been well contained by church walls today. When Sparrow parked, she lost her nerve. Her eyes filled and she couldn't move. He waited.

"My aunt and uncle got word a week ago . . . but they didn't say anything till Glenn had been shipped home and was actually here . . . as if somehow by not saying it, it wasn't real. I guess I've been thinking that, too." Her throat tightened and she said no more.

Sparrow opened her door and she knew at once the contrast in summer between San Francisco and here. The asphalt pavement oozed underfoot, giving her over to a moment's dizziness. Walking toward the gravesite, she took Sparrow's arm.

There was a cluster of people already gathered, so she and Sparrow stood at the fringe. The cemetery occupied a hillside, a smooth green carpet arranged with stone monuments overlooking a cypress grove, and beyond, hazy with heat, the ocean. A marine honor guard approached, bearing the flag-draped casket. When they had settled it carefully beside the open grave, Amy watched her aunt step forward and set a framed photograph on the coffin lid. It was Glenn, handsome in a dress uniform, smiling uncertainly, the way Amy remembered having seen him last, in San Francisco before he left. People quietly began to cry.

The minister, a pudgy man in a wrinkled tan suit, moved among the inner circle of mourners, murmuring words. Amy couldn't hear them, but there was comfort in his manner, and in the public voice with which he soon began to address the gathering. He had known Glenn and spoke of him in warm, familiar terms: a local boy, fine athlete, good son, and willing soldier. He took as his text First Samuel, the seventeenth chapter, the story of David and Goliath. It struck Amy as the wrong choice, given its bloodiness, and she fidgeted with the thought that the man was going to glamorize war. But he didn't. As he extemporized from the scripture, a chubby hand moving now and again to smooth down his hair, stirred by the hot wind, it occurred to her that the passage was fitting in its martial imagery, after all, and in the metaphor the man drew of death as a Goliath that, despite its might, is finally overcome. "And for those of us gathered here to remember and honor Glenn," he concluded, "we understand that grief is *our* wound, but we take our comfort in God."

A marine bugler played "Taps," which by rights she should have hated, but the pure spare grace of the piece pierced her and she wept. John Sparrow stood by in his dark suit, his brow pebbled with perspiration, solemn and somehow reassuring in his stillness, and she knew she had been right in having him come. Despite their differences, he was a good man.

When the marines had folded the flag into a neat cocked hat and the chief of guard presented it to the fallen soldier's father, family members and friends went forward to lay flowers at the grave. Out of respect, neither relative nor personal friend, Sparrow stood where he was. On the bright expanse of distant ocean, the tiny figures of surfboard riders were visible, bobbing in an uneven line. In their wet suits, they might have been blackbirds on a fence wire. Sparrow watched idly as one surfer detached himself from the others and went sliding down the glossy face of a rising wave, zigged fluidly to the left, then, as the crest broke, zagged, moving just ahead of the churning water. Sparrow wondered if Amy's cousin had once been part of the group.

After the ceremony, Amy led him over to her relatives. She and her aunt clasped hands at arms' reach a moment, then Amy drew the older woman to her. For an instant her aunt appeared to have no idea what to do, then she gave in, hugging her niece and crying freely. After a time, Amy made introductions. Amy's uncle was a tall, suntanned man, tie-less in a blazer, chinos, and Jack Purcell's that oddly seemed to dignify the occasion: "We're among friends here," his appearance and manner seemed to say. Still, he shook John's hand distractedly.

"Drive down from 'Frisco did you?"

"Yes, sir."

He tried to muster a smile. "That's all Glenn talked about. How he had to get up there and see what was happening. Check out the good 'vibes,' he called it." He made a thin sound and faced the ocean and said nothing for a time. Sparrow waited. "Several thousand miles out there is a place I'd never even thought about until Glenn enlisted. Yet our leaders tell us it's important, worth nine thousand American boys who've died there . . ." The man appeared to be searching the horizon; perhaps, Sparrow thought, imagining some threat that might issue from there. Or maybe having grave doubts that any ever would. He held the folded flag clamped tightly under his arm, as if afraid to let go for fear that all trace of his son, even his memory, might vanish.

Amy had been to her relatives' home once before, when she first came out to attend Berkeley, shortly before Glenn joined the marines. It was a tan bungalow, what they called a Craftsman cottage out here, though it was larger than the farmhouse she had grown up in. As people gathered, Amy donned an apron, glad to be useful. She and some of the other women went to work and soon, almost by magic it seemed, food appeared: cold fried chicken, rolled slices of ham, potato salad in Tupperware bowls, deviled eggs, pitchers of lemonade, an urn of coffee, a bucket of beers on chipped ice, and on the kitchen counter, in discreet array, an assortment of wine, liquor, and mixers: comfort food for the grieving.

Talk came more easily than it had at the cemetery, and she met distant cousins and people who had known and loved Glenn. If Sparrow felt out of place, he didn't show it; he joined conversations, helped shuttle chairs out into the backyard. She had the thought that he and Glenn would have understood each other.

She discovered an unexpected appetite and heaped her plate, and they found seats at a picnic table. At one end, a woman was commenting on the framed photograph, which had come back from the funeral and was set up on the mantel inside. "Glenn looks so nice in that uniform, doesn't he?"

"He made a fine-looking soldier," someone agreed.

"It was nice they sent an honor guard, but I broke down when they fired the guns. I just bawled like a baby."

"No need to," a bald man said tartly. "He died defending the country against communists."

Sitting across from Sparrow, Amy caught his glance, with its flicker of sympathy, and maybe a little warning, too. She didn't need it, though. She wasn't going to cause a scene by speaking her private views. Even so, she made sure to keep her mouth full of food. The drift of the conversation, however, kindled other sentiments. "I'll tell you this," declared the bald man, "if we don't nail the slant-eyed sons of bitches over there, we'll be fighting them here on the beach."

There were murmurs of disagreement and assent.

"Johnson's in a no-win situation," someone proposed. "I mean, how's he going to get out of this thing?"

"By winning."

"Or withdrawing."

"Spit on that!" said the bald man, jabbing his fork into a mound of potato salad as though there were something in it he wanted to kill. "We've never lost a god-damn war! Why should we run from this one?"

In a conciliatory tone, a woman said, "The president himself sent a personal note to Ev and Jen on White House stationery. Imagine. As busy as the man must be. It just goes to show . . ."

All at once, Amy's uncle, who was sitting at the end of the table pushing food around on his plate, shoved to his feet. In the motion, he upset a pitcher of lemonade, which poured across the oilcloth and set people to backing up, dropping napkins to stanch the flood.

"Glenn is dead!" he declared in a choked voice. "God, why can't we just tell the truth for once? My son is dead. And all this talk, and gun salutes and letters from the White House can't . . . can't . . ." His voice broke. Lurching away, he rushed inside. Amy got to him first. She put her hands on his shoulders and led him into the living room, where he collapsed onto a sofa in spasms of grief.

There were four of them as Sparrow and Amy got outside. They were suntanned and in trunks and T-shirts, standing by an old beach wagon. A cluster of surfboards leaned upright against the tailgate. Sparrow wondered if they were the kids he had watched from the cemetery. They were drinking beer—looked just old enough to be—and there were empty cans on the curbstone. Maybe it was just a casual thing, a chance to hang out and talk, perhaps even mourn in their fashion, and Sparrow was ready to give them this benefit; but something in the way they fell silent as he and Amy approached alerted him.

"Hi," Amy said.

The young man on the end held up his beer can in a toast. "So when you going over?" he asked, looking at Sparrow.

Rawboned and tough, his sun-bleached hair clipped short, he looked more suited to crashing defensive lines than balancing on a sliver of fiberglass and foam. "Over and serve your country," he elaborated. "You want to stop the war, right? Somehow you don't look like a flower-waver. I figure you mean to win it."

Sparrow remained puzzled. The kid rapped his knuckles on the nose of the Impala, and Sparrow saw the kid was referring to the sticker someone had pasted there in the Haight-Ashbury, still visible on the hood: DRAFT BEER, NOT MEN!

Before Sparrow could explain how it had come to be there, Amy said, "Don't you think that would work? And it'd be more fun."

"Dig it," one of the other surfers said, and they laughed, except for the rawboned kid. "The way to stop it," he said, "is wipe out the gooks."

Maybe because she'd been keeping herself in check all day, or because several glasses of wine had taken her inhibitions down, Amy didn't back off. "Explain to me how that ends a war."

"Real easy. You bomb the place back to the Stone Age, then stir-fry the gooks with napalm."

"Come on, guys," Sparrow said reasonably, wanting to break the tension. "Were you friends of Glenn?"

"Were *you?*" the one shot back.

Before Sparrow could answer, another of the surfers, the smallest of the four, said, "Cool it, Curt. No one's hassling. Yeah, we knew Glenn. He and my big brother were buddies. Glenn was a great guy."

Curt stepped closer to Amy. "I want to hear what *you* have to say, 'cause it's people like you who got Glenn fucking killed!"

"No." She shook her head. "You know that isn't true."

"Waving your goddamn love beads instead of a flag!"

"Glenn was my cousin," Amy said quietly. "I loved him."

It silenced everyone. Then, whether the kid intended to shove her or was reaching to make a point—or perhaps even offer comfort—wasn't clear, it happened so quickly. His hand went out and Amy stepped back off the curb. She stumbled and her shoulder hit one of the surfboards. The board tipped against the others, taking them down in a clattering domino effect. Sparrow grabbed for the kid, but one of the others stepped in. Reacting, Sparrow speared fingers into the second kid's stomach, making him buckle. Curt came at him, and Sparrow hit him in the nose. It was a short punch, but combined with the kid's momentum it landed with a *pop!* Blood spattered his white T-shirt.

"Jeez!" cried the small surfer. "Don't!"

Curt's hands went to his face. "By dose," he moaned froggily.

"Go on, get out of here!" one of the other surfers yelled.

"I thig you brogue by fugga dose," Curt went on.

Amy gripped Sparrow's arm, and after a moment's resistance he let himself be led to the car. He yanked off his suit coat and flung it into the backseat. He got behind the wheel.

"You didn't have to do that!" Amy said. "It was just so senseless."

"Are you all right?"

"I'm fine. But he's not. Anyway, it was John Wayne bullshit."

"He shoved you."

"He never touched me—and don't say you were defending me. That's an excuse men always use to rationalize violence. I could've talked to him. The others would've gone along."

"He didn't want to listen."

"Maybe no one does. The irony is you probably agree with their politics. You didn't put that sticker on your hood."

"No," he admitted.

Amy sighed. Silence pooled around them. He felt bad about what had happened, but there was nothing to say. The blond kid was pumping himself up to go down to the recruiter one of these days and enlist. Whether this would hasten the day or forestall it, Sparrow didn't know. He did know that the kid wasn't really hurt; Sparrow had pulled the punch. The kid would be cleaned up and back in the surf before they reached San Francisco. But as the miles passed, Sparrow found that nagging him more than the scuffle was his sense that he'd revealed a side of himself that he had managed to keep hidden from Amy till now. He remembered what he had glimpsed in her that day in the I/Thou coffeehouse and later in Golden Gate Park, but hadn't properly grasped. Now he did. However he might secretly scoff at her naive ideals of love, peace, and brotherhood, she desperately believed in them and was willing to take risks for them. She'd have talked to those kids, got them thinking, at least; would've connected on some level other than bone on bone. In Sparrow's world, the simple reality was that when push came to shove and there was no avoiding it, it made sense to hit the other guy harder than he hit you, and maybe more than anything else, that's what made them different.

They rode north like strangers.

The idea of showing Amy the sailboat didn't occur to Sparrow until they were almost back in the city. Its first form was only passing fancy, a peace offering, perhaps, with no more substance than the heat shimmers on the highway. They stopped for gas, and he telephoned the homicide detail and learned from Rocco Bianchi that the case had not been solved in his absence. Sometime after that the notion of showing Amy the boat took hold, and he suggested it. Listlessly, as though she were too dispirited to oppose, she agreed.

The *Blind Faith* lay in her slip, jaunty and self-reliant, her freshly cleaned hull and bright work aglow in the setting sun, as if to say, "See, sailor, I do just fine without you." Stepping aboard, he felt all at once renewed. Amy, too, seemed to become enlivened. For the time being, at least, it was as if the events of earlier had loosed their hold. They stood on deck and she was full of curiosity and comments about the sloop, not least of which was that the *Blind Faith* was an interesting name for a boat owned by a cop.

"Yeah, well, I gave long thought to the *Sea Pig*," he said.

It pleased him to see her smile, and he knew he had done the right thing in bringing her here. The chilly salt wind threshed her golden hair. The fading sun was igniting clouds, covering the bay with sparks. He fetched a key from its outside hiding place, unlocked the cabin, and went below. He brought out a fisherman's sweater that had been Helen's. Amy pulled it on. They stood by the starboard rail looking at the city, the green and brown geometry of its hills and buildings softened in the aftergleam of day.

"It's beautiful, isn't it," she said.

"One of the best," he agreed.

"Though a lot of what goes on in those shining towers is a pretty grubby business."

"Making money?"

"It's part of the problem, don't you think?"

"Mmm. Sometimes. I know that after my wife died I had a time getting the insurance company to pay some of the bills. No one gives you the runaround like those folks." He didn't mention having to go down there and threaten people, nor those actions being reported and put in his department fitness reports.

Amy looked at him. In the paling light her face had taken on another cast, her brow crested in a tiny fleur-de-lis of wonder and sadness. It was one of her qualities to keep surprising him. "You miss her, don't you," she said.

"Yes."

"Helen."

He nodded. Amy waited, perhaps giving him room to say more if he chose to, but he didn't. After a moment, she said, "Thank you for coming today."

"Thanks for having me."

"Bet you could've done without that blowup at the end."

He laughed. "I should peel that sticker off before I get into real trouble."

"I still think the sentiment is a good one."

"You want a beer?"

"Sure, if you've got one."

He fetched two cans from the galley and brought them out.

Amy was smiling one moment; in the next, as she turned, there was desolation in her face. Before he could think about doing it, he put an arm around her shoulder. After an instant's hesitation, she pressed her face against his chest and began to sob. He held her, wondering what he could do, should do, deciding it was probably best to let her cry. But even so, he was left with a helpless feeling. After a time she asked if they could go below.

In the cabin he turned on an overhead lamp. He got her some Kleenex and put several records on the phonograph spindle. John Coltrane started to play. As Sparrow made coffee, Amy looked around, pausing before a photograph. "Helen?"

"Yes."

"She was lovely. I'll bet *Blind Faith* was her choice of name."

Which was true, but it was he, Sparrow reflected, who had clung blindly to hope at the end. When the coffee was poured, they slid into the galley banquette, facing each other. "The music suits you," she said. "Cool, a bit distant and deliberate. But there's honesty there. And power."

"Thanks, I guess."

"It's your generation."

"I never thought of music as generational, but that day in the park—the solstice— I realized it probably is."

"At its best, though, it goes beyond." She drew her knees up under her on the bench seat. "I can remember lying in bed when I was a kid and hearing the radio playing in my folks' bedroom, and it filled me with a sadness because I realized that each one of us is alone, and yet music was a way of trying to touch that."

"That's precocious for a kid."

She laughed. "Most likely I'm thinking this in retrospect."

"Music is important to you, isn't it? To your crowd."

"It's a channel." She was holding the mug close to her face in both hands, speaking to him through the rising steam. "All our energy cycles from us through the musicians and comes out as music. The energy goes around. But a tribe needs leaders, too, and that's where the politicians are failing."

"What takes their place?" he asked skeptically.

"If the music's good enough, really in touch with the magic, *it* can. *Sgt. Pepper's* is doing it now. Have you heard it?"

"Bits and pieces, I guess."

"All over the world the songs are playing on radios and record players and in people's heads, bonding us. The Beatles are shamans, having visions . . . good, bad, inside and out, confronting things that need to be faced. There're other bands, too, some of the best right here."

The sentiments sounded nice, and being here talking with her was nice, too.

Outside, beyond the porthole, the night sky had deepened. On the bay a boat crawled past, reflected running lights bobbing in its wake. The record played out, and in the moment of silence before the next one dropped, a line creaked as *Blind Faith* drew against it. Sparrow could not escape wondering if at that moment a monster was taking energy from his own dark source, stalking his next prey. Chet Baker played his horn.

"Have you been a cop a long time?" Amy asked, perhaps sensing his changing mood.

He drew his thoughts back from the killer. "Twelve years."

"I came across a news photo of you and George Moon. It was taken during the murders in North Beach. Those were never solved, were they?"

He looked at her watching him in the lamplight and felt his pulse quicken. He set his coffee cup down. "No."

"I wasn't here then, so I don't know much about that. Only what I've read. But San Francisco isn't that violent as cities go. Four murders then, and now these . . ." She trailed off.

Sparrow provided the question. "Is there a link?"

"I'm wondering. You know more about that than I do, but is it possible?"

"The crimes are different," he said, resisting the idea. "And there's been a lapse of several years." He felt a sudden urge to tell her why he had left the North Beach killings unsolved, how Helen had been dying and he had turned away from the job. He let out a held breath, and with it his desire to explain. He poured more coffee. "As you said, no one's ever been caught."

After a time, the last record ended. The turntable shut itself off. Amy said that she should be going.

On deck, the fog had feathered in silently. The skyline was a blur. In the other direction, the Golden Gate Bridge was all but buried now, just the pinpoint glow of its red lights visible, like the ruby points of a coronet. Only directly overhead was the sky open, specked with stars. "Did you and your wife sail a lot?" Amy asked.

He looked at her, moved by an obscure desire to tell her about Helen and their final voyage, as though having been invited into Amy's sorrow today, here was a way of tipping the balance back toward equilibrium, mediating their tentative friendship. Huddled there in the cockpit against the night's chill, he was aware of her proximity, the light pressure of their shoulders touching. "Not enough," he said quietly. "Things always seemed to get in the way. Work, mostly. Mine."

Amy nodded. "When I first met you, that time at the press briefing, I pegged you as a nose-to-the-grindstone kind of guy."

"Shoulder to wheel."

"Can I be truthful?"

"Why do I think you're going to be anyway?"

She smiled. "You came across as an uptight fink."

"Ouch. A fink? Thanks for not rushing to judgment."

"It might've been premature." She paused. Her attention was unsparingly direct, and this stirred him. "I had the thought in there somewhere today that you're a good man, Sparrow. I was proud to be with you."

Proud. He wanted to go further, but just then a voice rose from the pier. "Ahoy, the *Blind Faith*."

A figure emerged and stepped into the glow of the slip light. It was the night man from the marina office. Seeing Amy, he looked surprised but nodded, then addressed himself to Sparrow. "A fella came this afternoon looking at your boat. I meant to tell you but clean forgot when you stopped in before."

"A buyer?"

"Visitor. Didn't leave a name, but I rec'nized him. The big fella who used to come by sometimes to see you." Sparrow drew a blank. "He's a cop, like yourself. Well, g'night."

When the man had gone, Amy said, "It's been a long day, I need to get back." Was she picking up on his reaction to the man's message? "We're working from home till the new office gets set up and we're facing a deadline. You've probably got things to catch up on, too."

He didn't want her to go—they had spent the day together, something he hadn't done with a woman in a long time, and the companionship felt good—but she was right. There were things to do. He locked the boat, put the key in its hiding place, and they walked to the parking lot. He insisted that he follow her back to the Haight-Ashbury in his car. She took off the sweater, over his protests, and gave it back. "Thanks for everything."

"Will I see you again?"

"You'll be around the Haight, won't you?"

"I meant . . ." He stopped. What had he meant?

She put a hand on his arm. "I don't think it's such a great idea, John. We've both got our jobs to do. And we're pretty different, you and I."

What could he say to that? That she hadn't seemed to mind Coltrane, or his coffee? He hadn't even listened to *Sgt. Pepper's Lonely Hearts Club Band* yet. "Good night," she said.

It was going on ten P.M. when he drew in behind the apartment building, into the area reserved for visitor parking. The address was in Pacific Heights, in a quiet neighborhood of genteel homes and fashionable apartment buildings, all at a far remove from the tumult of the Haight-Ashbury. As he started across the lot, he stopped. There in a first-floor window was his wife.

Of course, it was illusion. He was looking at Helen's older sister Elaine. Lit by a kitchen lamp, she wore a white sweater, which set off her dark hair, and the resemblance struck him with a force of old longing. For a moment he just stood there. Elaine didn't see him, working as she was at something on the kitchenette counter. Making dinner? He got the idea that she wasn't alone. But she was. She appeared startled when she opened the door, though the look passed quickly to mere surprise and she invited him in. There was a salad on the small ceramic table, which was set for one. On the record player, Sinatra was singing for lonely lovers.

"I didn't know if I'd ever see you again," she said with a note of hyperbole; she was his sister-in-law, after all. Still, it *had* been a long time. Three months? "I'm just sitting down to a late bite. Join me?"

"No, thanks. Elaine—"

"A drink?" There was a straw-basketed bottle of Chianti on the counter.

"Tell me about George and Helen," he said.

For a moment he was sure she was truly baffled by the request, and if she had said so he would have let it alone; as different as the sisters were, they shared a fetish for honesty. But her next reaction caught him unaware. Elaine tipped back her head and laughed. "John, you're one of a kind."

He sank into a chair at the table, his knees suddenly weak. She brought her wine over and sat, too.

"I know there was something between them," he said, though the notion had only come to him with anything like certainty just half an hour ago. The marina man had described Moon, and said a visitor used to come over to see Sparrow, but Sparrow knew Moon never had. So there was only one other explanation.

"That's an imperfect truth, if there is such a thing," Elaine said at last. She got a cigarette, and he fumbled with his lighter, applying flame. "Sure you won't have something? I don't like being a solitary drinker, unless I have to be."

At his silent waiting, she resumed. "You know George always had a special feeling for Helen. He liked to talk to her. God knows they had nothing in common when it came to their views, but I thought it was wonderful that he enjoyed my kid sister, and that you and he got along, even if you were never going to be best friends. Later, when things began to cool between George and me, I wondered if it was my sister he was taken with all along."

Sparrow sat like a man being presented with critical and potentially damning evidence he has missed. Elaine poured more wine. "He resented you, John, because you were a better cop, and because you had Helen."

"I wasn't a better cop," he said through dry lips.

"Let's say you were *happier*, and that made you better. Anyway, later, when we learned about her cancer and you took a leave of absence, the newspapers got on the department because the North Beach case wouldn't close. George imagined it was because you were no longer involved."

"Where did he get that idea?"

"I think I gave it to him. Was I right?"

"It's crazy."

"I was angry with him because if he'd done his share of work, instead of politicking for his own career, then maybe you would have been the one there for Helen."

It was an indictment; he'd lost a wife, she'd lost her only sibling. Sparrow wanted a drink now more than he could ever remember, but he didn't dare interrupt her.

"Before Helen got sick—or knew she was sick, anyway—George had shifted his affections. It was why he'd go to visit her when you weren't around. To talk."

And maybe Helen needed a friend then, too, Sparrow thought. "You knew about the cancer before the rest of us."

Elaine shut her eyes against the smoke from her cigarette. "She confided in me right after the first tests. 'Don't tell Johnny,' she told me. You were in the middle of that awful case, and she thought it would distract you. Dedicated, huh?"

"Go on," Sparrow said in a croak.

"I urged her to tell you, but she made me swear. You know how she could be."

He did. And so for several weeks, on the rare nights when he was home before Helen had gone to sleep, she would ask him about his day of police work, never mentioning her own rounds of tests, and later the diagnosis. Yes, he knew Helen.

Elaine filled another glass with wine and set it before him.

By the time Sparrow did learn of Helen's illness, the North Beach case was over for him, because he could no longer do it. Nor could anyone else, and after several months without a fifth killing, people wondered if the killer had left, or died, or if perhaps whatever dark impulse had moved him was gone. But by then Sparrow's enemy was cancer.

The moment he learned of it, he took a leave and devoted himself to Helen. After the last course of therapy, she asked him to take her sailing. They had gone out on a blue and gold October day, with a steady breeze.

Despite even the ordeal of the treatments, the systemic poisoning of her body in hopes of killing the malignancy, Helen was close to being her radiant self. It was possible to believe the physicians were wrong, that through sheer zest for living his wife would endure. They anchored in a leeward cove off Angel Island, and in a purple twilight, with the lights of the city winking like they might be a distant galaxy, so far away did they seem, they made love for the first time since her diagnosis. After, as he lay in the berth in a drifty doze, he heard the splash. When he got topside she was in the water. Having dived from the stern, she was swimming, as if to prove that she still could, even to suggest, perhaps, that being with him again had revitalized her.

"I shouted for her to come back, but she only waved and kept going. I got underway, and by the time I came about, she'd covered a good distance." He'd told the entire story just once before, to Helen's doctor, but he felt a need to do so again now. Elaine didn't stir except for the motions of smoking and occasionally to pour more wine. "She was chilled when I got her aboard, completely exhausted. That night, she went to the hospital for the last time. Two days later she . . ." He broke off.

The glass of wine stood before him, untouched. He picked it up and drained it, would have drunk anything, so dry had his mouth become. Elaine laid her hand on his. "I don't believe now," she said in a low voice, "nor will I ever believe, that she did it on purpose. Or that you should feel responsible."

Sparrow could make no reply.

"George, though . . . I honestly think he blamed you. If he could have, he would've killed you."

Sparrow almost wished Moon had tried; maybe it would have gotten things out where they could be looked at, agonized—even fought—over, set right in some way. But no, Moon had veiled his anger; and Sparrow had battened down the hatches. For a spell, whiskey had become a solace, but it offered so little comfort he stopped it. He submitted to counseling, but quit after a single session and returned to the job. He was given a transfer assignment to Vice; it scarcely mattered that his heart wasn't in it. And Moon had gone deep inside: deeper than Sparrow had suspected until now. But in displacing his pain, Moon had put it onto others. No longer just a tough cop, he had become badgering and mean, and now . . .

Elaine rose tipsily and went to a sideboard, to get another bottle, he thought, something stronger, perhaps. Instead she hunted in a drawer and came back with a framed photograph, which she clutched to herself. "It's one I managed to spare. That other one, the two of you . . . he crunched that under his boot."

Sparrow knew the picture she meant. It had hung in Moon's office for a time: the pair of them, young men, each with a fraternal arm tossed around the other's shoulder. Helen had engineered the pose. It was more show than real; they were simply too different.

"But this one . . ." Elaine's eyes had softened, though her voice had not. "I think he spared it because she's in it."

She handed him the photograph.

The Chianti was a heat in his cheeks. He gazed at the four of them as they stood years ago on the Embarcadero, windblown, smiling, and happy after a day of sailing. Of the four, however, Helen was by far the most incandescent, her dark hair gleaming, her mouth wide in a smile that seemed to say that all of life should be this joyful. Almost promised that it could be. He studied the other faces in turn—Elaine's cautious, as if she had foreseen something and was making peace with it; his own, angular and bemused, like that of a man not quite willing to believe his luck—coming at length to George's face. He searched its rugged features, looking for something lurking and tenebrous. If it was there, however, he couldn't find it. Moon merely looked sun-dazed and content. He handed the photograph back.

"Alive, she was the best of us," Elaine said, and her voice had lost its edge. "But with her dying, I don't know . . . I see what it's done, what's become of the two of you."

And of you, thought Sparrow: alone with your wine and Sinatra, that shaman for the lonely-hearted.

"George thinks you cheated him," Elaine said dolefully.

"What do you mean?"

"He lives with the idea that if Helen had lived, she'd have left you for him. It's foolish, but it's his unshakable belief. Now he's too far gone. You've noticed, of course?"

Sparrow thought of his encounter with Moon in the parking garage; but he didn't bring it up. If Elaine didn't know, what purpose would it serve? "He's different," Sparrow said carefully. "The attitude, the GI haircut . . . but then, he's been a hardcase for years."

She smiled at his neutrality. "Not like now."

No. It was true. Moon had been a sweeter man once. But, as if by a slow accumulation of poisons, his views had shifted for the worse.

"It's the cancer," Elaine said.

Cold dread stirred at the back of Sparrow's mind. "Cancer?"

"He's obsessed with it. Utterly. It killed Helen, and now he imagines it everywhere. In the city, the whole country. The land is being devoured with it, he thinks. He's half out of his head with rage. Haven't you seen it? He hates the hippies."

Sparrow glanced up, and as he did, a sudden look of something deeper invaded Elaine's sad mask—a sharp alarm, he saw, at the thought that he hadn't given voice to, but which she clearly suddenly shared: did George Moon hate the hippies enough to kill them?

Her hand came to her mouth, a gesture at once theatrical and chillingly real. "My God," she whispered.

20

AMY SPOTTED THE WINE BOTTLE GLINTING ATOP A STUMP IN THE UNDERGROWTH, AND took the otherwise unmarked turn for Windflower Love Farm. The phone call had come that morning, ringing in the rented space Seth had found for the *Rag*, a dusty storefront on the edge of the Fillmore district. "Are you all right?" Terry Gordon's voice had had a filament of tension running through it.

"I'm fine. Where are you?" she asked, puzzled.

"At a payphone, in Marin. I've been trying to reach you." She understood. The telephone had been hooked up in the new office space only that morning. She told him this, told him about Glenn's death. Terry's condolences were heartfelt; but it was soon clear he had other things on his mind. "Remember Naomi? One of the women here? She met a guy down in the city, and he mentioned he wanted to buy a gun. Naomi's trusting and told him my squatter neighbors are into guns." Terry broke off and Amy heard a ringing in the background. When it had faded, he said, "The guy said he might need one to protect himself—and to protect you."

"Me? Who is he?"

"Damned if I know. He seemed a little strange. Did you write a letter recently? Something addressed to the Death Tripper?"

The ringing sound came again, and she realized he was at a gasoline station. "When was this, Terry?"

"Whatever three days ago was. I tried to reach you. Your number's been out. But here's the thing . . . as I drove out today, I saw through the woods that his wheels are still over at the squatters' place."

"I don't follow you."

"That's what I'm saying. He drove Naomi back up here in this old beat-to-hell white van he's got."

The hairs on Amy's nape prickled. "What does it look like?"

"Like a planetarium. Moons and stars all over it. You know him?"

Terry Gordon was splitting wood in the yard when she got there. He peered under the flat of his hand at the car. Finally recognizing her, he set the ax aside and came toward her, walking hard. "What are you doing here?" he demanded.

"Hello to you, too, Terry."

"No, you turn around and go. I didn't call you to come up here."

"I need to speak to the person you said was here."

"I was passing along information, warning you, maybe."

"Where is he?"

"He's gone, I told you."

"You said he was still around."

"I said I saw the van." Impatiently, Terry glanced in the direction of the woods where they'd heard gunshots during Amy's previous visit. "And I said the guy was strange. What's this about?"

She told him about the white van in the Haight, and about John Sparrow. He clearly didn't like what he was hearing, especially the part about her involvement with a cop. "What do you figure to do about it?" he asked when she'd finished.

She had already considered this. Her best approach, she realized, was as a journalist looking for a story. "Perhaps this is all nothing, Terry—it may not even be the same van, and I don't know who the person might be, but I have to find out."

"Why don't you go back? I'll find out and let you know."

"I'm here now. I'm going to go over there."

Terry sighed. "All right, if it's that important, we'll go together."

"Wait." What would his role be? A trip-sitter? Bodyguard? She had the strong impression Terry and his neighbors didn't get along. "I'd rather have you here. I'll give you a number to call just in case."

"Whoa, in case of what?"

"Wrong choice of words, sorry. It's probably just better if I go alone. Some people don't like to talk if there's a crowd." He persevered about going with her, but she was equally firm and he relented at last, though only with her promise to come back at once if she suspected trouble. Amy wrote Sparrow's name and work number on a page of her notebook. Obviously unhappy with the idea, Terry took it. "I may have some talking to do," she said, hoping the confidence in her voice sounded real. "Give me an hour."

With its elegant hush, the gleam of old brass along the bar rails, and the green carpets and table linens, the Top of the Mark always made Sparrow feel as if he had entered an aquarium. The effect was heightened by the walls of surrounding glass, through which afternoon light filtered in pale rays, revealing a modest assortment of quiet people sitting over quiet drinks. A handsome black man in a tuxedo played a grand piano; the soft tinkle of notes might have been bubbles rising. Not that Sparrow frequented the Mark Hopkins Hotel, or anyplace on Nob Hill, for that matter. Earlier he'd had a call from Frank Austin, asking to meet him here at three o'clock. "And let's keep it between us," the homicide chief had said.

Now he wished he had taken time to put on a fresh shirt, but he'd stayed at the latest crime scene until the last minute, and so had to settle for pausing before a mirror to tighten his tie. Even so, he felt windblown as he approached Austin, already settled at a distant table, a drink before him. He motioned Sparrow into a chair.

"I never tire of this," Austin said. Sparrow supposed he meant the comfort. He certainly didn't mean dealing with yet another murder. "Any developments?"

The question hung a moment as a waiter took Sparrow's order for bourbon and left. Sparrow said, "We spoke with a few people who were on the street the other night and may have seen something, but they aren't sure, and no one could fix a time. They didn't pay much attention. The MO points to our guy. Hoagland promised autopsy results on victim number five later. Maybe we'll get lucky."

Austin took the news with a sip of his drink, and then set the glass to one side, the way a man might clear a desktop. "I didn't say much on the phone, because I wanted this between us." He drew himself closer to the table and lowered his voice. "Off school grounds, so to speak."

Sparrow felt a ripple of anxiety. "All right."

"Sometimes a little direct cooperation between branches keeps things moving, circumvents the bureaucratic bull. I've been at City Hall this afternoon. Just as you do up here"—Austin made a sweeping gesture that indicated the wraparound views of the city, fogbound at the moment—"you get an interesting perspective from City Hall. For instance, there are some voices there that speak for getting George Moon back."

"To join our investigation?"

"I'm afraid so."

"Not in your job?"

"No, Moon's better off where he is. The plan would be for a dragnet through the Haight-Ashbury using the TAC Squad." The idea struck Sparrow as reckless, absurd. TAC was trained for riot control, not criminal investigation. "They think they'll catch more fish than we're getting."

Breaking heads? Dammit, that was idiocy. Sparrow's face was hot. If the people in the Haight were wary of the cops now, what would be the effect of sending in TAC? He knew. Some people would abandon the district; but others, certainly the members of Mob Grope, would resist, even revolt—Off the Pigs!—and Moon would get what he was really after. "This is talk, right? The mayor's not considering it?"

"It isn't a given," Austin affirmed. "These are a few voices for now. But there's not a soul in City Hall who doesn't want this Haight-Ashbury business to end."

Did he mean the hippies or the killings? Or both?

"Tourism is starting to slide. People are changing vacation plans, canceling reservations. Some at City Hall are asking how long before one of the big conventions decides to bail out. It could set off a chain reaction."

And, Sparrow could not help thinking, there was an election year ahead.

"On the other hand," Austin went on, "if we could slam this case shut ourselves, find the killer . . . we could preempt Moon. And who knows? There could be some wiggle room in the Hall of Justice. Maybe for both of us."

More people had begun to come into the restaurant, drifting into the aquarium light as high tea time approached. All at once it occurred to Sparrow that everything till now had been preamble, that the drinks themselves were stage props and Austin would walk off leaving his barely tasted. This meeting wasn't about the killings; it was about careers. Sparrow was offended at this misuse of time—his as well as Austin's—the extravagance of pandering to City Hall, the presumption that he, Sparrow, needed a pep talk—or worse—a motive to do his job. He drank his bourbon down, desiring another, would've ordered one except there wasn't a waiter to be seen. He met Austin's gaze. "If the idea is that I need an incentive—"

"Only *added* incentive."

"It's not necessary. Regardless of who the victims are."

"Meaning no one at City is crying over the great unwashed?"

"Meaning that's the job, Frank. Okay, you got me out of the leper colony. I owe you. But I don't need a damn sales talk."

Austin bristled, but he maintained a faint smile, and his firm gaze. "How about allies? Can you use some of those?"

The man had a proven talent for navigating political seas; still, it wasn't a course Sparrow favored. Winds could change abruptly, and when they did it was amazing how quickly what you thought were shipmates proved, in fact, to be rats eager to jump. No, better to tie yourself to the mast of your own talent and capacity for work, even if it meant you sailed alone.

"I'm all right," Sparrow declared.

"That's what I told them, John. But just so we understand each other, I believe in laying my cards on the table." Which wasn't true; Austin had shown himself to be a shrewd bluff player. Sparrow hadn't forgotten the empty file folder Austin had used the day he broached Sparrow's return. "There are some who'd say you burned bridges after your wife died." Was he thinking he had taken too much risk by bringing Sparrow back? "*I* don't say that, but there are some." He glanced at the empty glass and the thought wisped through Sparrow's mind that this meeting was a test. Was Sparrow succumbing to pressures the way he had once before? Drinking too much? Being argumentative? Would he fail?

"Who is it?" Sparrow asked.

"What?"

"Complaining? Men in the detail?"

"No."

"They're the people I work with. Anyone else is irrelevant."

"One or two of the guys are probably waiting to see."

"But not Sandoval."

Austin shook his head. "The kid just wants to hump the boonies. He's glad being there."

Sparrow felt affection for the young cop, and even a grudging sympathy for Austin, like a spider in danger of becoming entangled in the intricate web of his own ambition. "I'm going to say it once then, Frank. Maybe I should've that day we talked. I didn't think I had to. Helen died. I buried her. That's the past. I don't expect it to come up again."

Austin had lost the moral high ground. He nodded. "All right. Where we're at, then—it's really this simple—I can keep City Hall and Moon off us a while longer. You find the killer."

Amy skirted the edge of a meadow speckled with Shasta daisies, brown-eyed Susans, and wild lilies. Part of her wanted to go sit among them and forget all this;

and a few days ago she might have done that. Groove in the grass. Hang loose. But she couldn't. With Glenn's death, the fire, Jester's odd withdrawal, and her conversations with John Sparrow about the killings, something had changed in her. She felt disconnected from that earlier self. Impelled by a sense of agitation and mounting curiosity, she turned her steps toward the trees flanking the rutted road and entered the woods.

The terrain sloped downward through pine forest. After five minutes of walking, just as she was beginning to sweat, she saw the van.

It sat at the edge of a small clearing, a pale boxy shape amid the greenery, still several dozen yards away. As she went nearer, it took her a moment to realize that the van had been ruined in some fashion. The window in the side facing her was shattered, and the side panel looked to have been spattered with mud. The tires were flat. But despite the destruction, there was no mistaking the vehicle, as its fanciful pattern of planets and stars made plain. It was the same one John Sparrow had chased in the Haight. His questions that day came to her now: Who was driving it? Who had they been watching? Why?

But now a more immediate concern insisted itself as she reached the van and discovered that what she had taken to be spots of mud were in fact bullet holes. The van was peppered with them, the tires shredded. This gave her a moment's pause. Overcoming it, she peered inside through the shattered side window.

Daylight leaked through the bullet holes in thin yellow pencils that lit the interior. The upholstery was tattered, the paisley curtain over the rear windows torn. On the carpet in back there were several large, dark stains. She stared at them, imagining what they might be, not quite daring to find out. She stepped back and looked around. Was someone else here? But the gloom of the surrounding woods was as before. A dragonfly landed on her arm, stayed a moment, then darted away.

Her heart beating fast with the possibilities of her discovery, she walked around the van. This close, just visible under the riddled paint job, she could make out faint words. KATSOUBAS'S BAKERY, ASTORIA, N.Y. The driver's door was sprung slightly. She tugged the handle. With a grating screech the door opened. She had changed her mind about trying to speak with anyone right now. She would quickly search the van, and then go find a phone. It was time to call Sparrow.

She leaned into the front compartment. On the dashboard, amid the chips of broken safety glass, were gas station road maps, old cups from fast food stands. In the ashtray there were several roaches. She was still aware of the stains on the back carpet, but put off examining them. On the passenger-side floor she found a thin brown strip of acetate, which she followed to its source under the seat. She pried out a broken cassette tape. Handwritten on the shred of label remaining on the shattered plastic casing were a few letters that didn't form a word. At just that moment, a cracking sound seized her. She turned.

Bolting into the clearing was a dog. It was a dark, heavy thing, and it was coming straight at her. Her heart began to pound so hard she could scarcely breathe. She froze. She heard the quick scrape of its paws on the ground, the exertions of its charge.

At the last instant, as it lunged, its jaws snapping and teeth bared, she scrambled into the van. She yanked the door partly shut—and not a second too soon. The dog hit the panel with a shuddering *whump* that Amy felt through the door. She looked out the broken window.

The dog lay on the ground. Reflexive spasms twitched its flanks, but it was otherwise still. Fearfully, Amy scanned the clearing and the surrounding woods. Were there other dogs out there? People? Should she cry for help? Wait for Terry to get worried and come looking for her? Should she get out?

She looked more closely at the dog. It appeared to be some kind of mongrel, with powerful legs and a heavy, barrel-like body, and it occurred to her now that the dog hadn't made any sound. Throughout its charge and its leap, it had been silent, and somehow this chilled her in a way that a loudly barking animal wouldn't have. That was enough. She scooted across the seat to the other door. She had to shoulder it several times till it opened with a grating creak. She jumped out and darted for the woods. Time to get back to Terry's.

She was partway up the slope, less worried about making sound than making speed, when she turned and saw the dog. The hairs at her nape prickled. It was the same dog, moving around the front end of the van, nose to the ground. Before she could react, it caught sight of her. For a moment they seemed to regard each other, then, like an image in a bad flashback, the dog started to charge.

There was a buzzing sound in her ears, and she felt her stomach go hollow. The road lay too far away. She'd never outrun the animal. Still, she had to try. Moving, she scanned the trees, frantically looking for one to climb. None had limbs low enough to reach. She glanced about for a fallen branch or a rock, something she could use to defend herself. The moment's distraction was enough for her to stumble. She went sprawling. One hand hit the ground, sent up a spurt of loam and pine needles, but miraculously she stayed on her feet. She was almost to the top of the rise when the dog hit her.

The impact knocked her forward, and she fell hard. Instinctively she rolled away, just ahead of snapping jaws. Even so, the dog caught hold of her sandal, tore it off. She struggled to get her breath.

The dog circled closer, its lips skinned back, mouth dripping. Amy sensed that it wasn't just holding her there, awaiting its owner. It wanted to maul her. Desperately she looked for a stick, something . . .

The dog lunged. She kicked, felt her foot jolt against its head. The dog leaped back. Again it came at her, and again she kicked. Her breath was coming in fast, hard bursts. She was pivoting on the ground, trying to keep the animal at bay. It lunged again, and she kicked, but too late realized the animal had outflanked her. It clamped its jaws on her ankle. She kicked it with her free foot, catching the dog on the side of its jaw, but it held on, making no sound beyond a strangled breathing. Teeth broke her skin, compressed the bone. Pain shot up her leg. And just then, at the corner of her vision, she was aware that two men had stepped from the trees. One carried a rifle. They made no move to call off the dog.

"Stop him!" Amy screamed.

The man carrying the rifle reached down and yanked the dog back by its collar. Shouting something that sounded like "Geddah!" he gave the animal a boot. It skittered back a short distance and stiffened, on the alert. The other man came forward and looked down at Amy. He had a beard that hung over the front of his dirty T-shirt like a brown bib. "Up," he commanded.

Shakily, breathlessly, she got to her feet.

"What the hell you doing here?" cried the bearded man.

The dog stayed where it was, twitching like coiled wire, soundless, as the second man stood over it. Amy's heart was pounding, her breathing still fast.

"Speak up!"

"I was looking at that van."

"You were, huh? Planning to buy it?" His voice had a fretful impatience.

The other man held the rifle cradled across his chest and looked on. They were a hairy pair, in soiled jeans and T-shirts that fit tightly over heavily muscled chests and shoulders, but in contrast with the dog, they were welcome. Some of her control returned. "Do you own it?" she asked.

The bearded man said, "Got a problem with that?"

"No. Were either of you looking for me? Amy Cole?"

The bearded one, who seemed to be the spokesman, looked narrowly at her, his eyes small and deep set. "Yeah, that's right." He glanced at the man standing by the dog, then back. "Amy, sure. Hey, how come you sneaked in here like that? C'mon down to the house with us so's we can talk. Ought to have a look at where you got dog-bit, too."

"It's all right. What did you want to see me about?"

"I think we'd best check it."

"No thanks. The denim of my jeans protected me."

"C'mon anyway. Chainsaw here's got a bad disposition."

The men had moved to stand closer to her, and she could smell them. They stank of stale perspiration and alcohol, and she knew with certainty that neither of them was the person she was looking for; knew, too, that if she went with them, she'd be at their mercy.

"No, thank you. I'm supposed to—"

"Let's go." The bearded man reached for her arm.

Panicked, she shoved him, catching him by surprise. He stumbled heavily backwards.

She ran, actually covered several yards before there was an explosion of light that had her waiting for the blast of the rifle. What came instead was swift and utter blackness.

THE TALL LONGHAIR PUSHED AWAY FROM A DUSTY BLUE CITROEN AS SPARROW DREW into the Texaco station lot. Dressed in coveralls, he appeared to be in his early forties, his eyes agitated behind circular steel-rimmed glasses. He bent toward the window of the Chevy. "Sparrow?"

"Professor Gordon?"

"Terry's good. Leave your wheels here and ride with me. It's best if no more strangers show up. We'll rap on the way."

Sparrow locked his car behind the gas station and climbed into the Citroen, where Gordon was already hunched at the wheel, gunning the motor.

Driving fast along backcountry roads, Gordon explained his phone call, and the one earlier to Amy, prompting her unexpected visit, first to him and then to his squatter neighbors, whom he knew little about except that he didn't like them. Amy had been insistent on going there but wouldn't say why, and wouldn't agree to let him go with her. Sparrow understood; she wanted to learn about the white van. "When was this?"

"A few hours ago. I hiked partway down there but didn't see anyone. That's when I decided to come call you."

"How many squatters are there?"

"I'm not sure. They're pretty reclusive. A couple anyway."

"You consider them dangerous?"

"Troublesome, maybe. I've let them be."

"Is there reason to think they'd hurt Amy?"

"Why don't you tell me?" Gordon glanced over. "Look, I don't know why she went there, or why she came running up here after I phoned her. What's this about? Who are you to her?"

Sparrow hesitated. "The same as you," he said. "A friend."

Only on the lay of the land was Gordon able to offer much information, describing the dirt road and the deep woods that sloped toward the edges of his land where the squatters had taken up residence in a pair of old shacks. Occasionally, said Gordon, there was gunfire down there, target shooting, he thought. It was clear that Amy hadn't told him much, yet in giving him Sparrow's name and number, she had foreseen the possibility of trouble. Worriedly, Sparrow wondered if she had found it.

At Gordon's farmhouse a pregnant woman in a peasant dress met them and said Amy had not returned. The old Volvo sat in the yard where she had left it. Gordon swung a U-turn and they went back along the dirt road. At last he braked and pointed downhill into thick woods. "This'll get us there." He yanked open his door.

"Not you."

"Bullshit. If I'd gone with her in the first place, none of——"

Sparrow's hand on his shoulder stayed him. "Let's assume the worst. She's in trouble. There has to be someone here in case I need help."

Gordon swore, clearly unhappy with the idea, but rational enough to see its merit. "How will I know?"

Sparrow checked his watch. "Go back to your place. If I'm not there in half an hour, call Inspector Sandoval at the number I gave you. You do have a clock, don't you?"

Each held the other's gaze a moment, then Gordon gave him the finger and put the car in gear. Sparrow waited until he was gone before he took his .38 Special from a belt holster under his coat. Gordon had been spooked enough without seeing the weapon. He knocked out the cylinder and checked the load. Then, hoping it was a needless preparation, he slipped the weapon into his jacket pocket and started down the bank to the woods. On the edge, before the trees began to thicken, he passed an old farm truck that sat rusting and forgotten, like an object lesson on man's impermanence. A leafy vine had wound its way up the radio aerial, like a line of bright green pennons.

There was no clear trail, so he was forced to bushwhack downhill through undergrowth. He was soon sweating. At length he came to a clearing, and there was a van. It sat on flattened tires, against a sandy berm. From the glint of broken glass ringing it, and the shredded rubber, he guessed that the vehicle had been shot up. If it was the van he had pursued in the Haight several days ago, as he suspected (and which Amy must also have suspected when Terry Gordon called her), how had it come to be here? He had to guess that Amy had discovered it, too, identified it, and gone to find out if the driver was around. So why hadn't she returned?

A shimmer of anxiety crept down his spine.

He resisted an impulse to rush forward to find answers to his questions. If something *had* gone wrong and she was in trouble, his haste might endanger her more. *If she wasn't already dead.* He shoved that thought away.

In the hot afternoon, insects sang. A Steller's jay screeched. He was scanning the clearing, looking for something to clue him, when he spotted it. The ground near the van was torn up, as though some kind of struggle had taken place there recently. Going quietly, he reached the van. A quick survey of it convinced him it was the van he had chased. Ghost words were visible beneath the paint: KAT-SOUBAS'S BAKERY. The bullet holes were recent, the edges without rust. He was turning to look inside when he heard sounds. Drawing the .38, he stepped around the rear of the van.

And saw the dog.

He'd expected he might, given what Terry Gordon had told him. A massive thing with a head the size of a basketball, it was groping among the trees on the other side of the clearing. It hadn't detected him yet, but it didn't have to; its presence was enough to hold him where he stood. Something else, however, urged him forward. Amy.

Moving as quietly as he could, he crept around the back of the van, but when he reached the other side and looked toward the sandy bank, the dog was gone. Gooseflesh tingled his arms. He mopped his brow with his coat sleeve, then scanned the woods. At the farthest point, he was no more than a dozen feet from the woods, which thickened quickly and seemed to ooze gloom. Amy might be lying in there injured, or worse. He stepped forward and heard a crash of undergrowth.

He spun. The dog had gotten around to his right unseen. Charging across the short distance it leaped, teeth bared.

Without thought, he dropped the gun and raised both hands. He seized the animal's forelegs and rolled backwards with its impact, curling his spine as he hit the ground, crunching his legs and getting his feet up under the dog. Rolling backwards, he gave a powerful two-legged kick and threw it in the direction of its charge. As it hurtled in an upside-down arc, he twisted in time to see the animal hit the van. With his heart thudding, he rolled to his feet.

The dog lay where it had fallen: eyes vacant, tongue lolling, breath coming in rapid pants. Sparrow picked up his weapon. Taking hold of the rope collar, he dragged the brute toward the rear door of the van. The dog was heavy, but he hefted it up into the rear compartment and slammed the door shut.

He moved in the direction where the dog had first been, toward where Gordon had indicated the shacks were. As he stepped into the woods, something chopped down on his shoulder. He staggered. A bearded, sun-browned shape stood among the trees. The man swung the rifle again. The barrel cracked against Sparrow's collarbone, and his left arm went numb to the fingertips. He started to sag. As the man raised the rifle a third time, Sparrow threw himself behind a pine tree. He rolled away, simultaneously pulling his handgun. He came up on the other side of the tree and wheeled the .38 level with the man's stomach. The man could bring the rifle around, but not fast enough, and he knew it. He froze.

"Drop it!" Sparrow said.

Sun shone on the .38's blued steel. The man hesitated a moment, then set the rifle on the ground. Sparrow got to his feet. "Where is she?"

The man looked as if he might deny knowing anything, but finally said, "Down yonder to the house. I ain't touched her."

"Who else is there?"

"Nobody." The man looked around. "Where's Chainsaw?"

"What?"

"My dog."

Chainsaw. Sparrow almost had to laugh.

A hundred feet along a trail they came to a weathered tarpaper shack. Just beyond it Sparrow saw a second, smaller structure in like condition, with boarded windows. Amy was in the first shack, in a dirty kitchen, tied to a chair and gagged with a dishtowel. She was pale, but her eyes widened at seeing Sparrow. He pulled the cloth away, and she cried, "Thank God!"

"Are you all right?"

"Yes, I'm okay." Her hair had come undone from a cloisonné comb, and hung in loose strands. She had on a denim shirt and her patchwork jeans, now ripped at the cuffs and dirt-stained.

"Untie her," Sparrow ordered the hulking man in overalls.

He went to work on the rope. "We caught her snooping, didn't know who the hell she was."

"Who's we?"

"There's a second one," Amy said. "He left to make a phone call. He could be back anytime."

As the man unknotted the rope, Sparrow looked quickly into the adjoining spaces, satisfying himself that they were alone. The small rooms were bare except for pallet beds and heaped clothing. The whole place had a rank smell of unwashed bodies: man and dog. When Amy was loose, Sparrow checked her ankle. The skin was broken in several places, but the bleeding was minimal. She said she could walk. "The van out there is the one we saw in the Haight. I don't think it's theirs, though."

"What the hell's this about?" the man demanded. "I want to know who you are, come busting in here."

Sparrow produced his SFPD star. The man didn't look happy. "Tell us about the van," Sparrow said.

"Never seen it before, or the guy driving it, neither, till he showed up a few days back, and that's God's truth."

"Who was he?"

"I don't know. He wanted to buy a piece. About like what you got there. Say, you mind puttin' that thing down? I ain't happy lookin' at it."

"Keep talking."

The man dragged a hand down his beard and grimaced. "The van croaked on him. He hung around trying to fix it. Day before yesterday he said he was gonna get a part for it. That's the last we seen him. He took the license tag, left the van and split."

"With a gun?" Sparrow asked.

"Yeah. He had a big-ass motorcycle in the van, all black and shiny. He rid out at night."

"You see the tag on either vehicle?"

"The van was New York, I think. It was bust for good. He burned the damned universal on the road in."

"So you used it for target practice."

"Christ, try gettin' parts. Wish he'd left that scooter."

"How about his name?"

"He never said it. Anyways, names don't mean squat, especially when someone ain't looking to be found."

Sparrow and Amy exchanged a glance. They were all standing in the filthy kitchen. "What makes you say that?" Sparrow asked.

"You being here—and her. That's what this is about, right? He wanted for something?"

Amy spoke up. "I heard he was asking about me. I thought he might still be around. We'd like to talk to him."

"So would I. Lay some hurt on the little sonofabitch."

Sparrow's interest sharpened. "Little?"

The man held a flat palm at the point where the bib top of his overalls ended. "Come to about here on me."

Which made him five-feet-five or so. It tallied with the estimates that Chang and Hoagland had made about the Haight-Ashbury killer. "You remember anything else about him?"

"If I do, I'll get in touch."

Sure you will, Sparrow thought. They went outside, and only then did he holster his weapon. "You okay to walk?" the man asked Amy. He was helpful now, eager to see them gone. Amy limped slightly on the wounded ankle but otherwise seemed fine. As they started away, the man called after them: "What about Chainsaw?"

"How bad?"

Terry Gordon was waiting at the farm, and now, as Sparrow helped Amy into the yard, he rushed to meet them. He led them inside where the pregnant woman Sparrow had seen earlier—Sister Sarah, she called herself—got Amy seated, cleansed the bite wound on her ankle, and wrapped it with clean gauze. Sarah went into the kitchen to prepare some food. As Amy went to clean up, Sparrow told Terry Gordon what had happened.

"Those creeps. I'm going to send them packing," Gordon declared darkly.

But Sparrow suggested that he wait a few days, that the squatters might save him the trouble. "You said you don't know much about them. Do you know what they're growing down there?"

Amy had been listening from the doorway. She came back over, her hair drawn back with the cloisonné comb. "That's what I was smelling. Pot."

Gordon seemed genuinely surprised, but he didn't need much convincing. It would explain things, he said. The dog, the guns, the attitude. "There's a sunny field beyond the shacks, and water. Is that what this is about? Is that what you're after?"

They told him the story, starting with the white van and the strange phone call from the person who'd read Amy's letter to the Death Tripper. Gordon listened intently, then, without a word, went outside. He returned accompanied by a big woman in a loose-fitting flower print dress whom he introduced as Naomi. She appeared to have been gardening: her hands were soiled, her face and arms red with sunburn. Recognizing each other, she and Amy exchanged greetings. She gave an uncertain glance at Amy's bandaged foot and sat on the edge of the couch.

"Naomi's the one who rode back from the city with the guy in the van," Terry Gordon said.

The woman looked at Sparrow. "You're heat, right?"

"I'm a homicide inspector."

"They're not here to hassle us," Gordon said gently.

The woman didn't look fully convinced, but Terry's endorsement encouraged her. Sparrow drew over a chair. Amy took out her notebook, so he didn't bother with his.

"I'd gone down to the city, to pick up supplies and catch some music," Naomi began. "I met this dude, we got talking. He offered me a ride, which was cool. I said he could eat with us, even crash a few days if he liked."

Terry Gordon, who'd been standing by the woodstove, came over. "Tell them what he asked you."

"About the gun, yeah. He gave me this trip how the law was after him. I thought he meant, like, right then, like pigs'd be coming through the door any second. No offense. He said they'd been after him a few months, said if they found him, his ass was grass."

"Did he say what pigs?" Sparrow asked. "Or why they were after him?"

"Just that he wanted to be ready. I told him we aren't into guns, like, we've got children and animals and we're growing vegetables up here, but I guess I mentioned that the squatters had guns." She shrugged. "I felt for him. He was a gentle soul, kind of lonely. Anyway, we rode back here in his van."

"When was that?"

"Three, four days ago. You remember, Terry?"

"Tuesday, I think."

"He was welcome to stay," Naomi repeated. "I mean that's what this place is about, you know? Right, Terry?"

Terry Gordon said, "That's when your name came up, Amy. He thought you could be in danger, but when I pressed him he wouldn't say how. He seemed a little strung out on nerves to me. After he left I tried to call you, but your phone was out."

Amy looked at Sparrow and he was pretty sure she was wondering the same thing he was. Was the van driver the same person who had telephoned her? The same person who had been watching them the other day in the Haight?

"He was uptight for sure," Naomi went on. "The whole ride up he kept checking mirrors, driving like he thought someone might be following. He'd been talky and friendly in the club when we met, but now he clammed, you know? In a way, I'm glad he didn't hang around here long."

"But obviously he went down to see the squatters," Gordon said. "Did he get what he was after?"

"He got a handgun," Sparrow confirmed. "The van broke down and he left it behind and apparently went out on a black motorcycle."

"He had it in the van," Naomi said. "It said 'Vincent' on the tank, but I don't think that was his name."

"It's a kind of bike," said Sparrow. Amy jotted it down. "Do you know his name?"

Naomi crinkled her brow in a show of concentration, as if the name might suddenly burst to mind. It didn't. Gordon didn't know it, either. Their description matched what the squatter had given: a lean man on the short side of medium height, dark hair just over the tops of his ears. Naomi found him good-looking, somewhere in his mid-twenties. There was disagreement on whether he had a mustache. "What's he done, anyway?" Naomi had grown agitated. "Is he the Death Tripper?"

"We don't know," said Sparrow. "We're trying to find out."

"Sweet Jesus. To think I was with him."

The pregnant woman brought in bowls of homemade guacamole and salsa and chips. From outside came the sounds of children at play. After a time, Amy said, "Naomi, where did you meet him that night?"

"A club on Divisadero. The stuff about being followed and wanting a gun, that was later." Her plump, sunburned face beamed with remembering. "At the club we were just grooving on the jams."

Terry Gordon walked them outside. In a wire pen, a few chickens were scratching in the straw. Sparrow noted a thin-chested young man in a loincloth using a hoe to break ground. Two women were plucking weeds from a furrowed patch of earth. The soil was dark, but the crops looked meager to Sparrow's eye, too far behind the growing cycle to give much hope for a bountiful harvest of anything but grubs and crows. The children didn't seem to mind, though, chasing each other and playing with the dogs. Despite the natural beauty of the setting, Windflower Farm didn't seem like much of an enterprise. Based on what Amy had told him about Terry Gordon, and what Sparrow had seen, Gordon was impressive in many ways, but he appeared out of his element here. It struck him that while Pete Sandoval had rejected a life of raising pigs in favor of a Berkeley education, Gordon's path had led him from the university to this hardscrabble farm.

As a gesture of appreciation for Gordon's hospitality, he said, "If your squatters make trouble, let me know."

"What will you do? Launch a tactical assault?"

"Not as long as they've got old Chainsaw. We'll napalm their cash crop and light 'em up."

Terry Gordon grinned. They shook hands and Sparrow climbed behind the wheel of the Volvo, which he and Amy would drive back to the gas station where his car was. She and Terry Gordon chatted a moment longer, hugged each other, then she got in. They had just started away when Gordon shouted. Sparrow braked. Naomi had come running out of the farm house, moving quickly for a big woman, her bare feet and the hem of her long dress sending up swirls of dust. She was winded from the dash. "The name I couldn't remember before . . . it popped into my head. He said to call him Bug Tooth."

A distance down the rutted lane, Sparrow drew over and shut off the motor. Amy looked at him questioningly.

"You wrote that name down?" he asked.

" 'Bug Tooth.' Got it."

"Along with a lot more." He studied her. She had sprung back from her trauma. "You did well."

"My journalism training." She smiled. "I thought it would free you up to ask questions."

"I meant the whole day. You showed courage and ingenuity. Maybe we can add some evidence." He hunted in the glove box and found a screwdriver and an adjustable wrench. "Rest your ankle," he said. "I'll be back shortly."

He went down the wooded slope to the clearing where the van sat. Neither the dog nor the squatters seemed to be about, and he had an image of the men hastily harvesting pot. If his guess was right, they would be gone in a few days, with no forwarding address. Using the tools and a handkerchief, he took off the inner door handles of the van, removed the vinyl sun visors, unscrewed the shift knob. He even took the ashtray and its contents. Who knew, maybe Chang could work some lab magic. When he got back to the car, Amy was gone.

He found her standing among the trees on the other side of the road, facing a meadow that was flecked with wildflowers.

"Isn't it beautiful?" she said.

"Yes," he said perfunctorily. "What about your ankle?"

"I need to be moving. Can we take a walk?"

He wanted to get back to the Hall to see if there were any new developments, and to get Chang working on what he'd taken from the van. On the other hand, it was three-thirty; if they went back now they'd be stuck in bridge traffic. And Amy was right, it was beautiful here. The grass was knee-deep, and birds and butterflies flitted among the flowers. As they walked, Amy removed the cloisonné comb and shook her hair loose. "What do you think of Terry?" she asked.

"He was your teacher?"

"Yes. Mostly Seth's."

"He doesn't seem like a natural-born farmer."

She laughed. "He's from Brooklyn." Her smiled faded. "Actually, the reason he came up here has more to do with one of your colleagues than with agriculture."

She told him a story that Terry Gordon had told her, of George Moon's infiltration of the university campus with informants. Sparrow's impulse was to dismiss it as fantasy (like the specter of mind-control experiments at Berkeley), yet he hadn't forgotten his sister-in-law's revelation about Moon's obsession with the hippies, or what Frank Austin had said about the TAC Squad's possible invasion of the Haight. Something twisted in his stomach. "Do you believe it?"

"Terry wouldn't make up something like that."

"Paranoia runs pretty deep on campuses these days."

"Couldn't you find out for sure? You know Captain Moon."

"We don't cross paths very often," he said truthfully.

She tucked a strand of hair behind her ear and took to gathering wildflowers, but as they walked, he began to imagine that her silence was an indictment of him somehow. Finally, to end it, he said he would look into the claim. She handed him the small tuft of flowers. When they reached the far side of the meadow, where it gave way to woods, he could see she was limping slightly, favoring her injured ankle. "Maybe we should go back."

"Can we sit for a minute? This is such a treat."

It was nice to be away from the city, even for a short while. Amy took off her denim shirt and spread it on the grass. She had on a black T-shirt with her jeans. Warmed from walking, her skin glowed. He handed her the flowers, and she began to weave them into her hair. "What I said about you and Captain Moon . . . I know you're not like him."

"I thought a cop was a cop was a cop."

"Pigs." Amy laughed. "I almost choked when you used that word at Terry's."

"I was in deep cover."

Her eyes were smiling, but they were serious, too, probing. "You and Captain Moon were friends once, weren't you."

"We had a connection. It's been a few years, though. He used to date my wife's sister."

She nodded, maybe surprised. He plucked a stem of grass. "Maybe we should get back, we've still got to pick up my car. And you may want to get that ankle looked at."

"All right." But neither of them moved to go. From the woods a bird called. Insects crackled in the high meadow. He said, "George Moon started on the force shortly before I did. We worked together. He was hard-nosed, a bit to the right in some of his views, but he knew where to draw the line between private opinions and public actions. He was a good cop."

And he began to tell it, as he'd known he would from the moment Amy had first asked. He told her about how Moon, a couple years older than himself, had become a mentor to him, teaching him things about being a street cop. Both single at the time, they had shared an interest in the job, and by a curious turn Moon had introduced Sparrow to the sister of the woman he was dating. It was how Sparrow had met Helen. But over time, as Moon made rank, his thinking started to change. Never one for open-mindedness, he'd nevertheless kept personal views to himself; but now they began to come out. He'd reached a low one time when they'd been called to a disturbance in the Fillmore, and someone had mouthed something about "whitey." Sparrow had to pull Moon off the man who'd spoken.

"He started to change in his attitude toward me, too. I see now that it had to do with Helen. Not what you might imagine, but . . ." He hesitated a moment, then told about Helen's cancer, his leave of absence from the police department, and what Helen's sister Elaine had revealed a few nights ago. He told about the assault in the parking garage. In telling all this to Amy Cole, it occurred to him that he had never really talked about it to anyone else; certainly not to the department psychologist he'd met with the one time. Amy listened with full attention. When he was done, she said, "So Moon blamed you for Helen's dying, and the North Beach case not being solved."

It was oversimplified, but, yes, in a sense it was true.

"But you know what?" Amy said gently. "It's Moon's number, not yours. You should let that go and deal with now. Like the attack in the garage. I understand your not telling anyone about it, because of that other stuff, but next time it might end worse." She was watching him with the intent gaze he'd first felt over coffee that day in the Haight. "I mean it. You're carrying the past. Let it be."

He sighed, uncertain he was capable of what she was suggesting. She studied him a few seconds more, as if to assure herself of his resolve, then she lay back.

Several moments passed and he felt himself drawn into a heightened awareness of the two of them here in the deep grass. Birds sang and a breeze whispered around them, carrying a country fragrance. Amy lay there looking up at the sky, her hair rayed on the spread shirt like a sunburst. The wildflowers had wilted and fallen and lay like confetti after a parade. "You're committed to this idea, aren't you," he said gently. She shifted her gaze to him. "Flowers and peace . . . the Summer of Love. You really want it to happen."

For a minute they were both very still, as though caught in a small web. Everything waited with a kind of heavy expectancy at what the next instant might bring. It was a false perception, he knew, but even the insects and birds seemed to have stopped singing. When she didn't speak, he closed the small arc of distance to her face and kissed her.

Her mouth was warm, and for a moment she returned the kiss, then stopped. He drew back, uncertain. She got to her feet, picked up her shirt, and without a word went into the woods. He was harried all at once by the insects that had been absent only moments ago. He wiped sweat from his forehead and went after her.

It was cooler in here, the ground spongy underfoot. He gazed about but could not see her. There was a suggestion of a trail leading farther in through thickets of manzanita and pepperwood. He took it. After a time the bushy trees gave way to a stand of redwoods which vaulted overhead in a green, cathedral gloom. The ground sloped steeply to a small gorge. It was lush with ferns and mossy, head-sized rocks. Had she gone there? He resisted calling out and made his way along the rim.

Pitched to one side of the gorge was a huge, moss-faced boulder. It was flat on top and sporting a wild headdress of ferns and small white flowers. Kneeling among them, looking down at him, was Amy. He tried to read her expression, but it was indecipherable in the shadowed woods.

"I'm sorry," he said, his throat dry.

He didn't realize until he struggled up to where she was that her jeans and the black T-shirt were lying there discarded, as were her sandals. She wore only the unbuttoned denim shirt. He saw where the shirttails spread over her thighs, and through the open front of it he could see her breasts, full and incandescent below the tan lines. The sight of her took his breath.

She handed him a flower. Taking it, he dropped to his knees, facing her. The flower was a small white woodland bloom—a violet or some such—so delicate it would already be in the act of dying, and yet for this moment it was lovely. *She* was lovely. Breathing through parted lips, she was watching him intently, her gaze both distant and penetrating, as if searching for her destiny.

His stomach fluttered. He felt a confusion of impulses: wanting to slide the shirt from her shoulders, to take her, hold her, but afraid to. For a long moment, they remained like that; then, slowly, he put his arms around her.

He inhaled the warmth of her sandalwood, the pine scent of the woods, the tang of her skin and hair, intoxicated by her. He kissed her brow, moving down across her cheek, and she turned her face and their mouths came together hungrily. This time there was no breaking away.

The woods were alive with the pulse of the afternoon: the motion of leaves, the noiseless flit of birds. When her fingers moved to his belt, gently persistent with the buckle, he gripped her shoulders and moved back. "Wait," he said hoarsely. "What about Seth?"

There was a fine dew of moisture on her upper lip, and her hair hung loosely over her shoulders. "That's not going on right now," she whispered. "This is."

A slow surf of objections rose—about age difference, and his not having been with a woman since Helen, and this outdoor setting—then rolled through him and was gone. The forest, becalmed only moments before, seemed to trill with sound.

She hadn't been aware of it at Terry's or in the car, but somehow, in that moment in the meadow when John had kissed her, the narrowness of her escape from death had come upon her with stark recognition. Her reaction had been to run. But that changed, replaced by a sharper sense of being alive. John had searched for her, found her, *saved* her, and in ways she couldn't fully fathom, she was connected to him. The feeling rocked her.

He knelt among the ferns and flowers in a splash of coppery light. She set his shirt atop her own clothes there on the rock. His torso was lean, hard-muscled, like he'd done physical work in his life. First one of his shoes, then the other, dropped into the leafy undergrowth below. She unzipped his pants. He started to speak, perhaps to object, but stopped as she bent and kissed his chest. His hands moved up under her unbuttoned shirt, traced the curves of her waist. He inhaled sharply as he cupped her breasts.

She took his cock lightly in her hand and felt it pulse. He drew her nearer and kissed her throat. Her nipples, aroused by the touch of his fingers, rose. Nerve endings sparked in her belly. His hands moved slowly down the curve of her back, drawing her to him. "You're so beautiful," he moaned.

The last word became something like a mantra, repeated until it was scarcely audible over the calls of birds and the cool sigh of wind in the trees, and then she could hear it only in the warmth of his breath against her.

After a long time, he drew her up. They shed the last of their clothes. He encircled her with his arms, holding her tight, and their kissing became a quickening need. They lay back on the soft bed of moss and ferns and he covered her body with his. The earlier weight of fear had lifted; even the pain in her ankle was gone. She gave herself to him, immersed in the joy of their lovemaking until a sound rose in her throat—Or was it his? She could no longer be sure—and she felt herself, and then him, coming in wave after tremulous wave.

Later, with the deep gold light of afternoon penetrating their bower, as she was leaning against John there atop the rock, pulling on her jeans, something fell from her pocket. He picked it up. It was the broken cassette tape she had found under the seat of the van. She had forgotten all about it. She must have stuffed it away when the dog attacked. John tipped it up to read the letters handwritten on the remaining scrap of label: *the Apo.* "Mean anything?"

There had been no time to make sense of it before, and now she didn't need time. She knew. "It's a bootleg of the New Riders of the Apocalypse."

FOUR

PURPLE HAZE

Something is happening here
But you don't know what it is
Do you, Mister Jones?
—Bob Dylan

AMY COLE KNELT ON THE DECK HATCH OF *BLIND FAITH*, WEARING ONLY A FADED DENIM shirt, the bay breeze tossing her long golden hair. Sparrow was trying to keep his eyes away from where the hem of the shirt lay on her smooth thighs. He glanced toward the marina parking lot, searching for the Volvo.

"What's the matter?" Amy asked.

"Where's Seth?"

"You've got this hang-up about Seth. I came alone."

"Isn't he your boyfriend?"

"My boyfriend?" She seemed to find the word amusing.

"I don't know. Whatever you call it these days."

"That makes it sound exclusive. We've been together a couple years. We met at Berkeley. What's that sound?"

"Seagulls."

"No. That."

Now he was aware of it, too. A thin, intermittent ringing, nagging in its persistence. He tried to shut it out and reached for Amy—and the telephone rang again. He blinked awake.

"Serial number matches. Same van." Just the bland voice, no greeting. And no Amy either. "You there?" Simon Chang asked. Mr. Personality.

"The one from New York?" Sparrow pushed up on an elbow, glancing around his apartment, feeling the full weight of its emptiness, and an accompanying jab of disappointment. "With those two missing kids?"

"I'll get back to you about fingerprints."

"When?"

But Chang had already hung up.

The notice is on page two of the *Rag*, a small item above an ad for longhair wigs, for "day-trippers who want to STAY COOL with their BOSS and HIP on the street!" Somebody trying to locate two kids, Christine Fallon and Edward McClain; and if they, or anyone who knew them, read the notice there was a number to call. This isn't one of the usual appeals to runaways you saw posted around the Haight: PLEASE COME HOME! No, this is after something else. Two kids driving an old white van. Anybody with information is asked to call a 415 number, which you're sure is the police.

You're also pretty sure the kids were the ones who picked you up in the desert after the cycle broke down, though you recall them as Christine and New York Ned. What really grabs your attention is a third name in the notice. "They may be in the company of a man known as 'Bug Tooth,' who rides a Vincent motorcycle."

Your gut cramps. Bug Tooth, and the Vincent. So the cops have got that much. What do you do? Run again? Drop everything and go? But how? Can't take the bike. After a moment's indecision, you realize that the situation isn't hopeless, that that's *all* they've got, a motorcycle and a nickname. They're scratching, but they won't get any closer than that.

For one thing, the Vincent is out of sight.

For another, Bug Tooth is dead.

God, you'd hated the name. Never said so, of course. You'd wanted friends too badly to voice real feelings about anything, and the name was just one more small anguish. You'd endured worse. In fact, you'd been reared from young to expect pain. Taught from the day your daddy found you on the shed roof and said to jump down, said he'd catch you, and then hadn't. "Let that be a lesson to you, boy. Trust only in God, for his burden is easy, his yoke is light." But Daddy's way was not light. Uh-uh. How you got the name, though—how you came to be Bug Tooth— was simple enough.

Happened one evening when you had the job at Tasty Chef. You went in the back door and the night manager looked at you and bust out laughing. He called the other workers back, and they all laughed, though you had no idea why. Finally, one of the window girls—Deb, the cute dark-haired one—shushed the others and said simply, "Children, we've got customers." And then, marching back to the service window, she paused to say sidelong, "Byron, there's a gnat on your front tooth," about the way you'd say your shoe's untied. You scraped it off, a bug you'd run into biking to work, and you pretended to laugh along with the others. The name stuck, and after awhile you didn't care, even took a certain pride in it because it gave you distinction. And though neither knew it at the time, that had also started you being friends with Deb.

Your daddy had begun his church by then. A quiet man with little more than a pretense of learning, he'd lost his mine job and had sought refuge in doing the Lord's work: visiting the sick, mending busted hearts, preparing long, dark sermons on the Word that no one in rural West Virginia needed to hear, even if they could've understood the arcane references, laboriously and erroneously drawn from Hebrew and Greek. And all the while, embarked upon his inspired mission, he'd neglected his own six kids, depriving them of a father, willing them over to the fierce care of his wife—a city girl, herself a college-trained teacher, far more learned than your daddy but frustrated by a society that saw no gain in a woman's having such skills. Your older siblings left as soon as they were able, one run off with a plumbing supply salesman from the North, another sister working the streets of Pittsburgh.

There was the greasy-dark patch of side yard, the one place where it seemed even weeds wouldn't grow, where several generations of your kin, mechanics for the coal mining company, had hauled truck engines slung on chains, and where your daddy had each year offered up an animal to sacrifice.

As you grew to adolescence, you took to spending most of your time alone, having developed a fascination with the empty mines that tunneled the area. Once prime country, it had yielded up rich blue coal for decades. Eventually, however, the shafts played out, the veins exhausted, no longer able to satisfy men's vast appetites. The company left, pulling out safely ahead of disaster. Too old, too cumbersome to move to newer locations, the machinery was simply abandoned, left to die in slow and elephantine agony, rusting away like relics of a forgotten war.

But the veterans of that war couldn't fade slowly, nor relocate. Rooted like weeds, untrained to anything but mining, they had to struggle on in the dying town, rank, hard-bitten men with perpetual raccoon eyes and hacking coughs, and their gaunt women and children, looking for something to sustain them. But even among their desperate kind, your daddy found stony soil for spiritual planting. " 'Some seeds fall upon the path and are trampled, some fall among thorns,' " he would quote and misquote scripture. "And some are left to wither . . ." To which your older brother—dead a few years later in a shoot-out with revenue agents who raided his moonshine still—would add, "And some get stuck up to their hubcaps in shit."

You were twelve when the town died. Around that time—perhaps because the operators sensed that people could use some excitement to lift their spirits, though more likely simply because it was passing that way and the operators saw a chance to skin a bunch of hillbillies—a circus came to the nearby county seat. You saw their banner nailed on a tree.

****
FIRST APPALACHIAN APPEARANCE
ELEPHANTS * HI-FLYING STUNTS * CLOWNS
CROCODILE MAN * HUMAN CANNONBALL
MAGIC * THRILLING RIDES!!!
****

The circus set up one October day in the fairgrounds. Looking back, you realize it was a tired little affair, one underfed Indian elephant hauling the posts, a moth-eaten tent, an alcoholic ringmaster—but to your eyes the show blazed with enticements. Walking the midway that evening, under the smoky gleam of lights, you saw the prospect of a world beyond the barren hills and hollows. You thrilled to the allure of barkers' voices, your imagination fired by the acrobats and the sideshows. But most exciting was the knife thrower, hurling the flat blades of glinting steel at the beautiful half-naked blonde strapped to a spinning wheel. Totally unaware of it at the time, you had eventually come to see the knife act as an emblem of the turning of the cosmic wheel. But that was years away, in Cu Chi.

The show stayed three days, and you hung around the tents so much a roustabout spotted you and asked if you wanted to work, be a pilot? You had visions of soaring in one of the aerial midway rides. "C'mon," said the man, leading you behind the animal pens, handing you a pitchfork and pointing at a dung heap. "First you pile it here, then you pile it there." And laughed.

But you didn't mind. You did the work eagerly, already in love with everything about the circus; and when the show left, you stowed away in one of the trucks. Your daddy found you two days later, three counties away, and fetched you home. He hadn't whaled you as you'd feared, or demanded the five dollars you'd earned working. Wordlessly, he led you far out into the autumn woods, pulling over logs and rocks until he spied what he was after. He drew you up to look.

At first you saw nothing among the brown leaves; then, with a startle, you saw it slither. It was big and leathery, thick as your arm. With a quick snatch, your daddy seized the snake behind its fist-sized head and hoisted it, writhing, aloft and began to pray aloud: "Lord God Almighty. . . ." Your marrow froze, for you knew what he meant to do.

It must've made a strange tableau, you've often thought: the two of you there in the woods, like Abraham and Isaac, your daddy praying, "Let this boy, my son, be a worthy sacrifice!" He made you grab hold of the snake, gripping it ahead of his hand, clamping your small fist upon the scaly hardness, you crying and begging him not to let go. But he did.

The snake surged, and you almost dropped it. You held on from sheer terror, feeling the muscles along the reptile's spine tensing like heavy springs, fangs jabbing like hooks, and you knew you wouldn't be able to hang on for long, that it would soon wrench free and bite you and you would die.

But it didn't, and your daddy said you were pure lucky, because you had little faith. He took the snake back, and with a sure, swift motion he slit its belly and drained the blood into the earth, and said that for your sin and all the other sins man had committed, going clean back to Adam, trouble would be yours and your own children's portion and only the precious blood of the Lamb could wash away the stain. "Be on your knees and pray with me, boy," he commanded. And you knelt.

"Do you believe?"

"Yes!" you said.

"Will you receive Him?"

Yes to everything. Terrified. Like you'd been most your life, except for that brief time in the green, crawling in the tunnels. And now that was gone. Your fault. All the others were dead, and you're alive.

For how long?

You snatch another look at the hippie paper. "They may be in the company of a man known as 'Bug Tooth,' who rides a Vincent motorcycle." And the cop phone number. They'd be coming. For Bug Tooth, okay, he was dead; but they'd figure that out soon enough. And the cycle. They quit making Vincents years ago; weren't a lot of them around. Sooner or later they were going to find it. But you have some time yet; not much, but maybe it'll be enough.

The seven-day clock seemed to keep watch, more ominous, Sparrow decided, than the grid map of the Haight-Ashbury, with its five red pushpins. The homicide task force had established an SOP for its daily sessions. With Frank Austin in charge, they went around the table, each member of the group recounting his activities for the preceding twenty-four hours.

Simon Chang was the man of note today. In addition to having made the match of serial numbers on the van, now there was the prospect of fingerprints. Granted, Sparrow had retrieved parts from the ruined vehicle, but Chang had found the prints on them. They were being cross-checked for matches. When it was Sparrow's turn to report, he circulated copies of the current issue of the *Rag* containing the information request he had placed.

"You going hippie on us, John?" Paul Lanin kidded. "An underground paper?"

"Why not the *Examiner* or the *Chronicle*," Hoagland asked, "where people are going to read it?"

Sparrow had wrestled with the same question. In fact, he hadn't wanted to involve Amy any more than she'd already involved herself by running her Death Tripper letter and going up to Terry Gordon's farm to find the van; but she had insisted that she was already part of the case. And she was. Maybe more than she knew. The thought of his hands on her breasts, her legs around him, had filled his sleep the past two nights.

"John?" Hoagland nudged.

"Anyone who has information about the runaways or the van is going to be in the Haight," he said. "Let's give this a try first."

The others had no objection, though they didn't believe the van was a strong lead, either, since there was no direct link to the killer. Sparrow didn't press the matter. As the meeting adjourned, Austin said, "Let me remind you that everyone is watching the city closely—and City Hall is watching us. Let's get something on those prints quickly."

Sparrow approached Rocco Bianchi afterwards. "Did you ever find that profile from the North Beach case?"

"The files are pretty scattered, but I'm still looking. I'll let you know."

"Check for the fingerprint records, too."

When he got to his desk his phone rang. "Detective Sparrow?" a man on the other end asked.

"Speaking."

"You remember the last time you were in?" There was twangy music in the background. "Remember what you asked me?"

"I'm trying. Who is this?"

"Joe, at Honey B's."

Ah, the cowboy bartender. "I didn't recognize your voice."

"It's been awhile. You recollect what you asked?"

"About that stripper."

"Dancer. Star Fleming."

"Have you got something?"

"I'll tell you this—the guy they have working Vice since you left? What a fucking winner."

The conversation's obliqueness grew clear. "I'll look into it," Sparrow said. "I'll let him know that you and I go back."

"I appreciate it. And Star Fleming . . ." Joe the bartender chuckled. "She probably decided she was underdressed and overeducated for this job. Word is she's a singer now, with a band. And I ought to know the name of it—it had a cowboy sound—but it definitely ain't country western."

"New Riders of the Apocalypse?"

"Now how'd you know that?"

He had gotten the address from Amy. It was a large pink Victorian on the upper end of Ashbury, with unpruned magnolias shielding it from the street. For no other reason than to save time, he badged the waif who answered the door, and she let him in. None of the musicians were there, she explained. "Who you should talk to, though, is Circe. C'mon in."

The girl led him through a foyer and into a cavernous, dark-draped room smelling of incense and smoke. A woman sitting in an ornately carved wooden chair, stroking a gray cat on her lap, looked up, and whatever doubt Sparrow might've had that Star Fleming and Circe were the same person was gone. She listened to his introduction and nodded. "I knew you were coming."

"Did Joe call you?"

"Who?"

He realized that Honey B's barman hadn't phoned her. He shook his head.

"I know you've been interviewing people about the murders," she went on, "trying to find leads. Sit down." She waved him to a chair. "You've changed."

"We both have." She wasn't the woman in the glossy photo in Honey B's lineup of dancers anymore—her hair was longer, and her face, while still beautiful, was fuller, with none of the lush come-hither expression of the glossy—but she was the same woman who had walked into the Hall of Justice two years ago to report that she'd had a "vision."

"I'm Circe now."

"Didn't she turn men into animals?"

"Swine." She smiled. "Being a singer in a band, I understand how that works."

He guessed she'd understood it before, undressing for the patrons in the Tenderloin. "What you told me that last time, about the man in the bathing suit . . . it proved to be right."

"North Beach."

"Yes. I'm sorry I never thanked you."

She tipped her head quizzically. "But the case was never solved."

"No."

"And now you're looking for something else?"

"Your band has come up several times lately." He was aware all at once of the irony in this: as she'd once come to him with nothing more solid than a psychic vision, so he was here with trifles. Still . . . "It could be coincidence," he said.

"Or maybe it's a sign of some kind." He couldn't tell if she was mocking him.

She glanced toward the bay windows that faced the street. Sunlight streaked the edges of the drapes, sparking a fern in a terra cotta pot, turning the graceful fronds to green fire. The cat sat on her lap, obliviously licking a paw. She said, "If I did know something, why should I think you'd believe me?"

"I'll take anything I can get."

She turned. "Yes. I see that. It's awful what's happening. This district, these people . . . so much promise for . . . good. For change. These folks are speaking truth. I'm curious to know what you've heard about the band."

Avoiding any mention of Amy, he told her about Naomi at the Windflower Farm, and about finding the broken cassette tape in the van. Circe didn't seem surprised at any of this. "That's what you hope for, of course. That your music will reach people. I didn't know for sure we'd been bootlegged, but every good band has people who want to capture the experience. All music is free in the end. I think of it as a counterforce, holding people together, leading and encouraging them."

"To do what?"

"To not be afraid."

It was an idea he had encountered before, one he couldn't entirely fault, although it seemed naive. She sat back, pausing, as though she'd foreseen a different conversation unfolding. "What else is on your mind, Inspector? I'm sure you're too busy to be entertaining my notions about the power of music or the origins of my band."

He had no more questions.

"Then I have one for you. Are you close to identifying the killer?"

"I wish I could say yes."

She stroked the cat a moment, then set it down. She rose and went over and drew back the drapes. Sunlight poured in a bright shaft onto a table. She waved him over. The table was inlaid with ivory and silver moons and stars, a motif, he realized, reminiscent of that painted on the side of the white van. "Are you familiar with the *I Ching*?" She picked up three Chinese coins and put them into his palm. "Toss them."

He looked at her. She nodded for him to go ahead. The coins clanged on the table, spun briefly, winking sunlight, then lay still. She noted the faces and had him toss the coins several more times, then she consulted a tattered book. " '*Kuan*. Wind and Ocean,' " she read. " 'In the midst of striving you have lost view of the larger whole. Step back, consider, watch.' "

He had begun to feel the way he'd felt one time when he had gone with Helen to City Lights bookstore to hear some poets read: the words teased but made nothing clearer. "Is that supposed to relate to the murders?"

She closed the book and set it aside. "That's for you to decide. But I will tell you this . . . he's here."

Sparrow's chest tightened. In spite of the warmth from the flood of sunshine, something cool brushed him like an invisible finger.

"But I can't see him, he's . . . hidden in some way."

The wood floor creaked. "Hidden how?"

"Masked . . . cloaked. Though that may be metaphorical. I truly don't know. And that's all I can sense."

On the edge of the Haight, Sparrow found a bar. A rundown cantina with cracked stucco and dusty potted palms, it was an oasis after several hectic blocks of boutiques and head shops. The grizzled bartender looked happy for a customer. "What'll it be, brother?"

"Bourbon."

A grin put crinkles under the man's eyes. "Fast forward, rewind, erase." He poured.

Rock'n'roll was issuing from a jukebox, a song Sparrow now recognized as one from the new Beatles album, the song with the same title as the album. You could hardly miss it; it was everywhere. He thought about what Circe had said about music. In a way, he envied people who could respond to something so powerfully as to make it part of themselves. His wife had been like that with her first-grade pupils, taking on their excitements and discoveries as her own. Sweet Helen. He pushed the thought down and drank. The clock on the back bar was a riddle for a moment, and then he saw that it ran backwards. Perfect. He had to smile. Rewind and erase.

He made notes on his talk with Circe, even jotted down the part of the *I Ching* reading he remembered: *Kuan*. Wind and Ocean. Step back, watch, consider. As he wrote, he thought of something else the woman had told him. He was changed, she'd said. Did she mean simply older? There certainly was that. But he sensed she'd meant more.

The barman refilled the glass.

With a clarity he'd not experienced before, he perceived that, since Helen died, his life had become like a house of whispers. He looked at the backward clock as if it might well be the measure of his time, because it was time unlived. He thought of *Blind Faith*, arguably the one vital thing in his life, and how after a day of busting peep shows and cut-rate pornographers, he'd taken to avoiding the boat and going home to his apartment for a deadening round of sitcoms and then the oblivion of sleep. It depressed him that he had settled for so little.

On the street, he found himself thinking about Amy, remembering her as she had been the other day in the woods. He wanted to see her, wanted to take hold of her, feel her nipples under his fingertips . . .

Circe's words intruded. *He's here.* And what Sparrow knew, more powerfully than he knew anything else right now, was that he had to find the killer.

You move in a crouch along the dark narrow tunnel, every muscle coiled. Even your dog tags are ready: one around your neck, the other laced inside your boot— "So when you get your sorry stinky ass blown to hell, trainee," the platoon sergeant in basic used to say, "we got somethin' to send home to yo mama!"—but the feeling of dread that you'd brought with you from home is gone. You creep around a bend, see the flicker of lights, and switch off the flashlight, and there's the small man squatting there on his haunches.

The sensation of lifting the knife. *Wsshhhh,* coming up fast, motored by adrenaline.

Wsshhhh . . .

Your brain jangles with the screams in it.

Nyoong bwong hum uh dow?

Shut up.

Done vee kwa um uh dow?

No.

Dear God, help me! I'm dying!

You scramble awake. Nerves scraped raw. The dream. You lie there breathing fast, and wait. The cries die slowly.

Too tense to sleep, afraid you'll dream again, you rise. You pull on your boots. You open the door and shuffle through the gloom of garden rakes and old auto parts to the bike. Moving by feel, you lift the saddlebags.

Your footfalls silent as the fog, you slip out into the night.

Almost closing time, and the frizzy-haired woman wasn't laughing anymore. Bad sign, Zephyr decided. Twenty minutes ago she'd been cracking up, making him feel like Shelley Berman. Now her manner had become mocking. She picked up the deck of Newport 100's lying on the bar beside her piña colada, knocked one out, and forked it into her mouth. He held a match for her, but she ignored it and used her lighter. Exhaling, she said, "Then how come twins can be different as day and night?"

"How come?"

From practically the moment he'd opened his eyes that morning, he had sensed today was going to be a Snake. Not that it was in the stars. With Mercury in Cancer, Venus and Jupiter in Leo, and Saturn in Aries, things promised to roll along blithely through the heavens for a time, so much so, in fact, that in his radio report that morning he had designated today a Horse. But in his *gut* . . . that's where he'd felt today was a Snake.

"Well, Professor Einstein?" Frizzy was waiting.

The line at Lynell's that morning had been maddeningly slow, and when he finally got a seat at the counter, the waitress—some new chick from East Pig Knuckle—had spilled hot coffee all over the front of his pants. He'd goofed on it, talking in a falsetto, saying it was cool, now he'd be able to sing with the Four Seasons, and got a laugh from the heads, but it wasn't funny. Then he'd gone out to find some lousy turd had knocked over his Vespa, crunched the fender. And if *that* wasn't enough, he'd been late getting down to the station for his report. He tried to tell Marty, the GM, about freak time; the guy read him the riot act, telling him freak, schmeak, a programming clock ran by *real* time! And on and on through the day, till here he was closing in on last call and Frizzy here was hassling him.

"See?" the woman declared triumphantly. "You can't explain it."

Cliff Durkin had come up with the rating scale one buzzed afternoon in Chinatown, half stiff on Fog Cutters. One of those Chinese New Year paper placemats had given him the idea of rating days based on the zodiac, and when he laid it on KPMX and the editor at the *Oracle*, they said, far out. What he did, he ranked any given day on an ascending scale: Roach, Snake, Rat, Dog, Horse, Dragon, Lion. As a campy touch, he called himself Zephyr. It caught on. The Zephyr Report. People planned their whole day around it. He'd once got a phone call from an entomologist at S.F. State weighing in on the survival skills of the cockroach; and then a mutt lover wrote saying even a dumb dog was smarter than a smart horse, and he'd explained he hadn't intended any disrespect or evolutionary sequence, it was just a rating system for the planets and stars, for God's sake, something he'd cooked up when he was three sheets to the wind and more than a few tokes over the line. He could've ranked the days with numbers or letters or green weenies for that matter.

At first it was a gimmick, but the more he studied, the more he'd begun to see that there were indeed secret meanings to the stars. And, even more important, there were people willing to listen.

As Zephyr, he had achieved status. Like Kesey had, and Chocolate George, and

Super Spade. He was *someone*. But Frizzy here was blowing smoke at him and giving him a ration of grief, and all he wanted was to float her fat ass on his waterbed.

"You sure you never heard of the Zipper Report?" he asked.

"You said 'Zephyr' before."

"Or read the *Orifice?*"

"What is this?"

A stranger sitting on the stool at the corner curve in the bar caught Zephyr's eye through the pall of cigarette smoke and rolled his own eyes to convey empathy. The woman's voice had hit a shriller note during the course of the last few drinks, all of which were on *his* tab. "Astronomy's not a science?" he asked, *feeling* more than hearing the words slur.

"Astro*logy*. You're shitfaced."

"Yeah, well . . . there's a moon out. Whachoosay we go outside, take a leak— a *look*—show me your moon?"

"Like hell. I'm staying right here where I'm safe." She poked an index finger against the bar rail hard enough to dent the Naugahyde. "For all I know, you could be the hippie killer."

"You see?" He gave a shrug of surrender. "It's destined. Fated and slated."

Her gaze fogged with momentary incomprehension. "What're you talking?"

"You were meant to sit here tonight, drunk and lonely. Was in the stars 'fore you were born." He slid carefully from the stool and dropped some crumpled bills on the bar. "Here. Hav'nother penis collapsa." He set a course for the door.

Outside, he paused, trying to clear his head. Man, he was cooked. Someone said, "That's a good line. I'll have to try it."

"Huh?" He turned and blinked the scene into focus. The guy from the bar was standing there with a leather bag slung over his shoulder.

"What you said—'It was in the stars.' I'll have to remember that."

"Why? You see me with her?"

"If you'd hung on for last call you might be."

"Any more drinks I'd need a *skyhook* to get it up. Take my advice, you wan' tail, get a better line."

"Smoke a bowl?"

"Now thas a good—whoa."

He grew aware that it wasn't meant as a line; the guy was offering him a pipe, a chubby little brass and bead affair. "It's cool. Go ahead."

They fired it there on the street, standing back against the closed storefronts in the shadows cast by the street lamps shining through the oaks overhead. "I'm Zephyr, by the way."

"I recognized your voice as soon as you started talkin' in the bar."

"Well, great. And you're—?"

"I've heard you on the radio, read your stuff in the paper."

Zephyr smiled; at least someone around here was hip. Smoking, they set off at a stroll, wandering to the accompaniment of the Haight's night sounds. Every once in a while the guy would shift the leather bag from one shoulder to the other as he passed the pipe.

"What you were sayin' before . . . can you explain it to me?"

Zephyr frowned, trying to recall what he had said. He could feel the ideas piled up in his head like unwashed dishes in a sink; he wasn't sure he wanted to deal with them right now. Man, he was buzzed.

"About the stars," the guy prompted. "How that works."

"Lemme ask you somethin'," Zephyr said. "You up for this?"

"Well—"

" 'Cause I don't know if I am. I mean, I can . . . I'm just . . ." He laughed. This was some primo shit here.

"I am curious," the guy admitted.

Well, why not? The truth was astrology interested him because he'd felt it work, an unfolding as orderly as the universe itself once you sussed it out, not that he did entirely, but he had his whole life to learn it. They headed for the park. "Okay," he said, scratching his scalp as if to stimulate thoughts. "Your birthday?"

The guy gave a small, self-conscious laugh. "October seventeenth."

"Libra. What year?"

The man told him.

"Awright . . . now, the moment you were born—when *anyone's* born—the stars are in a certain . . . position." Clumsily, he began shaping invisible orbs in the air with his hands. "And you were part of that. One little spurt of intergalactic goo, y'follow me? Speck of sand on the cosmic beach."

"A speck of sand," the man said.

"But your being there had an effect on the whole deal." He flung his arms wide. "By the laws of gravity and . . ." Sweet sonny Jesus, he was ripped. "Physics. And, uh, that caused other things to happen the way they have. Y'followin' this?"

They strolled deeper into the park, homing toward the dusty white moon staring through the trees, the night soft as mimosa and crickety cool, or at least that was how it seemed to him. "That chick was bustin' my cookies with that Einstein stuff, but it's true, s'all relative."

"So whatever happens, you're saying . . ."

"Meant to happen."

"Good and bad."

Zephyr burped smoke. "Fated and slated." He stepped over to a bed of ivy and unzipped. "Gotta whiz."

Peeing with wobbly imprecision, he jerked with a faint shiver as warmth passed out of him. For the first time he was aware of how cold the night had grown. Behind him he heard the man say, "It's me."

Zephyr half turned, tracing a silvery arc of water in the ivy as he did. "Wha—?"

"Me."

For one instant, he had a flash of knowledge—a Snake, he thought—before the knife skewered his heart.

CHE GUEVARA, KARL MARX, AND TIMOTHY LEARY HAVING BEEN IMMOLATED IN THE old theater, Seth had tacked an Escher print on the wall of the *Rag*'s new quarters, one of the artist's fantasy images: flights of stairs turning in on themselves in untenable ways, ultimately leading nowhere. Amy, who sat with late morning coffee in hopes that the caffeine would bevel the edge from her black mood, found the print disquieting, all the more so in the wake of the news of the sixth murder.

John Sparrow had phoned, and at hearing his voice, something in her quickened, catching her by surprise. His words, however, were a smack of reality. Had she heard about the killing? Gently, but directly, he told her. Zephyr was dead. She could barely believe it. She went silent with shock. The police had been in Golden Gate Park since dawn. He was calling from a booth; he could come by and see her if she liked.

Yes, she wanted to say. Yes, come and hold me and tell me everything will be all right, that the Summer of Love isn't some plunging, hell-bound flight of fun house stairs. "No," she said, "thank you, I'm fine." She was sure he had a ton of work to do. And anyway, she told herself, Seth was around to give comfort, right? Seth, who was her lover and soul mate and friend, with whom she shared so much—and with whom she didn't know where she stood anymore. "No." She thanked John Sparrow again. "I'm fine."

The intercom squawked in the night quiet of the homicide detail. Sparrow, alone in the bullpen, activated the speaker. "Yeah?" he said tiredly.

"Inspector." It was the desk officer in the lobby downstairs. "There's a girl here who insists on talking to you."

"Me?"

"Or someone up there."

"Who is she?"

"Calls herself Crystal Blue. That's all she'll say."

He glanced helplessly at the seven-day clock on the windowsill: 10:22. Beyond, the sky was blue-black. The normal shift in the detail was 9 to 5, with someone always on call, but since the killings had started, everyone was putting in crazy hours. He had been averaging five hours sleep a night for weeks now. Tonight, until Rocco Bianchi turned up to spell him, the call was his. "All right," he relented, "send her up."

Moments later a skinny young woman in a soiled tank top, frayed bellbottom jeans, and a gray sweatshirt tied around her waist, materialized from the elevator. She checked both directions along the empty corridor before spotting Sparrow in the doorway. "You the man I'm supposed to see?"

He said he was.

"Just got one thing to say." She giggled, like she had been rehearsing the line until now it seemed a joke. "I ain't dead."

He recognized her then. In spite of the unwashed pigtails that she drew away from her face with fingers whose nails were gnawed to the quick, he remembered her as the girl who'd been at the house on Ashbury the day he had visited Circe. She had a cute, gamine look, enlivened by a curious green-eyed gaze, like one of those Montmartre match girls you saw in Woolworth's reproductions, street-worn but innocent. It took her a moment, but she remembered him, too. "Well, John," she said, "as you can see, I ain't dead. Ned, neither—though he maybe ain't got a body anymore."

"Ned."

"New York Ned. He used to be Eddie McClain. The article in the paper? About the two people from New York, saying how they haven't been heard from, and someone wondering if maybe the Death Tripper got 'em, though it didn't come right out and say it?"

She was referring to the appeal he had placed in the *Rag*. "Is that you?"

"*One* of them's me. Before I was reborn."

He got her seated next to his desk. He got his cup with the Chinese characters on it, and poured coffee. She drank thirstily.

"What's this about Ned's body?" he asked.

"I don't mean for real. He's just gone spiritual."

Sparrow hunted for a copy of the article from the *Rag* and found it. "You're Christine Fallon?"

"Used to be, but like I told the cop downstairs, now I'm Crystal Blue. Uh, John . . ." She nodded at a pack of Winstons on his desk. "Can I bum a cig?"

He lit one for her, then flipped open a steno pad. "What can I do for you, Crystal?" he asked.

"Well, see, why our folks didn't hear from us"—again the gesture of pulling pigtails aside—"is because we didn't call them. Which I've got a right not to do, right? 'Cause I'm seventeen, and I ain't doing those numbers anymore."

"Numbers?"

"The ones they been laying on me all my life. Head games. Mind trips. My father used to get a little too free with his hands when he was drinking, liked to whack me one, even if I wasn't doing nothing. They didn't appreciate me."

"So you split and came out here."

"Down to the City first."

"Los Angeles?"

"The *City*. New York. Which is where Ned and me met. Washington Square Park. I became his old lady. He had this van, this cool old bakery thing, and we, like, did the pioneer trip and came out here."

"When was that?"

"Way back, it feels like. *Sgt. Pepper's* wasn't out yet. Three, four months ago?" As if it were time too vast to contemplate, she shrugged her thin shoulders and sucked deeply on the cigarette. Had she seen anything of San Francisco beyond the acid-drenched streets of the Haight?

"Where's Ned now?"

"There's this ashram down the coast, you can, like, sit and gaze at the sun going down. That's where he was, last I heard."

"He's not still your old man?"

"We don't do exclusive no more. No one does."

He nodded. "What about you?"

"Exclusive?"

"Where are you staying? Are you still in the house where that band is?"

Her green eyes narrowed warily. "You thinking to bust me?"

"For what? You came to volunteer information."

She'd been slouching in the wooden chair, but suddenly she shuddered and sat up, her gaze drawn to the window and the dark beyond it. "John?"

"What is it?"

"Can you shut that?"

He went over and closed the window. "A goose just walked on my grave," she said. "Swear to God. I've been in Hashbury since the Death Tripper started doing his dark thing, so how come I feel closer to the killings up here? Is that the cop vibes or something?"

"You're safe," he said reassuringly.

She nodded but didn't look quite sure.

"Are you still on Ashbury Street?" he asked again, wanting to keep this on track. She might be the closest they had come yet to someone with vital information. She may have ridden with the man they were seeking.

"Well, now, that's the thing. I *was* there, you know, up the hill from the Dead. It's a scene, man! Freak freely! I'm still a friend of them, and all, but, no, I'm not living there." The girl sank back again, and the spark, which had animated her eyes for a moment, dimmed. "Not anymore. They bad-tripped me 'cause I burned the rice. I mean, we were all getting off, and the music was loud, so how come I'm the one catches hell 'cause the rice burns and smokes out the kitchen? The Witch said I had to go. She didn't dig me being around, but she sure didn't mind having me run errands and be an all-'round house slave."

"Who are we talking about?"

"I call her the Witch. Circe. Who really was a Witch, like a hundred years ago in Ancient Greece and all? She's the singer. They're playing tonight over in Sausalito. I would've gone but I didn't have a ride, and hitchin' across the bridge gets cold as a—" She broke off with a laugh. "Hey, speaking of the Witch, right?"

He set his pen aside. This was a short story getting long. "Where are you living now?"

"Doing my own thing." She crossed her arms. "Getting it together. Nice nights I crash in the woods. Or on the beach. Wherever."

"Do me a favor? Don't. Stay with friends, stay indoors."

"On account of the Death Tripper?"

"Because it isn't safe."

"I ain't scared. I'm more scared here. This place creeps me out, you want to know the truth." As if to dispel the feeling, she blew a cone of smoke toward the ceiling and waved it away with a hand. He could see she had been a perky kid, precocious in ways; but she had slipped off the rails somewhere along the line, before coming out here, or since? Who knew? Now the energy was up and down. She was wearing out, the way the street life wore them out with drugs, casual sex, poor hygiene, till they were spent, yesterday's bright flowers, tomorrow's withered blooms.

"What happened to your van?" he asked.

She was looking beyond him. "Lot of red tacks. That's all the places where the bodies were found, right?" She nodded at the wall map. "I've seen them do that on *Felony Squad*."

"Crystal—your van?"

She shook her head, as if clearing it. "Okay. Yeah. Soon as we hit California, like some kind of sign or something, the van croaked. We'd picked up this hitcher a few days before, and were traveling with him, and he said he'd buy it. He had this motorcycle he was riding that broke down—that was in the *Rag*, too—and he had to get it fixed, so he said he'd fix the van, too. So Ned sold it for four hundred cash. We said 'Happy trails,' and hopped a bus."

"Was the name of the man in the article familiar?"

"Bug Tooth, yeah, that's what he told us."

"Did he have a real name?"

"What's this hang-up straights've got with names? I don't want to down-trip you, man—you seem cool—but names are names."

"So Bug Tooth stayed behind to get the van repaired."

"That was his plan, anyhow."

"Do you remember the town you were in?"

"Where we left him?"

"Or picked him up."

"The desert, I know that much. Can I have another butt?" He handed her the pack and she lit one. Blowing smoke, she said, "He was standing by the road looking bummed when we stopped. Right before a thunderstorm. We hung out a few days, like I said."

"Would you know Bug Tooth again if you saw him?"

"I've got a head full of faces lately, and, like, more and more they're all the same face. Ever notice that? Blue showed me we're all one."

"Who?"

"Some good acid, that's who. Blue Cheer. Don't got any on you, do you? Be a good thing around here, cheer up the boys in blue." Her laughter was brief. She hugged her thin shoulders again. He said she might want to put on her sweatshirt, and she did.

"Have you got family you can call, Crystal?"

She turned to him, her face knit with dismay. "What, you want me to go back there? Why you think we came out here? To get free."

He flipped the steno pad shut and stood. The girl pushed back her chair to rise but stopped. Something seemed to flash in the round, match-girl eyes. "Weird."

"What is?"

"How stuff comes back. I just thought of something." She stubbed the cigarette. "That night—or maybe it was the next—we camped in the desert, and he was talking in his sleep."

"Bug Tooth?"

"Bug Tooth, yeah. I was crashed when it happened, but Ned told me the next day. Gibberish it sounded like at first, but then Ned heard it clear. In his sleep, the guy said, 'I killed them all.' "

SPARROW CLIMBED OUT OF HIS CAR, SQUINTING IN THE HAZY SUNSHINE. THE ADDRESS was just north of the USF campus, a bungalow with a tiny front yard thick with unkempt flowering bushes, which gave off a rank perfume. *"Buenos dias, Juan,"* Pete Sandoval greeted, looking as alert as Sparrow felt tired. There were just Sandoval and Simon Chang, waiting on the sidewalk.

Sparrow had drunk a quick cup of coffee before leaving home, but only now, for the first time since Rocco Bianchi's call had roused him half an hour ago, did he feel awake. He and the other two conferred briefly, deciding that he would speak with the landlord. Sandoval would wait by the street should anyone arrive or try to leave. Chang, lugging his evidence bag, wandered up the driveway toward the garage.

Sparrow knocked on the side door. In the house a dog began to bark.

"I got a call about your newspaper ad," Rocco had said on the phone. For a moment Sparrow thought he was talking about the sale notice for the *Blind Faith*; then it occurred to him that he meant the item in the *Rag*. Rocco said, "Guess what the guy says is sitting in his garage?"

The inner door opened as an old man appeared, holding back a golden retriever with his knee. Sparrow showed his star and introduced himself. The dog had quieted and looked only eager and friendly now. The man pushed open the outer door with the rubber tip of a cane. He looked to be near eighty, his crinkled face buried behind oversized horn-rims. "I didn't know if calling was the right thing, but I felt it was my duty." His voice was an asthmatic wheeze.

"I'm glad you did, sir."

"I buy them underground papers. Because these kids are telling it straight. More'n I can say for that jug-eared bandit in the White House." He stepped outside, keeping the dog in. He had on a baggy brown cardigan, chinos, and carpet slippers. He indicated the garage with his cane. "I've been renting a room back there for years, students mostly. Never had no problems."

"Is your current tenant causing problems?"

"Never. That's why I hesitated calling."

"Is he here now?"

"I don't believe so, no."

From the corner of his eye Sparrow saw Chang appear on the far side of the garage. "Tell me about—" He broke off. With a yell, he jumped from the step, moving at a run.

Chang, startled, spun away from the garage door, nearly dropping his evidence bag. Sandoval came running, too, his .38 drawn. At Sparrow's hand motion, Chang scurried farther back and Pete moved to the left of the door and took a stand. Sparrow bent to examine the latch, and then eased his face to one of the dusty panes in the door and peered into the gloom of the garage.

"Anything?" Sandoval asked after a moment.

There didn't appear to be anything indicating a booby trap. The landlord arrived, winded from the hurried walk. "What is it?"

Sparrow's empty stomach was tight. "Just being careful."

Using a garden rake he found leaning nearby, he carefully lifted the latch. He hooked the tines of the rake into one handle and pulled slowly. The door creaked open.

Sandoval went in first, his weapon still drawn. After a moment, he called out that it was clear. Chang went in. The landlord stood planted where he was, propped on his cane. Sparrow resisted an urge to light a cigarette. "On the telephone, you didn't mention your renter's name."

"Brian, I think he told me."

"Is that his last name?"

"I don't know."

"You rent to people without getting a name?"

"Sometimes."

"What about references?"

"The only reference I'm interested in anymore is the president. Lincoln, Jefferson, Jackson. With good reason, too. I've had more rubber laid on me over the years than Firestone."

"So you've got nothing with your tenant's name on it."

"No."

"How long has he been with you?"

"Two months and some."

Since May: when the killings began. "Tell me, sir, what *do* you know about your renter?"

"He pays me." At Sparrow's silent stare, the old man sighed. "Nice enough fella. About the size and age of your young partner there, wiry build, dark hair. Keeps to himself."

"A student?"

"Don't know that. I barely see him. He comes and goes."

"John," Sandoval called from inside the garage. "Look at this."

Sandoval had produced a flashlight. Propped in a corner of the garage, amid the clutter of yard tools and old automobile tires, stood a motorcycle. It had no license tag, but on the side of the gleaming black gas tank, in gold lettering, was the word *Vincent*. Chang was already opening his kit. If anything might bear fingerprints, this was it.

"Told you," the landlord said. "Can't be too many of them babies around."

Chang was starting to apply powder as Sparrow joined the landlord at the doorway to the rented room.

A single window with a torn shade let in sunlight, which pooled on the worn linoleum like rancid butter. The unit was furnished with a bed and a wooden chair. There was an open closet with a few bare wire hangers on an iron pole. In a corner was a tiny bathroom. When Sparrow flipped a wall switch, a flyblown halo winked on overhead. It didn't reveal much worth looking at: plasterboard walls, a water-stained toilet and sink, a medicine chest with a cracked and dusty mirror.

"It's just right for a single," the landlord said, as if someone had questioned the accommodations. "Plenty convenient to the U."

Using a knuckle, Sparrow opened the medicine chest. The bottom shelf held a can of shaving crème and squeezed-out tubes of Brylcreem and Ipana. On the other shelf were a dispenser of blades, a stub of styptic pencil, and a safety razor.

Touching nothing, Sparrow left the trove for Chang and turned to the landlord. "When was he here last?"

"Couple nights back. He comes after dark, mostly, so quiet that Mello don't even notice."

"Who?"

"My retriever. Mello Yello, no *W*'s. A tenant left him with me, said she'd be back with the rent. Ha. Anyway, the dog don't bark when this fella's around. Quiet as a gravedigger. I only know when he's been here on account of something's different somehow, you know?"

"Is anything different now?"

The man surveyed the room. "Not that I can rec—. Hold on." He shuffled to the door and gazed back into the garage. Sparrow followed. Chang had brought a floodlight from the car and had it shining on the motorcycle as he worked. The old man snapped his fingers. "Saddlebags."

"What about them?"

"Gone."

Sparrow had come alert. "Are they the kind that have chrome studs?"

"That kind, yeah."

While Chang methodically dusted surfaces with his powder, resistant to Sparrow's urging to be quick about it, Sparrow and Sandoval accompanied the landlord back out into daylight. Sparrow gazed down the driveway to the road, where morning traffic went by. He felt a desire to be gone. "Does anyone else have a key, sir?" Sandoval asked.

"Just me and him."

"If he returns," Sparrow said, "it's best if he doesn't know we were here. Here's a card. I'd appreciate a phone call if he does come back."

Behind the horn-rims, the man's eyes grew even wider, perhaps at the prospect of a break in the presidential succession of currency. "You figure he might not?"

"If he saw the same newspaper you did, he won't."

Simon Chang came out at last, toting his evidence bag. At Sparrow's questioning look, he patted the bag. Sandoval went in to retrieve the flood lamp. The landlord, who'd been studying Sparrow's card, said, "Imagine that. Staying right here in my house. Funny if he turned out to be the killer."

"Hilarious," murmured Chang, trundling past.

The new office of the *Rag* didn't have the charm of the paper's former quarters, but here in the Fillmore the rent was cheap. As Amy entered the hallway, she almost stepped on a bundle lying by the door. It was a bouquet of flowers wrapped in florist's paper. Excitedly, she picked them up. From Seth? She unlocked the door. As she put her things down on a table, the telephone rang.

"Did you get the flowers?"

The speaker sounded vaguely familiar. "Just now."

"Open them. I'll hold."

She tensed. "Who's this?"

"Go ahead."

Bracing the phone with her shoulder, she peeled away the paper. Inside were half a dozen red roses. As she lifted them, she gasped. The heads had been severed, and they dropped to the floor. "Who is this?" she demanded.

"Where'd all the flowers go?" the caller said.

Simon Chang was sitting on a bench in the corridor outside the crime lab, a hand across his eyes as though he were asleep, or praying. He looked up as Sparrow approached, blinking without his glasses. If not elation, Sparrow had expected at least a sense of triumph. Nothing. Chang appeared tired, his skin papery, and all at once, for the first time, Sparrow saw him as he would be one day, a liver-spotted old man in black slippers doing t'ai chi in the park.

"You said you got something on the fingerprints?"

Chang patted the bench beside him. Sparrow sat. "I find a match between print taken from door of van and one from motorcycle. Also, I got name for person who bought motorcycle in Dallas, May second this year. Same person?" Chang shrugged. "I don't know. No ID on the prints yet. The man who bought motorcycle gave a military address at Fort Sam Houston."

"Texas," Sparrow said.

"I checked federal fingerprint file. No record."

"Could the prints belong to one of the kids from New York?"

"No."

Sparrow reflected on this information a moment. "Who bought the motorcycle?"

Chang handed him a piece of paper which had a name written on it: Byron Hoot.

There was John, already waiting at the Stanyan Street entrance to the park. It was four o'clock, and the sidewalks were busy. Amy stopped before he saw her, and she stood there a moment watching him. He stood alone in the eddies of people swirling about him, isolated and yet substantial in the transient flow, and she understood that what she had considered rigid in him before was also solid and dependable. Careful, too. Meeting here in a crowd was a precaution he'd insisted upon, for her safety, she knew. He turned then and spotted her, and she saw that his expression was relief. "Let's walk," he suggested.

She had transcribed what she could recall of the telephone conversation that had taken place just hours ago, including the echo of the line from "Where Have All the Flowers Gone?" Recovering from her shock at the beheaded roses, aware that the call was important somehow, she'd said, "Tell me."

"You don't know? What about the times?"

That had puzzled her. Steadier now, she recalled the conversation for John as they entered the park. "The times. As in they're a-changin'?"

"That's a song too, isn't it?" Sparrow asked.

"Yes. I was free-associating, thinking maybe he was playing music games with me. But it wasn't the right answer apparently. He said, 'Nine and ten, black and white and read all over.' And he hung up. It was him. The same person who called before, about my letter to the Death Tripper."

"Do the words make any sense?"

She shook her head, frustrated all over again. "I thought he might be referring to the *Los Angeles Times* or *New York Times*, so I went to the library and checked them both for the ninth and tenth of this month. I looked at *Time* magazine. Nothing. That's when I called you. Tell me that Seth was right about stoners, that I'm wrong and there is no message."

"You're convinced that there is."

It was true. He hadn't called for no reason. Or sent flowers. She shuddered again. They found a bench off the paved path and sat. John said, "Black and white and read . . . Could it be a reversal of the old joke and really is r-e-d?"

"Communist?"

"Or blood?"

"The killings?"

"Or war protesters splashing animal blood over draft board records, perhaps?"

Between them they had questions but few answers. Taking a chance, she asked, "Do you know the song? 'Where Have All the Flowers Gone?' "

"Come on, even I'm not that square. The Kingston Trio."

"It played over and over in the dorm my sophomore year at UMass. The refrain changes. 'Gone to young girls,' then 'soldiers,' 'graveyards . . . ' "

John tensed and sat up straighter.

"What is it?"

He glanced at his watch. "I'll tell you on the way. We have to hurry."

They entered the Presidio from the upper end, Sparrow using his SFPD star at the entry gate. The military policeman on duty directed them. They drove down a wooded and winding road until the pinewoods opened to the main post and views of the bay in the distance. Sparrow located the post library, a building more modern in appearance than the rows of red-roofed barracks and other buildings surrounding the large central parade ground. A wind was blowing from the bay, stirring palm trees in front. The only other vehicle in the library lot was a jeep. As Sparrow and Amy went up the walk, a pair of hemlock bushes flanking the door rustled dryly, as though whispering old secrets.

His weariness was gone. On the ride over, he told Amy about what had occurred to him. "The *Army Times*," she echoed. She'd used it when she was a news intern, writing obituaries. He also told her about the rented garage room near USF and what he had learned from Chang, including the name of the person who had bought the motorcycle, Byron Hoot. The woman at the circulation desk was Japanese-American, in her forties. As Amy and Sparrow entered, she gave a slight bow. "So sorry, we're closing."

Sparrow used his star again and explained that they were on official business that wouldn't take long. "We're open again tomorrow," the librarian said.

He was about to push harder when Amy's hand on his arm stayed him. "If there were time," she told the woman gently, "we would come tomorrow, but there isn't."

Maybe the woman recalled another war, when other bureaucracies had created Executive Order 9066, sending people, possibly her own family, to internment camps for the duration. After a moment, she said she had some paperwork that would take her twenty minutes or so. Sparrow said it should be enough.

The woman brought them what they requested, then vanished into an office behind the desk. They carried the newspapers to a long oak table. "May I make an observation?" Amy whispered. "We don't know squat about what we're looking for, do we?"

It was true. This was pure enigma, sutured with guesswork and hunches—like everything else about the case.

Opening the top issue on the stack of military newspapers for the month of July for the past three years, he located a list of casualties under the heading "Killed as a Result of Hostile Action". There were also categories for wounded and for missing in action. If "red" were in fact a reference to blood, this seemed a reasonable place to begin. They divided the pile and began to scan the columns. But beyond the grimness of the task, nothing came to them. Then, as he was starting to wonder if they were on the right track after all, Sparrow felt his pulse quicken. In the tally of the wounded for the second week of July 1966 was the name Corporal Byron Hoot. He showed Amy.

"The man who owned the motorcycle," she whispered.

"Look at this." He pointed to the names of men from the accompanying column, listed as having been killed in the same hostile action. Worden, Adair, Fischetti . . .

Amy wrote them down—twelve names in all: one wounded, eleven killed—all in a place called Cu Chi. They went through the remaining issues of the newspaper but found nothing more of interest. They piled the stack of newspapers on the counter as they left.

Exiting the parking lot, they had a view down the slope of the central parade ground. At midfield, a hundred yards distant, a company of men was going through a drill. Sparrow slowed the car. The men's shadows stretched long in the late-slanting light, and it took him a moment to realize they weren't U.S. soldiers. Standing to the side, watching them, was George Moon. The men were quick-stepping, jabbing batons forward in a thrusting motion. With a tingle in his solar plexus, Sparrow recognized the movement from the solstice gathering, though it seemed surer now, more efficient, honed by added weeks of drill.

"He's building an army, isn't he?" Amy said. And Sparrow was given over all at once to a scenario that Frank Austin had played for him at the Top of the Mark. The TAC Squad would invade the Haight if Homicide didn't find the killer.

Just then Moon looked in the direction of the car and brought a hand to his brow to visor the sun. Sparrow drove off.

The phone booth stood along the beach road. The floor was drifted with wind-blown sand, and old webs of mummified insects festooned the walls. For a moment he thought they had wasted time having stopped, but when he pressed the receiver to his ear, the dial tone was strong.

At Fort Sam Houston in San Antonio, it would be just after 3 P.M. To the woman who answered, Sparrow gave his name and title, and Frank Austin's, too, if she wanted to confirm it. He explained in only the briefest way what he was after. He spelled Byron Hoot's name.

"Sir, I'm going to pass along your request. Are you at a number where you can be reached?"

"When?"

"Very shortly."

He said he'd be waiting. He told Amy that the army medical center in San Antonio was one of the biggest in the country, that they might have something on Byron Hoot.

"But your crime lab person said he wasn't listed in the federal fingerprint file."

She'd been paying attention. "We'll find out."

A spider, perhaps stirred by a curiosity of its own, ventured out into its web to see what was going on, then set about adding intricacies to its design. The phone rang minutes later.

A man was on the line, and this time Sparrow got a name: Major Beckwith, a physician. Sparrow repeated his brief introduction and his question. The doctor listened and finally said, "A great many wounded returnees do cycle through the military hospital at Fort Sam."

"Was Corporal Hoot one of them?"

"Can you tell me more specifically what this is in regard to?"

"Major, his name has come up in a homicide investigation."

"He's dead?" the officer said instantly.

"He may be a suspect."

A pause. "I see. Do you have him in custody?"

"No, but we'd very much like to talk with him."

Beckwith admitted that the army had treated the soldier, that in fact Byron Hoot had been under Beckwith's care for a time. Sparrow glanced at Amy and nodded. "Can you give me some details about him?"

"I'm reluctant to talk about a patient."

"It could be of great help, Doctor."

"Look, I'm being paged."

"Is there another time we can talk?"

"I've got to go."

"I'm prepared to pursue this legally if I have to."

There was a brief silence, then in a halting voice Beckwith said, "Perhaps . . . we could . . . talk. Not on a telephone though."

Meet him? Sparrow doubted Austin would pay airfare to San Antonio and back on the strength of an uncertain line of investigation. And money aside, could they afford the time? Six people were dead. And Sparrow hadn't forgotten the image of Moon's troops. "Texas is a bit far right now, couldn't we—"

"What?" Beckwith sounded genuinely surprised. "Your call was transferred. I'm here in California. At Fort Ord."

Ord was two hours' drive down the coast. "When?" Sparrow asked.

The doctor hesitated, and Sparrow wondered if he was having second thoughts. Then he said, "Tomorrow afternoon. Say . . . sixteen-thirty hours?"

Sparrow did the math. "I'll be there."

"The Medical Services building. Come alone."

WHEN SPARROW GOT BACK TO THE HOMICIDE DETAIL HE WAS STARTLED TO SEE GEORGE Moon. He stood with his broad back to the doorway, leaning over one of the bullpen desks, talking in a low voice to Paul Lanin. An hour ago Moon had been drilling his troops at the Presidio. A big, unfamiliar cop sat on a desk by the window, swinging his booted feet like a bored child, the heels drumming softly on the desk's steel side.

At Sparrow's entrance, Moon turned. "Well, look who's here."

Lanin looked sheepish. "Hey, John."

"What's going on?" Sparrow wanted to know.

"I heard you've been hobnobbing with the great unwashed," said Moon. "Word is, you're not packing iron anymore. Traded in your piece for a string of love beads. Was that your chick you were with this afternoon? A study date at the library?"

Ignoring him, Sparrow looked into Frank Austin's office, but Austin wasn't there. Moon kept the floor. "You came up with a suspect. I applaud you," he said, and proceeded to do just that, slowly bringing his big hands together in several loud claps. "Now all you have to do is find him."

Sparrow looked at Paul Lanin. "Where's the lieutenant?"

Lanin, like Sparrow, had been with the detail when Moon ran it; his loyalties were mixed. "I'm not sure," he said with a frown.

"I know where," said Moon. They looked at him. "He's greasing his wheels over at City Hall, making excuses for why you people haven't caught the killer. You know this guy's whereabouts? Have you got solid evidence? Is there an APB out on him yet?" The questions were all rhetorical, the answers all no. "He's still out there, free as a fucking bird, and you people aren't doing squat to find him. I saw the chief to request that he use the TAC Squad. We're getting ready to mobilize."

Sparrow held onto his rising anger. "To do what?"

"What do you think? To stop the killings. To stop this Hoot."

So he had got the name. From Lanin? Rocco Bianchi? He doubted Chang would have given it up. Sparrow reined hard on his anger. "I'm going to the chief right now."

Whether at a signal from Moon or on his own initiative, the other cop hopped from his perch. With surprising speed for a man of his bulk, he moved to the door ahead of Sparrow, drawing the black truncheon from his belt as he went. He raised it as a crossbar.

If it hadn't happened so quickly, Sparrow might have given thought to his own reaction. As it was, he was taken by impulse. He grabbed the center of the stick in both hands and twisted left, then gave a sharp yank right, pulling the cop off balance. With his hip, he knocked the cop onto a nearby desk, Sparrow's own, sending the Chinese coffee mug smashing to the floor. He snatched the stick free. Lanin jumped up, but Moon warned him back, starting forward himself.

Sparrow raised the stick. Tight with rage, his fingers locked on the stick's ribbed handle; he could feel his arm tremble. Moon stopped his advance. Cunning curled his mouth. "If only your hippie girl could see you now."

"Shut up."

"You might lose all that good free love you've been getting."

Dizzy, Sparrow felt the heft of the truncheon, the swift, weighted swing it would have. He could see the spot on Moon's crew-cut scalp where the blow would land, where blood would flow the way it had from Seth Green's head in Golden Gate Park . . . What the hell was he doing? He flung the stick away. It banged the wall. Lanin shouted, and either that sound or Sparrow's motion gave Moon the split second he needed. He drove his shoulder into Sparrow, and they went down. Sparrow's breath exploded from his lungs as Moon fell on him.

Moon had size, and was in peak condition, but Sparrow's anger had reached a boil. He gave a heave, rolling Moon hard into the side of a desk, wedging him there. He punched him, smashing his lip. Blood spurted.

The other TAC cop grabbed Sparrow in a headlock and yanked him fiercely backwards. Pain wracked his neck. Sparks flashed in his brain. He foresaw a repeat of the night in the garage, the two cops beating him savagely. He couldn't let it happen. He twisted out of the hold. He got his gun from its holster and wheeled it up. It froze the others where they stood.

That was when Frank Austin came in.

"He's all over our case," Sparrow fumed when he was seated alone with Austin in the lieutenant's office. "He's got our suspect's name."

Lanin and the other TAC cop had been quick to back away from the scuffle.

When Sparrow and Moon were on their feet, Sparrow shoving his weapon away as Moon dabbed at his bloody mouth, Austin demanded to know what was going on.

"This maniac attacked me!" Moon shouted. "When Mike here tried to stop him, he pulled his gun!" He turned to the other cops. "Tell him. You saw it."

Lanin and the TAC cop nodded.

"I came looking for you." Moon addressed Austin. "We need to talk strategy."

Austin hadn't looked happy with the prospect, but he hadn't seemed surprised either. "Call me, Captain, and we'll do this the right way, following protocol. Right now," he said firmly, "I want some distance between our details."

Moon thrust a forefinger at Sparrow. "You're done!" he spat through swollen lips, and stalked out, trailed by the big TAC cop. When they'd gone, Austin gazed around the bullpen. There were fragments of the broken mug, upended wastebaskets and chairs, spills of computer punch cards. A tipped-over telephone whined until he slammed the receiver onto its hook. He took the seven-day clock from the windowsill, cradling it in his arms like a small pet that has had a narrow escape. "Get this cleaned up," he ordered Lanin. "Sparrow, in my office."

Which was where they sat now, with the door shut, Sparrow burning. "He's been shadowing the case for weeks. He's been after the ME for autopsy information. When I came in today, he already had Byron Hoot's name."

Austin's face was pinched. "What else?"

Sparrow told him what Moon had said about having spoken to the chief. Austin frowned, and Sparrow knew that Moon had been telling the truth, and that Austin was already aware of it. It took some of the fight out of Sparrow. "When?" he asked.

"The day after tomorrow. There's going to be a sweep of the Haight-Ashbury. Search and destroy. I opposed it, but the chief says it's time. I didn't want Moon to know we've got a suspect, but now he does. He won't need us anymore. With a name, maybe he'll come up with a mug shot. He'll want to act fast."

" 'Search and destroy,' " Sparrow murmured. "His words?" Austin nodded. So the TV war had truly come home.

"After the solstice incident," Austin said, "that mix-up over jurisdictions, it would've looked bad not to cooperate. And now, with the whole world watching the city, the last thing we can afford is a war inside the department."

So they'd have it in the streets instead, us versus them. Sparrow had an image of TAC cops goose-stepping up Ashbury. Austin gazed toward the wall with its photographs and citations, mementos of his civic service, perhaps wondering if there'd ever be any more. After a moment he turned back. His face looked fallen. "It might not be so bad."

But it would be; the TAC Squad was bigger, more combat ready than ever, but there was something else: Sparrow had a phantom recall of how the black truncheon had felt it his own hand, whispering to him, *Swing me, use me . . .* The solstice had just been practice. He knew that Seth Green and his cohorts in the Mobilization Group had been preparing for confrontation. Probably other factions had been, too. He had no doubt that some of them were armed. It didn't take much imagination to envision anarchy.

"We haven't built a single bridge to the Haight community," he said soberly. "If TAC pushes, people are going to push back. Moon knows it. He's counting on it. People are going to get hurt. . . ."

Austin glanced again at his trophies, like they were scaffolds he'd been building that would bring him to the height of his ambitions. But now it had begun to teeter, the ground beneath to shift. "I'll speak to the chief once more, see if I can get him to reconsider." He didn't sound hopeful. "But right now, I have to do something about what happened in there."

"I'll pay for the damage."

"You drew your weapon."

"That was wrong, I admit." It was too late to tell Austin about the night in the parking garage; the time to report it was right after it happened.

"What if it had gone off?"

Sparrow nodded. "I know."

"There'll be an internal review. I'll want your statement. And Lanin's. But one thing's clear, you did pull your weapon. You don't deny that?"

"No."

Austin tugged at his coat sleeves, regaining some measure of control. "Then for now, until it's investigated, I'm going to need your service piece and your badge."

"What?"

"That's policy. Mandatory suspension. I don't have any discretion."

"Nothing happened. The murders are what's important. You can—" He broke off. He didn't need to state the obvious. Austin *did* have discretion, but he already had set an unsolved case in the balance with a subordinate's violation of policy, and had weighed which was likely to be the greater impediment to his career. A certain number of crimes always went cold; but a man who wanted to command needed the total obedience of his men.

"The others will have to handle it," Austin said quietly. "I'm sorry."

Sparrow opened his mouth to speak, but he couldn't. The sensation was the one he'd had in the parking garage that night when Moon kicked his breath out. With shaking hands, he unsnapped his holstered .38 and set it on the desktop. He took the leather case from his pocket and twisted loose the inspector's star. It clattered on the desk, bounced once, and landed in Austin's lap.

The guy was friendly, even if he didn't have a stash. Crystal Blue would've liked a little weed, to mellow out the acid. The light of day was fading on Sutro Point, burnishing the cypress trees and the big orange carpets of nasturtiums growing everywhere. She remembered the first time she had come here, with Ned, soon after they'd arrived in San Francisco.

"Who's Ned?"

She blinked. Had she been spacing and talking aloud? The guy was watching her amiably. "You called me Ned." He plucked up a handful of soil, letting it sift away in the breeze off the sea. "Call me . . . Sandy."

Sandy. Had they met before? Something seemed familiar. "Ned was my old man. We were in Washington Square in New York and we kept hearing that song, about going to San Francisco . . . and we knew we had to."

Only now Ned wasn't New York Ned anymore, called himself Rama Chia or something, and he'd renounced drugs as a false means and gone down to an ashram in Big Sur. She imagined him sitting on the rocks at the edge of the continent, watching this same sun go down and meditating himself right out of his body. "When I picture him," she said dreamily, "he's so . . . incorporeal. I see him floating way up there somewhere." She stretched a hand to the sky over the darkening Pacific. "Looking down."

"But not you?"

"No way. I want to ride fast and free! Right to the last exit—and then the one beyond that!" She laughed as she said it, but she knew she was lying. She'd have given anything to be back to those first carefree weeks, when she was still Christine, riding with Ned in the old van across America, seeing the country, and realizing gradually that it wasn't *her* anymore, it was *them*! Sleeping under the stars, going west . . . *to* something. There'd been such promise. She and Ned, loving each other, loving all the gentle brothers and sisters. Glassy-eyed with excitement and weed, they drank down the songs which spilled in an endless stream from the radio—Airplane and Donovan, the Beatles and the Doors . . . and the Riders that very first time on a bootleg tape, popping the cherry of her virgin ears—all that righteous stuff before it started to go so sour. When had that happened? Where? "Think you could score some smoke, Sandy?" she asked tentatively.

"I could try," he said.

That sounded good. That's what she needed to cheer her up. She was suddenly thinking about the day Jerry Garcia came over to the house to do some picking with Eric . . . ol' Captain Trips himself, and he'd flirted with her and offered a joint the size of Castro's cigar. She laughed again. Everyone had something to pass around, turn you on, launch you, and she had become something of an astronaut, riding the rocketry of sensimilla and Panama Red, White Lightning, Blue Cheer, Sunshine, sugar cube, microdot, windowpane, blotter, electric Kool-Aid, mescalito, psilocybin, mushrooms, and right now the righteous Purple Haze sparking in her brain . . . and how Toad used to say you ain't ripped if you can still lie on the floor without holding on . . .

But what about love? Where was the love in all this?

A tear strayed down her cheek, but she kept smiling. "Okay, Sandy. Smoke sounds cool."

Sea mist hung in the air, and all that remained of day was a thin red line at the horizon. She had on a sweatshirt and the overalls she'd picked out of the free box at St. Vincent de Paul, like they belonged to some guy about eight feet tall, cuffs rolled up a dozen turns, but they were warm and the acid was starting to go visual and the guy's face kept changing, melting, kind of, the flesh oozing off like grease until suddenly the ridges of bone would poke through and build a whole new face, friendly and smiling and cute, with soulful eyes and dark hair, familiar somehow, and she thought maybe he had a place where they could crash later and ball . . .

"You okay, kid?"

"First ride's free, right?" she said.

It's what her dad used to tell her, warning her maybe. Pot leads to the hard stuff! "The way mother's milk leads by and by to Four Roses?" she wanted to ask him, but never did. He was seldom sober enough to fathom the logic, and he had as much appreciation for irony as a cinder block, and now she blinked and opened her eyes wide and saw silver light. *Wsshhh.*

The truth slipped into her at her breastbone . . . the harder stuff . . . a glint of steel, easiest delivery system yet, no waiting around wondering, would you get off? Just a thin red line and—*pain!*

Oh, God! *"Sandy?"*

He stabbed her again.

Ned! she called out, or thought. That was it; she was thinking. *Ned!* But Ned was gone.

Dad? *Dad?* Gone. The sonofabitch was *never* there when you needed him.

"Mommy?" Actually said that out loud, but her mother wasn't here, either, and all that was miles and months behind, and she had not followed the kind police detective's advice and phoned home or taken care. There was no Lucy floating in a sky full of diamonds . . . no, everything was all of a sudden dark.

The knife hit her a third time. And a fourth.

She had a flicker of memory but it was gone, too, and as quickly as it had gripped her, her panic flowed on past like a current of water, so it was like everything was flow, past-future-now, and she was running into the ground, would evaporate and condense and water the nasturtiums, the morning glories, and nightshade, and be part of the everlasting cycle, because for the first time she grasped the essential transcendent truth, and it was this: don't panic, it's organic. Her grin got so wide it hurt. *Everything* is one, always and forever, world without end, amen, ah man, for nothing . . . really . . . ever . . . *dies.* She was humming a song: "I went down to the cavern of the trees . . ." No, the word wasn't "trees," just sounded like it; Circe gave it that sound when she sang it but the real word was . . .

Sandy's face drew close, his expression knotted. "What's that?"

She laughed, happy to be able to turn someone on to the light, to share. "Only the greatest band in the universe!" she told him. "It's the Riders, man! 'Cavern of the *beast.*' "

She felt herself twitching, saw things sparkling bright as jujubes and understood that they were stars, that she lay among the orange flowers, hearing in the silence the moan of foghorns, and searching for the one essence, like the big crashing piano chord at the end of "A Day in the Life," a word . . . *the* word, since they were all the word made flesh and didn't need Steinways or Stratocasters or B-52s because it was within them and without them, and then she had it, a kind of gurgling, bubbly, buzzy vibration, which is exactly what it was—a vibe!—way deep down in her bursting body and coming up . . .

Ooommmmm . . .

 FIVE

BOOK OF THE DEAD

Take the highway to the end of the night. . . .
—The Doors

Sparrow learned of the seventh murder the same way half a million other San Franciscans did: on the morning TV news. The victim was a young female, no identity established yet, found in a cypress grove at Sutro Point. Unshaven, he stood in his apartment, angry and spooked, and watched the windblown reporter on the scene. Intercut with grainy footage, the story was told in that way that TV had of making an event both more and less real. He caught glimpses of Pete Sandoval, Chang, Hoagland, even Rocco Bianchi, pulled from the desk for one more blooding. There was no mention, of course, of flowers or mutilation.

He drove south in light traffic, pushing the Impala along at the speed limit. Earlier, he'd been about to call Austin, to ask him to send someone down to Fort Ord in his place, but the news of the murder changed things. He'd left a message for Amy with her friend Tess: he was on his way to keep the appointment; he'd be aboard *Blind Faith* that evening, could he see Amy then? No, there was no way to reach him; yes, she'd know what he meant.

A hundred miles south, cupped in the crescent of Monterey Bay, he came to the sandy barrens of Fort Ord military reservation. Off to the right, behind wire fences, armored personnel carriers scurried through the scrub like large ungainly bugs, in some kind of training exercise, apparently, though what bearing it might have on a guerrilla war in a jungle half a world away he could only wonder. At the main gate, an MP asked his business, detained him just long enough to log his plate number on a clipboard, and then waved him through.

Medical Services was at the end of a row of buildings, distinguishable from the others only by the caduceus pegged in the lawn. In a reception office, a Spec-4 sat at a desk, doing a hunt-and-peck on an old Remington. He took Sparrow's name, and said Major Beckwith was running a bit behind schedule but would be with him shortly. Too edgy to sit, Sparrow stepped out onto an outdoor stairway landing to smoke. A column of new recruits was marching past in the late afternoon heat shimmer. " 'WACS and WAVES are winning the war, what in the hell am I fighting for?' " It was classic call and response, a drill sergeant calling cadence, the trainees echoing the line and adding the refrain. " 'It's the Fort Ord Boogie, what a craaaazy sound . . . ' " He finished his cigarette and went inside.

The Spec-4 was still typing. On a corkboard affixed to the wall was a poster depicting a soldier with the top of his head being lifted off by a mushroom cloud of pills, syringes, and hand-rolled cigarettes. YOU ONLY GET ONE MIND! read the caption. DON'T BLOW IT! Just then an office door opened and a young soldier came through. Pulling on an olive drab baseball cap, he glanced at Sparrow, gave him a peace sign, and went on by, heading for the outer door. Behind him appeared an older man, forty or forty five, tall and clad in crisp khakis with a major's oak leaf and medical corps insignia. He laid some papers atop the Spec-4's Remington. "Triple carbons."

Turning his attention to Sparrow, the major nodded after the departing peace sign flasher. "He's filed for status as a CO. Are you the cop from Frisco?"

Sparrow said he was. The man's name tag said "Beckwith." He had a craggy face that gave him an eagle's intensity as he studied the SFPD card Sparrow handed him. Austin hadn't thought to take the cards along with Sparrow's star and his .38. Beckwith palmed it. "We're seeing a lot more of them than we used to," he said.

"Cops?" Sparrow asked.

"Conscientious objectors. Or young men claiming to be." The peace sign flasher, Sparrow realized. "We have to interview each one, to determine that they're sincere and not just angling to get out—or deluded somehow."

Or sane? Sparrow thought of Yossarian, the bedeviled bombardier hero of *Catch-22*. If you knew war was crazy, what did that make you?

In the office, Beckwith waved him into a seat and took his own behind a desk. The room was small and dim, its venetian blinds slatted against the day outside. The furnishings were drab chairs, file cabinets, and a desk, on which lay a folded sheet of paper. The one non-government-issue touch was an antique Regulator clock in a beautifully lacquered wood case on the wall behind the desk. It showed 4:50 P.M.

"Thank you for seeing me," Sparrow began. "This shouldn't take much time."

Beckwith rubbed his hands back over his wire-brush hair, then set them on the desk, flanking the folded paper. "So you're interested in one of our boys. Byron Hoot?"

"Yes, sir. We'd like to question him in connection with a series of murders. The seventh victim was found this morning."

Beckwith's eyes danced with astonishment, but only for an instant, then steadied. "Hippies. I heard. All killed by the same person?"

"We think so. Possibly Corporal Hoot." Sparrow paused. "Unless you know otherwise."

The major was silent, and Sparrow had the errant idea that so accustomed was he to dealing with body counts that seven was insignificant somehow. In the small office, the clock kept a slow, persistent beat. At last Beckwith shook his head. "No."

"You said on the phone yesterday that Hoot was under your care at the army hospital in San Antonio."

"That's correct."

"But not presently?"

"Not for several months now."

"May I ask when you stopped seeing him?

Beckwith hesitated. "Mid-April."

Before leaving San Francisco, Sparrow had jotted questions in his notebook, but he didn't look at them. "What was the nature of his wounds?"

"Minor. Some shrapnel, a phosphorous burn."

"His combat action was a year ago. He was still being treated?"

Beckwith paused a moment. "Not for those wounds. I'm a psychiatrist."

Now the surprise was Sparrow's. The major unfolded the sheet of paper before him. "I don't know how much you know. I had my clerk type some notes."

He gave the details, reading them off the sheet. Sparrow listened. Hoot's parents were deceased. His father had been a coal miner and later a preacher. Hoot attended school through age fifteen. Sporadic employment—laborer, restaurant worker, carnival roustabout. He enlisted in December 1965 and completed basic and advanced training at Fort Dix, New Jersey. With a job designation of infantry-man, he was assigned to a line unit and began a tour in Vietnam. He was wounded and was returned to the U.S. for treatment.

"As I said, Hoot's father was a pastor. The Church of the Rejuvenant God. Familiar with it?" Sparrow wasn't. "I am only because I checked. It's a tiny sect, a lot of it standard Pentecostal fare—speaking in tongues, trance states. What makes this different is sacrifice."

"Self-sacrifice, you mean?"

"Blood sacrifice. It seems to be part Old Testament law, part pagan rite. Once a year they offer up an animal, right around the summer solstice—an atonement for sin."

A chill arrowed up Sparrow's back. He drew himself straighter in the chair. "What do they kill?"

"A goat or a hog, usually." Beckwith paused, then went on. "Have you heard of a place called Cu Chi?" Sparrow knew it from the *Army Times*. "It's northwest of Saigon. By day, we control the district, but at night the guerrillas take charge. One reason they've been so hard to dislodge is they've got a network of underground tunnels they use to attack from, appearing and disappearing at will. They have everything down there—weapons, rice, medics. Whores. We send men in to check the tunnels out, blow them up. Tunnel rats. Hoot was good at the job. Fearless. Then, one night the small compound he and his squad were holding was sneak-attacked. His unit took heavy casualties. He was wounded. He was taken to Saigon, then Japan, and then home. I treated him at Fort Sam for several months. I was in favor of holding him for continued treatment. His regular separation date would've been next March, but . . ." Beckwith opened a hand, as if letting something fly from it.

"You released him?"

Beckwith frowned. "It never got to that. On April 18 of this year, he went AWOL. We've had no contact with him since."

"So he's a deserter!" Sparrow couldn't keep the pique from his voice. He was thinking of the time already lost tracking the soldier. "Did you notify anyone?"

"The Criminal Investigation Division has jurisdiction for deserters. If they thought civilian police should know, they'd have been in touch."

"They weren't."

"Well, that was CID's decision. I've got a lot more to deal with than every mixed-up kid that goes over the hill."

"Even if the kid turns out to be a homicidal maniac?"

Beckwith's face tightened, his brow compressed in hard ridges. "You don't know that."

Sparrow pushed down his own frustration. There was no point in alienating Beckwith; the officer had agreed to see him, after all. And he was acutely aware that his own position here was tenuous. He drew a calming breath. "May I ask what you treated Hoot for?"

The deep lines in Beckwith's face eased slightly. "My diagnosis was personality disorder—schizophrenia. He was carrying a big burden of guilt, that much emerged in his sessions. He was suffering nightmares, delusions of paranoia, night sweats. He heard voices. For awhile he even had some language loss."

"Caused by his war experiences?"

"Combat was likely a catalyst to bring things up, but I believe the root causes went back further."

"To what?"

"Childhood, perhaps?" He shook his head, in mystification more than denial. "I didn't treat him long enough to know."

"Had he ever been treated prior to the army?"

"Not that I'm aware. He grew up in rural circumstances."

"Aren't recruits given tests before they begin service?"

"The tests aren't very extensive. These are unusual times we find ourselves in."

Meaning, Sparrow presumed, that getting men processed and ready for combat was the primary objective. "So it was his experiences in Cu Chi that brought him to you," Sparrow coaxed, probing for something solid.

"Yes."

"What happened there?"

Beckwith rose, went to the door, and called out to the clerk something that Sparrow couldn't hear. He resumed his seat. "Inspector, I've been doing the talking."

Sparrow hadn't expected the information exchange to be one-sided. He gave a brief account of the case and the tenuous trail of evidence that had led to Byron Hoot. It corresponded with the time since the army had lost contact with him. Beckwith listened in silence.

As Sparrow finished, there was a knock and the Spec-4 brought in a sealed green folder, set it on the desk, and left. "Our troops are deployed over a wide area in the district," Beckwith said. "Hoot's squad was holding one particular hot zone. Hoot volunteered for duty as a tunnel rat. On his final op before the attack, he came upon a VC soldier underground. Convinced the man was about to pull a weapon, Hoot drew first. Figuratively speaking. He used a knife." Beckwith mimed the action, lifting an invisible weapon.

"And killed him?" asked Sparrow.

The major lowered his arm and sighed. He unwound the string seal on the green folder, fingered through a thick sheaf of paper inside and withdrew a page. "The enemy soldier, apparently believing he was about to die, was reaching for his prayer beads. When Hoot saw that, well . . . he says he had . . ." Beckwith found the passage he was looking for. "Had an 'experience of oneness' with the man."

"Oneness."

"His word. I believe he's sincere." Beckwith laid aside the green folder and frowned. "If only it ended there. Two nights later, VC sappers got into the compound and Hoot's entire squad—eleven men—were killed. Hoot alone survived."

The dead were the men listed in the *Army Times*, Sparrow realized, but hearing this hit him with a force that merely reading the lines of print hadn't.

"Several of the sappers were killed, too, their bodies found the next day. Guess who one of them was?"

The question was rhetorical, and Sparrow knew the answer. "The man Hoot spared in the tunnel."

"According to those who first treated Hoot, he had only superficial wounds, and displayed no particular mental trauma. Which is remarkable considering . . . what he'd had to do."

Sparrow bent nearer, the better to hear and be heard over the tick-tocking of the Regulator. Hoarsely, he said, "Go on."

Beckwith had begun to squirm, as if invisible bugs were biting him. Damp patches had appeared under the arms of his uniform shirt. "It was in the wee hours. I've read the battle action reports. All holy hell broke loose."

He looked as if he'd much rather have been interviewing the next soldier claiming to have conscientious objections to war, or worries about his feelings toward other men in the showers; but Beckwith told it, laying on details: of men abruptly awakened from dreams and plunged into nightmare, grabbing helmets, fumbling for weapons; the nighttime lurid with the light of flares and the stink of gunsmoke, the screaming confusion and the eerie yells of the sappers who penetrated the aprons of wire, the *pop-pop-pop* of assault rifles, the blast of satchel charges. There was something hellish in the image Beckwith was painting, like Dore's depiction of Dante's inferno. Now Sparrow fidgeted, as if the invisible bugs had gotten to him, too. The clock went on tick-tocking in the stillness, like a sewing machine attempting to stitch up some rip in the fabric of time, through which a terrible past was trying to seep into the present.

"No counteroffensive was possible," Beckwith said, speaking quickly now, as if just to get it told. "The sappers were already inside. Hoot was likely the only man in his squad not already dead or dying. He must've seen how it was, his buddies gone, the raiders closing in. How long before he'd be found alive and butchered? So what did he do? He saw that his only hope of surviving was to . . ." With a tremor, the doctor broke off.

"Was to lie among the dead," Sparrow finished in a whisper.

"All night long. Imagining that he, too, was a corpse."

Sparrow was dizzy. Beckwith said, "We didn't know this for some time. Not until Hoot was stateside, and even then it took time. Owing to trauma, he lost most of his language use. The extent of his speaking was stock Vietnamese phrases from the interrogation manual. *'Nyoong bwong hum uh dow?'*—'Where are the tunnels?' *'Doong yay!'*—'Stand up!' For a while there it was all he'd say. I believe he was reliving his combat experiences. I had him read aloud from children's books, I prescribed anti-psychotic medications. I honestly don't know if any of it helped. Eventually, his language did come back." He clapped a hand on the green folder. "These transcripts show that. If he'd stayed in treatment . . . who knows?"

"If he got involved in the hippie drug scene, what effect would that have?"

"I remind you, you haven't firmly established—"

"But *if?*" Sparrow persisted.

Beckwith frowned. "Psychoactive chemicals would most likely intensify his fantasies and paranoia."

"Could they cause violent behavior?"

"It's difficult to pinpoint cause and effect."

"Forget pinpoint. Is it possible?"

"Hoot could have flashbacks to the night attack."

"How would he react?"

"Withdrawal. Flight."

"Or fight?" Sparrow said.

Beckwith pinched at his eyes and sighed. "Speaking strictly hypothetically—and I mean that; I'd need much more proof than you've given me here—but it's possible that at some level he's reenacting what he sees as his failure to stop the forces that killed his men. But that's as far as I'll go."

Sparrow thought a moment. "May I examine those transcripts?"

"Negative. Patient files are strictly confidential. Now, I've said all I intend to. Our time is up."

"One last thing. On the bodies of the American casualties, was there any mutilation?"

Beckwith sat back, considering the question. "The enemy have been known to take body parts. But no, there was absolutely none of that there. Our men had been shot."

Sparrow was at the door when Beckwith said, "One detail I did note—the graves registration team reported that they found no dog tags for any of our men."

Outside the sky had grayed. Driving back across the post through the wavering heat, Sparrow passed another marching column of trainees. " 'Second lieutenants are at it again,' " they chanted, " 'winning the war with a fountain pen. It's the Fort Ord Boogie . . . what a craaazy sound.' " At the post entrance, an MP stepped from the gatehouse and held up a white-gloved hand. He bent to the window. "Is your name Sparrow, sir?"

Puzzled, Sparrow said it was.

"Would you pull over and step out of your vehicle, sir."

Puzzlement went quickly to alarm. "What for?"

The sentry pointed to the gatehouse. "Sir, you have a telephone call."

GRAY RAIN WAS SLANTING FROM A GRAY SKY, TAPPING THE ROOF OF THE CAR. SPARROW stared out past the sweep of windshield wipers he hadn't used since May, and when a motel appeared just north of Monterey on Route 1, the thin blood of neon declaring VACANCY, he drew in. The place looked serviceable enough: a single level of stucco and glass, boasting pool, color TV, and Vibra-Magic beds. But he was indifferent to amenities, interested only in the address: The Landing. He would need to let Vestri know.

The desk clerk pulled his face out of *Stranger in a Strange Land* and nodded greetings. "Weird, huh? The weather?" His muttonchop whiskers and delicate rimless glasses gave him a gentle, displaced appearance here a hundred miles south of San Francisco. Sparrow registered and got a key. In his room, he felt suddenly beached, possessed by a sense of having broken his momentum. He wondered what this might cost him. A few hours? Something more? He still wasn't sure what the telephone call at the army gatehouse had meant. On the line was the clerk in the medical corps office, "Spec-4 Vestri," he'd reminded Sparrow, his voice breathless and quick, as though he had run somewhere to find a phone and didn't expect to get his full message across. "Go to Moss Landing. Get a motel room and call me at nine o'clock." He rattled off a phone number.

"What's this about?" Sparrow asked.

"Got the number?"

Sparrow repeated it. The line went dead.

In the end, it was the urgency in the soldier's voice that persuaded him. He drove the few miles north to Moss Landing. In another context he might have found the small fishing village quaint; but under the cold, lowering sky—and still under the spell of Byron Hoot's history—he was aware only of squawking gulls, old trawlers marooned in a tide of weeds, and roadside lots full of rusting buoys and other flotsam, as though all of the town's hopes had been cast ashore and abandoned. With several hours to kill, he got a fistful of change, found a booth, and phoned the *Rag*, wanting to hear Amy's voice, to tell her that he was going to be late getting back to the *Blind Faith*. There was no answer. He tried Pete Sandoval at the Hall, but when, after too many rings, Lanin answered, he hung up.

He watched the motel TV briefly for any news from San Francisco, but there was none. He switched off the set. He felt edgy, like a person pinned in no-man's-land, vexed by a sense of time running out. Had he identified the killer at last? Was it the same person he had failed to find two years ago? Could he find him now? He got coffee from a machine in the hall and longed for some whiskey to doctor it with. He parted the drapes and watched the wet dark. At nine o'clock he made the call.

Twenty minutes later, headlights swept the rain-streaked window, then died. A figure emerged from a car and dashed for the door. Sparrow let him in.

Vestri was in civvies: a knit cap pulled down over his G.I. haircut, flared corduroys, and a dripping field jacket, though not of recent issue, more like one Sparrow had worn in Korea a decade and a half ago. He looked all of twenty, the age Sparrow had been then. Under his arm was a thick green folder, which he dropped onto the bed like something he was eager to be rid of. Sparrow recognized it as the file Major Beckwith had consulted at Fort Ord earlier. Sparrow unwound the string seal and lifted the rain-spotted cover. Inside were the several hundred pages of transcription of Byron Hoot's therapy sessions. He glanced at Vestri. "How did you get this?"

The soldier seemed fidgety and tense. "I'm Beckwith's clerk, for God's sake. I type and file everything."

"In Texas, too?"

"Join the army, see the world."

"Does he know about this?"

"What do you think?"

Sparrow understood. "I appreciate this, but I'll be honest—I'm not sure what I'm looking for."

"Then maybe you won't find anything. On the other hand, maybe it's there and you will."

Sparrow considered offering to buy him a drink, but Vestri's restlessness made it clear he wanted to be gone. "Do you know why Corporal Hoot went AWOL?" Sparrow asked.

"No idea. One day he was there, the next day the crazy sonofabitch went over the hill."

"Is Hoot crazy?"

Vestri twisted his mouth to one side. "Every dude who comes to see the major is crazy, isn't he?" He moved toward the door.

"I don't know why you're doing this," Sparrow said, "but I'm grateful."

"Screw that, I don't need it. I'm short. Twenty-eight days and a wake-up. First thing I'm gonna do when I get out is get high and stay high, a week, a month . . . who cares?"

Sparrow lifted the green folder. "Is this an attempt to set something straight?"

Vestri peered at him, sustaining eye contact for the first time. "You think I joined up to ride a Remington? I wanted to be a hero, another Audie-fucking-Murphy. I believed in this fight. Now that I've seen what I've seen come through the major's door, I figure maybe that needs reevaluation. I'll be back for that at dawn."

Sparrow wanted to quiz him further about Hoot and the war, but the soldier was out the door, darting through the rain to his car. Alone, he opened the green folder.

Except for the small pools of light made by scattered lampposts, the parking lot at the marina was dark as Amy drove in. Fog was feathering in off the bay, as if seeking shelter for the night. She couldn't see John's car, though he'd have returned from Fort Ord by now. The message he'd left with Tess that morning had said that he would be at the boat. The DJ on KMPX had announced the time at ten, and that was a while ago, before he'd begun playing side two of *Fresh Cream*. Now, as the sounds of Eric Clapton's guitar faded, she shut off the motor. Voices emerged from the silence.

In the rearview mirror, she saw a cluster of people scoot by on the boulevard, heading downtown. They were talking loudly, their words edged with nervous laughter, like kids passing a cemetery. That's how it was with the Death Tripper on the loose; if you went outside, you went in numbers, and you didn't linger. *So why am I out here alone?* She pushed the thought away and climbed out. This wasn't the Haight, after all.

The night air was cold. From the bay came the muted clang of bell buoys and the somber moan of foghorns. With a shiver she drew the collar of her woolen jacket around her throat. Moving quickly, she went through the marina gate and down a gangway to the dock.

The pier grew darker as she walked out, the lights of the parking lot dwindling behind her. Here there were only low dock lanterns at spaced intervals, casting just enough glow to illuminate the planking and reveal the outlines of boats. Most of them were dark.

In the distance, the beacon on Alcatraz swept the fog like a restless, occluded eye. She found herself remembering that evening after Glenn's funeral, when she and John had come here. Somehow, unexpectedly, in that long tragic day, they had formed a bond. She had wanted him to hold her, wondered if he would. Then the marina man showed up and said John had had a visitor, and intuitively she knew that it was Moon, understood that there were complexities to John Sparrow she didn't know. One thing she had recognized, however, was that he hadn't healed from the loss of his wife; it was there like a secret wound. That didn't take away what had happened between them in the redwood grove up in Marin. What had that been about? Lust, concocted from the intensity of the day? Or something else? In the days since, there'd been no time to wonder, but John came often to her thoughts, and although it wasn't fair to either, she found herself making little comparisons between Seth and him, weighing, balancing.

The pier branched again. She took the outermost branch. She was able now to make out sailboat masts, rising in a thicket from the dark. One of the boats would be the *Blind Faith*. With a backward glance, she saw that the shore was fading into the fog soup. The slosh of seawater was closer now, lapping against the pilings with a hungry sound. She could feel the chill the water gave off. She shivered.

With the killings, something malign had come, fraying the bonds that had connected people. Yet, oddly, in her role as journalist she'd felt inviolable, as if so long as she was *writing* about what was happening, she was safe. When she tried to voice this to Seth, he turned it around and questioned her commitment. By being the observer, he said, she was also an outsider. Not him, though. He was in the flow, linked to people and events, part of the Movement. But if his lack of a fixed place to stand failed him as a journalist, she nevertheless envied his involvement, his passion for the struggle; though in recent days she wondered if it was taking him down a dangerous path, toward some point of intersection where he would meet violence. She glanced over her shoulder and felt an odd little pulsation of fear. Behind her, the land was almost gone.

"Time was, Seth, all you white boys be coming looking for only just one thing." Nat Evans was perched on a stool in the auto repair shop where he worked in the Fillmore. On the workbench before him a small electric motor lay apart under the gleam of a gooseneck lamp, its innards sprouting colored wires like the veins and arteries of a laboratory frog. It was after hours, and several other black men stood around, a couple of them in leather coats and black berets. They had fallen silent at Seth's entry.

"Not no more," Nat Evans went on, expansive in his role at center stage. "Chicks be *givin'* it up now, nobody has to pay for poon. Next it was the weed you all wantin' to buy. Pass the giggle-stick, brother, form that guerrilla bond and shit." Nat shook his head and laughed. "But that's changin', too. So if it ain't poon, and it ain't weed—lemme see, can I guess . . ."

Seth was impatient with the put-on. Maybe Nat was tired of it, as well. He told the other men he'd check them later, and showing Nat clenched fists, they drifted into the night. "You and me now, Seth," he said, "talking supply and demand. You demanding, I'm supposed to supply."

"Save the lecture. We took that class together, remember?"

"Were you there, too? All you guys look the same to me."

"Have you got it?"

Nat's ribbing humor slid away, his face going to hard angles, one eye narrowing to a fierce stare, and he was once again the tough, bright grad student Seth had known at Berkeley. "You said there's no hurry."

"There's been a change. I'm going to need it tomorrow."

"Tomorrow!" Nat Evans sprang from the stool. "I can't get that shit that fast. I thought we were in agreeance. What you want takes time."

Seth frowned. How much time had *he* been given? An hour ago his contact at the Hall of Justice had told him the TAC Squad would be at the rally tomorrow night. Moon had a notion of smoking out the killer, but Seth knew better. It was a ruse to cause trouble. "That doesn't give you much lead time for a story," his contact had said, folding Seth's twenty-dollar bill into his shirt pocket. The fact was the next issue of the *Rag* wasn't due for days, and even that wasn't a sure thing anymore. He and Amy had been quarreling over the paper's goals. She still believed that the pen was mightier than the sword.

"Dynamite you got to liberate carefully," Nat Evans went on. "I've got a line on some, but it's gonna take time. It's a bounce at Quentin if I get busted with that shit. Jail for your pimply white ass, too."

"So you keep saying. How soon, Nat?"

"I'll be lucky if I get it by next week."

Which would be a week too late. Moon would win. Seth gazed around the little shop. An old fan creaked dispiritedly in the window, stirring the stale, gasoline-scented air. And suddenly he had an idea. "Okay. I'll pay you what we agreed on—but forget the dynamite. I want you to get something else for me. Something a little more . . . revolutionary."

It was nearing eleven P.M. Sparrow had been reading transcripts of psychiatric sessions for over an hour. What had seemed at first to be desultory talk, like that between strangers shooting the breeze, possessed in fact a concealed logic. With no sign of hurry, Beckwith, over a period of weeks, had gotten the shell-shocked Corporal Hoot talking. Mostly he spoke of the mundane, but at each point where opportunity presented itself, Beckwith pried up a small edge of protective armor to reveal something underneath. The revelations weren't big, or even very apparent, but taken together they were the rudiments of something more, as Sparrow was starting to see. In the session for 29 Apr 66, he read:

> *"How are you doing today?"*
>
> *"I'm here, aren't I?"*
>
> *"You've got to trust that this process can work."*
>
> *[Patient laughs] " 'Trust me, boy.' My daddy's own words."*
>
> *"Tell me about him."*
>
> *"Oh, you'd love him. A true servant of the Lord, my daddy. [Long silence] No. I won't talk about him. But I will tell about this one time. I must've been seven or eight. I was supposed to stay home and pile stove wood, one of my chores. But instead I clumb up on a shed roof. Just so's to have some fun, I reckon. That old town was flat boring most of the time. Small? Shoot. I'll tell you small. Anyways, I clumb on the roof and just set up there, thinking. After awhile I realized I needed to get on home 'cause I still had chores. Only I seen I was up pretty high, and was scared to get down. It came on to dusk, but I was nervous to call out to anyone, on account of they'd know I was afraid, or anyway they'd see I done something wrong. Eventually my daddy come looking and seen me up yonder on the roof." [Patient silent]*
>
> *"Go on."*
>
> *"He said, 'Let's go now, don't be a-scared, boy. Come on down.' I'm glad he ain't angry, but I'm froze stiff with fright being up there. 'Come on, then, boy,' he says, 'jump. Trust me. I'll catch you.' By this time, some them old boys who worked in the mines were coming home from work, and they stopped to watch. One of 'em said he'd go fetch a ladder, and I thought, I'm saved, but my daddy he told him, 'No, the boy's gonna jump and I'm gonna catch him.'*
>
> *"Finally I seen I didn't have no choice. He was bound and determined. So I pluck up my nerve and I jump. And as I'm dropping, he steps away. Bang, I hit the ground. Jammed my teeth up into my head, cut my lip. I'm lying there bleeding and crying, people standing around, and my daddy says, calm as ice water, 'Let that be a lesson to you, boy. Trust not in man nor mammon. Trust only in God, for his yoke is easy, and his burden is light.' And he walked away.*
>
> *[Pauses; laughs] "For the longest time I thought 'mammon' meant mammals. And it made sense in a way, which I figured was why he used to kill 'em."*

Beginning with the soldier's present situation, reversing slowly through his adolescence and childhood—both traumatic by any measure—and then, over a half dozen sessions, working forward again toward the more recent past, Hoot and the doctor were coming at length to Hoot's experiences in Cu Chi. It occurred to Sparrow that this subtle indirection was what the psychologist who had met with Sparrow after Helen's death might have sought to do, with some goal of getting him to examine himself and thereby, perhaps, heal. The man, however, seemed bored. After the first session, Sparrow hadn't gone back.

He lit a cigarette. He leaned back, wanting to empty his mind before returning to the transcripts. And for a few moments it worked, until a deep rumbling brought him back to the stormy night outside. He got more coffee and turned to the next page.

> *"Do you want to talk about the men in your squad? You were all close. What happened had to be deeply painful for you. [Silence.] Do you remember them? I've got their names here. Worden. Remember him? Heite, Fisch—"*
>
> *[Agitated, patient recites names in rapid alpha sequence.] "Adair, Fischetti, Ford, Heite . . ."*
>
> *"Tell me about them."*
>
> *"They're dead."*
>
> *"They were your buddies, weren't they? Your friends? It can be helpful to talk about that."*
>
> *"They're dead." [Long silence. Patient grows anxious.]*
>
> *"What became of their dog tags?"*
>
> *"What?"*
>
> *"When the graves registration team reached the compound, they couldn't find any tags. You weren't wearing yours, either. Do you have any idea what became of them?"*

A sea bird creaked in the fog.

At last Amy was able to make out John's boat. A light was on in the cabin, and she felt relief. He was aboard. But as she looked, the light went out. And why not? The poor guy had been running on nerves for days, had driven several hundred miles today. He must be exhausted. She quickened her steps.

As she neared the *Blind Faith*, a splash startled her. On a nearby boat a bilge hose spat a stream of water. She clapped a hand to her chest and laughed with relief. When the water stopped, she started forward again. At the edge of her vision, something flitted. It was farther out the pier, but when she looked directly, trying to penetrate the darkness, there was nothing to see. She listened. On the bay, the fog warnings moaned, like the demented ravings of beasts confined to sea caves. Behind her the land had vanished.

Nervous, given over to a sudden vague perception that something was amiss, she moved on. The planks ticked hollowly under her footsteps. She was spooked, her heart beating quickly now, but that was silly, she told herself. *Just get to the boat and see John.*

Something sprang from the dark.

A hand clamped her throat. Panic-struck, she spun hard to her right, trying to break free. Something sharp hit her shoulder. From instinct she threw a punch. But she had no power, could barely move her arm, in fact, and realized that whatever had hit her had sliced through the coat and cut her.

She swung her other fist. It hit something solid—an edge of jaw? A forehead— and glanced away. The sharpness ripped through the breast of her coat. A knife.

She made claws of her fingers, going for a face she couldn't quite see. She missed and stumbled back, stubbed her heel on a cleat, and slammed against a boat hull. She gave a small scream, and tumbling sideways she went off the pier.

Her eyes wrung shut. Ice-cold water rammed up her nose. But cold was nothing compared to the sear of pain in her shoulder as the sea enclosed her.

Underwater, she opened her eyes and saw the light above. As she rose toward it, a hand plunged down from the dock. There hadn't been time to take a full breath. Now she couldn't. She was being thrust deeper, wedged between a boat hull and the pier. She kicked harder, frantically trying to surface. The attacker pushed down. She could see her heartbeat, like a neon sign in an old movie, throbbing behind her eyelids each time she blinked. Above, she could make out a vague face. It was underlit by the dock-lantern. Gazing down through a distorted lens of water, it was all nose and heavy brow and deeply shadowed eyes, like the scowling face of a demon.

But it was no demon.

She had been badly mistaken in her sense of invulnerability. The knife plunged again, the blade arcing in a silvery trail of bubbles, like a scribble of lightning on a dark sky. It hit her shoulder, but she felt only a pinch of pain, for it wasn't the knife that was going to kill her she realized as air began to die in her lungs. Her eyes burned. The face was blurred and seemed far-off now, and she had a flickering long-ago memory of teaching Glenn to swim—*Relax, you'll float*—now Glenn was gone, and she was, too, the lights winking out one by one, and in another moment she would exhale a last breath and gulp in the endless night.

PETE SANDOVAL'S LINE AT THE HALL OF JUSTICE RANG A LONG TIME. SPARROW TRIED Sandoval's number at his father's ranch, but there was no answer there, either. He considered trying to reach Amy, but it was late, and there were other people in her house. Was she in Seth Green's bed? How did that work, this free love thing? Was that what they believed in? Had the afternoon she and Sparrow made love in the woods really meant something? He thought of them lying together among the ferns . . . He squeezed his eyes shut, voiding the image, and began to pace.

With each section of transcript read, he was coming more to see how Byron Hoot could be the Haight-Ashbury killer. Already a troubled young man when he'd entered the service, trained in weapons and fighting, concealment and stealth, he had experienced combat trauma, had lost his friends in a night attack that he alone survived. And Hoot had been AWOL since late April, not too long before he turned up in San Francisco . . . not long before the murders began.

But there was more. Hoot had also been in the Bay Area two summers ago, when the murders in North Beach had taken place. He had gone to Vietnam that September, and the North Beach killings had stopped. Coincidence? Those crimes were different, after all, in terms of methods and choice of victims. And what would the motive have been? Or the cause? And yet . . . Sparrow sighed. Was he stretching facts, looking for links where none existed? He needed to know more. And soon.

Outside the storm had intensified. Whips of rain, silvered by the strobe-flashes of lightning, lashed the window. He was exhausted. Why not lie on the bed for just a few minutes, let the Vibra-Magic mattress do its . . .

He got more coffee. And opened the next file.

> *"Do you want to talk about the tunnels?"*
>
> *"The tunnels, ohhh. What about them?"*
>
> *"Anything you want. What the experience was like, how you got involved in that. What you . . . found there?"*
>
> *[Patient seems unusually agitated]*
>
> *"It's okay to talk about. You volunteered, right?"*
>
> *"Did I? Raised my hand of my own free will and said, 'I'll do it'? I don't know."*
>
> *"One of the battalion action reports states that you 'repeatedly, and without thought for personal safety, volunteered for tunnel duties,' which you performed with*

courage. This even after the casualty rate among your unit went up and the risks became extreme."

"Extreme? [Patient laughs] I'd say the risk of just getting through each day was extreme. Was that really me? Crawling headfirst into those things? [Long pause] We go way back, tunnels and me."

By now the patterns of words on the pages had become so familiar that Sparrow was able to imagine voices giving them life. He heard Beckwith's calm tone, his compassion, read persistence in his silences. The patient, on the other hand, was more elusive, his words edged with an Appalachian nasality, his phrasing, at times, almost Biblical. It had taken Sparrow longer to imagine that voice. But now he thought he had it. Byron Hoot came across as wary, yes, but was there something else, too? An undercurrent of madness?

"When I was a kid I used to go down in the empty coal shafts in the town where I lived. The mines were mostly played out by then, boarded up. I had this fascination with them, the . . . mystery of 'em, I guess. Who knew what ghosts were in there? I remember this one shaft where four men had got killed in a cave-in. My daddy said it was on account of they'd been whoremongers. I had this fascination with being underground."

"Is that how it was in Cu Chi?"

"After a time, yeah. I got so's I wanted to do it. That sound dinky dow? *Crazy? I even liked it. Crawling in there with a flashlight. Most guys took a .45, but I liked a bayonet or a knife—quieter, and never knowing what I'd come on around the next bend. My heart'd be thumping so loud I'd think, there's no way someone else can't hear it. I'd be soaked with sweat. There were fire ants and rats, big spiders sometimes. Creeps me out remembering."*

"But it may help you. Go on."

"We had these little blocks of explosive. I'd run wire, then crawl back out, and Molloy—he was the sergeant—he'd use a battery-powered detonator. Bango! I got good at that. Afterwards, I'd go down again to see what I could find."

"And . . . ?"

"I dunno. Rice, weapons. Books. Sometimes bodies."

"And ghosts?"

"Ghosts. Yes, sir. I'd say so."

"Want to talk about that?"

*[Long silence] "I'm thinking, why was I so eager to go in there in the first place?
I mean, my whole thing, from day one, back at the induction center, was listen up, be
a good soldier, don't volunteer. So why'd I do it, deliberately put myself in a world
of hurt? Can you answer me that, Doc?"*

Major Beckwith had waited for the patient to provide his own response, which
Hoot failed to do, and five minutes later the session ended. There was a handwrit-
ten note stapled to the last page of the transcript, on letterhead from the U.S.
Army Medical Center at Fort Sam Houston in San Antonio. "Query MACV:
request copy orig. orders. How many tunnel missions? Check prior assignment to
DLI (6–65 to 8–65)." At the bottom were Beckwith's initials.

Sparrow's pulse quickened as some tendril of memory stirred, but it wasn't
enough to bring recall. MACV, he knew, was an acronym for Military Assistance
Command, Vietnam. But what was DLI? It was reasonable to assume it was a military abbreviation; beyond that though, he was in the dark. And yet Beckwith had
taken the trouble to jot and attach the note. Why? He would question Vestri when
the soldier arrived at dawn to reclaim the green folder. Meanwhile, why not try
something closer at hand?

Amy woke to the sensation of her clothes being pulled off.

She drew her legs up defensively. She was topless, wearing only her panties,
and lying in a narrow bed. Her teeth were chattering. A lamp swung slowly from
the low ceiling, painting the confined space with the zigzagging shadow of the
dark-haired woman undressing her.

"Thank goodness you're awake," the woman said.

"Where am I?" Amy sat up quickly.

The woman handed her a thick towel. "Maybe you should be the one to say. Do
you know?"

She looked around. Surrounding her were mahogany walls, and some kind of
nautical chart. She was in the cabin of a boat. *John's* boat. "Aboard *Blind Faith*."

The woman looked relieved. "And your name?"

Amy told her. But how had she gotten here?

"I was coming down the pier—coming to see John—and I heard splashing. You
were in the water." Amy couldn't remember it. "I wanted to get you into some dry
clothes. Put these on." She gave Amy a sweatshirt and some cotton deck pants with
an elastic waist. Amy drew them on. "When you've warmed up, we should go to
the hospital."

The woman seemed familiar somehow, though Amy couldn't remember ever having met her before. "Who are you?"

"I'm John's sister-in-law, Elaine."

Amy made the link: her resemblance to the photograph of John's wife was clear. Amy climbed out of the berth. "I have to see John."

"You've been injured. You must've slipped on the dock and fallen in. You gave yourself a good knock. Don't you recall that?"

She fingered a lump on her scalp.

"It's not just your head I'm worried about. You've got wounds on your shoulder and hand. I found John's first aid kit. I think you'll be all right. There isn't much bleeding, but that could be because of the cold water."

Amy reached under the sweatshirt. There was a gauze pad taped in place with adhesive.

"Here, dry your hair. I'll make some tea."

Amy settled at the little galley table, and Elaine put a kettle on the gas ring. Amy explained her own connection to John. Now other details came back. She *hadn't* slipped—she'd been attacked, shoved underwater. She told Elaine.

"My God! As soon as you're warm enough, we'll go to the marina office and call the police."

"Why don't we just tell John?"

Elaine seemed disconcerted by the question. "When did you speak with him last?"

"He left a message this morning. He was going to follow a lead, then meet me here tonight."

"You don't know, then, do you?"

Amy sat up. "Know what?"

"He was suspended from the force."

"Thank God. I was dreading the worst when you said that. When?"

"Last night." Quickly Elaine told of having heard it from George Moon: the scuffle, the drawn weapon, and the ensuing suspension. The welt on Amy's head began to throb. She sank back in the galley seat. "Do you want to go to the hospital?"

"I want to know where John is. He should've been back by now. What time is it?" It occurred to her she had no idea.

"After midnight."

Over two hours were gone, time she could barely recall; but right now her worry was for John. Where was he?

A small TV perched on the counter, its sound off, provided the light in the otherwise darkened motel office. In the shifting glow Sparrow noticed the sci-fi novel the clerk had been reading earlier tented open on the desk behind the counter. The clerk lay beside it, his muttonchop whiskered cheek on the desktop, his glasses off, his mouth slack, and for a moment Sparrow had the icy thought that he was dead. But as he stepped nearer, the man stirred and sat up, blinking.

"Sorry to bug you," Sparrow said.

The man hooked on his glasses and wiped his mouth. "S'okay, I was up." He switched on the desk lamp.

"Have you got a phone book that includes Fort Ord?"

There was nothing under the listings for the post. "What do you need?" asked the clerk, awake and helpful now. Sparrow told him. "DLI is no sweat," the clerk said. "Defense Language Institute. Soldiers get assigned there to learn languages. Russian, Cuban Spanish. These days I imagine Vietnamese is a big one."

"*Dinky dow*," Sparrow murmured.

"Huh?"

"Where is this place?"

The man motioned with a thumb. "Right over in Monterey."

Sparrow read the handwritten note on the transcript again. ". . . Check prior assignment to DLI (6-65 to 8-65) . . ." Had Beckwith ever followed up his query? Sparrow was stuck on the idea that Byron Hoot had come *back* to the area, because he had been here once before, on assignment in Monterey. That in itself was intriguing; but it was the dates that sent a tingle up his spine. Prior to going to Vietnam, Byron Hoot had been here, less than a hundred miles from San Francisco, from June through August: three months coinciding with the murders in North Beach.

"Three and two the count, and Allen waits. The pitch—crack! And it's going, going . . ."

PFC Jimmy Hazen watched the pebble vanish into the night and a second later heard it ping distantly off the roof of one of the armory sheds. "Foul ball. Richie Allen and the Phils stay alive."

He bent and plucked another pebble from the small pile at his feet. Continuing the commentary—"Three and two, still, and the delivery . . ."—he lofted the rock gently with his left hand, and gripping the nightstick with his right—

He froze. The stone fell with a soft plop. Quickly, he hooked the nightstick onto his web belt, snatched up the M-14 rifle that lay on the ground, and started to walk along the woven-wire fence that ringed the armory compound on the lower end of the Presidio. And not a moment too soon, as a figure emerged from the darkness into the diffused glow of a perimeter light.

Hazen stopped and brought the M-14 to cross arms. "Halt!" he said, using the standard challenge. "Who goes there?"

The man came nearer, cloaked in shadow still, so it took a few seconds to spot the the 1st Lieutenant bar on the epaulets of his field jacket. Shit! Probably the Officer of the Day.

"You hoping to stay out of the war, soldier?"

"No, sir, I—"

"At ease."

Hazen lowered the M-14. The lieutenant peered at him, and Hazen saw now that he wasn't the OD. He didn't recognize the man.

"You're not one of those draft-dodgers who'd rather be poking daisies in the muzzles of rifles than sighting down one, are you?"

"Sir, I—"

"Stand at ease."

Hazen cursed himself for having volunteered for guard duty. The first, most basic lesson a soldier learned was never, *ever* do jack if you weren't directly ordered to! But he'd volunteered tonight because he knew from a certain company clerk (who took five bucks for the information) that upon seeing Hazen's name on the duty roster, the Old Man would be favorably inclined to grant Hazen's request for a 24-hour pass. He wanted to be in Golden Gate Park tomorrow night for the big free concert and antiwar rally. Not that he cared about politics—it was useless to worry about what he couldn't change—but it would be a chance to catch some music and toke a little marihoochie; maybe even scoop a chick if he was lucky.

Now he was dead certain to do none of those. In fact, if the officer was a hard case, he'd be lucky not to get an Article 15. He stood at ease, wondering if he ought to try to explain, admit he was bored and had made up this little game. Hell, it was pretty patriotic when you got down to it, baseball. No, shut up. Say nothing.

The lieutenant was inspecting Hazen's boots, his uniform. Hazen wanted to check his gig line—the vertical line from shirt buttons down through freshly Brassoed belt buckle and on down his fly—that a soldier was supposed to keep straight; but he didn't move.

"You're a pretty sorry-ass soldier there, troop. What do you do, sleep in that uniform?"

"No, sir. I'm a little low on fresh starch right now."

"A *little* low?" But the officer wasn't pushing it. He peered into Hazen's face now. "You hoping to give the ladies a joyride when you get back home?"

"Sir?"

"That pussy bumper on your lip. It's growing long."

His throat tightened. He had let his mustache creep down past the corners of his mouth. Bad enough he'd have to go to the concert with a whitewall haircut— everyone else in shoulder-length, him in *soldier*-length hair—but at least he had a halfway decent 'stache, almost like Paul McCartney's on the new album. But he didn't say this, because this nimrod wouldn't know who McCartney was, and regs did say that facial hair couldn't extend beyond or below the corners of the mouth. He said nothing about this chickenshit duty, either: pulling sentry on an armory that probably didn't have anything in it in the first place, and was a million miles from the war in the second, and while he was standing around in the cold guarding it, longhairs with big righteous mustaches were right this moment over in the Hashbury plunged to the hilt in sweet snatch.

"Where you from, soldier?"

"From, sir? From Philadelphia."

"That's a draft-dodging town if there ever was one."

"Sir, I—"

"Tench-*hut!*"

Hazen clapped his boot heels together.

"What are the general orders?" the officer barked.

Aw, man, Hazen thought, *don't do this.*

"I can't *hear* you, troop! Sound off like you had a pair!"

"Sir, the general orders are: One, to take charge of this post and all government property in view. Two, to walk my post in a military manner . . . um, keeping always on the alert and observing . . . everything that takes place within sight or hearing. Three—" Hazen went on reciting the orders.

The officer was lean and suntanned and sort of good-looking, probably some gung ho type. He had turned his gaze toward the armory Hazen was supposed to be guarding. He surveyed the coils of wire along the top of the fence, and the lit- tle sign that said DANGER: EXPLOSIVES. Fog was rolling in whitely from the bay. He turned back. "Present arms for inspection, soldier."

Hazen quit his recitation and handed over the rifle. The man shot the bolt and peered in. "Keep going."

"Seven, yes, sir. To talk to no one except in line of duty. Eight, to give alarm in case of fire or disorder."

The general orders were coming out of rote memory, locked there by hours of drill in basic training; Hazen, however, was thinking about something else now . . . something nudging his mind like a june bug on a screen door. What was it?

"This here's a good weapon. Over there you get sixteens. Haven't been over yet, have you, PFC?"

"No, sir."

"Goddamn Tonka Toy, the M-16. The thing jams up with dust, or with the damp. Trouble gets close, she freezes, or your ammo runs out, you're KIA."

Gripping the rifle in one hand, the officer drew back the hem of his field jacket with the other, revealing a belt scabbard Hazen hadn't noticed before. From it the man slid out the gleaming length of a bayonet. Hazen watched, transfixed.

"Keep going."

"Eleven, to be especially watchful at night and during the time for challenging . . . uh . . ." He faltered as the man affixed the bayonet to the M-14. *Who the hell is he supposed to be? John Wayne? What is he doing with a bayo?* Almost done . . . " ' . . . during the time for challenging and to . . .'" His mind went blank.

The officer glanced up. "Well?"

And then Hazen got it: "To challenge all persons on or near my post, and to allow *no* one to pass without proper authority." He gushed a breath. "That's it, sir."

"Outstanding, soldier."

"Thank you, sir. Uh—may I see your ID, please?"

The officer's eyes went round with surprise. "What?"

Hazen almost smiled. It'd been a test, a challenge. Well, now the dude would know PFC Hazen was doing the job, being alert, had a *pair*! "Sir, I see your uniform, and the rank insignia, but I don't know you. I have to ask for ID."

The man's eyes were intent on Hazen's own now, darkly shining in the shadows. Silence stretched around them. Hazen's excitement began to falter. "You want to know who I am?" asked the man.

A trickle of sweat snail-crawled down the crack of Hazen's ass. He was full of doubt all of a sudden. "I think so. Sir."

The man gave a sad smile and nodded. He offered back the M-14. With a flood of relief, Hazen reached to take it.

The motion was swift. The man spun the rifle in a one-eighty and thrust it forward. The bayonet punched through Hazen's field jacket, fatigue shirt, and T-shirt and made a small *pop* as it pierced his stomach. The blow jacked him backwards as the polished steel sliced intestines, bashed through his spine, and hit the back of his canteen belt, knocking his nightstick to the ground. But that was crazy. Why would an officer bayonet him? He was imagining it. He had fallen asleep on duty and was having a nightmare, because he was still standing there, after all, straight and tall, and there was no pain, just . . .

A soft splashing sound drew his gaze down. A sluice of dark liquid was running out of his jacket as if a small hose were concealed inside. The liquid frothed on the ground, wetting his boots. The sight made him woozy, like he wanted to puke. But he didn't. His head reeled. He was aware of dropping onto the little pile of stones that Richie Allen was supposed to knock out of Connie Mack Stadium. Was aware, too, of the man detaching the bayo from the M-14 and setting the rifle down.

He was aware of the wheeze of his own breath, the sound a straw makes when a kid sucks the last of a root beer float through it. He was aware of a soft voice saying, "That's who I am . . ." The words seemed to echo away among the fogged-in tin sheds of the armory. "Who I am . . . who I am . . ."

As the man walked away, PFC Jimmy Hazen of Philadelphia got hip to something else, too, washed in a bright light somewhere in the back of his eyes: the detail he'd been trying earlier to seize. "Boots," he murmured, wanting to show he was vigilant after all, an alert sentry, not deserving of this shabby treatment . . . but the word was a soggy croak in his throat. What he wished to call attention to were the man's boots. Not government-issue stateside black cowhide leather. Uh-uh, these were just plain old civilian work shoes.

On which the man moved off, quiet as the night itself.

SPARROW SPED NORTH IN THE FADING NIGHT. HE HAD LEFT THE GREEN FOLDER WITH the motel clerk for Vestri to pick up at dawn, and now he was mentally working the material he had dredged from the psych files, searching for a pattern.

The details of Byron Hoot's boyhood were intriguing: his relationship with his father, the church with its practice of blood sacrifice, the pounding message of sin and guilt. Of more immediate interest were Hoot's combat experiences and the loss of his squad, men whose dog tags had been missing (what that might mean, he had no idea). What had Hoot been doing before going overseas? Was he linked somehow to the killings in North Beach? Was he the Death Tripper?

Sparrow put on the car radio, twitching the dial past country music and farm reports. Paul Harvey was commenting on a great countercultural outbreak that had visited the land, a plague of almost Old Testament proportions: long hair, protests, love-ins, even murder. Things were going haywire. Sparrow snapped off the radio. At a filling station outside Palo Alto, he was served by a polite attendant in neat blue coveralls. As Sparrow paid, the man asked, "You want your stamps, sir?"

"What?"

"Green Stamps. For the gas."

He was almost back to San Francisco when the car died.

"Authorities at the Presidio this morning made a grisly discovery."

The transistor radio has a tinny vibration, and you want to reach behind the counter to adjust it, but you resist. You need to be extra careful now. Closing your eyes in hopes you can filter out the coffeeshop babble, you key on the newscaster's voice.

". . . was found stabbed to death. Military and city authorities are on the scene. An undetermined quantity of explosives is missing from the armory Hazen had been assigned to guard. Police have not said whether these events are linked or if the murder is related to a recent series of killings in the Haight-Ashbury, but an unconfirmed source says . . ."

On the street again, you shoulder the saddlebags and set off.

God, you're tired. If you could, you'd go back to the room and sleep awhile, then get on the Black Shadow and ride. But you can't, they've got the bike. Anyway, no time. There's something you have to do tonight, something you should've done already.

And there's the Cole woman.

A short walk, a stop to ask directions, and Sparrow found the place. It was a small, weathered ranch on rolling land: the home where Pete Sandoval had grown up and lived now with his father. The faded name on the mailbox was "M. Sandoval."

The air had the rank, sweet stink of pigs. He knocked on the ranch house door but there was no answer. A faint metallic squeaking was coming from the barn, and he wandered to it. As he reached the door, he jumped at the sudden appearance of a man in a blood-spattered apron. They had startled each other. But after Sparrow's quick explanation, the man, who looked to be in his late fifties, with a cap of tight, graying curls, grinned and nodded enthusiastically. "Ah, *Señor* Sparrow. *Mucho gusto.* I've heard about you. I'm Miguel Sandoval. *Con respeto, señor* . . . welcome to my home!"

In his excited hospitality, he offered a bloodstained hand, but drew it away before Sparrow could take it. "I been working." He motioned over his shoulder at the barn. "Pedro, he has told me of you. Your car broke down, eh? Come."

They went into the barn. At the end of a short hallway, Mr. Sandoval hung up his apron and began washing his hands in a soapstone sink. Beyond a large window was another room, lit with pale purple light. Suspended from stainless steel hooks, a double row of pigs' carcasses hung on rollers, and Sparrow identified the metallic squeaking he had heard. The room was a refrigerated storage room. By the door was a wooden box with gloves and boots and the tools of his trade. "Come," Mr. Sandoval said again, waving him past and into a small office area. Sparrow used the telephone and dialed Pete Sandoval's extension. On the wall, tacked among various FDA certificates, was a snapshot of a small boy holding a piglet and a prize ribbon. Sparrow tapped the photo. "Is that Pedro?"

"*Si*. At the 4-H fair. Later, it broke his heart to learn a pig cannot stay a pet forever."

There was no answer at Pete's extension. Outside, the man listened to Sparrow's account of the Impala's demise. It sounded like something he could fix, he said; but at the moment he was *muy ocupado,* getting pigs ready for market. Sparrow said he would call a taxi, but the elder Sandoval wouldn't hear of it. He led the way out to an old Dodge pickup truck parked behind the barn. It was an extra vehicle, he said, his insistence prevailing over Sparrow's reluctance. The truck started on the third try. Sandoval leaned to the open window. "If I can fix your car later, I will telephone you." He took Sparrow's card. "*Vaya con dios.*"

TENSE FROM COFFEE AND THE HIGHWAY MILES, HE MADE IT BACK. HE DIDN'T GO TO THE hall. Austin would be impossible to talk to, and Sparrow had neither the energy nor the inclination to try. When he needed to, he would get hold of Pete Sandoval; his first order of business, however, was to reach Amy. From a booth he called the *Rag,* but the telephone rang unanswered. She had no phone in her apartment, and he knew of no other way to reach her. He hesitated a moment, redeposited his dime and dialed another number.

The house was on Baker, an old building divided into apartment units. In the foyer, Sparrow checked the row of dented mailboxes. On the third box was a card with names typed on it.

seth g.
tess ferriera
f. o'neill--'the jester'
amy cole

He found the bell push and pressed it.

Earlier, from the phone booth he had made a second call.

"John? Thank God," his sister-in-law Elaine had said. "Where are you?" He told her, being deliberately vague with the location. Paranoia was running deep in him now, like an infection. "Is Amy with you?" Elaine asked.

The question took him by surprise. How did she know about Amy? Elaine told him about last night's attack at the marina, of their having gone aboard the *Blind Faith*. The news was a blow. "We got her checked at the hospital," Elaine said. "She's okay, or was when I dropped her at her apartment."

"When was that?"

"After midnight. I'd hoped she'd be with you now."

"She's not."

"I'll call her at once."

"There's no phone there," Sparrow said.

And there didn't seem to be anyone here now. He went across the street to a laundromat and found another pay phone. He called Elaine at work and let her know. Elaine took down the number for the *Rag* and said she'd keep trying there. "Amy could be out doing a story, right? There's that big rally tonight." She tried for a note of confidence, but it didn't fully work.

"I'll call you back," Sparrow said.

"John—"

"Yes?"

"She's lovely."

Elaine let a small silence grow, giving him a chance to speak. He said simply, "She is."

Sparrow found the house near USF again. He rapped sharply on the screen door. Inside, the landlord's dog started to bark. The inner door opened. Behind the screen, the old man, looping suspenders over his shoulders, blinked through his horn-rims into the weak daylight. "Oh. I was sacked out. Didn't recognize you for a moment."

"Has your renter been back?"

"Brian?" Sparrow didn't correct him on Hoot's name. "I've kept an eye peeled, but I ain't seen no one except you cops."

"Get the key. And a flashlight."

When Sparrow unsnapped the padlock and pulled open the garage door, dust and gasoline fumes drifted out. He shone the flashlight in. The motorcycle was still propped on its kickstand, but he gave it only passing regard on his way to the back. The rental room was as before. He flipped the light switch for the adjoining bathroom, and the fluorescent ceiling ring flickered palely a few times, and then winked on. His eyes went to the mirror in the medicine cabinet above the sink, and suddenly his heart beat faster.

The old man shuffled into the cramped bathroom behind him.

"I thought you said no one's been here."

"Brian, you mean? Can't have been. I've kept the place locked since—" He broke off as Sparrow stepped aside and he caught sight of the mirror. The glass was shattered in a spiderweb pattern, and on it were some reddish-brown lines. The old man squinted. "Is that blood?"

Sparrow touched it. It was. Careful to touch only the very edge of the door, he opened the cabinet. A cockroach, startled by the intrusion, zipped along the empty middle shelf and vanished into the slot in the back wall for the disposal of used razor blades. A Vietnamese phrase rose to Sparrow's mind. *Dee dee mao!* Move out fast! It was what Byron Hoot had done, evidently. Except for the stub of styptic pencil and the Brylcreem, the stash of toiletries that had been here before was gone. "Got that flashlight?"

With it he explored the small bedroom and then the garage. He looked among the garden tools and old auto parts. The dog was snuffling in one dark corner. Sparrow went over. The retriever had its nose to the ground near the wall where the cement floor gave way to packed dirt. "What've you got there, doggie?"

Several pieces of pine board, each about three feet long, lay side by side on the ground. The landlord said he'd never noticed them before. With cobwebs brushing his face, Sparrow bent to lift one of the boards. Instead of pill bugs and spiders, as he might have expected, he found a hole underneath. He moved the boards aside.

"God almighty," croaked the old man, gaping at the hole, "where'd *that* come from?"

For a moment Sparrow wondered the same thing, but only for a moment. "Go call the Hall of Justice," he told the landlord. "Ask to speak with Inspector Sandoval in Homicide. If he's not there, get Lieutenant Austin. Only them, no one else." He repeated the names, told him what to say. When the old man had shuffled out, trailed by his dog, Sparrow got on all fours and aimed the flashlight.

The hole was recently dug, cut to a width of about two feet, but he could see into it only for a short distance before it angled away into darkness. *Nyoong bwong hum uh dow?* The words from the transcript came back to him. A sense of warning touched him, like a dark wing. Had he made a mistake in not posting surveillance? Too late now. He hesitated; then he crawled headfirst into the hole.

The dirt was coarse and dry. He dragged himself down on elbows and knees, following the flashlight beam. It was tough going in the narrow confines. Several feet in, he got a sudden claustrophobic conviction that the ground would collapse onto him, trapping him. He crept on. Thankfully, the tunnel soon sloped up to a plywood surface. Sweating from exertion, he put a hand against it and pressed. There was a grating sound. Grit and dry leaves sifted down on him, then the second makeshift door moved away and daylight poured in.

When he'd pulled himself all the way up, he was beneath a clump of bushes in the narrow alley that ran behind the garage. Brushing dirt from his clothes, he pondered the stealth with which someone, presumably Byron Hoot, had come back unseen and taken his belongings. And shattered the mirror? Whatever that meant.

He was closing the garage door when the landlord reappeared, breathing as if he'd hiked to the Hall of Justice and back. "I phoned. Neither of them people was in."

Sparrow thanked him for trying and returned the flashlight. As he headed for the street he could see small, ash-gray clouds moving across the sky above the trees and rooftops like puffs of gunsmoke. He was about to start the truck when he stopped.

The old man was still standing with his dog by the garage, braced on his cane. "Forget something?" he called at Sparrow's return.

Sparrow opened the doors again and went in. From an assortment of garden tools in a corner, he got a shovel and carried it into the bathroom. He paused before the medicine cabinet. In the cracked mirror, his distorted image gazed back. He knew that he shouldn't touch anything, was aware, too, that the shovel in his hands could've been the one used to excavate the tunnel and therefore should be held for Chang's analysis; but he wasn't concerned with that. Such details seemed of tiny consequence. Even cornered at last, it seemed, the killer had eluded detection and capture because Sparrow and the others had failed to take proper account. Now, if the killing and theft at the Presidio were the work of the same person (and Sparrow believed they were), the killer had more weapons than ever, and Sparrow could harbor no hope that he wouldn't use them.

He drew the shovel back the short distance the cramped bathroom allowed and drove the spade end into the wall beneath the sink. The blade sliced through with a gritty crunch and sank to its middle in the plasterboard. Using the handle as a pry bar, he levered down and popped loose a chunk of wallboard. The dog began to bark.

Sparrow repeated the process several times, kicking away slabs of wallboard that clattered to the floor and began to pile up like jigsaw pieces awaiting assembly into some meaningful whole. Soon he could see the studs and the darkness between them.

"What the hell—!" the landlord yelled, coming in, grabbing Sparrow's shoulder.

He shook free and hacked out another piece of wall. He set the shovel aside. He squatted to peer into the hole he had made. In the light he could see only the plumbing and hunks of rubble inside the space between the studs. Numbly, after a moment, he stood.

"What got into you?" the old man demanded.

"I'll pay for the damage," Sparrow murmured. He turned the tap and cupped cold water to his face, holding it there till it had leaked away. As he dried his hands, he saw that the landlord had bent over and was aiming the flashlight into the gaping hole. Plaster dust sifted through the beam. The man pulled out several of the bigger pieces of broken wall. At the bottom of the space lay a litter of rusted razor blades that had been dropped through the slot in the medicine cabinet, going back who knew how many years.

"There," the man wheezed, pointing at something.

Sparrow saw it too, shiny amid the litter. Carefully, as though he were reaching in among booby traps, he picked it up.

"What is it?" the old man asked impatiently.

Sparrow gazed at the small, untarnished rectangle of metal in his hand. Only slightly larger than a razor blade, it was shiny because it wasn't steel and therefore not subject to rust. It was aluminum. Stamped into it, so that the symbols were indented on one side and raised on the other, was:

HEITE, KENNETH S. 001-34-6707
BLOOD TYPE: O POS.
RELIGION: PROTESTANT

He drew out more broken plaster and reached in to retrieve a second rectangle. *Adair, Douglas R.* And a third. *Molloy, Warren.*

Only when he was reasonably sure he had recovered every one did he stop his exhumation. There were twelve tags in all. Twelve names. The landlord's question was a humid breath on his ear. Sparrow didn't have to think long to answer.

"They're dead men."

SIX

DEATH TRIPPER

Went down to the cavern . . .
cavern of the beast. . . .
—The New Riders of the Apocalypse

31

Sparrow's discovery had brought him back from the brink of exhaustion. The way he imagined an injection of amphetamines might, finding the dog tags had charged him with energy. It was illusory, he knew; ultimately it would leave him more wasted than ever, but for as long as it lasted, he would use it.

Briefly, he considered going directly to Austin, revealing what he had learned at Fort Ord and since; but the idea was fleeting. He had been acting without authorization; he had failed to preserve evidence, and committed a host of other infractions. But the more pressing reality was that there wasn't time. Hoot knew he was being tracked, would be preparing to kill; perhaps, in light of the news report about stolen explosives, with greater violence than before.

From a phone booth, he called Elaine again, but she hadn't been able to reach Amy. As he got ready to hang up, she said, "John, have you . . . heard from George?" He hadn't. "He was looking for you earlier. I made him tell me why. He wanted you to know that he got the green light. Does that mean anything?"

He drove back to the Haight, hoping Amy had returned. As he stood inside the hallway with the mailboxes and bell pushes for the rental units, he could hear music playing beyond the door to Amy's apartment. He knocked.

The dog tags were wrapped in a handkerchief in his pocket, and his mind returned to the moment he had found them, telling the landlord that the tags belonged to dead men. Brushing aside plaster dust, he had laid the tags on the bathroom floor, clicking them down on the linoleum in alphabetical arrangement, the way the living men might once have fallen out in squad formation. The names were those from the *Army Times*, casualties in the sapper attack in Cu Chi, which Byron Hoot alone had survived. So what Major Beckwith had hinted at as only a possibility—of Hoot's having taken the dog tags from the other men—was true. What did it mean?

In Amy's apartment, music went on playing, but no one answered his insistent knocking. Like everything else about the building, the door was old, flaking paint. Gripping the knob in both hands, he twisted hard and simultaneously shouldered the door. It popped open without resistance. He stepped inside.

The music was louder. He looked into the kitchen, where there was a table stacked with papers. On a wall someone had begun to create a mural depicting animals and flower children in a fanciful garden setting that resembled Golden Gate Park. The artist had sketched the scene and started filling it in, but evidently had run out of paint or ambition; only half the figures were complete.

He went down a hallway, off of which were several closed doors. At the end of the hall was a narrow open room. Looking in, he saw it was scarcely more than a large closet, lit with a blue bulb in the ceiling that cast the room in a weird, other-worldly light. The music played on a record player that sat on the floor, set so the album would play continuously. Sitting cross-legged on the bare mattress was a heavyset kid with wild, uncombed hair, which in the blue light seemed to spring from his head in gorgon coils. For a queasy instant, Sparrow thought of the first of the Death Tripper's victims he had seen: the youth in the crash pad near the Pan-handle. But this kid wasn't dead. He appeared to be tuned to some psychedelic lul-laby. He had an American flag affixed at his throat and hanging cape-style over his shoulders. Otherwise he was naked. Recovering from his surprise, Sparrow recog-nized him. They'd met at the *Rag* office; he was the one they called Jester. Sparrow lowered the volume of the music. "Sorry to bust in on you."

If the kid was startled or offended by the invasion, he gave no sign. The tiny room smelled of stale clothes and sweat and the bitter underlay of pot. "My name's Sparrow. I'm looking for Amy."

The kid went on staring into a dim distance.

"Have you seen Amy?"

No response. Like a wind gusting across his mind, an image of the poster he had seen at Fort Ord came to him: YOU ONLY GET ONE MIND! DON'T BLOW IT! Is that what had happened here? Had drugs shriveled the kid's life into nothing? Spar-row stepped nearer. "When did you see Amy last? Has she been here at all?" No change of expression. "What about Seth?"

Nothing. It was as if the person in there had vacated the body. Maybe, Sparrow thought, Amy and Seth had gotten word of Moon's impending invasion and had left the city together, gone up to Terry Gordon's farm, or. . . . No, he knew bet-ter. They wouldn't have left.

He went back down the hallway, opening doors. Amy's room wasn't hard to find. On a bentwood chair next to a brass-framed bed sat an Underwood type-writer. He wanted a note, some sign as to when she'd been here last, where she might be now. Rolled into the platen was a sheet of paper with a single word typed on it. *REVOLUTION! S.* He pondered it a moment. *S.* Seth?

Starting with a dressing table set before an antique oval mirror, he searched. There were silk scarves and beads hanging from the mirror frame, a small cache of lipsticks, mascara, vials of scented oils, tiny boxes of soapstone and teak. In her closet hung blouses and jeans and a few dresses, including the one she'd worn to her cousin Glenn's funeral. On a shelf was a straw basket, which he went through, giving only fleeting consideration to its contents: journals, a slim book of Sylvia Plath poems, a tattered copy of *The Dharma Bums*, envelopes addressed from Massachusetts, and others from an APO address (her cousin's, he realized).

A window faced the street. Beyond the row of houses on the other side, and the glowing laundromat, the sky was deepening. Amy's sandalwood scent came from her belongings, conjuring her. In another set of circumstances, being here would have been an exotic experience; now he felt he was moving against a heavy flow of time. He turned back to the dressing table, and as he did he noticed something he had missed before. Tucked in the corner of the mirror frame, half concealed by a silk scarf, was a snapshot. He slipped it out.

In the fading light from the window, he saw that the photo appeared to have been taken on the campus at Berkeley. It was of Amy and Seth, their arms around each other. Seth was looking at the camera, Amy gazing at him with tender regard. They made an attractive couple, Seth as darkly handsome as she was fair. In a simpler day they'd have been king and queen of homecoming. He remembered the fantasy he'd had of Amy and himself sailing together, and he was chagrined at the foolishness of having let himself think that he could ever really mean anything to her, that their worlds could coalesce across the gulf between them. She had her man, and the man had her. But where were they now? In trouble? He slipped the photo back.

In the tiny room at the end of the hall, the record had become stuck in a groove: " 'Feed your head . . . feed your head . . . feed your head . . . ' " In the kitchen, atop the papers on the table lay a steno pad marked for household expenses. He tore out a blank page, and with a pencil wrote: *Amy, if you get this, please wait here. I'll be back.*

As he signed it, he found himself thinking that amid the odd disharmonies of time and place, some things were coming clear. Not fully yet; he was still nowhere close to resolving the mysteries he probed, but for the first time he thought he could sense the significance of the summer. There was something in the air, as people had been telling him for weeks now, and he had chosen to disbelieve. But that feeling, multiplied a thousandfold, ten thousandfold, among the pied ranks provided a momentousness to the experience he could no longer deny. Nor did he want to, for strange as it seemed, he also was part of it. The feelings had embraced him, too. Not the drugs, or even the music—though he couldn't escape the excitement for the music that Amy felt—but in other, fundamental ways he felt himself drawn. Hadn't one of the season's own bright flowers restored him to something approaching hope? He found himself remembering that day in the woods up in

Marin. The thoughts excited him, and although he could not foresee how it might be worked out, what he began to feel now, more powerfully than he felt anything else, was that he wanted to be with her. But was that likely? Was it even possible? Probably not; but he couldn't think about it now. There was much to do first—most important, to find her.

There was a bunch of flowers in a jar on the windowsill. Wanting to be sure that Amy saw the note amid the clutter of papers if she returned, he plucked a daisy and set it and the note on the counter. He reread his message. On an impulse, he added one word before his name. For an instant he hesitated, thinking of the snapshot in Amy's room, and almost erased the word; but he let it stand, like a tiny blossom of hope.

Looking out through the steamed windows of the laundromat you can see her place. The guy over there in the apartment right now is heat. Okay, so he's driving an old pickup truck and hasn't shaved in awhile, but he's a cop all right. Even the kids sitting on the stoop had seen it and split, teenyboppers, who'd looked all of fourteen. They'd been sitting there getting ripped when you'd gone over earlier and asked was this where Amy Cole lives.

"Yeah. In there," one said, pointing with the roach clip, which was a hemostat.

"The fat funny guy, too," said another. "Haven't seen him in days, man. He cracks me up."

"What's in the saddlebags?" a girl asked.

Passing the roach. They wouldn't know what a hemostat was really designed for, definitely had never seen a man screaming in the dirt with his blood squirting and a terrified medic clamping them in. How could they? They were too young. Hell, you were *all* young. Adair, Fischetti, Ford, Heite . . . Nineteen, twenty-year-old kids.

You let out a breath and draw back from the window, aware of how tense you've grown. Luckily this place is practically empty, only one head, sitting down there in his Skivvies and staring into the glass porthole of a washing machine, watching his clothes go round and round. You sit clutching the saddlebags, breathe in and out, zoning, like the army shrink showed you. Letting your thoughts go. Slowly in . . . slowly out. The warm air smells of laundry soap. When you're calm, you look out the steamed window once more, and decide. No more waiting. You'll have to catch up to her later. Time to hit the park.

No fog. That's what was different, Amy thought. This time of day it was common to see it drifting in off the cold ocean, something about the heat up in the Sacramento Valley, drawing it in, she'd been told; but today there was no fog. Instead, an ominous dark cloud loomed in the southwest, like the coming edge of a storm. The radio had been plugging the concert all day—Big Brother, the New Riders, the Dead—but she hadn't heard a word about bad weather. It wasn't the season.

Approaching the Golden Gate Bridge, she saw hitchers lined up before the southbound entrance, heading over for tonight's concert. She was in the wrong lane to stop. Anyway, she didn't want passengers right now. She needed to think. Ahead, standing on the bridge sidewalk, separate from the hitchers, a long-bearded man in a tattered suit was holding a cardboard sign. As she neared, she recognized it as an image of Kali . . . who lived among the dead, and whose time, Circe said, was come. With a shiver, Amy sped past, more eager than ever to get home.

The laundromat was empty save for a man in his Skivvies, sitting in an orange molded plastic chair, oblivious to everything but the whirling eye of a clothes dryer. Sparrow used the phone directory. There were lots of Changs listed, but only one Simon Chang.

If the evidence tech was surprised at hearing Sparrow's voice, it didn't come through the line. After a cool exchange of greetings, Sparrow said, "There were flowers left at each of the crime scenes, but no prints, you said. The flower on the first victim, a daisy, as I recall—"

Chang grunted. "What you after?"

"Were there any prints on it?"

"The evidence was spoiled. How many times I got to tell you? Thank College Boy."

They weren't going to let go of that. "Did Pete touch it before or after the crime scene photos were taken?"

"What are you doing, Sparrow? You on something besides suspension? You smoking pot?"

"Before or after?" Sparrow pressed.

Chang sighed. "Photographs taken before anyone allowed on the scene. I always make sure."

"If you were to enlarge a photo from that first killing and examine it microscopically, there might be something on the flower from *before* Pete handled it."

Chilly silence. In the laundromat, Sparrow could hear only the soft whirring of the dryer. He'd been grasping at straws. The thorough Chang already would have considered every possibility. He was about to say forget it when the tech said, "Call me at the lab in one hour."

Outside the sky had thickened, massed with menacing, plum-colored clouds, like an armada beating across a stormy sea. Sparrow could almost believe that the weather had stalked him north from Monterey; and now he had the unsettling thought that Amy was out there somewhere and he wouldn't be able to find her. "Where would she go?" he asked aloud, expecting no answer but needing to hear himself ask. And then suddenly he remembered what Elaine had said about the rally and concert in the park. Of course.

He grabbed a rain slicker from the truck and set off on foot.

Almost nine P.M. With the overcast sky, daylight quivered on the edge of extinction. George Moon drove the unmarked Ford along Fell, moving toward the Haight. He ought to have been thinking about tonight's operation, reviewing tactics one last time, anticipating resistance. But he wasn't. For reasons he didn't fully understand, he found himself remembering the afternoon he had driven over to the elementary school where Helen taught and had waited for her across the street. It was a day in early spring. Trees were in bud and yellow busses came and went. On the flagpole in front of the school, the flag waved gently like a bright postage stamp pasted on a pale blue envelope. Helen was one of the last teachers to leave the building. She came out with a small cluster of her first-graders. He could see the children's excitement as they talked, and her beaming approval. It was a quality she had, of drawing people to her, making them feel valued, loved. As she saw the kids onto their school bus and started for her own city bus stop, she noticed him. He had climbed out of his car.

"George. What are you doing here?" There was a look of sudden alarm on her face. "Is something wrong?" With John, she meant. Johnny.

No, Sparrow was working, as always, putting in the long hours. "Everything's fine," he said, and Helen relaxed. "I want to talk to *you*."

Adjacent to the school was a playground, empty in the late afternoon, the swings hanging motionless, the seesaw a static diagonal line. Helen sat on one of the swings. He stood, but he didn't speak right away. In the school yard, a janitor took down the flag, bunching it unceremoniously in his arms as it came. A student spanked erasers, making silent white puffs. The late sun lit half of Helen's face, emblazoned her dark hair, but she didn't press him to speak. The swing chains creaked softly. At last, gripping one of the swing poles, he said, "What if I'd met you first? Would we be together?"

She smiled her beautiful, patient smile. "George . . . you're such a boy. You love Elaine."

"I'm in love with you."

If she felt shock or disapproval or even surprise, she didn't show it. Did she know? Had she been aware of it happening slowly, over time? Did he dare hope she felt it, too?

"Go away with me," he said with urgency. He almost went down on one knee, might have if he hadn't felt his world begin to swim under him. His hands trembled on the iron pole. "Anywhere you want. Someplace simpler."

"I'm an illusion to you, George."

An illusion. The *illusion* was that Sparrow loved her. He wasn't capable of this kind of love. "Please," he said, hearing the desperation in his voice and not ashamed of it. "Whatever you want, just ask. I can change. I don't like what's become of me. We can—"

Now the dashboard radio spat his name. He seized the mike. "What?"

"Alpha here, Cap," said his second-in-command. "We're in the park, in position." In the background, Moon could hear sounds, like the noise of a ballpark crowd on a radio broadcast. "The first band's tuning up, if you can call it that. And guess who's doing security?"

"Well?"

"A biker gang, by the looks of them. Down there by the stage, armed with pool cues. Any instructions?"

Damn. It was more of the tiptoe shenanigans of City Hall. They didn't want to make waves by insisting on a police detail, so the organizers had opted for goons. How long before trouble broke out? Moon checked his watch. Just after nine. Early. The hippies wouldn't be there in force yet. These scraggly do-nothings didn't follow clocks. They'd never punched in at a factory or reported anywhere for duty. And they'd damn sure never waited while time stole from them someone they loved. Now they were overrunning the land. Life was just one big funfest—listen to music, get high, protest against your own president and country, burn the flag. He tried to conjure Helen again, dream her as his wife . . . but he couldn't. Her radiance was gone forever.

"Cap?" the voice on the radio prompted.

Christ. Months of training and they couldn't be patient a while longer? "Sit tight. I'll get back to you."

As he drove across Divisadero, a young couple carrying an infant in a papoose stepped off the curb directly in front of his car. He braked hard and fried their ears with the horn. The man flipped him two fingers. *A peace sign!* Idiots.

As Sparrow headed for the park, scraps of paper skipped past in the rising wind. One wrapped around his ankle. He snatched it, his eyes falling momentarily on the image of a ghostly horse, smoke flaring from its nostrils. The Art Nouveau script seemed clearer now than it ever had before: BRING HOME THE WAR! FREE CONCERT AND RALLY! THE GRATEFUL DEAD, BIG BROTHER & THE HOLDING COMPANY, AND THE NEW RID—The rest was torn off. He let it fly. Bring home the war. George Moon was going to be glad to oblige.

The dog tags made a soft jingling in his pocket, and he thought of how war was always like that: politicians sending young people off to kill and be killed, justifying it in the name of this or that noble cause, but it was never their asses that went on the line. A dark and unexpected anger had begun to churn in his heart.

Amy found a parking spot in front of her apartment house. Under the splotched gray quilt of clouds, day was fading fast. Street lamps had come on. Key in hand, she hurried for the doorway. As she entered the dim hallway, a figure emerged. She gasped.

"Hey, sister."

The man stepped nearer, and it took her an instant to realize it was Nat Evans. He was wearing his old surplus field jacket and a black beret.

"Didn't mean to freak you," he said. "I was looking for Seth."

"Isn't he here?"

"No one answered. Anyway, I gotta be someplace. Here, you see him, give him this." Nat handed her a twenty-dollar bill.

"What's this for?"

His expression told her he realized that he'd goofed. "Just tell him I want the goods back."

"What goods, Nat?"

In the dim gleam of hallway light, his eyes were evasive. "He'll know." Hastily, he added, "Make him see this shit's not for him."

"He'll know what that means, too?"

"If he's smart."

She knew Nat wouldn't reveal anything more. "All right, I'll tell him." With a nod, he started away.

"Nat." He turned. "What about you?"

"Me?"

"I haven't seen you wearing a beret before." She meant not just the beret, but also the panther image on the front. He reached as though he were going to touch it, then dropped his hand. "Nat, why? You've almost got your doctorate. Couldn't you finish, get a job teaching? You'd be so good at it."

"Like Terry Gordon? Where's he at these days? Besides, you know any school gonna hire a man with more felony busts than degrees?"

"Joining the Panthers isn't likely to help."

Coldly, Nat said, "Fuzz in Oakland rousted another bunch of brothers last night. Strip-searched them at gunpoint. The other day they shot a kid seventeen years old. We can't take it sittin' down."

She was thinking all at once of the TAC Squad's plan for using force. An image of an Old Testament battleground, with bitter, warring armies, came to her mind. "Things can get out of hand. You must have some influence with the leaders," she said hopefully. "Can't you reason with them, call for restraint?"

"Ain't nobody be looking for a hassle, but we got to be ready if it comes. That sitting around waiting for Michael to row his boat ashore ain't cutting it anymore."

"What is, then?" she asked.

Nat lifted the hem of the field jacket and revealed the shape of a pistol butt in the waistband of his jeans. He yanked the jacket back down. "Be cool, girl." He went out the door into the night. With a gnawing in the pit of her stomach, she looked at the twenty-dollar bill in her hand.

In the apartment, she turned on lights. In the back bedroom, where the blue bulb still burned eerily, Jester lay asleep. Quietly, she drew a light blanket over him. In her room, she put on a sweater and got her rain poncho. That's when she saw the sheet of paper rolled into the typewriter. She cranked it out.

REVOLUTION! S.

Her heart gave a small clench. Another time, she might've dismissed the note as just more Movement rhetoric, Seth's flair for the dramatic; but in light of her encounter with Nat Evans and the report of the TAC Squad's plans, she couldn't. Seth would be in the park, but he wasn't going to record the story; she was pretty sure he was determined to *be* the story. In the kitchen, where she went to gather some food to take, she saw the second note. It was handwritten.

Amy, if you get this, please wait here. I'll be back. Love, John.

She read it again. "Love, John." The words seemed old-fashioned somehow, quaint-sounding, like a chorus spinning out of a jalopy's dashboard radio in an earlier time, before Dallas, Birmingham, Oakland, and Vietnam. Love. How often had she heard the word used that summer? Read it? Sung, spoken, and written it herself?

There were love-ins, love beads, love vibes, love burgers, love oils, love candles, love potions, love, love, love, until the magic had been leached out of the word and it was just a sound. *Love, John.* This from a man who'd sentenced himself to isolation, holding onto some hidden misery that he refused to let go. So how could the word, scrawled in pencil on the page of a note pad, be any different? *Please wait here. I'll be back.*

And she could stay, she realized. It was a nice offer. Safe. She could cook up a batch of spaghetti, toss a salad. There was wine. She liked Sparrow, he was a decent man. But he just didn't understand.

REVOLUTION! S.

Get out of the Haight, Terry had warned on her earlier visit. *It's going to go bad.*

Be cool, girl. Nat Evans's words, Nat with a gun in his pocket.

In the quiet of the apartment, she could hear the faint passage of the wind outside. She thought of Jester, his humor gone, thought of the lonely doomster on the bridge, with his placard proclaiming the time of Kali. She thought of the dead. Of her cousin Glenn. Of last night at the marina.

Revolution!

Be cool.

Love. Death.

Lightning crackled, making her jump. In the flash she saw the painting that Tess had started on the kitchen wall but had never finished: the jungle and the figures of lions and lambs and children. She thought again of her image of warring armies, and in that instant she knew with an abrupt clarity that it was down to choices. It couldn't be all ways. In maintaining a distance from which to judge, she'd stayed outside too long. It was time to choose or be chosen. Problem or solution? On the bus or off the bus. Revolution. Love. Folding both Seth's and John's notes together, she slipped them into her jeans pocket. Food would have to wait. She snatched the poncho, stuffed the twenty-dollar bill in her pocket and went out.

Although it was totally out of season, rain had started to fall. On the corner, the laundromat glowed with light like a steamy oasis, but no one was inside. Despite the weather, people would be going to the rally. As she inserted the key in the ignition slot, there was a tap on the passenger-side window. She jumped. Through the rain-streaked glass she saw a person bending to look in, holding up his hand in a wave. She leaned across the seat and rolled down the window an inch.

He looked to be about her age, his dark hair pasted on his brow by the rain; despite that, however, he was smiling. "Heading for the park?" he asked.

He was disheveled, and wore a leather jacket that was dirt-stained, like he'd been crawling on the ground in it; but his manner was friendly enough, his gaze direct. "It's cool if you're not," he said.

Her thought was to lie, say she had errands to run downtown, but she hesitated.

"In fact, a walk'll do me a world of good." He raised a hand palm up and squinted at the sky, an almost comic gesture, like Gene Kelly's in *Singin' in the Rain*.

Deciding, Amy unlocked the door. "Come on."

"Thank you." He slung a heavy-looking pair of saddlebags onto the floor and climbed in.

32

THE BOTTLES WERE FROM SOME CHEAPO BRAND OF VODKA, SETH SAW. SO NAT EVANS had a sense of humor. Actually, Seth had seen it yesterday when he'd told Nat to forget the dynamite, that he had something else in mind. "Molotov cocktails?" Nat gawked at him. "That some fancy-ass hootch the snobs out at the country club drink?"

"That's what I'll take instead. I'll pay you the same as we agreed on."

"For a bottle of gasoline and a rag?"

"Two of them." Seth took out a pair of twenties and laid them on the work-bench. "Tomorrow. You got the ass to swing it?"

Nat pushed one of the bills back and poked the other into his shirt pocket. "Do you?"

They agreed on a time and place for delivery. As Seth reached the door, Nat called him. "Remember, you fall on bomb charges, man, you fall hard."

"I'll keep it in mind."

"Take this." Nat held out an unlit joint. Seth waved it away. "Acapulco Gold. 'Fore you do your bad-ass 'Burn, Baby, Burn' number, smoke it and ask yourself, is this what I really want to be doing. 'Cause if it ain't, you maybe want to slide on back to Beverly Hills."

"Go to hell, Nat."

"Been there all my life, boy."

But Seth had taken the joint. He had it with him now in the pocket of his field jacket as he sat in the locked office of the *Rag*, holding the two firebombs Nat Evans had left as per their plan. For the money, Seth could've ordered more Molotovs—Nat was right, they were cheap to construct—but since he was doing this solo, two were all he could manage. As Nat had warned, getting caught with fire-bombs would mean jail. He'd lie low awhile longer, until it got darker, rainier, then make his way over to the park.

The bottles had got Seth thinking back to the days when his father and his step-mother would host fund-raisers at their home: people in dinner jackets and spaghetti-strap dresses, plucking canapés off plates and sipping Veuve Cliquot and Stolichnaya (because it was *real* Russian vodka) as they talked about the plight of the Negro and the Chicano farm worker, then getting into their Cadillacs and weaving home to Brentwood and Bel-Air. Americans for a Democratic Hypocrisy.

The first politics he'd ever talked with Amy, one afternoon over coffee on Tele-graph, had revolved around that. She told him he was being unfair to his parents, that they were doing *something* to support their beliefs, that's what mattered. Why was giving money for a cause less worthy than some other act? But Amy hadn't grown up with wealth, and therefore, he believed, she had mythologized it. Still, he liked her spunk, and soon they found the aphrodisiac of heated debates on weekday afternoons at a cafe or in the student union, then hurrying back to his place, or hers, to make love.

But so much had changed since then. Politics didn't move Amy the way he'd once imagined. Maybe that had just been hot pants thinking. "You've been co-opted by the system!" he accused her. "And you've lost your objectivity," she shot back, still spunky. Well, if objectivity meant seeing all activities as equally valid, he was happy to lose it. There was a distinction between just dancing a fountain pen across a check and being willing to take action for a cause. The situation here was no different than what Che faced in the Bolivian jungle. You had to struggle against the machine—pigs busting heads, the government ordering you to kill people you didn't hate—a big machine *clank-clanking* away. Seth locked the door and stepped out into the rain. Sometimes you had to lay yourself down in front of the wheels.

Or toss a firebomb.

The Haight was quiet in a way Amy couldn't remember it ever being before, the streets strangely deserted. Her passenger was preoccupied, gazing out the fogged side window at the night. After a brief initial conversation, each had fallen into pri-vate thoughts. With the rain pelting softly on the car roof, drizzling down the glass, they might have been passengers in a bathyscaphe, probing cold ocean depths.

All summer, even with the grim menace of death, the Haight had pulsed with life, the entire world eagerly attuned to what was going on here. But tonight the district seemed faded: a sidewalk chalk drawing dissolving in the rain. Except for a trickle of people, the streets were empty. She shuddered with the vision that, like the children of Hamlin in the fairy tale, the Haight's children had been led away to some unnameable fate. As she reached JFK Drive, however, she was relieved. She began to see people heading toward the park. On Fulton, traffic crept along, and more on Balboa. People were bound for the concert and rally.

Since the Be-In in January, each public event had surpassed the one before. The solstice gathering had brought sixty thousand. Tonight, even despite the rain, there would be many more.

"You know what this is about?" her passenger asked, as if he had read her thoughts. She looked at him, giving him her attention. "A judgment," he said.

Again, she had the feeling that there was something familiar about him, but she couldn't pin it down. "On what?"

"Everything."

It was a weird remark to make. "Whose judgment?"

He shifted in his seat, glancing at the wet saddlebags on the floor as he moved his feet. He seemed kind of pathetic, in his damp clothes. He had a stained bandage around one hand. "We'll see," he said.

She wanted to press him to elaborate, but he turned to peer out once more. Suspended somewhere between hope and dark dread, she quelled a shiver; then she gazed out to concentrate on the traffic and the rain and the gleaming streets.

33

WAITING AS A PARK POLICE OFFICER IN A YELLOW SLICKER DRAGGED ASIDE A BARRICADE to let him drive past, George Moon keyed the two-way radio mike.

"Go ahead, Cap," came the voice of his second-in-command.

"I'm just entering the park at Nineteenth. Anything?"

"Negative. Got the usual chuckleheads playing guitars too loud, and some little wild-hair singing. Her voice is black, but she ain't." Garbled music filled the car, making Moon cringe. The cop had apparently thrust the mike out the window of his van for a moment. "Belts it out pretty good, doesn't she, Cap? Janis something or other."

"Who're you?" growled Moon. "Dick Clark? What're the bikers doing?"

"Nothing yet. It's pretty calm."

Hesitating, Moon said, "I think the killer is here."

"Tonight?" The cop's voice rose.

"Or will be."

"In the park?"

"Listen up. You have his description. He's armed, may be carrying explosives. Alert the others." He signed off, and was waved past the barricade into the park.

Hoot would be here; he had little doubt of it. Hoot was on the run now, and tonight would be his last stand. If he intended to up the body count, what better place? But that was Austin's problem. It was TAC's job to defend the city against chaos. And to Moon's mind, before the night was over, the moorings of order were going to break loose.

There was an explosion. He clenched the wheel. Thunder. He let out a breath, but he didn't relax his grip.

At Park Presidio, where it crossed Balboa, Amy swung toward the park. She'd hoped to enter there, but it was clear at once that that wasn't an option. Vehicles were parked haphazardly along both sides of the road, squeezing traffic to a single sluggish lane that inched along. She'd be lucky to go another block. Ahead, she recognized the old International Harvester bus that Kesey used. Painted across its Technicolor back end, the message CAUTION WEIRD LOAD was visible. Its destination board, she knew, read FURTHER, but the bus had stopped, unable to travel anywhere. It looked to have been abandoned by its merry crew. She eased the Volvo past, but there was nowhere else to go. She squeezed into a space beneath some overhanging bushes.

Her passenger glanced over, looking concerned.

"We won't get any closer," Amy said.

"What time is it?"

"I'm guessing. Nine-thirty?" More rain beat on the car. On an impulse, Amy pulled the twenty-dollar bill from her pocket and held it out. "Take this. Maybe you can find someplace dry to sleep tonight."

He looked at it and frowned. He shook his head. "Too late for that." He leaned down to get his saddlebags. He began to unbuckle one flap when suddenly there was a rap on the roof of the car, startling them both.

Through the rain-streaked glass, Amy saw a cop. She cranked down the window a few inches. "Can't leave it here," the cop said. "Move it." With the cop standing by, her passenger got out to guide her into another spot, and when she'd parked the car, both of them were gone.

No matter what else might go down tonight, Seth's most vivid impression would be the smell of gasoline.

He was dizzy with it, having sloshed his way to the park with two Molotov cocktails concealed under his coat. In need of a short rest to gather himself, he propped the bottles upright among wet ferns and sat back against a tree.

If the mimeograph machine hadn't burned in the office fire, he might've equated tonight with the smell of copy fluid. He could've done up leaflets to hand out, warning folks to be cool, to get their stashes hidden, draft cards and IDs in order, be ready for the Man. Thanks to Moon, that wasn't a choice. The cop had craftily pared down the options, and Seth accepted the terms. The pen was mighty, as Amy insisted, but sometimes you needed a sword.

It was funny, all the times he had imagined this moment he had seen it in hot light, full of people to share it with. But here he sat, alone in the wet dark.

From his pocket he fished the joint Nat Evans had given him. He didn't need it; better to be clear-eyed about these things. Still, a few hits might calm him—and take the stink of gasoline out of his head. He shut his eyes and toked deeply.

He remembered the day in Sproul Plaza after he'd given a speech, and he and Amy had gone back to his place and made love for the first time. God, he'd wanted to leap out of his skin and into hers. But her passion and commitment . . . they weren't the same as his. He understood that now. They'd been drifting apart. Amy had been the one finally to say it. It was sad, but what could you do? He sucked in more smoke, feeling the Gold ignite the fumes in his brain. When he opened his eyes he was startled to see someone emerging from the bushes.

He held the joint, poised to ditch it, and squinted through the rainy mist, trying to make out who it was. Could it be? It was.

Excitedly, Seth started to push to his feet, but Terry Gordon waved him back. "Glad I found you," Terry said.

"Man, me, too! How'd you do it?"

Terry peered around, blinking owlishly through his John Lennon glasses. "You solo?"

"Not anymore. Welcome back. Here." Seth offered the joint, but Terry stood where he was, a dozen feet away, still half concealed by the dripping undergrowth. "You all right? You seem kind of . . ." He'd been about to say "blurry," and indeed, Terry did look insubstantial somehow, but that was the weed.

"Give it up, Seth."

"What do you mean?"

Terry made a slow, sweep of his hand. "These people aren't ready for what you've got in mind."

"Revolution? The people never are, you know that. They've got to be led."

"Okay, we know that peace is preferable to war, tolerance better than prejudice, love better than hate. Everyone does. We don't have to push people's faces in it."

Terry's words surprised him, as did the odd hollowness of his voice. Seth scrambled onto his haunches, cupping the joint to keep it dry. "How do we smash the system, then? Oh wait, wait—I get it." Terry was playing devil's advocate. This was like the days in Terry's classroom, when they would go at it head to head. "Last week it was Farmer Gordon's back-to-the-land rap. Now you're going to give me the old work-within-the-system trip."

Terry shook his head. "No more trips. That's been our problem. No one's here tonight for politics. It's the music, the fun. Let them just listen to it, to their hearts. I mean, this is the Summer of Love, right?" He spread his arms, and in the mist, backlighted, they fanned from his side like crooked wings. "Beautiful people with flowers in their hair."

"That's bullshit, a collective hallucination."

"Amy believes in it, doesn't she?"

Seth frowned. He didn't like Terry taking things out of context, taking sides he didn't really endorse. "Okay, say peace and love were *supposed* to be part of it. Good vibes and all that. It's been co-opted."

"Love can't be co-opted."

"The Man's got no love."

"So, forget the Man. Who needs him? Poke flowers in his gun barrel, tie bells on his billy club. Laugh at him, for God's sake. Moon him. Hey, if he can't take a joke . . ."

It was something that Jester would say, not Terry. Why was he being so weird? "Are you forgetting your Marx so conveniently? 'There's a time to crack a whip for the masses.' "

"That was Lenin."

"Close enough. I'm just—"

"Close only counts in horseshoes . . . and Molotov cocktails."

It caught Seth unawares. How did Terry know about that? He laughed to cover; but Terry's expression was sober. "What are you doing, Seth? When I first knew you, you were a tennis ace."

Seth frowned. Was this like an exam, Terry testing him to see if he'd evolved? "Why'd you come? Did you see Amy today? She was going up to see you."

"Was she? I must've missed her. I had a little . . . mishap with the Blue Lunch."

A worried thought wisped across his mind. He wasn't sure he believed him. "Terry . . . something I've wondered about . . . did you and Amy ever—" He swallowed, the taste of pot sharp on his tongue, tinged with gasoline. "I mean, it's okay, I'm not into a possessive number, but I always wondered. Back at UC . . . did you two ever . . ."

"It kind of just happened," Terry said softly. "A rainy night—like now—bottle of wine, some Stones on the stereo. I thought maybe you knew."

The realization hit him like a punch. He threshed a hand through his hair. "No, but it's . . . it's cool. I mean, people's bodies are their own, right? Nobody owns anybody else." He felt woefully sure, but he pushed on, speaking faster. "Anyway, there're more important things. The struggle, resistance, stopping the machine. It's time to bring the war home."

Terry clearly wasn't enjoying the repartee any longer. In fact, he was starting to look pained. He gestured away, toward where the concert was. Mist swirled about him. "You want to put a bunch of kids up against riot cops? You were always one of the brightest, Seth . . . think about it."

"I have."

"Think some more. Don't get reckless." In the distance, lightning flickered, bleaching away Seth's vision for a moment. When the thunder passed, he saw that Terry was beginning to recede back into the mist from which he'd emerged.

"Hey, where you going? Wait. *Terry*—?"

Silence.

He was gone. Fuck, had he hallucinated the whole thing? Fog hung in the air. Seth whirled at the sound of movement, but it was only rain pattering in the ferns. He felt uncertain all at once. Terry had always been like a big brother, had made sense; but this rap he was talking . . . had he totally sold out? Music began to play again. He sucked the joint, but it had the stone cold taste of ashes. He flicked it away. Drying his hands on his pants as best he could, he picked up the Molotov cocktails.

34

NO UMBRELLAS. IT WAS A DETAIL THAT STRUCK SPARROW AS HE MADE HIS WAY INTO THE park. Huddled together under towering trees, or moving along paths toward the meadow where the concert was, people wore raincoats and ponchos; some had stripped to considerably less as they danced to the distant music; but there were no umbrellas. The rare summer rain was something to be welcomed, not warded off. Walking in it had helped clear Sparrow's head.

When he reached Speedway Meadow, he saw that lights had been set up at one end and tarps strung over a stage where a band was playing. He thought of that day all those weeks ago when people had gathered in sunshine and high spirits to celebrate the solstice, unaware of how it would play out. He felt a grudging respect for their resiliency, for their longing to be part of something larger than themselves. But there was something else in the air tonight, too: a mood of edgy anticipation that he didn't like.

As he neared the stage, he observed a small scuffle in the crowd. Almost immediately several men converged and began swinging sawed-off pool cues. The scuffle ended. Sparrow realized the men were bikers, here to handle crowd control, probably paid with drugs and booze. The idea angered him, but there was nothing he could do. Sending a wary eye in their direction, he moved on toward the stage.

The woman singing, he discovered, wasn't Circe, nor was the band the New Riders of the Apocalypse. This singer had a mane of brown hair, which she flung this way and that as she moved, clutching the microphone to her mouth while she poured pain into it. She was inviting a lover to rip her heart into pieces.

Sparrow edged along the crowd to approach the stage from the back. A large man in a Prussian helmet and greasy denims who was leaning against the stage, swigging beer, noticed him. He set the bottle aside, picked up a pool cue, and moved to intercept him. With no badge to show, Sparrow raised a hand in greeting. "Are the New Riders back there?" he called above the music pouring from the speakers.

"Scrape off, crud, nobody gets back here."

"I have to speak with someone. It's important."

"What've you got, shit in your ears? I said, *blow!*" The man shoved the cue hard against Sparrow's chest.

The impact sent him backwards a few steps. Bracing, he gripped the stick at both ends. He brought his knee up into the man's crotch. The biker's face drained. As he hunched forward, Sparrow slammed the cue down over his helmet, snapping the stick, knocking off the helmet. With a groan, the man sank.

"So much for love and peace," someone called.

Sparrow looked up. Under the edge of a tarp that covered the backstage area, several longhaired young men stood passing a pipe, which they made no effort to hide as Sparrow climbed the steps. "I'm looking for Circe."

A short, round-faced man came over. "Who's asking?"

He looked familiar. "You're in the band, aren't you?"

"Toad, yeah. But that don't buy you no privilege. Who are you?"

Sparrow considered explaining his purpose, but it would be difficult over the volume of music, too involved. "A friend. I need to talk to her."

"We're going on in a few minutes."

"That's all this'll take."

"Ah, shit. C'mon, then. But it ain't up to me whether you see her or not."

Sparrow glanced back to look for the biker, but he was nowhere to be seen. He followed Toad. On one side of the covered area, madras bedspreads had been hung to create an enclosed inner space. Toad paused there. "Soon as Big Brother's done, we're on." He lifted a corner of the madras curtain, and Sparrow saw Circe on the other side, seated alone at a card table, in profile. There were flowers on the table, and a bottle of Southern Comfort. Before her lay a spread of Tarot cards. Toad said something to her that Sparrow couldn't hear over the music and the rattle of rain on the tarp. She turned and saw Sparrow. At her silent regard, Toad appeared to grow uncertain, on the verge of telling Sparrow to leave, perhaps; but then Circe nodded. "Come get me when it's time," she told the musician. Seeming reluctant, he left. She glanced up at Sparrow as if she'd been expecting him.

"You look tired," she said. He felt it, too: haggard and frayed, as though the past span of days had laid too heavy a hand on him. "Are you here for the music or the politics?"

"Neither."

She raised her eyebrows. "*Cherchez la femme?*"

His exhaustion fell away. "Is she here?"

"Amy, right?"

He slid into a chair. Circe's eyes were shiny and intent. "Something happened last night, didn't it. To her. To both of you, maybe."

These weren't questions. He leaned nearer so that the card table was pressing his chest. His heart was beating fast. "She was attacked," he said, "but she escaped."

"When did you see her last?"

When had it been? He was losing track. He thought of Amy on that day at the I/Thou. "Don't get hung up on details," she'd told him, "grasp the ambiguities."

Cryptic. Like what Circe had read him from the *I Ching*—"Wind and ocean. In the midst of striving you have lost view of the larger whole."—words he had written in his notebook. Step back, consider, watch. Grasp the ambiguities. It's what he had failed to do. When was that? A week ago? A month? He didn't know. It was as if time, that oddly useless commodity in the Summer of Love, had been backing up behind a dam; but it had breached, and now was pouring down on him without mercy because he had stood oblivious too long, and so was helpless before its flow. Dimly, he was aware that the music had stopped and the crowd was yelling. The madras curtain was drawn aside and Toad reappeared. Behind his spectacles, his eyes seemed to dance without focus. "Two minutes." Beyond him, the other young men had begun strapping on guitars.

Circe waved him away. She said, "I think she's here. And the killer, too."

Even though he'd feared and expected them, the words rocked him. Beyond the curtains he could hear a growing commotion of the crowd. "Has he got Amy?"

Circe rose. "I have to go."

He stood, too. He dug in the pocket of his coat, drew out the folded handkerchief and spilled the dog tags onto the table, atop the tarot cards. After the briefest glance at them, she snapped her gaze away, refusing to look again. "I don't want to know about this."

He gripped the card table, feeling how flimsy it was, like everything here: this tiny space with its bedspread curtain, the stage, the security—like papier-mâché, makeshift and unreal. The Southern Comfort bottle fell over, rolled off the table, and smashed into bits. Circe jumped. Beyond the curtain, he could hear Toad and some of the others arguing with somebody: bikers, he realized. He reached across the table and grabbed Circe's arm. "Tell me what you know!"

She tried to pull away. "This isn't a game, damn you!" Color had risen in her cheeks. "I can go only on what I sense."

He let her go. "Then, tell me," he said desperately. "Please."

With a pained expression, as if they posed a danger, she frowned at the dog tags. She hesitated, and then touched one of the tags, running a fingertip across the raised letters and numbers. She touched another, and another. Tightness was congesting Sparrow's heart. Finally, she spread her hands lightly over all of the dog tags. He waited. In a voice just audible above the tatter of rain on the canvas, she said, "Where did you get these?"

He exhaled a held breath. "They belonged to soldiers in Vietnam."

"They're dead. All but one of them. And . . . he's here."

"Where?"

She glanced around, almost as if she expected the person to materialize there before them. "There's something more," she said. "What I told you about once before . . . in North Beach."

Sparrow's heart was drumming hard. "It's him?"

Circe held her hands in place on the tags, frowning. Then she shook her head. "No. Not the same. But find Amy. Get to her. To *them*."

Their gazes locked together. The arguing voices beyond the curtain had faded. The crowd was cheering. On the public address system a man was announcing the New Riders of the Apocalypse. With broken glass crunching under his shoes, Sparrow gathered up the dog tags, put them in the handkerchief, and stuffed it back into his coat pocket. "Thank you." When he reached the curtain, Circe called his name.

He turned. Her dark eyes probed him. "The past," she said, as if the word had swum into the damp air before her. "Does that mean anything?"

"What past?"

Mystified, she shook her head. "I don't know, but it's important somehow. Go there."

In a blue-white strobe of lightning it's there, just for an instant, then gone, leaving only an afterimage of wires. Your impulse is to hurry, get this done. Close call with the bikers, but then they'd gone up onto the stage and you managed to slip in here, underneath. In the returning silence, as thunder rolls off, the music has ended. You open the saddlebags and take out the explosives, the timer. You crawl over to the back of the audio board that the New Riders use, got their name on it and everything. Your hand hurts and feels clumsy with the wet bandage, but soon, with familiar skill, as if no time has gone by, you're hooking up the wires, making the connection. Then the clock. Okay . . . enough time for the band to get into its act, get cooking with one of its crazy songs, and then . . .

Time to split. You buckle the saddlebag flap. Peer around to be sure no one sees you; then you move into the crowd and walk steadily away. Once, you turn and gaze back and see the band taking the stage, and you remember how, in another storm, out in the desert after the Black Shadow broke down and the hippie couple picked you up, the three of you turning on, listening to a bootleg tape, you'd only sensed the music's power, felt something running through the sounds like a slow, dark current wanting to take you under. Now, finally, it will.

Amy watched knots of people drift by on branching paths, moving in the direction of the meadow where the stage was set up in the far distance. Big Brother had just stopped playing. She patted her pockets, looking for her notebook, a pencil, but she couldn't find either. She wasn't ready for this. Any of it. She wasn't a cop—this wasn't a game anymore, with some foolish idea that she'd been helping the community, helping John. If anything, she'd been in the way the whole time, distracting him.

Go. Back to the apartment, lock the doors, wait for him. He'd said he'd return. She didn't move. She'd been here at the beginning, at the Love Pageant last October, the Human Be-In in January, the gathering on the solstice, and she was here now. It was as if the killings, indeed the entire summer's unfolding, had taken on an aura of destiny, and, for better or worse, she was woven through it, too. Whatever went down tonight, she needed to be here.

Just then she heard her name, an actual voice this time, coming out of the rainy night: "Amy." A woman's voice, somehow familiar: "If you're out there, listen to me."

It was Circe speaking from the stage, her words coming through the sound system and moving across the crowd.

"Meet John . . . in the past."

John. The message was for her. What did that mean? It was important somehow. But how? She drew a slow breath and shut her eyes. Meet John in the . . .

Then she knew.

THE *PAST*. CIRCE HAD ASKED HIM IF THE WORD MEANT ANYTHING, AND HE'D FELT HIS resistance. What could he have said? That he'd left a case unsolved there, a killer uncaught? A wife buried? "You have to go there," Circe said. He didn't want to, and yet . . . Then he heard Circe announce Amy's name and a thought came to him. The *Portals* of the Past. He hurried toward the section of the park known as the Portals of the Past.

And there was Amy.

With her back to him, her long hair and muslin peasant blouse clinging wetly to her, she moved to the music. She was in a group of people dancing among the upright columns on the edge of Lloyd Lake, all that remained of the old mansion that had once stood on the spot. Antique lamps cast rings of light on the marble stairs. He climbed up, took her arm, drew her around.

After an instant's surprise, a stranger tipped back her head and laughed. The man with her put a hand on Sparrow's shoulder, evidently intent on raising some objection at being cut in on, but one look at Sparrow's face and he broke off, took the longhaired girl and moved away.

"John."

He turned and this time it was Amy. Her green poncho glimmered. She'd just arrived. They met on the steps. He threw his arms around her. He held on tight, breathing in the rainy scent of her hair. After a moment, he drew back.

"I want you to go back to your apartment. I'll get someone to take you."

"No. I'm staying with you."

"Out of the question. It isn't safe."

"Where is safe?" The sharpness of her words brought him up short. "Where were you last night? I went to your boat."

"I know," he murmured. "I wasn't there."

"I only meant that this involves me, too. If you're going after Byron Hoot, I want to go."

"Why? For a story?"

"I have to know."

The man had tried to kill her last night—might try again if given the chance. "I'm not armed. Hoot will be." He was trying to imagine ways this might play out. There was almost certain to be more violence. There'd been too much already. Nobody was invulnerable; he'd learned that. Suppose something should happen to her? "No," he said, deciding. "I can't let you."

"Why?"

"Because . . . I've fallen in love with you."

In the lamplight, Amy's eyes flickered with what might have been surprise and she took a half-step back. "It's true," he said.

She looked at him with an expression suggestive of waiting: for the punch line of a joke perhaps, or a swift recanting. He felt the pressure of her gaze, but he held it. "Sparrow," she said softly, "you're such a gentleman. Gallant and old-fashioned and given to the grand gesture."

Was there mockery in her words? Pain? His pulse beat in his temple. His face was hot.

"Earnest declarations of emotion at a time of high tension. I got your note." She patted the front of the poncho. "I have it right here. You're really something. One time in bed with a gal, and you want to do the right thing." His stomach twisted. "Not a bed, no," she went on. "A bower in the woods."

"You're wrong."

"Am I? How many women have you been with since Helen died?"

The question was like a punch. Inwardly, he recoiled.

"I was the first, wasn't I."

"What's that got to do with anything? Nothing."

"You still feel her loss, like a wound. You do. I saw it that night on your boat, after Glenn's funeral. And in the meadow that day. You haven't healed. Elaine told me about Helen. I can't replace her. No one can."

Lightning seared the sky. Thunder banged. There was a feeling in the air of immense forces in motion, realigning themselves. He kept his eyes on hers.

"Ah, John . . . this isn't the time for this."

He suddenly wanted that to be true, wished he'd never brought it up. He wouldn't have, he realized, if she'd just agreed to leave as he had asked; but it was too late. Whatever might happen in the next short span could change everything forever, might well be all the time there was, and he needed to speak. "I've been telling myself it's crazy. I'm just under some spell . . . exhaustion. I don't know. Our worlds are so far apart. Our ages, the music we like . . ." He looked away. When she said nothing, offered no argument, he turned back. "Is it the badge?"

Now it was her turn for consternation. "What?"

"If it's me, I can easily believe it. I saw the photo of you and Seth. Tell me. I'll accept it." He mustered an unhappy smile. "But don't let it be an old prejudice."

"The hell with that!" she cried. "I don't care about it. It's this whole . . ." She had her hand out, as though trying to find words there in the misty space between them. In the lamplight she looked tired, and he saw that it wasn't only on him that the past days and weeks had pressed so heavily. She had been in the thick of it, too, and he hadn't properly valued that fact. He'd seen only her youth, her sparkle. Her eyes shone with fatigue, the lines around them etched finely. He reached out and took her hand. He felt her tremble as she spoke.

"I don't know anything anymore. The Summer of Love. What does that mean? It promised so much . . . yet, so much has died."

There was an explosion of thunder, the loudest yet, like something rending the earth. It brought them back to now, shoring up the breach of emotions. He let his hand drop. "All right, we'll stay together and try to find Byron Hoot. If we can."

36

LONG YELLOW HAIR FRAMING HIS FACE, ERIC LINDGARD STRETCHED A HAND TOWARD the sky, as if invoking spirits, and brought it down across the Fender's strings. Sound wailed from the amps and went searing across the crowd like a flight of demented valkyries. Gooseflesh rose on Toad's skin. Almost at once, the sound was answered with a slash of lightning, so bright the crowd shrieked, and seconds later there was a detonation of thunder that made the lights flicker and momentarily silenced the amps.

Joe Williams hunched his shoulders and shot Toad a "Yikes!" glance, but he, too, went on playing. He was driving the rhythm, firing volleys of chords from the Rickenbacker, which gleamed like a shank of anthracite across his pumping hips. Under the billow of hair, his face, streaming sweat, was a dark and changing mask.

Even Vince Russo had shed his torpor. His eyes were wide, lit, no doubt, with the White Rabbit acid they'd all dropped, but there was something else in them, too: fear of the storm, perhaps, or of the killer stalking the night; anger at what had befallen Crystal Blue. He prowled the stage, his bass notes as fierce and steady as the pursuing hoofbeats of the pale horse with its pale rider.

And from where Toad sat at his drums, like a troll in a dank forest, he saw that all the work and dreams, the freak-outs, the sweat, the toilets where they'd paid dues night after night, had come together at last. Circe glided to her microphone, and with the crowd roaring, she resumed singing. As he picked up the beat, he knew that whatever else might happen, right this moment, the Riders ruled.

Seth was sheltering under a clump of jacaranda, a bottle in each hand, trying to decide what to burn. To his left, some distance away, he noticed a car groping up the park road. It had its headlights off, just the parking lights on, windshield wipers batting at the rain. The park entrance roads had been barricaded for hours, which meant the car had to be an official vehicle of some kind, though he couldn't make out any insignia.

When the car was twenty yards away, it eased off the road onto the grass and stopped. Carefully, Seth stood the bottles in the underbrush. The driver shut off the lights and motor and got out. He was big, clad in a raincoat and a fedora. He locked the car and started up the path on foot. As he passed where Seth hid, Seth's heart clenched. It was Moon.

Seth watched him walk in the direction of the rally. Then, carefully, he bent to retrieve the Molotov cocktails. As he lifted the first, the wet glass slipped, the bottle upending as he tried to grab it. Moon turned. Seth froze, helpless as the fuse slopped out of the bottle and the gasoline gurgled into the ground. Moon didn't see him; perhaps wasn't sure he'd even heard anything, what with the patter of falling rain and the distant music. After a moment, he moved on. With a curse, Seth kicked the bottle away. Why hadn't he just scored the dynamite!

Trembling, he dried his hands as best he could and picked up the remaining bottle. Clutching it tight, he could still feel a tremor, but it wasn't from nerves. What was inside the bottle might well have been his own thwarted emotions, stoppered now for too long and ready to burst forth. He thought of Moon kicking over the can of duplicating fluid, lighting a match and letting the *Rag*'s office burn, of Jester's furtive, phantom face in the crowd. In his heart he felt the stirring of something primal. He wanted to kill Moon. Of course, he couldn't, not directly—he wasn't a murderer, after all—but symbolically, taking the fight straight to the Man, letting history overtake and destroy him . . .

And all at once he saw how.

He gripped the bottle, savoring the weight, wishing once more that someone were here with him to bear witness, but it was down to him. Experiencing a mingling of dread and jubilation, he struck a match. The flame wavered, threatening to go out as he applied it to the fuse. For a moment, the strip of rag only smoldered—then it caught. He loped partway down the path to gain momentum, and heaved it.

Flaming, the bottle wobbled through the long arc of his throw; but almost at once he saw he'd misjudged the distance. His heart sank. The bottle fell short. Astonishingly, it didn't shatter. It bounced and tumbled forward, pinwheeling fire, and struck the grille of Moon's parked car. In a noisy spangle of glass, the bottle burst.

The banner was slung between two poles some hundred yards away, but it had enough intensity to bring George Moon to a halt. Hand-lettered with red paint, the words blurring in the rain and streaking the white canvas like blood, it said:

☮ STOP THE WAR! ☮

Sure, as if that's all it took. Just declare peace, say the fighting is over, chant it, set electric guitars skreeling behind it, and dance on the graves of eight thousand American boys who weren't coming home, leave their ghosts to wander restlessly around the jungles and rice paddies of some stinking hellhole on the other side of the world. Jesus, didn't that frost his ass. His knuckles tightened on his truncheon.

If he'd been given a free hand a year and a half ago, none of this would be happening. When the first longhairs started climbing off Greyhound busses to parade barefooted along the city streets, if he'd been allowed to roust them then, this never would've gone so badly awry. If he'd been authorized to bust the anarchists, the freeloaders, and chickenshit peaceniks, shut down the propaganda sheets, things could've turned out differently. Ah, but they hadn't, and it was too late now. Might as well wish that Helen were still alive.

Ahead, the crowd was an indistinct mass. At the far side of the meadow was a lighted stage where a band was performing, pouring noise over the crowd through big amplifiers; but closer at hand, like a finger right in his eye, waved the banner.

☮ STOP THE WAR! ☮

A chant rose from the people surrounding it. "Hey, hey, LBJ, how many kids did you kill today?"

To which others rejoined, "Peace now!"

"Hey, hey, LBJ, how many kids did you kill today?"

"Peace now!"

Moon started toward them.

"Hey, hey, LBJ, how many kids—"

At the explosion, he whipped around. Several hundred feet back, in the direction he'd just come from, a fireball sizzled into the air. A vehicle had gone up in flame. Agape with shock, he took a moment to realize it was *his* car!

The bastards had bombed it!

He thought about racing toward the blazing wreck, ready to spill some hippie brains. But he didn't. Instead of shaking with rage, what he experienced instead was a cool wash of relief. He understood that what he'd sought from City Hall but hadn't received had come to him after all. This attack wasn't random. It was personal— the way Sparrow's causing Helen to die had been personal: *done* to Moon because of his power and the threat he represented to lesser men! But what hit him most was the fact that he was now free. Stop the war. Well, the hell with that. Time to *make* war.

37

AT THE BLAST—A FOUNTAIN OF GREASY ORANGE FLAME—THERE WAS A SUDDEN RICO-
cheting of radio messages from the TAC units spread around the meadow's rim.
Bravo, the second-in-command, tried to raise Moon on the two-way without luck.
He opened the channel to all units. "What exploded?" he demanded. A vehicle, he
was told, but no one knew anything more; it was still burning. Delta said it was in
his sector; he'd check it out and get back ASAP.

Bravo took up binoculars. The thought of having to make any decision without
Moon made him nervous. He scanned the crowd. No one was reacting in any big
way that he could see—a little stirring around the edges—mostly, people still
appeared to be intent on the music. He tried Moon again, but got nothing. Now
the other units vectored on him, requesting instructions. His apprehension growing, Bravo said, "We're still assessing the situation," emphasizing the "we," hoping
it sounded as if cooler heads were part of the debate. In a moment, Delta was
back. "The vehicle that blew up was Alpha's!"

"The Captain's?" He went boneless with shock. "God help us. Was he—?"

"God help *him* if he was! I can't get near it. The car's melting like candle wax."

At a second explosion, Bravo jerked as if he'd been hit. Near the stage a geyser
of sparks spat into the air. What the hell was happening?

"Orders?" Charlie pressed.

Was Moon dead? Was it war? Was this what their months of training had been
for? Bravo's mouth went dry.

"Sarge?"

Commands sprang to his mind. Deploy tear gas! Close ranks! Advance! Stand
down! Withdraw! But it was ragtime. Bravo realized he didn't know *what* to do.

Just starting to peak on two hits of White Rabbit, Toad watched the forms of people moving beyond the curtain of rain, dancing the light fantastic in the fantastic
dancing light, Williams out front, right there in the face of the crowd, his Afro
standing defiantly against the rain that beat at it, the tip of his cigarette a bright
orange eye that yo-yoed from his mouth to the neck of the Ricky with streaking
speed. Russo's bass ran through the music like a ground wire, steady and primal.
Lindgard was the power line. Deep into his own head, he bent over the Strat, in the
same posture in which Toad had first seen him, and it occurred to Toad that in all
the months the band had lived together, smoked, tripped, played together, he could

count on one hand the conversations he'd ever had with Eric Lindgard. Now, at last, Toad was able to make sense of the silences, of Eric's withdrawal to the place where he communed with his own strange muses. The gleanings of all those wordless times were coming out in the tales he was telling with his ax—creating a mind-shattering melodic line, then attacking with frenzy, sending feedback and distortion gnashing into it like rabid wolverines, chewing it up, spitting it out like bones. Toad followed. Whereas earlier he'd felt cold and disconnected, he was ablaze now, his flesh oozing, and the crowd was a vast living thing bawling its ecstasy as the terrible drum rolls of darkness itself thundered overhead and rain rattled on the tarp and snake-hissed in the trees, and far off there were flames—a vehicle ablaze!—as if lightning had come to ground. No cheesy liquid-slide lightshow for the New Riders, Toad thought, Christ no, what you had here was hell's own fire!

George Moon was weeping. It was a reaction to the tear gas, but he also felt a gnawing loss. He was thinking of that day when he and Helen had talked in the playground near her school. "What if I'd met you first?" he'd asked her. "Would we be together?" Helen stopped swinging and the creaking of the chains died softly away, and with it some piece of him fluttered on the dividing line between hope and extinction. "George," she said with quiet affection, "who can say? I met Johnny, and I love him."

He knuckled his eyes. Except for the tear gas, which was already thinning, he could detect no other evidence of the TAC Squad's presence. At the very least he'd have expected them to commandeer the stage, shut down the noise pouring from there, order the crowd to disperse or face arrest. But that hadn't happened. The music went on in a rampaging torrent. He wondered if his men had been ambushed, set upon by the crowd. Or had they deserted? Were they getting high, dancing naked with the crazies, their helmets tossed aside and stuffed full of flowers? No. The probability was they weren't doing much of anything beyond awaiting his command. But with radio contact gone, along with his car, he wasn't going to be able to give it.

He pulled off his raincoat and dropped it. Underneath he wore combat fatigues. He would have liked to have had his helmet and shield, but he'd make do. He still had his sidearm. And this. From his belt he drew the black truncheon. Okay. As a start, he would get to the stage, find the power source, kill the noise. From there, he'd decide what to do next.

Things weren't what Sparrow had feared. He gazed down on the floodlit meadow. An automobile that had been set afire was pretty much burned out and now only smoked in the rain. Most of the crowd remained in place, involved in the music, dancing. The TACs hadn't overreacted. They'd used a few canisters of tear gas to keep people away from the burning car, which looked to be more a safety measure than anything else. For a change, Moon was exercising restraint.

"What happens now?" Amy asked.

She seemed remarkably steady and in control of herself. He hoped it wasn't shock. He looked at the crowd, aware that the Death Tripper could be there among them, aware, too, that they had no way to find him if he were. It was time for reinforcements; time to get the task force involved.

"Let's find a telephone," he said.

Moon trudged on, having closed half the distance to the stage without interference. He saw no sign of his men. The ground underfoot had been tramped to mud, which he felt clogging on his boots. The tear gas had wisped away. His eyes had ceased to burn, but his ears took the assault of the music. The hippies didn't seem to notice or to care. Holding his truncheon in view, using it like a prod to open a path through the tightening crush, he passed among them, feeling their dangerous energy, smelling them, hating them.

Toad felt "The Valley of the Shadow" expanding out of itself, the song going someplace none of them had ever taken it before, drawing energy from the music, and he felt so illuminated that he had the kooky notion that if he were to look at himself from a distance he might see himself bathed in light, as though electricity were discharging out of his skin, sparking in the wet air, which, of course, was just weird chemical mind noise from the White Rabbit making him crazy as a full-moon dawg, taking his desperate and unrequited longing for Circe into the music, as the entire band was giving vent to the longings of the whole hungry-hearted crowd, and he could *feel* that the power that'd been pent inside of them, waiting for the moment of perfect alignment when all the auguries were right, was *here!*

Moon had closed to one hundred feet from the stage, in a zone where the sound was a shock wave, beating him back. How could they stand it? His mind was numb with noise. His teeth ached. He would shut the control board down, climb the stage if he had to, rout the musicians and—

That's when he spotted the couple.

They stood to the left, facing the band. Wrapped around them like a blanket was a flag. The cloth was wet, clinging to them, so it was impossible to know for certain, but he could see yellow and some red, and he was pretty sure of what it was. He'd seen it at the solstice. Changing course, his brain pounding with sound, he angled toward them. As he neared, he shouted.

The pair didn't hear him.

"*I'm talking to you!*" he roared.

They didn't respond.

Rushing them, he grabbed an edge of the flag and yanked. The force spun the two people out of the cloth, dumped them onto the muddy ground. The kid recovered first, and scrambled to his hands and knees. He looked around, and spotting Moon, sprang at him from a four-point stance, screaming words that were lost in the music's roar. Moon bludgeoned him. The kid dropped, his legs tangling in the flag, and for a second time Moon tore the cloth away, saw now that it wasn't Ho Chi Minh's NLF flag, but rather some kind of a frat house banner: red Greek letters on a gold field. He whipped it aside.

Several people standing nearby jumped him. He slashed the stick around and sent one of them reeling backwards, clutching his bleeding face. A second kid got an arm around Moon's neck. With a strangled roar, Moon bucked forward, but the kid, surprisingly strong, clung. Now a third person tackled him. They all went down together. Moon lost hold of his truncheon. He rolled sideways, elbowing and kicking. His attackers dropped away. He forced himself to his feet. Wobbly and mud-covered, he looked around at the meaningless faces. No one moved. He picked up his truncheon and pressed on grimly toward his goal.

From a pay phone just outside the park, Sparrow called Homicide. Lanin answered. "John, did you hear about it? Explosions in the park!"

"Is Austin there?"

"No one is but me. They're all out looking for whoever did it. Hey, where are you?"

"In a booth."

"Did Sandoval get hold of you?"

"No, when?"

"He was looking for you earlier. He said he had something to show you. You can try him at his place."

But when Sparrow dialed the number, the phone rang unanswered.

The audio mixer sat to the right of the stage, protected by a makeshift tent of plastic sheeting, which fluttered under the storm surge of noise like wings. A girl in a black vinyl raincoat was operating the board. As Moon reached her, she turned and saw him, too. Maybe it was the truncheon and his ripped, muddy fatigues, or something in his expression—or her own noise-addled confusion, for all he knew—but her eyes slitted with uncertainty for a moment, then went wide. She stood and flung up her hands in what appeared to be surrender.

But he didn't want prisoners. He was tired. He wanted quiet. He speared the girl in the stomach and she dropped.

He stepped over her to the audio mixer. He looked at the knobs and switches and little needles bouncing inside glowing dials, too delicate-seeming to have any relation to the sonic blast of noise from the stage. He raised the truncheon to smash the board . . . but something made him turn.

A half circle of people had gathered over the girl in the black raincoat. No one bent to help her. She was slithering in the mud toward the stage, like a beetle whose carapace has been broken and wants only to crawl under something and disappear before it can be stepped on again. She was no threat, but it didn't matter, because all at once she was them. *All* of them. Crotch-rot crazies, too chickenshit to defend themselves or their country or even each other. *Them.* Everything that had spoiled the city and was cancer at the heart of America, that had helped kill Helen and shriveled his hopes and had set to ruin George Moon's life.

They needed to pay.

He slashed the truncheon in a sweeping motion, driving everyone farther away. Then, getting his back and shoulders behind it, he raised the truncheon in both hands and swung it down onto the girl, like a man splitting stove wood with a maul. The bitch writhed with a shriek that rose over the music, and something in the sound inflamed him all the more. He stumbled over a power cord. Spreading his arms to maintain balance on the slippery ground, he booted her. He was peripherally aware of onlookers fleeing back in horror, leaving a broad clearing around them. He raised his foot for another kick, bumping against the audio mixer as he did, and in that instant something exploded.

Sonofafreakin'—!

At the blast, Toad sprang off his stool, which tumbled backwards with the motion and rolled off the side of the stage. There was a sizzling *pop* as sparks spurted from the mixer, and Toad had a flashback of a man in an army field jacket monkeying with the system earlier, not Raimes. But this just came and went as he kept drumming, no longer sure what was real or what his head might be cooking up, the way the sound system was doing its own crippled thing now, still working on some circuits, like the acidified circuitry of his brain, and like an elaborate Escher structure finally aware of its own impossibility, the music was collapsing in on itself, coming back to the melody ("Valley of the Shadow"—he had actually spaced out enough to have forgotten) and the music went on spilling from the shredded speakers, channeling in and out and in and out . . .

As the audio mixer exploded, a slab of plywood and metal the size of a child's sled, and jagged as icicles, ripped into George Moon, all but severing him at the waist. For one mad instant he stood braced against the impact, his arms spread like a man riding a surfboard through a choppy sea. Gripping his truncheon, he gazed around with a sense of baffled regret, wondering who or what to hit. But there was no one, nothing. He saw the world grow dim. The roaring had stilled and he heard, or perhaps imagined he heard, the soft, slowly diminishing creaking of swing chains . . .

He fell like a cut tree.

Seth could barely believe it: but there it was. He'd been the spark! Trembling with excitement, he stared toward the meadow and saw another explosion near the stage. (A strike of lightning? Someone else with a firebomb?) Sparks shot into the air and the music cut out for an instant before surging on again. Elsewhere, puffs of tear gas moved over the crowd.

He was juiced! He wanted to tell everyone that it had begun . . . that *he* had started it, with a vodka bottle, a strip of rag, and eight cents' worth of gasoline!

But something was wrong.

Except for the people at the fringes of the crowd, nobody was moving. They were just standing there in a lumpen mass, listening to the music. Worse, he saw now, the people on the rim weren't engaging the pigs: they were scattering, fucking running. It was the solstice all over again.

Don't retreat! He wanted to shout. *Tie rags across your faces to cut the tear gas! Join arms! Face the bastards!* But his voice was useless over the music, and the tear gas had grown so thin it was hardly even there. The pigs weren't doing anything. They were keeping a distance. Closer to the stage, nothing was happening at all. With a sinking hope, he watched.

If only the people had stood together, really mobilized this summer, they could have done anything! But they hadn't. They were scared or weren't angry enough or just didn't care, and now it was too late.

"Green!"

A man in an old jacket and a black beret was heading his way. Nat Evans. For a moment, Seth imagined that Evans was going to clap his back, tell him "Right on!"; but Nat wrinkled his face. "What'd you do? Drink that stuff? You stink."

"It worked," Seth said, his hope surging again.

"Somebody ID'd you, man. You'd best go."

"Come on," Seth cried, "let's get some more."

"You ain't listening. The cops are looking for you."

"The hell with that. We can do this!"

Nat shook his head emphatically. "I've done some thinking. Maybe like Terry Gordon finally did, too. This ain't how you change things. Maybe that's what he was doing this morning." He paused, looking closely at Seth.

Seth grew wary. "What are you talking about?"

"Terry went back. He's gonna teach again."

Seth stammered a moment, lost for words. "But that . . . that's crazy, I just—I—"

Nat Evans lifted the hem of his jacket and drew a pistol from his waistband. He gazed at it like a man contemplating a lost past and an uncertain future, and wondering if there was any safe passage between the two. "You'd best book, man. If they catch your ass, it's Quentin." Holding the gun by the barrel, he flung it toward a thicket of bushes. "Later."

THE VOLVO WAS JUST OUTSIDE THE PARK, SNUGGED ALONGSIDE A BUS WHOSE CRAZY colors seemed to run riot in the rain. Sparrow drove. Eureka Valley wasn't far. En route, he told Amy what Lanin had said. He located the farm road and then the mailbox. A light burned in the house and another over the barn door. In the yard, he shut off the motor.

The damp air smelled of animals, but the pens beyond the fences were silent. Had it been only that morning when he'd been here before? When no one answered his knock at the house, he waved Amy from the car and they went to the barn. The interior was dark, but even so, he called out, "Pete? It's John."

To their left was the small office from which Sandoval's father ran his business, but Amy was pointing toward a faint purple glow coming through a window deeper in the barn. He told her about the chiller, where the pigs were hung after slaughter.

In the office, he switched on a lamp. The desk was paper-covered: farm catalogues, invoices, and receipts. On the wall hung the picture of ten-year-old Pete hugging his 4-H pig, each blissfully unaware of impending doom. Sparrow's glance fell on a manila folder stamped with the SFPD seal. It took him a moment to realize that it was from the case files on the North Beach killings. In the folder was a black-and-white photograph of Sparrow and Moon standing beside an unmarked Ford. It had been taken on the street just before the two of them and Rocco Bianchi went into a nearby alley to view the final victim of the North Beach Strangler.

"That's the one I saw in a newspaper," Amy said. "It's why I associated you with Moon."

The folder also contained fingerprint reports and a profile that a psychologist had worked up on the killer: materials that Bianchi said he had tried without luck to locate. Had Pete been working the cold case on his own and found something? With Sparrow on suspension, and no one else he trusted to reveal it to, had he brought the files here for safekeeping? From whom? His mind groped toward some understanding.

"John. Check this."

Amy was holding a note. "It's for you."

John. I checked the prints—just to rule out any link to our guy. No connection. Hope you don't mind my taking the initiative. See you soon, partner.

He stared at it. Amy said, "Is this what he wanted to see you about?"

"Yes."

"What's it mean?"

That I've been wrong. Chasing an obsession, he thought. *Looking for atonement.*

She didn't ask for elaboration. She took his hand and squeezed it. He said, "Let's find Hoot."

They started back out to the car, but he recalled something he'd seen earlier in the day, in a box by the chiller, among rubber boots and gloves. "Wait. We should get a weapon."

At the window that gave a view into the chiller, he stopped with a gasp. He tried to block Amy's view, but too late. She was already peering into the purple-lit room. She gripped his arm hard with one hand and clapped the other over her mouth. Even so, he heard her moan. Partly hidden by the suspended carcasses of pigs, the fabric of his shirt bunched behind his neck and pierced by a stainless steel hook, hung a man. Though the face was swollen and splotched with death, Sparrow recognized Pete Sandoval. On shaky legs, he hustled Amy outside.

They stood by the car, recovering from shock, trying to make sense of what they'd just seen. In a monotone, he told what must have happened. Hoot had once told her he had their addresses. He'd evidently tried to find Sparrow at the boat last night and had missed, had failed to get Amy, too. Now he had come here. They held each other. Overhead, moths spiraled around the barn light. Somewhere a nighthawk cried.

"Shouldn't we . . . take him down?" Amy's voice shook.

He'd felt the same impulse. There was something monstrous in the man's being hung like that. But it was a crime scene. Was that ludicrous? What had any of the Death Tripper's grim work ever offered up as evidence before? Still, the point returned him to a measure of control. "Wait right here," he said.

He made a quick search but found no trace of Miguel Sandoval.

In Miguel Sandoval's office, when he lifted the handset, the line was dead. Near where the cord went into the baseboard he saw that it had been cut. Hurriedly he gathered the SFPD files and stuffed them into a big envelope. As he was leaving, he thought he saw a shadow flit past the glow thrown from the chiller.

He checked on Amy. She was standing against her car, her arms crossed as if warding off cold. He went down the short aisle to the chiller window. The room was as before. Pete Sandoval hung among the pigs his father had slaughtered that afternoon. In the box by the door was a knife. To free his hands, he slid the file folder inside his jacket against his chest and zipped it. He picked up the knife. Its blade was heavy and double-edged for cutting through gristle and bone. He opened the chiller door.

"Hello?" he called. The word was a frosty puff. From somewhere farther in, a compressor hummed softly.

He stepped in and let the door close behind him. Ahead hung the row of pigs, and behind it Pete Sandoval. An odd tingle of premonition swept along his spine, and all at once he felt drawn, on the brink of something. Answers? A discovery? Gripping the knife, he started forward. He checked Sandoval for his gun, but it was gone. At the edge of his vision he saw movement. He spun. Right beside him, between two of the hanging carcasses, a hand rose in what looked like a greeting. *No!* Something slammed hard into his chest.

Light flickered. The floor lurched. He dropped the knife. Trying to steady himself, he grabbed cold flesh. A pig carcass squeaked away on its overhead roller. The room began to whirl, the light drawing inward like a camera eye wringing shut. In the instant before it reached pinpoint size and vanished, he heard a voice calling him from across what seemed a vast landscape.

Cold. He hadn't been down long. Minutes? Above him, bodies still swung like pendulums, slowly.

He got to his feet. The floor tilted left, then right, before stabilizing. He picked up the big knife, which had fallen under him. Whatever had hit him had penetrated his jacket. Stiffly, he unzipped it and found the file folders and the envelope he had stuffed in there. They had taken some of the blow. He peeled open his shirt and saw a red stain on his T-shirt, not very big. Holding the knife, he stumbled out.

The Volvo sat in the yard as before; but Amy was gone.

He took the car. At the paved road, he hesitated just a moment, then swung left, following lingering traces of dust, picking up speed. Fence posts and trees were a passing blur. A neon clock on an Esso station showed nearly midnight. When he reached the coastal road, he turned north. He kept the pedal down, his stomach a sick knot. He tried to form an impression of his attacker, but there was nothing there. After a mile or so, when he still hadn't seen another car, doubt began to gnaw him. As he was slowing, considering alternatives, he spied taillights far ahead.

Any idea of overtaking the other vehicle was out—the Volvo didn't have the speed—so he settled for keeping the red lights in view. At the periphery of his vision, his imagination played tricks. He passed the long, fog-bound stretch of Ocean Beach, where the flower girl had been found, and Sutro Point, where victim number seven had been discovered yesterday morning. And now Amy was—

A car swept out of a side road, right across his path. He braked hard and swerved. The other driver gave a long blast of his horn. Recovering, Sparrow kept driving. His heart was thudding fast.

As the road twisted east toward the Presidio, he briefly lost sight of the taillights, then they reappeared. A half mile farther along, their red merged with a carnival glitter of yellow, blue, and white. He approached, and with relief saw several patrol cars and a cop dragging a wooden sawhorse into place to block an entrance lane to the Golden Gate Bridge. He drew up to the barrier. But his relief went to dismay as he looked around for the vehicle he'd been following. The only cars here belonged to the SFPD. The other vehicle was nowhere to be seen. A young patrolman in an orange reflective vest came over. "The bridge is closed, Mac."

"A car just came this way. Where did it go?"

"Sir, you'll have to turn around."

"Who was in it?"

"We're shutting the bridge down."

Sparrow blinked his raw eyes and felt anger eat at him like an ulcer. "Was there a woman inside?"

"Sir, you can't go through."

Sparrow climbed out. "Who's in charge here?"

The cop's hand began making tense little arcs near the butt of his .38. "Get back in your vehicle, sir."

Off to one side, Sparrow noticed a man in a trench coat marching this way. "Hold him right there!" the man called.

Frank Austin. Austin made recognition, too. "What're you doing here?" he demanded.

Sparrow glanced past the line of sawhorses toward the bridge, ghostly in the mist. Where had the other car gone? A small coil of anxiety turned in his belly. "Chasing the killer," he said.

In the winking lights, Austin looked bewildered. "What the hell are you saying?"

"The Death Tripper." The coil in Sparrow's stomach tightened. "Frank—what's going on?"

Hesitating a moment, Austin said, "George Moon is dead."

Sparrow felt like he'd been punched. Moon. He could barely believe it.

"We've got all units out. We'll find whoever's responsible. Now, get in the car."

"But you don't—"

"You wait right here!"

"I have to get through."

Austin hammered a fist on the Volvo's hood. "Wait in the goddamn car!"

Overruled, dizzied by what he'd just learned, Sparrow obeyed. Taking this, and the fact that the men knew each other, as a good sign, the patrolman relaxed a little. Austin trotted over to the cluster of men he'd been with moments ago. Sparrow watched them conferring, some dissonant note sounding in his mind.

George Moon dead, too? And Sandoval. Reflexively, he clenched and unclenched the steering wheel. One of the men gestured to Austin. Austin gestured back. What was the holdup? Sparrow noticed the knife on the seat and put it into his jacket pocket. He still had the police files and the other papers. He laid them on the floor and pushed them under the seat with his foot. The discussion continued, distant and removed, like the talk of generals in a war room, far from the front. On the fogged-in bridge, if the other vehicle had been there, it was gone now. Was Amy in it? He couldn't wait any longer.

He flung open the door. As he stepped out, the heavy knife fell from his pocket and clattered on the wet road. The patrolman gawked at it, wide-eyed, then shouted something, whether at Sparrow or to Austin wasn't clear. Sparrow considered explaining, but the cop was unsnapping his holster. Sparrow grabbed the knife and dove back into the car.

The cop's gun boomed into the air.

The old car didn't have much pickup, but it was rolling pretty well when it hit the center sawhorse. Broken planks spun away from the impact. A headlamp shattered; a front tire blew. He chugged past, gaining speed. In the mirror, he saw the cop level his weapon, glimpsed Austin giving chase on foot, shouting, but his words were lost, and soon he was, too.

Fear was trying to pry her open. In her darkness, Amy felt the car stop again, heard the motor quit this time, the door open. There was a metallic scratching and the trunk lid rose. Orange light stabbed her eyes. She screamed, or thought she did; she wasn't sure; it might've been only a tiny noise at the back of her throat where something felt lodged. There were tears on her face, but they were cold. She wasn't crying now. All her emotions had been compressed into terror. Her vision was blurred. Wordlessly, the man gripped her arm. Her legs were weak from her confinement, and as she stepped uncertainly onto the road they almost buckled, but she straightened.

Her captor tugged a wadded cloth from her mouth. The scream that had been bottled inside her came out as a cry of help, but it was small in the chilly, surrounding night. Blinking her eyes into focus, she realized that the man was the man she'd given a ride to earlier. Her heart raced. It took her a moment to perceive that they were on the Golden Gate Bridge. The stanchions were hung with webs of fog. Except for her and her captor, the bridge appeared totally empty.

The acrid chemical taste remained, but she could breathe freely, at least. Her head cleared a bit. The man left her hands cuffed in front of her. His attention was drawn now by something behind her, and she looked, too. A single light was emerging from the fog a few hundred yards away. Another vehicle was on the bridge. A motorcycle? Drawing Amy back away from the car, he shouldered his saddlebags, then he pointed a gun and fired it into the trunk. With a *whoosh,* flames began to leap from under the car. Sending another glance toward the headlamp emerging from the fog, he pulled her across the empty lanes to the raised sidewalk that ran along the outer edge of the bridge. He went to the rail and looked over.

A cold wind gusted at them. She jerked her head to get her hair out of her face, and glanced down. All she could see was a blanket of fog. Behind them, the car was a ball of flame. The man pushed her against the railing. She struggled and pulled away. He jabbed the gun painfully into her ribs. He seemed to be debating a moment, then he said, "Climb."

Forty feet from the burning car, Sparrow braked and got out. He shoved the heavy knife into his belt. Even from here the heat was enough to make him raise a shielding arm. The blaze was a crackling intensity, the flames reflecting off the red iron structures of the bridge. It was impossible to tell anything about the car or if anyone was still inside. Just after the fire erupted, he had seen two figures scurrying toward the sidewalk. One of them, he thought, had been a woman.

He crossed the traffic lanes and climbed onto the passenger walk. For the thirty or so yards he could see in either direction, there was no one to be seen. On foot, they wouldn't have been able to get farther than that. At the rail, he peered down. His heart felt sick. Hundreds of feet below, shrouded in fog, the ocean was a chasm. He climbed to the top of the barrier fence. He hoisted a leg over. He lowered himself on the other side, holding on tightly. The wind buffeting him now, he gazed down and saw what he was looking for. He moved a few sideways steps to his left, adjusting his position, summoning courage. For an instant, he determined to wait for Austin, who was surely on his way; but that was no option at all. He jumped.

AMY WAS IN THE CENTER OF SOME FIERCE NIGHTMARE. SHE HELD THE WET RAIL WITH her cuffed hands, desperately hanging on as the man led her down a steep flight of steps to a catwalk. The structure seemed absurdly flimsy. Except for a huge girder just below, there was nothing but a long drop to the ocean.

Earlier, waiting outside the barn as John used the phone, she'd been startled by a car's appearance. A police car—Pete Sandoval's, she realized now. It drew near and the driver peered from the open window. As she bent close, the driver reached out and grabbed her and pressed something against her face. A chemical smell filled her head. Had she called out John's name as she swam into the void? She wasn't sure. She'd wakened in a confined, moving dark.

The grillwork underfoot was treacherously slick. High overhead, the wind made a rising, falling moan in the bridge's cables. Through a drifting membrane of fog, she saw the dark form of the Marin headlands appear and then disappear, as if by a trick of sorcery. So far away. They'd never reach the other side. "Come on." The Death Tripper tugged her onward.

Her nightmare was intensifying.

With a sense of unreality, made more so by the fog lights glowing on the empty bridge, Sparrow peered down the stairway into pooling darkness and realized that it led to a catwalk used by bridge painters. They must have gone that way. The stinks of burnt gasoline and rubber were riding a dragon of smoke up into the night behind him. Clutching the pipe railing, he began to descend.

Halfway down, a flutter of dizziness began to swarm him. He slowed but kept moving. The wind rose to a whispery crescendo, like taunting voices. His vision started to blur. *No, not now.* Eyes shut, clenching the rail, he drew a long breath. Some of the dizziness passed. Here, without the glow of lights, he could see along the catwalk a short distance in both directions. Empty. Gingerly, as if uncertain the structure would take his weight, he stepped onto it.

For some reason, he found himself wondering if he could have foreseen this. Not the particulars exactly, obscured as things had been by the havoc of the whole strange season, but were there instants when he might've peered through a break in the wall and sensed an unexpected reality? That day, for example, when Amy had talked of chaos and ambiguity. Or the afternoon they had made love in the woods. Or even today, when he had literally burst through a wall and discovered the dog tags. Was it possible that a shrewder observer might have seen there was an inevitability to events, running like a dark thread through the bright fabric of the summer? He hadn't, encumbered as he'd been by the past; and now he feared it was far too late. He began to jog desperately along the catwalk, chasing wraiths, as blind to the ways things might end as he had been to their beginning.

This time she had no doubt. The catwalk vibrated under her feet. Breathless with fear, she half turned to look back. She was startled. Far behind, hurrying toward them from the San Francisco side, was a man. Some instinct, whether of dread at what lay behind, or of having her captor discover they were being pursued, told her to keep moving. But soon, when she craned another glance back, she saw the pursuing man had closed the distance and was near enough to see. It was John.

A wave of hope splashed over her; then, instantly, alarm. He was close. She mustn't give him away. She turned forward again, but her captor was alert. Stopping, he yanked her to a halt, and looked back. Amy threw up her hands to show John she was handcuffed, to warn him. She opened her mouth to shout.

But it was the man with her who spoke.

"This is the end."

At the words, Sparrow skidded on the slick iron and stopped. They were words he'd been hoping to hear from that day when he had gone to the murder scene in the boarded-up house in the Haight, the first day of the rest of his life. The end of it all. For a stunned moment he stared at Amy, wanting her to be all right. She was shivering, her hair wind-tangled, but she was okay. Then, for the first time, he looked at Byron Hoot.

Shaggy hair, ragged clothes. A kid, really. His mind was reeling with questions, but with knowledge now, too. It was almost more than he could bear. He stood where he was, trying to breathe.

"Throw away your gun," Hoot said. Even his voice was strangely young sounding.

Sparrow showed his empty hands. He hadn't had a gun all day. The knife was in his belt, concealed by his jacket. "What happened to you?" he asked, needing to hear some other sound than the wind's cry. Back in Hoot's childhood, he meant, back in Cu Chi, or in the desert. How had he come to be this?

Hoot said, "I've done what I set out to do."

"Reclaim your dead?"

"I was going to kill her, but I don't need to now. She'll come with me to tell the story."

"Let her go."

Hoot looked as though he might deny everything, or not respond at all. His face was waxen in the diffused light. He glanced over the catwalk rail. Instinctively, Sparrow looked, too. Below was a line of girders and, he knew, the ocean, several hundred feet down. At some dizzying distance in between, the fog shimmered seductively. It looked almost pillowy enough to soften a jump. Sparrow pulled his gaze back. "Let's all get out of here," he said, his throat dry with tension.

Amy was staring hard at him. He grew aware of the swiveling reflections of lights on the bridge as patrol cars crawled past, moving south to meet their counterparts coming north. They'd reach the burning car momentarily, and from there it would be short work to put things together. Sweat was pouring down his brow, icy in the wind, burning his eyes. "We should give up."

"*Me* give up, you mean."

"You can."

Yellowed by the vaporous glow overhead, Hoot's face looked like the page of an old book. He was motionless, as though waiting for instruction, perhaps; but aside from the distant approach of more sirens, there was only the sigh of wind through the cables and the high iron.

Spotlights drew their attention. From the roadway above, beams had begun to stab erratically through the blowing mist, like iridescent probes. Sparrow swallowed back his rising terror. At the rim of his vision, he could see fuzzy shapes moving on the bridge. Marksmen taking position?

"She and I are going on," Hoot said. "I've gotta kill you, though."

Amy gave a cry, but Hoot yanked on the handcuffs and she fell silent.

"It's too far," Sparrow said. "You won't make it."

Hoot unlocked the handcuff on one of Amy's wrists and slipped it onto his own. It snapped with a smart *click*. He pointed his weapon—was it the one he'd bought from the squatters? Or Sandoval's?—at Sparrow.

Sparrow didn't wait. He grabbed for the railing and kicked. The gun clanged on the girder once, twice, and was gone. Before Sparrow could recover, Hoot drew a knife. Menacing Sparrow backwards with it, he forced Amy down onto the catwalk's floor. He wanted her to crawl under the railing. He intended to go down onto the girder.

"No," Sparrow pleaded. "You'll fall."

"Move and I'll kill her."

And Sparrow knew he would. Hoot slipped under the bottom rail, drawing Amy with him. In an instant, they dropped down onto the girder and were gone.

Amy's heart was beating with rivet-hammer speed as they climbed awkwardly down a diagonal support to the lower span. In the fog that boiled up off the black cauldron of ocean far below, she felt the soles of her feet tingle. There was a booming in her ears, an enormous weight crushing her chest. Hoot drew her on.

Getting by each crossbeam there was a moment when she had to let go with her free hand, take a step, grab hold of the other side and be tugged around. The steel circlet on her wrist yanked at flesh and bone, but it was a small anguish. John had tried so hard . . . but the Death Tripper had won.

Sparrow squirmed under the rail and dropped. The support was a line of two massive girders, one above the other, tied with zigzagging crossbeams. The span he stood on was five or six feet wide. The surface was slick, puddled in places, studded with huge bolts, which threatened to trip him. Hoot and Amy would be on the lower girder, making their way north. Despite the massiveness of the bridge, he could feel it tremble, flexing with the forces of wind and ocean currents, oblivious to the trivial events being played out on its span. *Kuan.* The word from Circe's *I Ching*—wind and ocean. Ambiguity and chaos. Gooseflesh pimpled his neck and arms.

He didn't see the bolt head.

He stumbled and went over the edge. With a lunge, he just managed to get his arms onto the top of the girder, but there was nothing to cling to. Hands flat, fingers spread to gain traction, he held on. His heart beat madly. He started to try to hoist himself back up, but he realized the effort would break his grip and he stopped. Sweat was pouring off him in buckets.

A spotlight that had been probing the dark swept the girder ahead and found Amy . . . then Hoot. The light steadied. A bullhorn voice said, "You are targeted by sharpshooters. Return to the bridge."

Austin. Sparrow could have laughed. Return. How he wished he could. His palms were burning, his arms trembling. And now his hands began to slip.

He saw one chance to save himself. Letting his body dangle, putting more pressure on his already slipping hands, he swung his legs toward a crossbeam. Missed.

His hands were sliding fast toward the edge. His arm strength was about gone. He swung his legs again, felt his kneecap crack against the steel and his hands lose the girder—just as his feet found the crossbeam. He drew himself onto it and crab-walked down the angled steel to the lower girder, heart dancing in his chest. He stopped there, trying to breathe.

More lights splashed the area just ahead, dazzling in their brightness. Amy and Hoot weren't as far along as he'd imagined. They stood linked to each other, Hoot holding his knife out.

"Lower your weapon!" Austin commanded, but even amplified, his words seemed small and ridiculous in the wind.

Hoot took a step, but missed. He teetered away from the crossbeam. Amy's arm jerked out, yanked by his weight. She screamed. Clutching the crossbeam with her free arm, she pulled, trying frantically to keep them both from plunging over.

Sparrow scrambled toward them. But it already was too late. Hoot had tipped out too far to grab. Amy's arm was stretched to the limit. Her hold was being pried loose. Hoot waved the knife impotently in the air. There was only the hypnotic voice of the wind. In the crisscrossing lights, the handcuffs gleamed.

Sparrow was out of time. He found the heavy knife in his own belt. He raised it like a hatchet and leaned as far forward as he could. For a moment, his gaze met Hoot's and some complex communication passed between them—or maybe it was nothing at all. Then, with the hardest swing he could muster, he brought the knife down just below the circlet of steel. With a gritty crunch, the blade cleaved sinew and bone.

Far away a voice calls, "Jump boy, I'll catch you," and suddenly you're free, streaking away across vast open spaces of light, the sun starbursting off the Shadow's ebony gas tank, the cool wind in your hair, the screams silent forever . . .

EPILOGUE

SPARROW JERKED UPRIGHT WITH A GASP. THE DREAM. THE BAD ONE. BUT IT WAS COMing less often. He lay back, letting his heartbeat slow. The Death Tripper fell, tumbling away, fading, paler and paler until he was gone. When Sparrow looked up, he saw Amy clinging to the crossbeam. For a moment, he could not budge; then he got to her and they both held on.

On a bright Tuesday in September, as seagulls screamed on the bay, he sat aboard his sailboat at the marina, drinking coffee and gazing at the Golden Gate Bridge. It was one of those sights that continually surprised even the most jaded eyes, but he viewed it differently now. Some of its grace was gone. Maybe that would change. He hoped so.

The dog tags had been turned over to the Army and sent home to the families of the men of Byron Hoot's squad. Pete Sandoval had been buried with departmental honors; his father, who had been away on the night of his son's death, accepted a posthumous award for Pete's valor. George Moon had been given a quieter ceremony. The TAC unit was being reexamined, its future uncertain. Frank

Austin was now a deputy chief, so City Hall had paid off—as it should have; after all, Austin had closed the Haight-Ashbury killings. He had sent a note to Sparrow, acknowledging Sparrow's role in the investigation, and officially ending the suspension. He'd suggested they talk. Sparrow hadn't gotten back to him yet.

Seth Green had vanished, gone underground, it was believed, with a militant group who'd begun to refer to themselves as Weathermen, a name reportedly derived from a Bob Dylan song, though Sparrow didn't know which one. The FBI was pursuing the matter. In Sparrow's last conversation with Amy, a week after the frenzied events, she confided that she'd heard from Seth just once, in a postcard with a single word on it: "*NEVER!*" Whatever that meant. The larger issue, the one he kept grappling with, was what had set Byron Hoot in motion in the first place?

"You kept her."

He turned to see Amy standing by the top of the gangway. His heart clutched. He had missed her coming along the pier. He missed nothing now. She wore round sunglasses and a blue paisley dress that the wind swept around the lean contours of her body, and her hair was aglow in the sun.

"The *Blind Faith*. You didn't sell her."

"I thought about it. But on a day like today . . ." He shook his head.

"She's looking good. Shipshape."

"She isn't the only one." Amy had never looked more beautiful.

"Thank you. I feel rested. Have you been sailing?"

"Around the bay some. Not far. It's always more fun sailing with somebody. Come aboard."

"I haven't much time."

"One cup of coffee?"

"For a minute, then. I've got a taxi waiting."

He took her hand. There was a moment as she stepped on deck when they might have embraced, but neither one moved into the small intervening space and the moment passed.

"I've meant to come by sooner, but I was away on a writing project, and with one thing and another . . ." Her words trailed off. "I heard that John Coltrane died."

He nodded. "I missed it at first. Busy summer."

"I phoned police headquarters. They told me you'd taken vacation. Well earned. Your hair is longer."

"Whose isn't?"

"LBJ's."

He laughed. Her own smile was brief. "I wanted to say good-bye before I left."

"Off on another trip?"

"I'm going back to Boston."

"Ah. Home." He felt a twist of regret. He tried not to show it; it wouldn't be fair to send her off with it, especially if the regret was his alone. He even managed a smile. "Does your mom still think she understands everything?"

"Not altogether. She's willing to admit she's as confused as everyone else. They're glad I'm okay."

"They must be proud. Your piece in the *Chronicle* was good. More than good."

"You were a big part of it. The inside details made it work."

"You wrote it. I can't imagine it was an easy story to do."

"It took some digging, much of it right inside me. I wasn't always wild about what I found. But I am glad you appreciated it."

"A few others did, too, apparently. I saw in Herb Caen's column that you got an offer to work for a magazine."

She gave a little laugh of wonder. "In New York."

"Congratulations." God, he hoped he didn't sound grudging. "That's a great opportunity," he said, and if it wasn't effusive, it was sincere, and that tempered his regret because it confirmed the truth of what he felt for Amy. He wanted her to be happy.

She took off the sunglasses and was watching him now, studying him in that way she had. Her eyes had the blue of the surrounding bay. "It is a wonderful chance," she agreed. "For someone."

He tipped his head, uncertain.

"I'm not taking the job. I want to come back here."

"To the Haight?"

"I haven't thought that far ahead. I'll have time to while I'm back East." She drew a windblown strand of hair behind her ear, but it leapt free again. "Anyway, I . . . guess I wanted to know I'd still have a friend here."

A friend. "What I said that night in the park, Amy . . . I meant it."

"I know." She shifted her gaze, glancing about as if there might be prompts tacked to the railing. "Hey, you know Emily Dickinson?"

"Married to Burt Bacharach."

It took her a moment, but she smiled. He did, too. "You still think cops don't read anything but Miranda."

"I'm learning. One of her poems says, 'After great pain, a formal feeling comes.' With all that we went through, I sensed maybe we both needed some space. Was I right?"

"Probably." He considered telling her his thought about the Golden Gate Bridge, but he wasn't entirely sure it applied. And time was short. He said, "The answer is yes. You have a friend here." And this time he followed his impulse. He circled her with his arms and he held her close, inhaling the warmth of her, his body tingling with the feel of hers against him, her hair soft on his lips. She hugged him, too, and for a long moment the world around them faded to mist. He felt anchored.

They walked up the gangway to the marina gate, where a cab waited. "A newspaper taxi," he said.

Amy brightened. "You've been listening."

"I'm trying."

They hugged once more. In the backseat, she rolled down the window, as if remembering something. "Today's the equinox. Happy autumn, John."

He watched until the cab had gone from sight, then he started back to the *Blind Faith*, which rolled gently against the backdrop of the sparkling bay. A white bird had perched atop the mast, probably a seagull, but he imagined a dove, aware that he very much wanted symbols. Amy was right; today was the official end of summer, the end of the Summer of Love. But perhaps, in ways he could not yet see, it was only beginning.